TARGETED

John M. Wills

A Chicago Warriors™ Thriller

TotalRecall Publications, Inc.
United States, Australia, Canada,
and United Kingdom

ISBN: 978-1-59095-795-0
UPC: 6-43977-77954-0

Edited by Adele Brinkley

TotalRecallPress.com
1103 Middlecreek Friendswood, Texas 77546 281-992-3131 281-482-5390
Fax
6 Precedent Drive Rooksley, Milton Keynes MK13 8PR, UK
1385 Woodroffe Av Ottawa, ON K2G 1V8

Printed in the United States of America with simultaneously printings in Canada, and England.

1 2 3 4 5 6 7 8 9 10

FIRST EDITION

To my children: John, Amy, and Tina.
I could not be any more pleased and
proud of each of you.

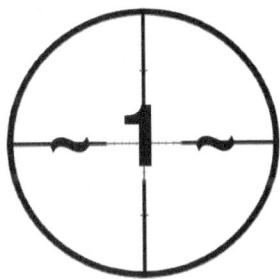

The shot shattered the cool, calm morning, causing birds to soar skyward. A frightened squirrel dashed up a tree, and the sound of barking dogs peppered the air. Chicago Police Officer Eduardo Gonzalez had just started down the front steps of the brick bungalow where he had been dispatched to take a report on a vehicle stolen during the night. As he exited the house and took his first step, he heard the shot break. That sound was the last thing he would ever hear. The round entered his right eye, penetrating deep into his cerebrum, fragmenting on the way, and destroying brain matter along its path. Mercifully, the bullet severed his brain stem, ensuring that he felt nothing. Officer Eduardo Gonzales was dead before he hit the ground.

Seconds later, a vehicle pulled from the curb and departed the area; its driver content with his first kill. Driving slowly from the scene, he could hear the whining of sirens as a legion of cops responded to a fallen brother. Revenge!

His lifeless body splayed awkwardly on the steps of a stranger's home, Eduardo never knew that that his colleagues were en route to help him. The life sustaining blood that once coursed through his body now formed a crimson pool, like a halo, around the fallen warrior's head.

Soon investigators would try to determine who killed Officer Gonzales and why. It would prove to be a daunting task for them, but the shooter had no such problem. He was clear about his mission.

"Lockup!"

"Yeah, yeah . . . hold your horses. Can't you see I'm busy?"

The grizzly old timer continued fingerprinting a prisoner, not turning around to see who had called out to him. He finished up with the last print, escorted the man to the bullpen, opened the cell door, and then re-locked it after the prisoner had gone inside. Turning toward the locked cell door that led to the 8th District station, the jailer saw Pete Shannon and Marilyn Benson with a prisoner. "Hey, Pete, long time no see. Whaddya got?"

The lockup keeper shuffled over to unlock the door and take custody of the prisoner. Pete drew his weapon from its holster and handed it to Marilyn. "Hold onto it for me, will you? I'll join you in a minute. I want to make sure he understands what's happening."

"Sure, partner. I'll meet you in the break room." Marilyn took the weapon and waited until Pete and their prisoner were inside and the door re-locked before she left.

Pete handed the paper work to the lockup keeper. "Here you go, Billy. He'll be going to court in the morning."

"What's the beef?"

"Aggravated criminal sexual abuse."

"Let me guess, another kiddie porn scumbag?"

"Not exactly." Pete pulled him over to the side. "Billy, I need you to take care of this guy—he's a priest."

"Yeah, so what? I've had his kind in here before. You don't spend twenty years doin' this job without gettin' just about every kind of creep there is."

"I hear ya, but listen; I have a strong feeling about this case. I really think that this guy's innocent."

Billy looked over the arrest report. "Yeah, yeah, they're all innocent. If I had a dime for every time I heard that, I wouldn't be waitin' to take my pension, I'd be rich."

"No, Billy, I actually believe that he's telling the truth."

"Whatever . . ."

Pete lowered his voice. "Do me a favor. Don't put this guy in the bullpen or, for that matter, with anyone. Give him his own cell. If these guys find out that he's charged with child molestation, they'll be all over him."

"Well . . . I'll see what I can do, but I can't make no promises. If they bring a load of drunks in, I gotta put 'em somewhere."

"Thanks, Billy. I owe you."

"Yeah, yeah. Say, how's that partner of yours doin'?"

"Marilyn's fine, stronger than ever."

"She's quite the cop. Took care of that rapist in fine fashion. Ya know, in my day, I wouldn't of partnered up with a woman if ya paid me. Most of 'em couldn't even pull the trigger on the gun, much less hit what they was aimin' at. But that partner of yours is one tough gal."

"Yes, she is. She can probably outshoot most of the guys on the job."

"Well, you keep lookin' out for her—she's a keeper."

"I'll do that. Good talkin' with you."

Pete turned to the prisoner. "I'll see you in the morning at the Criminal Courts building. In the meantime, Billy will take good care of you."

"Thanks, Detective."

Removing the big, brass cell key from his waistband, the lockup keeper let Pete out. "See ya later, Pete."

"Take care, brother."

"Awright, mister, let's get you printed and put away for the day."

Father Ed Matthews was still in a state of shock. As the cop took him by the arm and began to fingerprint him, he was hoping that he would awaken from this nightmare and find himself in his room at the rectory of St. Nick's parish.

"Just relax. Let your arm go limp, and I'll control your fingers and hands. If you stiffen up I can't roll a good print."

"Yes, sir."

The priest had, thankfully, never experienced being booked, nor had he even visited any of his parishioners in jail, although he knew that there were several. Father DeSalvo, the pastor of St. Nick's, normally assumed that duty. Truth be told, Ed was glad. He didn't like being in confined spaces, didn't even like being in the small confessional where he heard the sins of his parishioners. After an hour or two of sitting inside the three foot wide box, he was always ready to stand outside in the fresh air.

The cop took Ed's right hand and finished up with the four finger tips together on the print card. "There, all done. Now, give me that belt and your shoe laces. Don't want you hangin' yourself on my watch. Empty out your pockets on the table there. I'm takin' all your personal property."

Ed did as he was told, placing his wallet, a rosary, keys, and a few dollar bills on the table.

"You'll get a receipt for all that. Now, let's put you to bed." Billy led the priest past the bullpen, which held four prisoners, and down to a row of smaller cells, a couple of which were still empty. He put the huge key into the lock, turned it, and pushed the cell door aside.

"Here's your new home for the time being. Baloney sandwiches and coffee will get here in a couple hours. It's all you'll get till tomorrow so I suggest you eat it, even if you ain't hungry. You don't get no breakfast before you go to court in the morning."

The priest stepped inside, and the lockup keeper slammed the door shut. It was an awful sound, so loud and harsh that it seemed to signal the beginning of the end of life as Ed knew it. The sounds of church bells, choirs, and students in classrooms seemed just a memory. Father Matthews' new reality was cold and stark. Nothing good could possibly come from this world of concrete and iron. His existence was now defined by measurements of eight feet by four feet. His amenities consisted of a steel bed attached to the wall, a wool blanket, and a combination sink and toilet, sans a seat. His entertainment—overheard conversations and screams from his fellow prisoners.

Father Matthews sat down on the bed that felt as hard as it looked. He never imagined that his life would ever have taken such a dramatic turn. Surveying his cell, with its battleship gray painted walls and steel bars, he now understood the despair that people felt after they'd been arrested. He also saw the reasoning in taking prisoners' belts and shoe laces, lest they use them to hang themselves. Despair hung thick in the air, smothering any breath of hope.

Over the years, he had counseled a couple of parishioners about the evils of suicide and had even performed a funeral mass for one man who had killed himself with drugs. His message had always been the same: things are never so bad that they should cause people to want to end their lives. Now he was rethinking that advice. The joy that he used to feel was gone, just like his freedom. He was a prisoner. Accused. Shamed. Alone.

"Any problems?"

"No, Billy said that he would take care of him as long as it doesn't get too full back there."

Marilyn handed Pete back his weapon. "I think that Father Ed is in a state of shock."

"Yeah, he's out of it. When we arrested him at the rectory, I thought he was going to pass out on us."

Marilyn took a sip of coffee while Pete got his own cup in the break room at the Chicago Lawn police station. "I'm glad that you told him to change his shirt and not wear his collar. That would have been like putting a target on his back for all the lowlifes inside to use him as a punching bag."

Pete sat down with his coffee. "Well, he's not out of the woods yet. He still has to get on the bus with the others who have to go to court in the morning. Lord only knows what that experience may bring."

"I know. Once they read the charges at his initial appearance, the cat will be out of the bag. Everyone will know that's he's been arrested for child molestation. Jail is the worst place for someone accused of that type of crime. Word spreads quickly, and unless they put them in isolation, it's open season."

Taking a sip of the steaming brew, Pete said, "My gut tells me that the victim's mother isn't telling us the truth. Little Rodrigo didn't seem at all that traumatized to me."

"I agree. It all seems too well packaged—the father has gone back to Mexico, they live in subsidized housing, the mother doesn't have a steady job . . ."

"Yeah, I hate to say it but someone may have put a bug in Magdalena's ear, cluing her in about the big payouts the Catholic Church has been making to sexual abuse victims. She may think that her son has become her future meal ticket, like she could win the lottery by making an allegation against a priest. It's like you said, Marilyn, it's just all too convenient. We need to knock on some more doors and dig a little deeper. If Father Ed is guilty, then he deserves to be in jail, but if he is not we need to do our best to exonerate him."

Marilyn finished her coffee and got up from the table. "Ready to head back to the office?"

"Sure, let's go. We need to fill out the rest of the paper anyway. Do you want me to handle the court appearance in the morning?"

"Thanks, Pete, that would be great. I could spend some extra time at the gym."

"Yeah, like you really need it. But that's okay. I want to see how he made it through his first night in jail. I hope that he'll be able to get some rest tonight and recover from the trauma of being arrested."

"That and the bus ride," added Marilyn. "Wait 'till he finds out that he'll be in belly chains and leg irons for the trip to court."

"I'm going to pray for Father Ed," Pete said quietly. "I'm afraid he's in danger. Bad things happen in jail."

Ed awoke from a fitful sleep. Anxiety had plagued him throughout the night. The sounds and sights that he experienced were things he had found only in books and movies. The cell next to his had erupted at some point while he dozed. Two prisoners had decided to gang up on their cellmate. From the ruckus, it sounded like two Black men had taken exception to their fellow prisoner's inability to communicate with them—he was Hispanic. They took his silence as a sign of disrespect and meted out what they thought to be the appropriate punishment. The lockup keeper was slow to respond, and the victim had been transported to the hospital a short time later.

Plenty of other things haunted him throughout the night. Men were crying out, some to the jailers about needing this or that, some requesting phone calls, medical attention, or some about their discomfort with being either hot or cold. But one prisoner in particular caused him the most consternation. Several cells away a man confessed his sins to God, pleading with Him for forgiveness. He bared his soul for more than an hour, and Father Ed's first instinct was to comfort the man. After all, Ed was a Catholic priest and healing people was what he knew.

But was he indeed still a priest? After all that had happened, were his priestly powers still intact? Moreover, did he still have the authority to act in that capacity? And even more important, should he even let on that he was a priest? Detectives Shannon and Benson had cautioned him to keep that piece of information to himself, telling him about what happens to those accused of what he had been arrested for. He was in limbo, literally and figuratively. Even if he was somehow cleared of the charges against him, would he ever be trusted again, either by the Church or by people in general? Could he still function as a man of the cloth?

Lying on his steel berth, he was startled back to reality.

"All right everybody, wake up!" the jailer called. "It's time to go to court, time to see the judge. When I call out your name, I want you standing tall by your cell door. If I have to come in and get you off your rack, I'm not going to be happy. Believe me, if I'm not happy, you're not happy. Listen up! Hoffman, McBride, Williams, Hinkle, Matthews."

The lockup keeper walked by the appropriate cells and unlocked the doors, allowing those whose names had been called to assemble by the intake area where they were met by four uniformed officers, all of whom carried numerous pairs of handcuffs, leg irons, and chains.

"Okay, pay attention. Form a single line so we can get all of you cuffed and chained. Keep your mouths shut, and we won't have any problems. Once we get on the bus I don't want any chatter. If anybody gets frisky, I've got a nice, fresh can of pepper spray to settle you down. Don't make me use it. Now, let's get started."

The four officers worked quickly and methodically, first handcuffing each person and then placing each one in leg irons. Then they ran a long chain through a ring on each prisoner's belly chain, connecting all of them together. They marched the prisoners down a narrow hallway and out through the parking garage where they boarded a waiting bus. Father Ed grimaced in pain as he walked, the leg irons constricting his gait and rubbing against his ankle bones. Going up and down the steps caused the restraints to rub and gouge his skin, but he dared not to complain.

He was thankful that he was at the end of the column. At least he didn't have to worry about anyone behind him.

The group was loaded on the bus. A steel mesh partition separated the driver from the prisoners, and another enclosure separated them from the other three officers. Steel bars covered the windows. As they began their journey through the city streets, the hard composite seats magnified each bump and pothole in the road, jarring the priest. He winced, for he felt the impact through every bone in his body.

Looking out through the bars as they traveled slowly toward the court, he saw the familiar sights of what used to be his comfortable, peaceful existence. The southwest side of Chicago had been his home for all of his thirty years. He had been born and raised here, educated, and ordained a priest. His family, friends, and favorite restaurants were all here, yet they all seemed so distant now. He felt like he was in a parallel universe, living someone else's life.

The bus soon reached its destination at 26th and California Avenue, the Criminal Courts building. It was an imposing structure, housing both the Cook County Jail and the largest court system in the nation. Ed had only seen it on the news, but now he was on a bus being driven deep into the bowels of the massive monolith. Shortly, Father Ed and his fellow prisoners were herded into a padded elevator that made a non-stop trip to the holding cell behind the courtroom where they would wait until each of their cases was called. The only convenience afforded the men was the removal of the belly chain that had linked them all together.

"What time is it, Turnkey?" A voice cried out.

"Why, you got some place you need to be?"

"No, I'm gettin' hungry; what time do we eat?"

The prisoners were now in the charge of the Sheriff's Department, the authority responsible for court security. A middle aged Black woman with close cropped hair and wearing a uniform that seemed barely able to contain her ample girth, answered quickly. "Don't know if y'all will eat or not, depends on if we go past lunch time. Judge Olsen likes to get through the docket fast as he can . . . he's a golfer."

"Well, I'm hungry now. What can you get for me?"

"Can't get you nothin', fool, you shoulda thought about that before you got yourself arrested." She turned back to her desk and continued to snack on donuts and chocolate milk.

Soon the activity began. The judge arrived, and each prisoner was escorted to the bench when his case was called. Shortly after the second man returned to the holding cell, Father Ed's name was rang out—it was time.

"Matthews," shouted the female deputy as she unlocked the door and motioned for him to move out. He got up from the bench along the wall and shuffled toward the door that led into the courtroom. Dragging the chain that connected his leg irons, he looked out over the benches where the visitors were seated. He spotted his parents and mouthed the words, "I love you," to them. Seated next to them was his best friend, Dan Walsh. His eyes beginning to tear, Ed was directed to stand beside the public defender in front of the bench.

Several feet away, Detective Shannon stood next to the Assistant State's Attorney. While the clerk read the charges, the public defender spoke with Ed. "Father Matthews, this is a serious charge, a felony. Do you have the financial ability to retain counsel?"

"Sir, I'm a priest; I have no money."

"What about your family? Are they able to provide you with an attorney?"

"No, my father works for the city and my mother volunteers at the parish rectory. They have little, if any savings," Ed answered nervously. He stole a glance at his family.

"What about the church, can they give you any financial assistance?"

"I'm not sure," Ed replied. "I have no idea whether they can help me in any way."

The PD shook his head. "If that's the case, the Public Defender's office will provide you with a lawyer, but my advice to you is to somehow retain a private criminal defense attorney."

Judge Olsen addressed the PD. "Counsel, are you prepared to proceed?"

"Yes, your honor. The defendant advised me that he is unable to retain a private attorney in this matter."

The silver haired judge looked over his bifocals at the priest. "Father Matthews, our purpose here this morning is to inform you of the charge and set bond. Mr. State's Attorney, do we have any criminal history associated with the defendant?"

The ASA answered quickly, "No, your honor, no criminal history, not even a traffic ticket."

"I see."

"Your Honor, may we approach the bench?" asked the ASA.

Judge Olsen nodded and signaled for them and the PD to come forward for the sidebar.

"Your honor," he began, "Detective Shannon has informed me that although he has a statement from the victim and his mother, he feels that something isn't quite right. His interview with Father Matthews did not produce any inculpatory evidence. In fact, his answers and demeanor were such that the detective has a strong feeling that the priest may be innocent."

The judge stroked his chin while he pondered his next move. "What about the child? Has he been examined? Are there any injuries or evidence of sexual molestation?"

"No, your Honor. There's no medical evidence to substantiate the charge, and Shannon indicates that his interview with the victim and his mother left him with more questions than answers."

"So, all that being said, what is your recommendation for bond?"

"I know this is going to sound strange coming from the State, especially with the type of offense being charged, but we're inclined to go PR on this, if you'd have no objection."

"You're right. Coming from you, the recommendation does sound strange," he laughed softly. "If I didn't know any better, it almost sounds like you have a bit of compassion left in that old body of yours, Counselor."

"Thanks, I guess."

The group returned to their positions.

"Father Matthews, I've spoken with the State regarding its case, and it appears to me that there needs to be more investigation undertaken in this matter. Inasmuch as you lack any criminal history, I'm going to issue a Personal Recognizance Bond and set the next court date for ninety days from today. Is the State amenable to that?"

"Yes, your honor."

"I thought as much. Now, Father Matthews, listen carefully to my instructions. You are not to have any contact with the child or his mother until this matter is resolved. Is that clear?"

"Yes, Sir," a grateful Ed Matthews replied softly.

"Additionally, you are not to travel outside the state of Illinois. If you get into any trouble at all, or violate the conditions of your bond, it will be revoked immediately and you will be held in the county jail until your case has been resolved. Is that clear?"

"Yes, Sir."

"I remind you again, these are serious charges. My advice to you is to somehow retain counsel to defend yourself against them. The State does not take these allegations lightly, nor should you."

"Yes, your honor."

"Very well then, Mr. Sheriff, take custody of the defendant and have him execute the bond. Mr. Clerk, please call the next case.

It's a beautiful day to be out on the golf course."

Ed was escorted back to the holding area where he resumed his position on the bench along the wall. The prisoner seated next to him, the same one who had asked for something to eat, spoke to him.

"So . . . you a priest, huh?"

Remembering what the detectives had told him earlier, Ed remained silent, not wanting to cause any problems for himself.

"Hey, man, I'm talkin' to you," he shouted, as he shoved Ed with his manacled hands. "Judge said you was a priest. You like foolin' around with little boys, huh? You better watch your ass. Dudes in the joint know how to take care of your kind."

The sheriff's deputy sensed that the conversation was about to get out of hand. She quickly interjected. "Fool, shut up. Quit running yer mouth before you get into more trouble. If I have to come in there, you gonna get a whuppin'."

Having been through the system numerous times before, the prisoner wisely followed her orders.

An hour later, those who could make bond were taken to the outtake area and processed. Ed signed his paper work and walked through a door that led to the outside of the building. He breathed in the fresh air and gazed skyward, the warmth of the sun gently caressing his face. *Thank you, Father.* Watching people walking, driving, and engaging in their daily activities, captured his attention like never before. He noted the freedom with which they moved, coming and going as they pleased. It was a gift that had been taken from him the past couple of days. He would never again take his liberty for granted, for freedom was now of paramount importance in his life. What used to seem important, lesson plans for his classes at St. Nick's, preparing the children's choir, working on his homily for Sunday Mass, all those things he used to fret about, had now taken a back seat to one thing—freedom. He knew from his short experience in jail that if he were found guilty, he would never survive being locked up.

Walking around to the front of the building, he spotted his parents. His mother rushed up to him and held him. "Edward, are you okay?" Tears streaming down her face, she kissed him repeatedly as she held him tightly. "Are you hurt?"

"No, Mom, I'm fine."

His father wrapped him in a bear hug, the same embrace that had always made Ed feel safe and protected throughout his life. Now, although still welcome, it didn't hold the same power. "Son, we've been so worried, what's going on? What's this all about?"

Seeing his parents suffering tore at Ed's heart. He had always been their pride and joy. An honor student in school, Eagle Scout, and athlete . . . they had supported him in everything, boasting about their son to anyone who would take the time to listen. On the day of his Ordination to the priesthood, they were absolutely ecstatic. His mother beamed, her smile so bright that it almost seemed to sparkle. Now they appeared to have aged overnight. Her eyes were sad and tear-filled, sunken in her head, she appeared pale and fragile. His father's posture, slumped, his face etched with anxiety, his self-confident, strong persona, replaced with a broken spirit.

"Let's talk on the ride home."

"Sure, son," his father answered. "We're parked in the lot across the street."

Driving south on California Avenue, Ed seized on what used to be mundane things. Riding in his father's car, unlike his journey on the police bus while shackled to other prisoners, gave him an appreciation for this simple pleasure that he had never felt before. He looked out the window at the neighborhoods, the trees and parks, all clearly in focus now, part of the Artist's palette.

"Edward?" His mother's voice snapped him back to reality.

"Yes?"

"Please, tell us what's going on. This charge . . . sexual assault, is it? What does it mean?"

This situation was going to be difficult to explain to his parents. It was humiliating enough to have had the police arrest him at the rectory in front of the pastor, but now to actually have to tell his parents the nature of the charges was something no son should have to put his parents through, especially an innocent son. He felt a rush of shame fill his neck and face as he pondered how to begin.

"Mom, Dad, let me begin by telling you that I've done nothing wrong. I say that with complete honesty and respect to you as the two people in this world who I love the most. Yesterday, after I was arrested and brought to the police station, the detectives questioned me about an allegation that is completely false. One of our parishioners, Magdalena Mendoza, told them that I had molested her ten- year old son, Rodrigo."

"Oh, no, Edward...how could she?" His mother gasped.

"I know, Mom, it's hard to believe and I still don't quite understand what's going on. Rodrigo has been an altar boy for close to a year. He's done a great job and loves to serve at mass. He's also in the children's choir and tells me that he enjoys being at church and having a role in the parish. His mother and I have not had many conversations other than talking with her about her son's scheduling and such, but she's never given me any indication that there was anything wrong."

"Will it be on the news?" His father asked as he navigated the city streets.

"Probably."

"Don't they know what a fine priest you are?" his father complained.   "You're probably more well liked than Father DeSalvo."

"I know, Dad, but that has no bearing on anything. The detectives did their job, questioning me about the allegations made by Rodrigo's mother. I'm not about to get into the graphic descriptions that they related to me, but after several hours with each of them taking turns asking me to admit to even the most minor of transgressions, they changed their attitude. They didn't say as much, but my feeling is that they think that Mrs. Mendoza may be lying."

"But why, Eddie?" cried his mother. "Why would she lie about something like that?"

"I'm not sure, Mom, but I thought about it all night as I lay in my cell. Over the past several years the Church has suffered through dozens of these same types of allegations, some true, others having no merit whatsoever. Regardless, the media has covered this topic enough for people to know that the Catholic Church has doled out millions of dollars in settlements to victims of abuse."

"It's not right."

"I know, Mom, but absent any other rational explanation, maybe that's what's going on here. The problem now becomes one of how to prove I'm innocent. It comes down to my word against the child and his mother. Chances are that I wouldn't fare very well in that scenario."

His father eased the car to the curb in front of the rectory at St. Nicholas of Tolentine parish. "Son, would you rather stay at our house?" His father asked as he put the car in park.

"No, Dad, this is where I live, but I appreciate the offer. Besides, I have to find out where I stand with Father DeSalvo and the Archbishop."

His mother leaned over the seat and gave him a kiss on the cheek. "We love you, Eddie. Our door is always open for you. I know that God will eventually get us past this horrible day. In the meantime we'll be praying for you."

"Thanks, Mom and Dad. I love you both so much. I don't know what I'd do without you."

Ed got out of the car and headed up the steps to the front door and then turned to wave. He opened the door to find Father DeSalvo standing in the hallway. Waiting.

Driving through the city streets after court, Pete opened his window and breathed in the crisp autumn morning. The trees had just started to morph from monotone to eye-catching kaleidoscope. He loved the fall; especially during his early morning workouts. Running in the cool air was invigorating and a welcome change from the hot, humid mornings that characterized the summer.

Minutes later, he arrived at Chicago's Police Headquarters. Making his way up to his office on the third floor to the Violent Crimes Unit, Pete walked in and spotted his partner, Detective Marilyn Benson, seated at her desk.

"Hey, Bens, good morning."

"Hi, Pete. How did it go in court?"

Pete put his duty bag on the floor beside his desk, sat down, and took a sip from his cup of coffee. "It went well. The ASA had a sidebar with Judge Olsen, and they agreed to give Father Ed a PR bond."

"Good," Marilyn replied, smiling. "I don't think he's guilty of anything, particularly what the kid's mother accused him of."

"Yeah, I don't see the priest having anything other than a pastoral relationship with the boy. The little guy seems to idolize the priest, and the mother was just too well prepared and forthcoming with information, knowing just the right thing to say."

"I know. The kid's answers seem rehearsed, like she had gone over them with him. There was no spontaneity. "

Taking another sip of coffee, Pete said, "The problem is the kid's age. Even though my gut tells me that all this may very well be bogus, we'd catch hell if we didn't arrest the priest."

"You're right, but in the process of covering our own butts, we may have destroyed the life of an innocent man. The stigma of being labeled a pedophile never goes away. That spotlight quickly shines brightly when you're accused but dims slowly once you've been cleared. All that people remember is you were arrested."

"Well, I don't know how you feel about it, Marilyn, but depending on how busy we get with other cases, I say we dig a little deeper on this one. I think it's just as important to prove a man's innocence as it is to prove his guilt."

"Agreed, partner."

"Shannon . . . Benson . . . my office," barked Lt. King.

Lt. Jerry King was the Commanding Officer of the Violent Crimes Unit. A Marine Corps vet, he was a no-nonsense boss who performed his job with military precision and commanded his troops with a firm, but fair hand. A divorced father of two, one of which was presently in the Corps, he had two loves in his life—the Marine Corps and the Chicago PD. He valued loyalty and integrity and expected his detectives to do the same. Pete and Marilyn enjoyed being on his squad.

The partners walked into his office.

"Have a seat," he said pointing to the chairs near the window of his office. "You've no doubt heard about the murder of Officer Gonzalez yesterday."

"Yes, sir."

"Well, the homicide dicks have come up with zero. They've done a canvass of the neighborhood, interviewing people who live on both sides of the street—no one saw anything."

"What about the shot, anyone hear that?" Marilyn asked.

"A couple people, but that only gives us a fix on the time. The crime scene guys searched for a bullet casing but failed to find one.

They even had a class from the police academy come out and do a grid search of the entire block, but they came up empty handed as well."

"Had to be a shoulder weapon, right boss?"

"That's my guess, Shannon, but we'll have to wait and see what the lab guys come up with after the autopsy. Anyway, I didn't call you two in here for idle chatter; you're both being assigned to the case."

Pete and Marilyn looked wide-eyed at each other before she spoke up. "Lew, we've never worked a homicide case. Why us?"

"I know that, Benson, but the Chief of Detectives wants this thing solved ASAP. The only problem is that Homicide is buried under a mound of dead bodies, no pun intended. Last weekend there were ten homicides on top of the eight that occurred during the week. He's running low on manpower so he's reaching out to us for help. I tried to tell him that I don't have the bodies to give him, but I may as well have been talking to the wall. You two are all I can spare. Everyone else on the squad is weighed down with a caseload that won't allow them the hours they need to work on this murder. You two, as the least experienced, have the lightest load." King leaned over to take a file from his desk drawer.

Pete quickly thought about the fifteen cases that he and Marilyn were working and silently disagreed with King's assessment.

"By the way, good work on arresting the priest on that sexual assault. That's another reason why you got the ticket on the homicide. I know you both did a lot of legwork on that case. That frees you up to do the same on this one."

"Boss," interrupted Pete, "we're not really finished with it yet. Marilyn and I think the guy's innocent, that the mother might be lying."

"It wouldn't be the first time a witness lied, would it? Whatever plans you have to flesh out your theory will have to be put on the back burner. This case takes precedence. And one thing I didn't tell you is that you'll be working with two guys from Homicide who'll be the lead detectives on the case. Before you get all upset up about that, let me work out the logistics on this thing with Lt. Darcy of homicide. The Chief told me she would be in charge of this joint effort, but I hate to have my guys answering to anyone but me.

"Anyway, you've got a meeting with her and whomever she's assigned the case at 1500 today, in her office. Hopefully, with four people assigned to the investigation you can solve this thing quickly and get back to work on your own caseload. Any questions?"

"No, sir."

"Good. One last thing . . . I realize that neither of you have worked a homicide before, but I wouldn't have given you the assignment if I didn't think you weren't capable of handling it."

When the two stood up to leave, Pete said, "Thanks, Lew. That means a lot."

"You're welcome. Dismissed."

Heading back to their desks in the bullpen, the partners discussed their new assignment. "What do you think, Pete? A homicide case; think we can handle it?"

"I don't know. In a way I'm glad to be assigned to help find whoever murdered a cop, but I don't know if I'm up to the challenge."

"Well, let's stop and analyze this for a moment. We're getting hung up on the fact that it's a homicide case and that we've never worked one before. But it's all the same, partner. We do the legwork—canvass neighborhoods, do interviews, background work—just like we do with all of our cases."

Pete smiled. "You're absolutely right. We don't approach this any differently than we do with any of our cases. We work logically and methodically to find the shooter. Brilliant."

"I know."

Pete laughed. "Okay, I know, you've got beauty *and* brains, but you are right. We shouldn't let this case intimidate us, and King wouldn't have given us the ticket if he didn't think we could handle it."

"That's right, partner," Marilyn said, grabbing her ID off her desk "What do you say we go grab an early lunch before our meeting this afternoon?"

"Good idea. Now I'm excited about being assigned to a murder case. I just wonder who we'll be partnered with in the Homicide Unit."

"Yeah, me too," replied Marilyn, "but most of those guys have a lot of years on the job and are pretty set in their ways. I'm not sure they're going to welcome us with open arms."

"No sense worrying about that now. Let's grab some chow; I'm starving," said Pete, as they walked down the stairs. "I ran a hard six miler this morning before work; I need some carbs."

"Good for you. I don't know how you get up that early every morning. I've tried it, and I find myself dragging the rest of the day."

"Once you get in the habit of doing it, it becomes easy. Besides, I like to get it in early so that when I get home after work I can spend time with Beth and the baby."

"How's she doing?"

"Gettin' bigger."

"No problems with the pregnancy?"

"No, thank God. The doctor said she's doing fine."

"Good," replied Marilyn as they reached the parking lot behind the building. "Who's driving, you or me?"

Pete tossed the keys to her. "Why don't you drive, I want to call Beth and check in on her and the little guy."

"Okay. Hey, Pete, when we get back I want to review the statement from the boy's mother again. I've got a hunch about something."

"Sounds good. Your hunches are usually spot on."

"I hope you're right about that, for Father Ed's sake."

Ed walked into the rectory and closed the door behind him. Looking at the pastor, he said, "Hello, Father."

"Hello, Edward. I'm glad to see you're out of jail."

Ed felt the tension in the air; it was as thick as a swarm of gnats. "Thanks. I'm glad to be out, Father."

"We need to talk," said the pastor. "Let's go into the study."

Ed followed the older priest into the large room that had served as a study and library for dozens of priests over the years. Three of its walls were adorned with floor to ceiling book shelves, containing tomes on Theology, Christianity, the Catholic faith, and Church doctrine. A small section was devoted to contemporary subjects, both non-fiction and fiction. A huge mahogany desk that each pastor had claimed as his own occupied one corner, while a smaller table used by the other priests stood alone on the opposite side of the room. In the center, three burgundy easy chairs formed a semi-circle around an ornate coffee table that held several photo books containing pictures of cathedrals and churches from around the world.

As the pastor sidestepped the easy chairs and went directly to his desk, Ed knew this meeting was not destined to be a pleasant one. Father DeSalvo sat in the high-backed leather chair behind the glass topped desk; Ed chose one of the two wooden chairs on the opposite side. The older priest folded his hands in front of him on the desk and began.

"Father, we have a very serious situation here at St. Nick's. Your arrest has not gone unnoticed by the press or our parishioners. I've had dozens of calls since yesterday, asking me to explain what happened. The papers and television have been after me for a statement, but frankly, I don't know what to tell them. So, I need you to explain to me what you've done. Is it true, did you harm that boy?"

Squirming in his chair, unable to fully comprehend that this was indeed happening, Ed answered. "Whatever you've heard, Father, is simply not true. The allegations made by the boy's mother are totally false. My relationship with Rodrigo has always been nothing more than priest to parishioner. Has he spent time alone with me? Yes, within the confines of his duties as an altar boy in the sacristy, both before and after mass. Beyond that I've never been alone with him."

"Have you done anything special for the child . . . given him any gifts?"

"Yes, I've given him a rosary and a St. Joseph's Catholic Prayer Book."

Father DeSalvo sat straighter in his chair. "Have you done the same for any of the other servers?"

Father Ed shook his head. "No, Rodrigo is poor. His mother is out of work, more often than not. She doesn't have the means to buy things for him other than the basics."

"I see," said the pastor. "What else have you given him?"

"Nothing."

"Really? His mother told me that you gave him a baseball cap."

Pausing to think, Ed replied. "Oh, yes, don't you remember? I took the altar boys to the White Sox game during the summer. The other boys had money to buy snacks and souvenirs. Rodrigo was the only one without any money, so I bought him a hat."

"What else have you done for the boy?"

Ed didn't like the direction this line of questioning was headed. In fact, it felt like he was back at the police station being interrogated by the detectives.

"Father, what are you getting at? My relationship with the boy is no different than how I've treated all of the children of the parish. He's a good kid who treasures his assignment as an altar boy. Because of his circumstances, I try to brighten his life by giving him a little extra attention at times. Have we come to a point in society where showing another person you care is misconstrued as criminal?"

The pastor sat back and folded his arms. "Father, all I know is that you were arrested for molesting a child. The Archbishop called me this morning after he had been contacted by the newspaper. He was not happy; he gave me orders that you are to be relieved of your priestly duties at St. Nick's. You are to use the chapel here in the rectory, and you are not to have any contact with the child or for that matter, any of the children in the parish, which means no altar servers are to assist you."

"Father, what about my classes and the children's choir?"

"You will be assigned administrative tasks to be performed either here in the rectory or downtown in the diocesan office."

His heart racing, his face flushed with anger and embarrassment, Ed replied. "That's it? I've been judged guilty before ever having gone to trial? Father, do you believe that I'm innocent?"

Shaking his head, the pastor said, "I don't know what to believe. I know that we've had problems such as these in our past. The Church has suffered many indignities because of this type of behavior, yet She has survived. I pray that what you say is true, Father, but all I can do is be obedient to the Archbishop. He controls both our destinies, and right now it's his call. You are prohibited from entering the school, and from conducting any extracurricular activities with the children. You are not to say mass in public. And one more thing, Father, the Archbishop has ordered that you not wear your clerical collar outside of the rectory."

Hearing the decree from the Archbishop, Ed sank in his chair. Feeling faint and slightly detached from what was happening to him, he felt as if he was watching someone else's life being destroyed, not his own. Father DeSalvo may as well have given him a death sentence. To be restricted from saying Mass in the church and not being able to teach the children was too much to bear. Helping people, saving souls, and serving the Lord by serving His people were the very reasons he had entered the priesthood. What would become of his vocation? Would he ever again function normally within the Church?

"Father, may I ask one question?"

"Yes."

"I need you to answer honestly. Do you believe that I molested the boy? I'm asking as a friend, and it's important that I know."

The pastor rested his head in his hands and looked down toward the desk for a moment. Uncovering his face, he looked at Ed. "I'm not sure, Father. I'm sorry to have to say that, but I just don't know what to believe."

Ed stared at the priest, a person whom he considered his friend, confidant, and spiritual mentor, and at that moment Ed realized the enormity of his situation. If his fellow priest didn't believe in his innocence, how would a judge or jury be expected to believe him? He felt the last drops of hope drain quickly from his body, like a bucket of water with a hole in the bottom. He stood up to leave; it was finished.

"I need to be alone," he said.

He walked from the study and up the stairs to his room on the second floor where he encountered the housekeeper, Mrs. Dumbrowski, on the way. "Father, may I get you something to eat?"

"No, thank you, Margaret."

"I put your clean vestments in the sacristy today. They're all ready for tomorrow's mass."

"Thank you, but I won't need them."

Ed walked into his room and closed the door behind him. Exhausted from his night in jail, he collapsed on the bed. His back was sore from lying on the steel rack, as were his wrists and ankles from the cuffs. The thought of being confined terrified him. He looked at the crucifix hanging on the wall. *Dear Lord, why? Why this test . . . what are your plans for me? Please, if it be Thy will, take this burden from me.* Then, mercifully, he slept, dreamless.

He awoke around nine. The rectory was quiet, the pastor and housekeeper in their rooms for the evening. His stomach queasy, still anxious and fearful about his future, he decided to give his best friend a call. Reaching across to the nightstand, he picked up the phone and dialed.

"Dan, it's me, Ed."

"Ed, are you okay? You looked terrible in court."

"I'm fine, now."

"I don't know if your parents told you or not, but I couldn't see you after you made bond. I had a couple of other cases scheduled and barely made it to your hearing."

"That's okay, Dan. Listen, do you think you could meet me somewhere for coffee in the morning? I need to talk with someone, and right now you're about the only one I feel comfortable discussing this with."

"Sure, if you can come out my way . . . say, the coffee shop on 95th Street, around seven-thirty? That way I can head north and catch the Stevenson to work."

"I'll be there. Thanks, Dan."

"No need for that, Ed. Get a good night's rest, and I'll see you in the morning."

His friend's advice to rest would have to wait. Ed had too

much to think about, too many plans to make. He turned on his laptop and began to set his ideas in motion.

Pete and Marilyn arrived at the Homicide Unit for their meeting with Lt. Darcy. The office was set up much differently from their own at Violent Crimes. Their boss, Lt. King, liked the open bullpen scheme, which gave him the ability to see all of his people. In contrast, homicide's space afforded each detective an individual cubicle, allowing them some small measure of privacy and individual expression. As they walked around, they saw an assortment of family photos and other paraphernalia adorning each person's work area. They made their way to the commanding officer's office, which occupied the far corner of the huge room. The door was closed; the name plate on it read, Lt. Pat Darcy, Homicide. Pete knocked.

"Stand by," came a female voice from inside the office.

Moments later a petite woman with black hair and a faultless smile, highlighted by teeth as white as a snow capped mountain opened the door. She extended her hand, first to Marilyn, then to Pete. "Hi, I'm Pat Darcy; welcome to Homicide. I feel like I already know you two. I've seen stories on the news about your work on the serial rapist case and the Wrigley Field robber; Jerry King filled me in on your backgrounds before I approved your TDY here. Come in, please, have a seat."

Pete looked around the room, which was filled with photos and plaques chronicling her career in the department. Unlike Lt. King's office, which was stark by comparison, having only the Chicago Police Star and Marine Corps logo hanging on the wall,

Darcy's was filled with memorabilia and souvenirs. It was the quintessential "I love me" wall.

Darcy took a seat behind her desk, while the two detectives sat on a couch, reserving the two chairs for whoever their partners turned out to be.

"Thank you for your promptness. McKinnon and Russo should join us momentarily; they seem to operate on a different time schedule than the rest of us." She shuffled some papers on her desk. "When I learned the two of you would be temporarily assigned to me on this case, I was pleased. I know all about the good work you both did on Operation Cleanup. Marilyn, I hope that you've completely healed from your encounter with that cave dweller."

"Yes, ma'am," Marilyn replied with a smile.

"Good, let's . . ." Before she could finish her sentence, there was a tap on the open door, and two men entered the office."

"Sorry we're late, Lew. Traffic was heavy," said the taller of the two men, who spoke with a toothpick in his mouth. They moved to the chairs and quickly sat down.

"Harry McKinnon . . . Bobby Russo. . . meet Pete Shannon and Marilyn Benson. They'll be your partners on the Gonzalez case."

Pete was about to stand to offer a handshake to his new colleagues, but the pair remained seated and simply turned and nodded in acknowledgement of Darcy's introduction.

"McKinnon and Russo are my most senior detectives, having been in homicide for a combined thirty years. They've seen just about all there is to see in the way of murders. They'll be the lead on this case and will determine the direction of the investigation. For now, I want both of you to conduct another neighborhood canvass," Darcy said, looking at Pete and Marilyn.   "One has already been done, but it didn't yield anything worthwhile. Maybe you two can come up with something that may have been overlooked. The problem is we're two days out from the murder.

The further we get from the incident, the more difficult it becomes to solve. I also want you to do a detailed analysis of the murdered officer's arrests. Find out if anyone he arrested in the past has recently been released from jail, or if he had any altercations on the street that might give us a clue as to who may have wanted to kill him."

Taking notes as the lieutenant spoke, Marilyn asked, "What about his family? Have they been interviewed?"

McKinnon spoke up, his toothpick dancing between his lips. "Yeah, we've already talked with them, but not much there to go on."

"If you think it's worthwhile to sit down with them again, go ahead and do it." Darcy slid a folder toward Pete and Marilyn. "Here's the file. Take the rest of the day and review what's been done thus far. There's a cubicle on the far side of the office that you'll use while you're temporarily assigned here," she said, pointing to an area by the coffee maker.

"I'm giving you free reign to decide what else needs to be done. The problem thus far is no witnesses and no evidence. My concern is the Chief of detectives. He wants this case solved ASAP. Do what you need to do to get it done. Let me know if you need anything in the way of equipment and the like. Make your own hours; I'll authorize all the overtime you need.   Any questions?" Darcy asked.

The two homicide dicks shook their heads.

Darcy looked at Pete and Marilyn. "And you?"

"No ma'am," answered Marilyn.

"Good. One more thing, I'm sure we all know this team was established at the direction of the Chief. I didn't request the extra help, although I think it will be beneficial, and Lt. King wasn't keen on giving up two of his people. That being said, let's put aside any differences or hard feelings anyone may have and get on with the job of finding whoever killed our brother officer."

The four detectives got up and filed out of the lieutenant's office.   They walked halfway down the aisle separating the cubicles when McKinnon and Russo stopped abruptly and turned toward their new partners.

"You two do like the boss ordered, look over the file," McKinnon said, taking the toothpick from his mouth and pointing it at the pair as he spoke. "We'll catch up with you in the morning; right now we've got things to do."

"But . . ." Before Pete could finish his sentence, the pair turned and walked out the door.

"This isn't quite the beginning I had envisioned, Pete."

"I know. The vibes are pretty strong. They're not pleased to have us along for the ride."

"Yeah, it reminds me of working with Geraci and Carone on the Wrigley Field stick up man," she said. "They weren't thrilled about working with us either. What have we gotten ourselves into?"

"I'm not sure, but let's not lose hope just yet. Let's find our cubicle and study the file. Maybe we'll find something someone else missed."

"Good idea," Marilyn said.   "We can also plan the neighborhood interviews. There's plenty to keep us busy."

The two detectives located their temporary space and surveyed their domain. "Computer, phone, file cabinets. Looks like we've got all the basics, Bens."

"Tell you what, Pete, let's approach this from the standpoint of not having any partners. Let's just move forward as if it were just the two of us working this murder case."

Pete smiled. "Sounds like a winner, and frankly, that appears to be the case anyway. My sense is that as long as we find the killer, no one will care if it was solved by the so-called team or not."

"Yeah, and we're probably doing Mutt and Jeff a big favor by staying out of their way."

Pete laughed. "Mutt and Jeff? I like that tag, I just hope I don't let that accidentally slip out some day."

In comparison to how their new partners were referring to them, the nicknames, Mutt and Jeff seemed tame.

Ed arrived early at the coffee shop and ordered his favorite beverage while he waited for his friend to show. He breathed in the rich aroma of brewed coffee and fresh baked goods. His incarceration was still fresh in his mind, causing him to be thankful for just about everything he did. The ability to go places freely, like the coffee shop, and order whatever he wanted to eat or drink strengthened his resolve to go through with the decision he had made yesterday.

Ed hoped Dan would lend his support and maybe even give him some ideas. They had been friends since the sixth grade when the Walsh family lived next door to the Matthews' house. The two had attended St. Nick's grade school, and upon graduation, both had been accepted to Brother Rice High School where their friendship grew even stronger. They had played together on the baseball and football teams and maintained near perfect grades. It was in their junior year when they felt God was calling them both into the priesthood. They set off for Mundelein College to prepare, but after two years, the once raging fire in Dan's heart to become a priest turned to mere embers. He transferred to the University of Illinois and went on to the John Marshall Chicago School of Law, finally becoming a criminal defense attorney.

Ed brought his coffee cup to his lips, and looking through the steam rising from it, he spotted Dan coming in the door. He stood and waved, signaling for him to come over.

Dan gave his friend a hug. "How are you? This is such a tragedy, Ed. I can't believe what's happened."

"I know, neither can I."

Dan pulled a newspaper from under his arm. "Here's yesterday's *Sun Times,* and you're in it. The good news is that you're not on the front page." He dropped it on the table and walked over to the counter to get his coffee.

Ed didn't bother to look inside the paper; he'd had enough bad news to last a lifetime. He didn't need to see it in black and white. A minute later, Dan was back with coffee and a bagel. Sitting across from his friend, he asked, "So, tell me, how in the world did all of this get started?"

"It's not complicated. One of the parishioners went to the police and accused me of molesting her son. The first I heard about it was when the cops showed up at the rectory to arrest me."

Dan took a bite of his bagel. "I'm not even going to ask whether it's true or not because I know you too well. I know that your heart is pure. If there was ever a perfect fit for the priesthood, it's you."

Ed sighed, his eyes moistening, and for the first time in the past couple of days, his body relaxed. "Dan, thank you. Your words mean so much. Other than my parents, everyone has treated me like a criminal. The jail experience was something I never want to go through again. I know I was there only overnight, but believe me, the thought of having to go back . . ."

"I can only imagine what it was like," Dan replied. "In my practice, I deal with mostly repeat offenders. They're so used to being locked up that they consider it part of the risk of doing business. In fact, for some it's like old home week. They get to visit with their buddies. Every once in a while, I'll get a first timer like yourself who finds being incarcerated a horrible experience that either makes or breaks him."

"Dan, I can't go back to jail, I won't go back. And I know the way it looks now, it will come down to the mother and the boy testifying against me. I don't have a chance; who's going to believe me when they see this little boy on the stand?"

Dan nodded. "Do you have a lawyer?"

"C'mon, you know I don't have the money to hire anyone. I barely make enough each month to pay for my car, gas, and a few meals out with friends. Mom and Dad don't have enough savings either, and I wouldn't ask them anyway. They're close to retirement and need what little money they have to survive."

Dan took another bite from his bagel and looked toward the ceiling while he chewed. He took a drink of coffee and said, "Ed, what if I took your case, pro bono?"

"You mean for free?"

"Yeah. Heck, I owe it to you and your folks. Besides, that PD who represented you at the hearing is green. He's okay for things like bond hearings, but a trial? A seasoned prosecutor would chew him up and spit him out."

"That would be fantastic, but I'm still worried this whole thing is beyond my control. The damage seems too major to repair, especially my reputation. How will I ever be trusted again by anyone?"

"I won't lie to you. You're in big trouble, and there's a chance that, like you said, the boy's word against yours is going to be difficult to overcome. We may have to work out a plea agreement to keep you out of jail."

"But I'm innocent, Dan. I haven't done anything wrong; I never touched Rodrigo. I couldn't, I care too much about him."

"I know, and ironically, that may just be the problem, the fact that you care for the boy. Look, I know that right now the future looks bleak, and you're probably at the lowest point you've ever been in your life. Just give me some time to analyze what evidence the State has, go over the file, and see where the holes are. Then we can sit down and mount a defense."

Father Ed offered a half smile to his friend. "Dan, I appreciate your offer, and I accept it. I know you'll provide me with the best possible defense. The problem is when I look at cases like mine that I've seen in the news, the priests have either gone to jail or been given fines and probation. In either case, the bottom line is they were found guilty and subsequently labeled as sex offenders. I can't handle that; I can't live like that."

"Wait a minute, Ed. Before you give up all hope, what's the alternative? It is what it is—you've been charged with a serious crime. Yes, it's one that has dire consequences, but you're innocent until proven guilty. That will be my job, to prove your innocence. After all we've been through, don't you trust me?"

"Yes, I just don't trust the system."

There was a moment of silence between the two, and as Ed looked around the coffee shop he spotted a couple at the register. He recognized the woman as one whom he'd seen at mass on several occasions. She was talking with the man standing next to her and pointing in Ed's direction. He didn't know if his reaction was fear or humiliation, but her finger pointed in his direction may as well have been a gun, for all the pain he felt.

"Ed?"

"Yeah, uh, listen, Dan. You're the best friend a guy could ever hope for, but right now what I need most is some time to myself. I've got to think about my future and what my options are."

"That's okay. You're most likely still in a state of shock. I'll be in court today on several other matters, but I'll stop in at Judge Olsen's chambers and inform the clerk that I'll be your attorney of record. We've got plenty of time to sit down and work on a strategy. In the meantime, what has Father DeSalvo said?"

"I'm ostracized. The Archbishop has ordered me not to say Mass or have any contact with the child, his mother, or any of the children in the parish. No classes; no choir. It's bad. I don't even feel like a priest."

"I'm sorry. I thought that at least DeSalvo would support you."

"I thought so too, but he won't even tell me that he thinks I'm innocent."

Dan picked up his cup and put a travel lid on it. "I've got to go, but for what it's worth, I'm absolutely in your corner, and I know you could not have possibly done what you've been charged with. The man I know is a child of God, one who walks with our Lord each day, but, at least for the moment, Satan has you in his grasp. Through prayer and hard work, we'll set you free."

The two men stood and Ed moved to hug his friend. "Dan, I'm so afraid of what's going to become of me."

"I know. Just try to hang in there and let me see what I can do."

"Okay. Bye."

"Good-bye. I'll call you in a couple of days." Ed's new lawyer walked out and got in his car.

Don't worry about calling, I probably won't be around.

Ed got in his car and drove to the public library in Palos Hills, a southern suburb of Chicago. He needed to use the Internet, but he didn't want to do his research at the rectory, lest Father DeSalvo or the police get wind of what he was up to by searching his computer. He also didn't want to use the local libraries in the parish where people knew him there.

When he arrived at the library, he walked up to the woman seated at the desk where the computer assignments were made. "Good morning, ma'am. I'd like to use one of the computers."

"Yes, sir, we have several available. Do you have a library card?"

"Uh, no . . . I'm visiting some friends. I'm from out of town."

"Okay, that's not a problem. Just sign in here. You'll use terminal number seven. Here's the password for today, and your hour will begin once you log in."

Ed signed the sheet, John Smith. The woman glanced at the sheet and said, "Mr. Smith, we limit our patrons to one hour per session, but since we have no one waiting in line to use the computers you may log in again after your session expires."

"Thank you."

Ed walked over to number seven and logged in. He thought about how he lied by using a false name to sign the register. Obviously he wasn't good at lying . . . *John Smith*? The woman must have known immediately that he was not telling the truth. Beyond his inexperience with not being truthful, what bothered him most was the act of telling the lie. How easy it was. Easy or not, he didn't like how it made him feel inside.

No time for introspection. He needed to get busy finding answers that would allow him to place his plan into action. Dan would no doubt be a great lawyer on his behalf, but Ed thought it best not to divulge his plans to his friend. The criminal justice system couldn't be trusted, not at all. Unfortunately, Dan was part of that system. Ed was determined to take control of his own life and not leave his future in the hands of a system that time and again had proven to be corrupt—especially in Chicago.

He opened the browser and Googled two words: new identity.

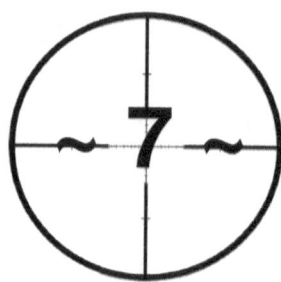

"I bought a latte for you, Bens. I thought we'd start our day with a cup of coffee, a good way to ward off this chilly fall weather."

"Thanks, partner. What's new at home? Beth and little Pete okay?"

"Yeah, they're good. They're anxiously awaiting the arrival of little Pete's sibling. Beth might have had a bout of morning sickness, but it quickly passed. The baby was kicking up a storm overnight."

"You two still plan to hold off on finding out the baby's sex?"

"Yeah, I guess we're old school when it comes to that. The element of surprise adds to the beauty of the birth."

"Good," Marilyn said and then changed the subject. "You know, I was thinking about the murder last night, wondering if it might turn out to be one of those cases that go unsolved for years. The officer's file didn't show anything extraordinary. His arrests were rather run of the mill, and the only guy ever charged with assaulting him was that domestic case, and that was dropped later. I didn't find anyone with a grudge who might want to murder him."

Pete grabbed the file from the cabinet in their cubicle. "I know. His five years on the job were all spent in patrol. A beat cop just doesn't make the type of enemy who hunts him down and kills him."

"Well, let's stick with our plan. We do another neighborhood, especially the two homes where no one answered the door during the first canvas, and then re-interview the family."

"You know, Bens, I was thinking it might not be a bad idea to talk with the guys on his watch. Maybe he hung out with someone, stopped for drinks after work or something, or maybe shared an incident with them that we're not aware of."

"Good idea. That's something that his family members wouldn't know about either."

"Yeah, that should keep us busy for awhile. Before we hit the street, let's stop by the Crime Lab and see if they came up with anything on the bullet."

The pair made their way to the fifth floor and walked into Bill Sherlot's office. Bill was a respected cop with plenty of street time under his belt. His passion was firearms, not necessarily shooting them but knowing everything about them, inside and out. His specialty was being able to identify whether a certain gun was used in a crime by using ballistics and markings specific to a certain weapon. Bill was the department's resident expert on ballistics and tool marks, having testified about them at hundreds of trials.

Sherlot was looking through a microscope as Pete and Marilyn walked in.

"Bill . . ."

He looked up and saw the duo. "Hey, Pete . . . Marilyn, what brings you two here?"

"Hi, Bill. We're wondering if you've got anything for us on the round that killed Officer Gonzalez."

"I didn't know that was your case, Pete. The evidence came in under McKinnon's name."

"It's a long story," said Marilyn. "The chief thought that four heads were better than two on this one, so Pete and I were sent TDY to homicide to give them a hand."

"Oh, man, McKinnon must be steaming. He doesn't like anyone working cases with him. Heck, even his partner, Bobby, sometimes feels like he gets in the way of Dirty Harry."

"Dirty Harry, as in Clint Eastwood?" Pete asked.

"Yeah, he likes to play the role, even carries a six inch 44 Magnum, same gun Dirty Harry carried in the movies."

Pete smiled. "Now that you mention it, he does bear a resemblance to Eastwood. He's tall, lean, with the same black hair, combed straight back. Marilyn's got her own name for him and his partner—Mutt and Jeff."

Sherlot chuckled. "Be careful with that one, Marilyn. McKinnon's got a huge ego and a temper to match. He's been in a few tussles with the bosses over the years. They consider him to be a lone wolf type, kind of a rebel. I think he's been partners with Russo for so long only because Harry can control Bobby."

"I'll heed your advice on that, Bill."

Sherlot grabbed a file from the corner inbox on his desk and opened it to a photo showing bullet fragments. "Here's what's left of the round that killed Gonzalez. There's not enough there to make any identification from the rifling, the pieces are too small. Some of them were lost when they exited his skull. However, I've seen enough of these types of rounds to make an educated guess. It looks like a .223, which is used by some police departments and the military. And it would make sense, since the shot was obviously taken from some distance. If you can come up with a shell casing, I can make an ID from the markings made by the extractor and the firing pin impression."

Pete shook his head. "That's going to be tough. There were already two searches done. The mobile lab came out, and then later, they had a class from the academy do a grid search."

"I know; I heard, but that casing is somewhere."

"Well, it's something we'll keep in mind when we go out there today."

"You find that casing and a gun that you think is the murder weapon, and I'll make the match."

"I have no doubt," Pete said. Thanks for your help and the information. We're going to head out to the scene and maybe take a look for it ourselves." Pete turned to leave.

"One more thing, guys," Sherlot stopped them. "I don't know if you've thought about this angle, but the shot that killed Gonzalez was a brain stem shot. He was killed instantly. All law enforcement snipers train to shoot at a one inch band that covers the eyes. A shot delivered anywhere in that area will sever the brain stem where it connects to the cerebellum and the spinal cord, causing immediate incapacitation. Military snipers aren't required to deliver as accurate a shot. Any shot that hits its target and takes the combatant out is considered a kill, but they are aware of the brain stem shot and try to take it if they get an opportunity."

Marilyn stroked her chin in thought. "So you're thinking that our shooter may be law enforcement or military trained?"

"That's my guess, Marilyn. Unless I'm completely wrong and the shot was pure luck, I think our guy is a trained killer."

"Holy cow," said Pete, "This case gets more complex by the minute. Thanks, Bill, you've been a tremendous help. I hope we can somehow come up with the casing and the weapon."

"I hope so too before our guy finds another victim. Good luck, guys."

That was an ominous warning, one that the detectives hadn't considered. Until now.

Ed's weekend had been horrible. Sundays were normally the highlight of his week. Saying Mass and visiting with the children during Catechism classes were the essence of doing the Lord's work through spreading His word to the flock. But this was the first Sunday of his priesthood that he was unable to do those things. He had been banned from his duties and been relegated to the chapel in the rectory. Alone at the small altar inside the tiny room, he once again felt the fear he had experienced during his night in jail. Confinement. Although he was doing what he loved, celebrating Mass, it wasn't the same as leading the faithful in prayer and calling them to share in the Eucharist. His banishment was intolerable.

Besides excluding Ed from parish activities, Father DeSalvo had become distant. He was no longer the friend and confidant he had been since Ed was first assigned to St. Nick's. His deliberate avoidance was painful. The only saving grace was their housekeeper, Margaret, who continued to treat Ed as if nothing had happened. She seemed to sense that the whole matter was a lie and that he had been set up.

His mother had called several times over the weekend, asking him to come for dinner, but the news of his arrest had spread, and he didn't feel comfortable being out in public anymore. He loved his parents. He couldn't bear to see them in pain. His arrest had shattered their well being. He had spent most of the weekend in prayer, asking God to lift this burden from him, but after much introspection, he realized that his plan was probably his best option. His research on the Internet had given him the answers he needed to leave this untenable situation behind. His new identity had arrived; he was resigned to say goodbye to what had been a rewarding and blessed life as a priest. The old neighborhood, family, and friends would become but cherished memories of a time when everything was right in his world.

Picking up his suitcase, Ed made his way quietly down the steps of his second floor residence in the rectory. Father DeSalvo and Margaret were asleep in their rooms this late at night. Placing on the kitchen table the note he had written explaining that he was on his way downstate to visit a friend, he slipped quietly out the back door. *More lies. It was becoming easier to be dishonest.* Walking the half block to where he had left his car parked earlier in the day, he looked back toward the rectory—no lights. He normally parked in the garage, but tonight he didn't want to take the chance of waking anyone when he pulled out. Placing his suitcase in the trunk, he started the engine and drove off. He made a right turn on Lawndale, stopping momentarily at the main entrance to the church. Blessing himself, he prayed: *Father, may this journey be favorable in your eyes, and may you be with me as I travel down this road of uncertainty.*

A priest on the run, Ed headed toward the Interstate, enroute to Fredericksburg, Virginia, a place where he hoped he could begin anew. Two years ago, while attending a conference in Washington, DC, he took a day trip and visited this small town that rests comfortably on the banks of the Rappahannock River. He fell in love with the city and spent the entire day walking around the historic downtown district and visiting the many quaint shops that helped maintain its colonial complexion. Founded in the early eighteenth century, the city had connections with many of America's historical figures, including George Washington.

What helped attract him was the lack of modern day stores and fast food establishments.   There were no McDonalds, Burger Kings, JC Pennys, or Walmarts.   The beautiful little town was a throwback to the old days when times were simple and uncomplicated.   Ed hoped that he could somehow just blend into this seemingly anachronistic burg and leave back in Chicago the despair that filled his heart.

Driving east, he thought about Dan, his friend and now attorney.   Ed knew that when Dan opened the email from him, he'd be upset.   His departure would no doubt cause a major problem with whatever defense Dan had been considering, but Ed saw no other way to escape the problem.   No one could know his destination; it would be easier that way, especially after the authorities discovered that he was gone.   He would eventually have to tell someone where he was, probably Dan, hoping the attorney-client privilege would keep his whereabouts a secret.

Ed wasn't sure if he could make it non-stop to Fredericksburg, but driving through the night wasn't as bad as he had envisioned. The farther he got from Chicago, the more relaxed he became. He could feel the tension dissipate.   Rolling the windows down, he allowed the chilly autumn air to keep him awake.   A couple of hours later, he stopped for a break in Pennsylvania, eating a sandwich and getting a large cup of coffee to go.   The sparse traffic and hum of the tires began to lull him to sleep.   However, the closer he got to Washington the more traffic increased, and by the time the sun burst over the horizon Ed had entered the DC area and found himself gridlocked.   Two hours later, he finally entered Virginia, travelling the last fifty miles to Fredericksburg without a problem.

Spotting a sign that read, "Fredericksburg East," Ed exited the highway.   He drove along Route 3, down a gentle hill leading to the historic downtown area.   He passed St. Mary's Catholic Church, and a few blocks later, he saw the University of Mary

Washington nestled quietly in a residential area hidden by trees and rolling landscape. Continuing on William Street, he found a parking spot at the corner of Caroline Street. Getting out of his car, he decided to reacquaint himself with the town.

Walking along the main drag, Ed remembered why this place had stuck in his mind. It was serene. Shopkeepers were out sweeping the sidewalk in front of their stores, while some restaurant owners placed chairs around tables in front of their businesses, hoping to attract those diners who wished to eat outside. The town was quiet, orderly, and attractive. No police or fire trucks screaming past, no traffic jams, no gangs on the corners, and no litter spoiling the view of a wonderful little city that just might be the key to his future.

His first order of business was to find a place to stay. He made his way back to his vehicle and headed west, over to Route 1, Jefferson Davis Highway. He recalled that he had seen a drive up motel during his bus trip. He headed in that direction, and moments later was at the TwiLight Hotel, a two story building that sat in front of a strip mall, anchored by a grocery store, post office, and bagel shop. Parking in front of the office, he went inside and found a plump, elderly man seated behind the counter. He wore a NASCAR tee shirt that strained to contain a stomach that appeared to have been spawned from too many bottles of Bud Lite. Its design depicted a race at the Richmond Speedway. The man also wore a baseball cap with the number 48 on it, presumably the man's favorite driver. His long, stringy hair hung like strands of spaghetti from underneath the cap. The clerk was thoroughly engrossed in a movie and snacked on chicken wings while staring at the small TV set. Ed let the screen door slam behind him to alert the man that a customer had entered the office.

"Hey there, young fella, what can I do fer ya?"

"I was wondering if you had any rooms available."

"How long ya need it fer?"

"Well, I don't know for sure, maybe just a couple of nights."

The man swiveled on his chair and looked at the pigeon-holed configuration mounted on the wall behind him. Ed had never seen anything like it, except in old movies.

"I got one on the second floor, down at the far end. It's better up on top. Riffraff from the street don't bother nobody up there. We charge a hundred twenty five bucks a week, even if ya don't stay the whole week."

"Okay, I'll take it," Ed said as he reached into his pocket. "Do I pay up front?"

"Sure do, I ain't stupid, son."

"No, I didn't mean to imply . . ."

"Don't worry about it," the grubby little man said, as he took Ed's money. "Cash, huh? Better'n plastic in my world." He slid an index card toward Ed.

"Here, fill this out with yer name and address, and I'll get ya a receipt."

Ed took out his pen and began to write down the information but stopped short. He had almost written his real name down before remembering that he had a new identity. Concentrating, he completed the card and slid it back to the clerk.

"Okay, Mr. Edward Michaels," said the clerk, reading from the card. "Here's yer key and a receipt for the week's rent. Let me know by Friday if yer fixin' to stay another week sose I don't promise that room to nobody else. We got parking right in front of the hotel, but make sure ya keep yer car locked. Sometimes fools 'round here like to take stuff don't belong to 'em."

Edward Michaels took the key from the clerk and returned to his car. Parking directly below his room, he took his suitcase from the trunk and walked up to the second floor. Opening the door, he surveyed the room. It was dark and smelled of smoke; one small window facing the street provided the only ambient light, and that was only after the heavy red velvet curtains were pulled to one side. The single bed had a matching comforter with tassels hanging from the bottom, most of which had long since vanished. The nightstand held a small lamp and wind up alarm clock, its face cracked from one too many collisions with the wall. The sink and a small mirror were just outside a small room containing the shower and toilet. The sink's counter top was white Formica and had so many cigarette burn holes on its forward edge that the markings almost looked like a planned design.

Ed placed his suitcase on what had once been an easy chair, but now was anything but, its broken springs allowing the cushion to sink almost to the floor. Tired from the long ride and anxious about what he was embarking upon, he laid on the bed for what he thought would be a short nap. He had difficulty falling asleep. Being in a strange place with spartan accommodations took his thoughts back to that night in jail. He couldn't go back; he had to follow through with his plan, even if it meant staying in places like the TwiLight Hotel. He eventually fell asleep and didn't awaken until ten o'clock the next morning.

With no responsibilities to meet, no Mass to say, Ed walked across the street to a coffee shop. He had breakfast while reading the classifieds in the local paper, *The Free Lance-Star*. The TwiLight would suffice for several days, but any long term stay in Fredericksburg would necessitate finding a comfortable place of his own. He found an ad for an apartment located on Caroline Street, the town's main thoroughfare. Writing down the address, he finished his breakfast and walked back across the street to his car. He'd have to get different tags; the Illinois license plates stuck out like the ribs on an anorexic teenager. The money from his closed bank account would last for a little while, but he decided that he may as well begin a job search sooner rather than later.

Driving over to Caroline Street, he tuned the radio to the local station. Might as well find out what's happening in town. While there was still much uncertainty in his future, he was feeling good about once again being in charge. He wasn't sitting around doing nothing while others determined his fate. He was adamant about starting over and not just giving up. Having goals buoyed his spirit so much that a smile formed on his face.

Pulling into a parking spot on Caroline, Ed walked to the address listed for the apartment rental. He passed several people on the way and exchanged greetings with them. They treated him with respect and kindness, something that had been in short supply this past week. *So far, so good, Mr. Edward Michaels.*

~ 9 ~

"Did you get the text message from Lt. Darcy?" Pete asked his partner.

"Yeah, Pete. Meeting at 11 o'clock."

"I wonder if it's a meeting with the team or just the two of us."

"The team, that's a good one," Marilyn replied, curling her lip. "Neither of our partners has responded to any of the phone messages I've left for them. How 'bout you?"

"Nope, haven't heard from either one since our first meeting two days ago. I don't mind telling you it's beginning to bother me. I get the fact they're not happy working with someone else on their case, but they could at least fake it."

Marilyn pulled out the files from the cabinet in their cubicle at homicide. Two days of legwork at the crime scene had netted hardly anything new. The two residents that hadn't answered the door during the initial canvass were accounted for and proved negative as well. They had also come up empty handed on their search for the casing. It seemed they were about out of leads to pursue.

"The only other thing I can think of is to hit the streets and work a couple of informants. Maybe there's word on the street about this guy or his vehicle. Somebody out there must need some money."

"Yeah, Pete, let's ask Darcy at the meeting how much cash we can spread around."

"Okay, you ready?"

"Yeah."

They were about to leave their cubicle when Detective McKinnon appeared in the opening. Flipping a toothpick over and over in his mouth, like a pancake on a griddle, he blocked their departure.

"Listen, before we go into this meeting with Lieutenant Feel Good, let's get something straight. I don't work well with partners. Bobby Russo's been with me since day one. I'm used to him; he knows how I work. I don't need any rookies hangin' on my coattails."

"Hey, wait a minute, McKinnon," Pete started.

"No, you wait, and by the way, I got your calls. I was busy so I didn't answer, but unless you've got our guy in cuffs, I don't need to hear from either of you. Now, we're gonna go to our meeting and smile for the little lady like we're all one big happy family. Got it?"

"So you don't even want to know if we've come up with anything new?" Marilyn asked.

"Lady, I already know you don't have squat. And I know you were at the lab askin' about the bullet. That evidence had my name on it; I could've told you the results before you went stickin' your nose in it."

Pete felt his face flush, and his blood pressure rise. "McKinnon, you're an idiot. In case you've forgotten, we're supposed to be a team which means we share information so that we can solve this case. What is your problem?"

"I'm lookin' at it. You two spend your time in the freakin' office lookin' at reports and computers. Well guess what? You don't solve cases workin' at your desk—the answers are on the street. You've got to talk to people, man, get down in the gutter with 'em. That's where you'll find the dirt."

"Harry!" Lt. Darcy shouted across the room. "Are you and Russo ready for our meeting?"

"Be there in a sec."

He took the toothpick from his mouth, broke it in half, and dropped it on the floor. Looking at Marilyn and Pete, he said, "Do yourselves a favor. Don't make no waves here, it ain't worth it. Me and Bobby will solve this thing, and you'll be back in your own unit where you belong."

McKinnon reached into his coat pocket, put a fresh toothpick in his mouth, turned, and walked toward the lieutenant's office.

"Damn him!" Pete slammed his fist on the desk.

"Pete, easy . . . calm down. Don't let him get under your skin." Marilyn put her hand on his shoulder. "I've never heard you swear before. He must have really gotten to you."

"I'm sorry; I don't know what got into me. I'm just frustrated I guess. I thought the reason we're here is to catch the guy who murdered a cop. Why can't he see that?"

"I don't know, but let's go to that meeting and let Darcy think that everything's fine. We can deal with McKinnon later."

Pete grabbed his notes and got up to leave. "You're right. Smile. But I'll tell you, Mutt and Jeff have not heard the last from me."

The duo headed toward the meeting, Pete's anger boiling beneath the surface. He wasn't comfortable with the way he was feeling, but he wasn't ready to let McKinnon walk all over him and his partner either. He knew there would come a day when the two would butt heads again, but today's skirmish was over.

The partners took a seat on the couch in the CO's office, while McKinnon sat alone in one of the chairs facing Darcy's desk. It was the same seating arrangement as their first meeting, almost as if each opposing team knew their positions. The lieutenant set her can of diet soda on her desk and looked at McKinnon.

"Where's Russo?"

"I've got him tracking down an informant. I'll let him know what went on here."

Truth be known, Bobby Russo was lying on the couch in his apartment nursing a hangover. It was a well known fact that the two detectives spent many nights at a cop bar called Bob Richards Tap. The place was well stocked with women, cop groupies, who were infatuated with all things blue. Harry usually had his choice of gorgeous ladies who were ready to please him in any way they could. High stakes poker games were known to take place in the back room as well. The two o'clock closing time was actually to satisfy licensing regulations, but once the front door was locked, it was strictly "cops only" until the sun came up.

Darcy frowned. "I expect that when I call a meeting, everyone will be here."

"Hey, Lew, you know how informants are. They operate on their own time schedule. Besides, there's not much else out there. Nobody eyeballed the shooter."

She looked over at Pete. "Okay. So how did the canvass go? Anything new come from your house to house?"

"Not really. The two houses where no one answered on the day of the shooting came up negative. We looked over the twenty-four hour incident report for the day before and the day of the murder and came up with a hit-and-run accident."

"At our location?"

"Just down the street, Lew," said Pete. "As you know, the shooting occurred early in the morning but later that night a man who lives down the block and across from the crime scene was going out to the store. He noticed that the driver's side rear bumper of his car had been damaged. It looked to have been sideswiped by a vehicle pulling out of a parking spot. We sent the lab guys out to get some paint scrapings from the damage."

Nodding, Darcy said, "That's good work. Now all we need is the car that matches it. Anything else?"

"The Firearms Section said that there wasn't enough left from the bullet that killed Officer Gonzalez to make any ID," said

Marilyn, "but Sherlot thinks that the round is a .223."

"So the bottom line here is that we're no closer to finding the shooter now than we were the first day. The Chief's not going to be happy, especially with four detectives assigned to the case."

McKinnon let out a sigh and shifted in his chair. "Listen, Lew, we won't find this guy wasting our time in meetings. The answer's on the street somewhere. We need to be out there talking with people and knockin' on doors."

She stared at McKinnon. "Harry, I know you're not a big fan of meetings, but unless I bring something to the old man, he's going to be riding all of our butts and making life difficult. Okay, we're done here. Go back out there and let me know if you develop any new leads. I'll go upstairs and try to schmooze the boss."

McKinnon left without a word; Pete followed him out the door. As Marilyn was leaving, Darcy stopped her. "How's it working out with McKinnon and Russo?" she asked.

That was a loaded question. Marilyn didn't want to complain about the complete lack of cooperation, at least not yet. "They're obviously working their traps, and we're looking more toward the logical leads. Hopefully between the two teams we'll come up with something very soon. Can we spread some money around to stir up some interest?"

"Sure, just don't go overboard. And hey, I know McKinnon is tough to work with. I have a difficult time reining him in on occasion. Let me know if there's anything I can do to help, or if things get too uncomfortable."

"Will do."

Uncomfortable is putting it mildly, Marilyn thought.

They don't have a clue. The day after the murder, news of Gonzales' death had been all over the news. Now hardly a word about a cop being killed. He fidgeted, restless and eager to hunt.

Ready. It was easier than he thought it would be. Just keep your eyes open for a blue and white, get into position, and then take the shot. They're no match for his skill. Soon he'd target another unsuspecting cop. He'd make them all pay, have them shaking in their boots, fearful to get out of their cars. He'd show them.

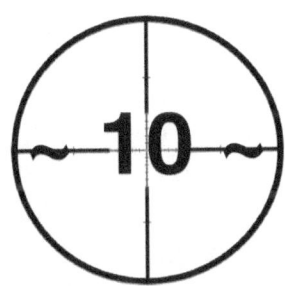

Father Ed couldn't believe his good fortune. After renting the furnished apartment, he was walking back to his car and passed the Fredericksburg Visitor Center. Spotting a "Help Wanted" sign, he went inside. An hour later he had both a place to live *and* a job. Things were finally looking up; his plan seemed to be coming to fruition. Maybe this was God working in his life; maybe he was supposed to do His work in another capacity.

A slight breeze picked up, blowing orange tinted leaves down the cobblestone sidewalk as if making a clear path for him. It was autumn in Virginia, but compared to fall weather in Chicago, it seemed summer-like. The mild temperature and vivid colors matched his new disposition. He no longer felt the cold darkness of despair, but rather the warm light of hope.

Reluctant to go back and sit in his dingy hotel room, he decided to walk to the library, which was only a couple of blocks away. He needed to get on a computer and find out what, if anything, might be in the news about him in the Chicago papers. He wished that he had his laptop with him, but it belonged to the Church. To take it would have been stealing.

Minutes later, he was walking up the steps of the three-storied Fredericksburg Headquarters Library, a huge red brick building that had formerly been an old school. Entering through the front doors, he spotted a room identified as the computer lab. The wooden floors creaked as he approached the desk.

"Hi, I'd like to use a computer, please."

"Certainly," replied the woman, whose smile revealed perfect, snow white teeth. Looking at Ed through emerald green eyes, she asked, "May I see your library card?"

"Uh, I don't have one; I'm new in the area."

Flipping her red hair aside, she asked, "Would you care to apply for one? It would enable you to utilize all of the library's services."

"Okay."

She handed Ed the application which he took over to a nearby table to complete. Stealing a glance at the woman, he noticed her name plate, Lisa Lewis. *Very attractive.* Pausing, he recalled that it had been years since he'd entertained these types of thoughts, trying always to keep his mind on the Lord and away from looking at women superficially. Yet, at least according to the Archbishop, he was no longer a priest. And if his plan was to begin a new life, shouldn't noticing a beautiful woman be natural for him? He took the completed card to her.

"Just take it over to the . . . no, never mind. Wait here, I'll take it to the circulation desk and have your card for you in a few moments."

Ed watched her walk over and hand his application to another librarian. After a brief conversation, the woman sheepishly looked in Ed's direction. A new set of emotions sprang to life as he felt his face fill with color. He tried to be nonchalant and feigned looking around the room, but in the process stole several glances at the young woman to whom he felt attracted. Her trim figure and inviting personality were magnetic. She soon turned and walked back to where he was waiting.

"Here you are, Mr. Michaels. You may begin using your card today to check out books and CDs."

"Thank you, ma'am. You're very kind."

"You're welcome, but please, call me Lisa." She sat back down and logged him in on her sheet.

"You can use computer number four in the second row, sir. Our policy permits patrons to remain on their terminal for one hour, but since hardly anyone is here today I can waive that restriction."

"Thanks, and please call me Ed."

"Okay, here's your password to log on. Let me know if you need any assistance."

Sitting down, Ed logged on, opening the browser to a Chicago news site. He scanned the two major papers and the local neighborhood edition as well. There wasn't any news about his arrest in any of them. Next, he logged into his commercial email account and scanned the inbox—nothing that needed his immediate attention. There were a couple of emails from friends, but he dared not reply for fear of being traced. He wasn't sure about the ability of law enforcement to track someone's whereabouts through a computer and didn't want to take the chance of tipping them off.

While surfing the net, he occasionally glanced at Lisa as she sat at her desk tending to her duties and waiting on other patrons. Once he caught her staring at him. When their eyes met, they both quickly averted their gaze. He tried his best not to look her way, but he found himself doing so anyway. *Such a beautiful woman.* Finishing his session he got up and walked over to Lisa and returned the card with the password.

"All finished, Ed?"

"Yes, thank you. How late does the library stay open?"

"We're open until nine o'clock during the week and five-thirty on the weekends."

Before he realized it, he was asking her, "Do you work in the computer lab every day?" *Will she think I'm being fresh?*

"I work from nine to five, Monday through Friday."

"Oh, um, I was just wondering. You're so helpful. I know that I'll probably need to use the computer again."

"I'll be here. I look forward to seeing you again."

"Thanks, Lisa. See you soon."

Ed walked out the door and down the steps, feeling excited about his day. Passing two massive oaks on either side of the walk, he breathed in their sense of strength and permanency. He'd made his first friend, or at least he hoped he had. Walking to his car, he realized he was eager for this day to end and for tomorrow to begin. He had a new apartment to move into and a new job to begin. This new beginning was starting to feel better. Still he felt a hole deep inside his soul. His identity had always been something he'd been proud of. Being a priest was his life, it meant everything to him. Now it seemed as if it had all been a dream—like he'd never been Father Ed. Could he live his life this way? Uncertainty filled him, but one thing he did know: he was anxious to see Lisa again.

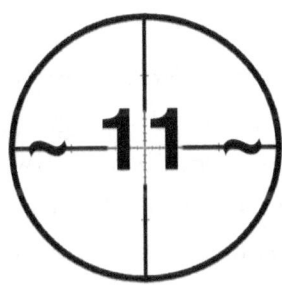

"What's wrong, honey? The past couple of days you've seemed out of sorts."

Toweling himself dry after stepping out of the shower, Pete hesitated before answering. "I'm mad at myself. I let McKinnon get to me, even swore at him because I was so mad."

"That's not like you, babe. You haven't done that in years. What did he say that made you so angry?"

Pete grabbed a pair of boxers and pulled them on. "It's not so much any one thing that he said, it's his attitude. He looks down on Marilyn and me like we're two rookies who couldn't find a blood trail in freshly fallen snow."

"Did you tell him about the rape case you two worked? That was one of the biggest cases ever. The papers loved it."

"Beth, he doesn't want to hear it. I really don't think it matters to him what we've done. His style is strictly working Harry's way, which includes skirting the rules and making the arrest without any help from anyone. Even the boss said she has trouble controlling him."

"What about his partner? Is he the same way?" "I really don't know. I've never had a conversation with him. Harry does all the talking for that team. Bobby appears to be there only if Harry needs a backup or a poker partner."

After Pete finished dressing, they went into the kitchen. The baby was asleep in the playpen next to the table. Beth poured a cup of coffee for herself and Pete. "I was going to scramble some eggs. Are you hungry?"

"Yes; that would be great. You know, I was thinking about this problem during my run this morning. Last night, before I fell asleep, I decided that I was going to go see Lt. King and discuss it with him, but the more I thought about it this morning, I decided to handle it myself, even if it comes down to a confrontation with McKinnon. I'm not going to allow him to disrespect me or Marilyn."

"Pete, what's got into you? I've never heard you talk like this before, and, frankly, it's not very Christian."

"I know. I've prayed about it, hoping that God would take the anger from me, but I think that McKinnon needs someone to stand up to him. I think he's cowed all of the people in that unit to the point that they tolerate him and his stupid antics."

She popped a couple of muffins into the toaster. "I just hope you'll be careful, honey. This guy sounds dangerous."

"I know. Believe me, I will be." He grabbed her around the waist as she set down a plate of eggs in front of him. "I've got too much to lose," he said, as he kissed her obviously pregnant waistline.

Wrapping her arms lovingly around him, she kissed the top of his head. "No more talk about it; let's bless the meal and turn it over to Him."

"Amen."

"So what're we gonna do, Harry? We got nothin', no leads, no snitches . . ."

The pair sat in a corner booth that years ago they had claimed as their own. Elliott's was a rundown breakfast joint that catered to bookies, junkies, and cops nursing hangovers. A throwback to the 1960s, it was furnished with chrome legged tables and chairs sporting plastic covered seats. It opened at two in the morning and closed at ten—no lunches or dinners. Just eggs, bacon, ham, grits, and toast, all washed down with thick, scalding coffee. Decaf had never seen the inside of Elliott's Home Cooking.

Harry smashed a roach that scooted across the table. "Damn, I thought Bubba said he had the pest guys out."

"Maybe these roaches are immune to whatever's bein' sprayed."

"Yeah, Bobby, especially if it's watered down. Bubba's good at spottin' a bluff in a poker game, but he's blind to most other scams."

Harry took another drink from his third cup of coffee. "Listen, when we get in today, throw a couple of reports in the file sayin' we shook the bushes last night but came up with nothin'. Put in an expense report for three hundred bucks, just say we spread it out among five or six sources."

"Hey, man, we only handed out a hundred bucks last night."

"Just do it, Bobby. Don't give me any crap. I still owe a couple hundred on that all night poker game on Saturday."

"Yeah, okay, okay; take it easy. I just don't want Darcy breathin' down my neck when I go in and get her to sign it."

"Don't worry about her. She couldn't find a dollar bill in a vault full of money," said Harry, as he finished his coffee and pulled a fresh toothpick from his pocket. "Besides, she's got the two Jesus freaks keepin' her busy with their canvases and reviewin' old reports. Those two should be directin' traffic down in the subway."

"Yeah, right in the middle of the tracks," laughed Russo, as he stuffed the last strips of bacon into his mouth."

Harry took the toothpick from his mouth and pointed it at his partner. "You got the tip?"

Russo knew that the toothpick pointing in his direction made Harry's request a mandate, not a question. It was McKinnon's way of adding emphasis to a veiled command.

"Yeah, I got it."

Russo dropped a five dollar bill on the table and the two walked out the back door. It had been years since they'd paid for a meal at Elliott's. Not since the day they walked in on a robbery in progress. Some knuckle dragger high on coke and looking to score another eight ball had stuck a gun in Bubba's face and demanded the money from the till. Harry took one look at what was happening, drew his gun, and dispatched the would-be robber to the morgue. Bubba never laid another check on Harry's table after that.

They got into their unmarked unit, and Harry pulled out onto Garfield Boulevard and headed toward headquarters.

"Whoever this guy is that killed the cop is good. No physical evidence; no eyeballs . . . nothin'."

"So how we gonna grab this guy, Harry?"

Harry pulled his toothpick from his mouth, broke it in half, and dropped it on the floor. "We wait till he kills another cop."

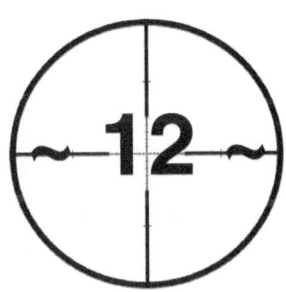

Easing his vehicle into a parking spot in the lot at the Field Museum, he slid into the back if the van to check his field of vision—perfect. From here, he had an unobstructed view of the cop directing traffic on Lake Shore Drive. The football game at Soldier Field, adjacent to the museum, was almost over; the Bears had wrapped this one up early. Some fans were leaving, trying to get a jump on traffic, not wanting to wait until the inevitable crush of cars at the end of the game. The mass exodus always turned Lake Shore Drive into a huge parking lot, despite the best efforts of cops trying to feed them down secondary arteries and away from the lakefront.

The bright sun belied the fact that it was a typical Chicago fall day. The temperature was chilly and the ever-present lake wind, called The Hawk by Chicagoans, swept across the multiple lanes of traffic, making the day seem even colder. No matter, weather conditions would not affect his marksmanship. The government had spent time and money training him to make a kill shot under the most adverse situations. His sniper hide inside the comfortable vehicle, sans hot, cold, rain or snow, afforded him ideal conditions. With so much traffic noise and the roar emanating from the crowd inside the stadium, it was unlikely his shot would be heard. The only real problem he faced was ensuring a quick escape afterward.

Grabbing the rifle, he slid open the glass window. Cold began to seep into the van, the same cold that enveloped his heart. Fan noise and honking horns did their best to distract him, but he remained undeterred. Focused. Sitting down in a comfortable position, he removed the lens cover from the scope and stuck the muzzle outside, allowing only several inches to protrude beyond the glass. He located his target; the animated cop who was waving his hands in sign language universally recognized by drivers. The killer dialed in the power, filling his scope with only the officer's face. The traffic whistle danced in the cop's mouth as his cheeks alternatively filled and emptied with each blast from the black appendage between his lips. He, too, was focused.

It's time. Closing out all distractions around him, oblivious to all sounds, smells, or anything else that might compromise his mission, he took aim at the center of the officer's head. As was his routine, he took three deep cleansing breaths and on the fourth, during the exhalation, he began his slow, deliberate pull on the trigger. The shot came as a surprise when it broke, just as his instructors in the Army had taught that it should. Looking through his scope, he saw that his target was gone. He reached forward to the focus ring and opened up the field of view. He found the officer on the ground and not moving. *Got him.*

As was his habit, he placed his weapon on safe and put it on the side of a box on the floor of the van, covering it with a green army blanket. Climbing back into the driver's seat, he quickly pulled from the lot and melted into traffic on Lake Shore Drive. Safe. Feeling neither happy nor sad, he drove deep into the bowels of the city, critiquing himself as he went. The news would be his ultimate evaluator, telling him if his shot did what it was meant to do. Until then it was time for more reconnaissance, time to find another cop.

"What was that?"

The noise startled the two teenagers, causing them to sit up. They had been parked in the lot at the museum for a couple of hours, exploring each other's bodies. The boy's parents had agreed to allow him to use the family van to take his date to the Bears' game. One thing led to another, and pretty soon kissing was no longer sufficient to satisfy their puppy love. At half time, they decided to leave the game and return to the van.

"It sounded like a firecracker," she offered.

"I don't know, Barb. I think it kinda sounded like a gun going off. My dad took me to the range a couple of times...that sounded like a gunshot."

"Ray, the van next to us, the engine just started." She grabbed him and pulled him back down. "Be quiet, it's moving."

The love-struck teens lay quietly while the vehicle next to them pulled from its parking spot and drove off. When the boy took a quick peek, Barb quickly pulled him back.

"I'm scared, Ray. Let's get out of here before something happens."

"Okay, the game's probably over by now anyway. My Dad will be suspicious if we get back late."

The pair quickly dressed, folded the blanket, and placed the rear seats back in an upright position. By the time they pulled out of the lot, police sirens began to rise in an angry chorus.

"Something bad happened, Barb. Maybe whoever was in that van next to us did something. Maybe that was a shot."

"Should we tell the police what we heard?"

"No. How would we explain that we were parked in the lot at the museum? My Dad's parking pass is for the main lot at Soldier Field. He'd figure out that we left the game early."

"I don't know; it doesn't seem right. Just take me home. I'm not feeling well."

"Okay, but remember, not a word."

"Where do you want to go for dinner, honey?"

"I don't know, something quick. I don't feel like a big sit-down meal. How about beef sandwiches at Portillo's?"

"Okay, Mike, but first you've got to get us out of this gridlock. I thought leaving the game early would help us avoid the traffic jam we usually encounter, but it looks like it doesn't really matter when we leave."

Her husband did his best to weave in and out of traffic, but the police had strategically placed cones out on the street, funneling the cars exactly where they wanted them and slowing them down in order to gain more control. Mike was eager to get away from Lake Shore Drive and onto the freeway. His mouth watered as he thought about the beef sandwich dripping with gravy and the hot spicy peppers adorning it.

"What's the holdup? Leticia, can you see ahead? Why are we slowing down?"

"Looks like a police officer is directing traffic and . . . Oh my god!"

"What? What's wrong? Leticia?"

Sobbing and covering her eyes, she said, "It's horrible . . . how . . . why . . . .?"

Mike looked over at his wife who was shaking and covering her eyes. As his car approached the spot where the officer had stood directing traffic, Mike saw him. The officer was lying on his side, the whistle still in his mouth, but the back of his head was almost gone. The pool of blood that was quickly forming around his head reflected a beautifully clear nighttime sky filled with brilliant stars. Officer William Wright would never see that beautiful sight again.

Pulling his car in front of the officer's body to shield it, Mike stopped and pulled out his cell phone. He dialed 9-1-1. "Send help, an officer's down on Lake Shore Drive! I guess . . . well, I guess he must have been shot!"

"How do you want your steak, Mar?"

"Medium well. I thought you knew that by now, Joe."

Marilyn was at her fiancée's house helping him fix dinner. It was one of those rare weekends when their days off coincided. Joe was also on the job; he worked a beat car in the 8th District.

Cutting up some lettuce, cucumbers, and tomatoes, she took down two bowls from the cabinet and equally divided the salad. "How much longer on the steaks, honey?"

"Ten minutes."

"Okay." She picked out two potatoes, wrapped each of them in a paper towel, and started them cooking in the microwave. This was going to be a treat. Home cooked meals were rare for both of them; neither was ever home long enough to cook. Most of their meals were eaten in restaurants or take outs. Tonight was special. Marilyn had even brought a bottle of wine to top off the evening. They had agreed to discuss their wedding plans and set a date. Minutes later, Joe brought the steaks in from the patio deck, the cuts still sizzling on the platter. "Brrr, it's chilly out there."

The aroma filled the room and jogged her memory, reminding Marilyn of her childhood. She missed the cooking smells other people took for granted. She was eager to marry Joe and finally have a real home, not just a place to live.

"Did I tell you that I spoke with Sgt. McNamara about the Tac Team opening?"

"No, what did he say?" Marilyn answered.

"He said it's between me and Dotson, but if it were his sole decision to make, he would choose me, based on my previous stint as a detective." Joe took the two steaks to the counter while Marilyn prepared the plates.

"I hope the watch commander takes that into account. Your time on the job and investigative experience should make you number one. It's time you got out of uniform."

The microwave sounded and Marilyn took out the baked potatoes and placed one on each of their plates. "Joe, bring the wine, will you?"

"Yes, ma'am," he replied, carrying the bottle and two glasses to the table.

Marilyn went back to the counter and retrieved the two candles she had hidden in the bag along with the bottle of wine. Taking them back to the table, she lit each one and then sat down.

"Hey . . . now that's a nice touch," said Joe, as he turned down the lights. "I feel like we're dining out someplace fancy."

"Bless the meal, honey."

"Okay. Father, we thank you for this day, for good health and good friends, for your continued blessings and protection as we work to protect your children from evil. We ask for your guidance as we embark on our journey toward married life. Bless this meal, that it might keep us strong in order to do Your will. In Jesus' name we pray, Amen."

"Amen."

Cutting into her steak, Marilyn took her first taste. "Mmm, Joe, this is perfect. I think we've determined whose going to do the cooking in the family."

"Fine with me. I like cooking, especially when it's for you."

She picked up her wine glass and raised it toward him. "To us, honey. May we always be together."

"To us."

Just as the pair finished the toast and sipped their wine, Marilyn's phone rang.

"Detective Benson."

"Marilyn, this is Lt. Darcy. There's been a shooting at Soldier Field. Another officer's been murdered. Call Shannon and get down to the scene ASAP."

"Will do."

Joe slumped in his chair. "No, don't tell me you have to leave."

"Sorry, honey. That was Darcy. Someone just killed a cop at the Bears game. I've got to call Pete and head over there. I'll call you when I know what's going on." She got up from the table, grabbed her purse and headed for the door.

"Are your other two partners going to be there as well?"

"Don't know; Darcy didn't say, but if we are indeed a team, I suspect they will be."

Kissing Joe, she leaned into him and lingered for a moment in his arms. "I'll make it up to you; I promise." She went out the front door, got into her car, and drove east toward the freeway, dialing Pete's number at the same time. He would not be happy, especially if McKinnon and Russo would be meeting them at the crime scene. Her gut told her that a fire was smoldering within the foundation of the team, one that could flash at any moment and turn into a raging inferno.

~13~

Ed stuck his head into the room where a movie describing the Civil War era in Fredericksburg had just ended. "Trolley tour leaves in five minutes, everyone please get your tickets and assemble outside," he called out.

Holding the door open, Ed directed the group to the front desk where they could purchase tickets to ride the two hour tour of historic Fredericksburg. He was enjoying his new job at the Visitors Center. It meant that he was teaching and talking with people, something that he had done as a priest. Although his days didn't begin as they used to with saying morning Mass, he was at least attending Mass each morning at St. Mary's. As he watched the priest on the altar during the Consecration of the bread and wine, he experienced a deep sense of loss, almost as if a vital organ had gone missing from his body. At that sacred moment, the reenactment of the Last Supper, Ed felt a longing for a return to the altar.

The first week at his new job went by quickly. Trying to bring himself up to speed meant studying the history of the town during lunch breaks and at home after work. He had little time for anything else. Today was Friday. He hadn't had time to check email or peruse the Chicago news all week. Today, he decided to visit the library and use one of the computers. And, if he were completely honest with himself, he was eager to see if Lisa would be there.

He opened the door of the office and herded the tour group outside. After the last person boarded the trolley, Ed brought the ticket stubs inside and told his supervisor he was going on lunch break. He quickly walked toward the library, all the while hoping that Lisa would be working. A few blocks later, he opened the front door and stepped inside.

There she was, at her desk. Sighing, he hesitated momentarily, watching as she waited on a library patron. Today she wore a navy blue dress, cinched tight at the waist, accenting her trim figure. Her red hair was worn up, giving her face a much leaner look. He approached the desk as she finished with the elderly woman. Standing in front of her, he was taken by her bright red lipstick and how it framed her perfect white teeth.

"Hi, Lisa."

"Ed, how good to see you again. How are you?"

"I'm well."

"Do you need to use a computer?"

"Yes."

She filled out the sheet as Ed offered her his library card.

"I won't need that, Ed. I know who you are."

"Thanks."

"Here you go," she said, handing him a card with the password. "Number nine, over to the right. How much time do you need?"

"Oh, I'm on lunch break so I only have about thirty minutes."

"Okay; I hope you saved enough time to eat."

"I'll grab a sandwich on the way back and eat at my desk."

"Good. At least you're out getting some fresh air. I look forward to my lunch break, getting out of the library. It's a long day inside."

"You're right." Ed took the card and went to his terminal. Sitting down he looked over toward her desk *So beautiful.* He quickly logged on and opened his email. Two missives from his mother wondering why he hadn't called, one from Dan, telling him that he was now officially Ed's attorney and that they should sit down and discuss strategy. There were also several emails from parishioners, all supportive, reassuring him that his arrest in no way diminished their love and respect for him.

Ed reflected on that for a moment. He'd given little thought to the good people of St. Nick's with whom he'd bonded and loved. Suddenly, he realized that they were probably hurting as much as he was, and now he'd abandoned them. But what choice did he have? If he stayed, he had no priestly authority. He couldn't say Mass, hear their confessions, or minister to their needs. No, he was better off doing what he was doing, starting anew.

He checked the Chicago papers and news sites, searching his name, but nothing about him appeared in any of them. Was he being paranoid? Did he expect that he would continue to be news, even after the fact? Of course, no one yet knew that he had violated the conditions of his bond and fled the jurisdiction. Once that became known, he would probably become a news item again. He finished and logged off and then walked back to Lisa's desk.

"Here you go," he said, handing her the card. "Time to get back to work."

"Do you work here in town?"

"Yes, at the Visitors Center," he said, smiling. "Do you know where it is?"

"Of course," she replied, waving her hand at him. "Wow, you work fast. New in town and already you have a job?"

"Guess I was at the right place at the right time."

She filed his card and asked, "So, any big plans for the weekend?"

"Not really, just run some errands on Saturday and try to get settled into my apartment. Sunday morning I'll go to church and probably explore the area a little bit."

"Oh, what church are you attending?"

"St. Mary's."

"Me too. Ten-thirty mass is my favorite. The choir sings during that service."

"I'll try to make that one. Maybe I'll see you there."

"Okay. I'll look for you."

He started to leave. "Bye, Lisa, it was good to see you again. Have a great weekend."

"You too, Ed. Bye."

He stopped at the deli and bought a sandwich to take to the office. Walking back, he thought about Lisa. He was definitely going to attend ten-thirty mass on Sunday, and if she was there, he would make sure he sat with her.   Things were changing in his life. Rather than saying Sunday Mass, he was now a worshiper. *Was this God's plan for him, or was he going down a path that would lead him further away from ever regaining his vocation?*

By now, darkness covered the crime scene like a wool blanket. The lights above the playing field at Soldier Field still shone brightly as crews tended to their post-game cleaning ritual. Outside, the crime lab had set up their own spotlights, bathing the area in an eerie glow while illuminating the killing field. Officer Wright's body was en route to the Coroner's office, but his blood marked the spot where he breathed his last. Barricades ensured that no one would contaminate any evidence and that throngs of media wouldn't get close enough to defile this now sacrosanct slab of roadway.

Scores of cops dotted Lake Shore Drive, replacing the thousands of vehicles that would normally be jockeying for position on the five lane thoroughfare. Gathering in clusters, each group worked reverently trying to uncover clues to the identity of this cold-blooded cop killer.

Pete and Marilyn had been at the scene for over an hour, conferring with crime lab personnel and trying to pinpoint the location where the shot had been fired. "Pete, this was the perfect storm for the shooter, plenty of traffic, noise, and a crisp, clear day."

"Yeah, so many distractions, no one would pick up on someone secreted somewhere, taking the shot, and then departing the area—just too much noise and activity."

Shaking her head, Marilyn said, "Yeah, I guess, but I'm still confused. How does a guy with a rifle go completely unnoticed *twice*?"

"Do we even know our shooter is a male?"

"C'mon, Pete."

"Well, why not? Look what a great shot you are. Let's not rule out anything just yet."

"But the motive, what could it be?"

"I don't know, Bens. Maybe our shooter is a gal who was dumped by a cop, and now she's getting even with all male cops. It sounds crazy, I know, but right now everything's in play. You're right about the conditions though, it was perfect for a shot. What a contrast this is to the first killing that happened on a quiet Sunday morning."

Pete pointed toward the Field Museum. "According to the crime lab guys, the trajectory of the bullet indicates that the shot may have come from that direction. We need to comb that area and see if we can find a casing or possibly a witness."

"Casing, yes, but a witness? It's Sunday night, and the place is closed. What's the likelihood of anyone being around?"

"I know, but what else do we have, Bens? Besides, I think the Museum's lot is used for overflow parking on game days."

Marilyn stared out over Lake Michigan, momentarily mesmerized by the moored boats dancing in Burnham Harbor. "Pete, the harbor."

"What about it?"

"People fish there day and night."

His eyes widening, he replied. "Yeah, and it's salmon season. Someone's bound to have been there. Excellent, Bens. Let's go."

"Okay, you head over there. I'm going to talk with the on scene commander and get the parking area by the museum cordoned off. We need to do a grid search there at first light. I'll have a beat car drop me off at the harbor after I've made the arrangements."

"Roger that. Hey, one more thing. See if there's anyone in the security office. There may be some surveillance cameras on the exterior of the building. We can review the footage."

Smiling, she replied. "Pete, we may just uncover some pieces to the puzzle tonight that will help us solve this case."

"I pray that we do. By the way, have you seen McKinnon or Russo?"

"Yes, they were in a group of uniforms when we first arrived. I looked over toward them and noticed that when McKinnon saw us, he turned his back. I think that was a clue."

"What is it with that guy?" Pete clenched his jaw. "I don't really care whether he likes us or not, but I wish he would put his feelings aside and work with us so we can find the lunatic who's killing our brother officers."

"I know," Marilyn said, shaking her head. "Hard to believe someone can be that cold."

"Hey, we need to run down the 9-1-1 caller, too. I want to talk with whoever it was that put the call in. Maybe we can get something there as well."

"Good idea, Pete. I'll see you in a little while over at the harbor."

A few minutes later, Pete was slowly moving along Burnham Harbor Drive looking for fishermen. Spotting several lanterns out at the end of the docks, he parked and got out on foot. He walked across a grassy area and then onto a pedestrian walkway leading to where the boats were anchored. He'd always loved the lakefront; it was a treasure that too few Chicagoans took advantage of. Fishing, boating, swimming, and a bike path that paralleled the lake for twenty miles should have been constantly teeming with people, but that wasn't always the case. He made a mental note to bring Pete, Jr. here when he was old enough, and teach him how to fish.

Walking to the end of the first pier, he took out his ID. The thirtyish looking man had already turned around. Pete's hard soled shoes and the vibration he caused by walking on the dock had announced his presence.

"Police Officer," Pete said. "Can I speak with you for a minute?"

The man put his rod into a makeshift holder on the pier. "Hey, I got my license in the car, officer. I fish here every fall; it's snaggin' season."

Pete chuckled. "I'm not here to check your fishing license."

"Didn't really think so. You're kinda overdressed for that."

"Right. How long have you been out here?"

"I guess a few hours, got a couple of twenty pounders already . . . Coho."

"Good for you. While you've been here have you heard anything strange, maybe something that sounded like fireworks or maybe a gunshot?"

"Damn. I figured that's what it was. I heard what sounded like a rifle shot. I know that's what it was 'cause I was in the military. I spent enough time behind an M-16 to know what one sounds like. At first, I thought I was imagining it. Ya know ya get kinda hypnotized staring at the water. Then about five minutes later I heard sirens and looked over toward the Bears game and I saw a bunch a cop cars swarmin' like bees. Figured somebody got shot."

"You're right. A cop was killed."

"Damn. Sorry, Officer."

"Thanks. About what time was it when you heard the shot?"

"It was about four thirty. I know 'cause I take a break every half hour and have a smoke and a Bud. I didn't use to wait for the break, just kept poppin' a Bud, ya know. Pretty soon I'd run outta beer before I was done fishin'. Ain't no fun fishin' if you can't drink."

"I'll remember that. I know this is a long shot, but did you see anything or anyone that may have attracted your attention at that point?"

"Naw, but I can tell ya where it probably came from. I was lookin' out over the lake and I heard it from over my left shoulder, so probably from Lake Shore Drive or maybe somewhere near the museum."

Pete had his note pad out recording the man's information. "Can I get your name and contact number?"

"Sure can, anything to help catch somebody would shoot a cop."

Pete took the man's name and contact number and began moving back toward the pedestrian path to check the rest of the docks. At least now he had some information that might help nail down the time of the shooting. It felt good to have something concrete, a piece of the puzzle, albeit a small one, to help piece together a portrait of a cold blooded killer. *Lord, please let there be cameras at the museum..*

"So what is it exactly that you're lookin' for?" The private security guard employed by the museum asked as he led Marilyn into the security office.

Following him into the temperature controlled room, Marilyn saw a bank of cameras whose job it was to capture not only the rooms containing the exhibits but also the exterior of the building as well. "I'm interested in any footage you may have of the south parking lot."

"That's no problem; I can bring that up for you. It's all digital now, no more tapes. The problem is narrowing it down to a specific time period. What time frame are you lookin' at?"

Trying to remember when she got the call from Lt. Darcy and working backwards, she answered. "Let's try the fourth quarter of the Bears game, maybe ten minutes before the end."

"Okay, shouldn't be too much activity on camera. It's a madhouse before the game starts. Cars streamin' in wantin' to park real quick so they can get over to Soldier Field before the game begins. After we get all 'em parked, the attendants leave; it's like a ghost town. Then, at the end of the game activity picks up and it's every man for himself cuz everyone's in a big hurry to beat the traffic home."

The guard sat in front of a screen and typed in some numbers on the console. "Here's about the point you were lookin' for. I remember when there was about ten minutes to go, was watchin' it on TV. Bears intercepted a pass and ran it in for a score."

Marilyn sat down beside the man and they reviewed the disk. It was boring; no cars moving out of the lot, an occasional pedestrian walking through, taking a shortcut. "There, that red van's pulling out," said Marilyn. "Back it up to just before it pulls out. Can you zero in on the front license plate?"

"Sure."

The guard rewound the disk to the point Marilyn asked for and used the zoom control to enlarge the frame. "That's strange, there's no front plate."

She looked at the frame and saw the same thing. "Any chance of getting the rear plate?"

"No, that's the only angle we got of that lot. The camera's fixed. We can't move it to follow anything."

"Okay, let it run awhile longer."

A couple of minutes later, a blue van that had been parked next to the red one departed as well.

"How about that blue van, can you get the tag on that?"

He dialed down the power and enlarged the area of the rear license plate and got a clear read. "There you go, Detective. It's plain as day. Funny how that red van was the only car in that whole row that was backed in."

"Yeah, funny." Marilyn copied down the plate number. "Can you make me a copy of this footage we just reviewed?"

"Sure. Give me a sec, and I'll put it on a CD for ya."

"Thanks, you've been a big help."

Armed with the disk, Marilyn walked back toward the crime scene, stopping at the section of the lot where both vans had been parked. It was not well lit, but as she did a cursory search of the immediate area where the two vehicles had been, she noticed a cigarette butt. Needing any bit of evidence she could find, she pulled a plastic baggie out of her jacket and collected it. She'd have to remember to ask the guard if they employed a parking lot clean up service. The butt didn't look weathered, like it had been there very long. If she could establish the clean up time and maybe get some DNA from the cigarette, it may come in handy in the future by placing someone at the location of the murder.

She headed back to the crime scene and had a blue and white take her over to the harbor. She'd get the DMV info on the tag now, but it was getting too late for an interview. She and Pete would contact the owner of the vehicle first thing in the morning. Right now she needed to find Pete. *Hopefully, he came up with an eyeball.* They needed a break in this case; they had to find this madman before another cop was murdered.

"That lady detective's already been here and got the information."

Damn. "What did you tell her?" Harry didn't want to get scooped by his two interloping partners. "Did she come up with anything . . . a car or suspicious person?"

"Not sure, but I gave her a copy of some surveillance footage from the parking lot."

"Did you get the license plates?"

Squirming in his seat from the rapid fire questions thrown at him by the tall detective, the security guard replied, "One of the vans didn't have a plate, but I got the other one okay. It's on the CD I gave her."

Harry stared at the guard, causing him to sink in his chair. Taking the toothpick from his mouth, he pointed it in the guard's face. "Make me a copy of the same footage you gave her—now. I don't have a lot of time; a cop's been killed."

"Okay, Detective, okay."

"Bobby, take a look at what he puts on that CD and run the tag. Call me in an hour with the info. I've got a stop to make."

"It's gettin' late, Harry. You wanna just wait till morning?"

"Damn it, Bobby. That plate might be our guy or at least someone who may have seen him. I'm not waitin' around while Captain America and Wonder Woman process their information and beat us to the punch." Taking the toothpick from his mouth, Harry broke it in half and threw it at Bobby's feet.

"We're going to find out to who that plate is registered and pay a visit there—tonight."

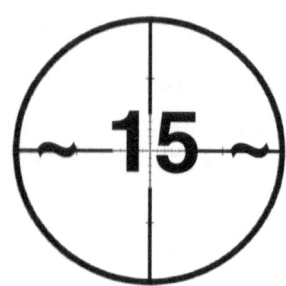

Pete parked his pickup on the driveway. It was late, and he didn't want to awaken Beth by pulling into the garage. Unlocking the back door, he slipped as quietly as he could into the house only to find Beth waiting for him in the kitchen.

"Hi, honey. It's so late. How are you?"

Kissing her, he replied. "Tired. Looks like the same guy struck again. The officer never knew what hit him."

"That's just horrible. Why is this happening?"

"I wish I knew."

"Are you hungry?"

"Not really. Anyway, it's too late to eat now. Breakfast will be in just a few hours. We did come up with some leads this time. Marilyn and I will run them down first thing in the morning. Pray that they pan out, babe."

"Pete, I'm scared. This guy is targeting cops."

Taking her in his arms, Pete reassured her. "It's okay, babe. Our shooter appears to be looking for uniforms, so, at least for now, I'm flying under the radar."

She kissed his neck. "Honey, we've been through so much already, and with the baby on the way. I don't know what I'd do if . . . ."

"It's okay. Marilyn and I will be watching each other's backs, and I'm praying to St. Michael every day. He's right beside me."

"I hope so. Hey, what about your new partners, any progress on that front?"

Shaking his head, "I guess all I can say is that all four of us were at the crime scene at the same time. They did their thing; we did ours."

"Can't your lieutenant do something about them?"

"Not really," he said, as he took his coat off and went to the hall closet to hang it up. "McKinnon seems to walk on water as far as she's concerned. He does whatever he pleases, and she doesn't question him."

"I'll be happy when you go back to your own unit. You and Marilyn work well together there, and Lt. King knows how to handle cops who cause problems."

They headed into the bedroom where Pete began to undress. "I know, I'll be happy to go back to Violent Crimes too, but for now, this case has become personal. I want to catch this killer, quickly, before McKinnon does."

"Just make sure that you worry about McKinnon as much as you do about the killer. I don't trust either one."

He crawled into bed. *Good advice.*

Getting up from the bed, Harry walked the few steps to the bathroom. "That was good, baby. You've got the magic touch."

"Thanks." Lt. Darcy pulled the sheet up to cover herself while she waited for him to re-emerge. As usual, she began to feel the pangs of guilt immediately following their coupling. Each time she allowed him into her bed, she swore it would be the last. She knew it was wrong; after all, she was his boss, but the act itself seemed to overrule what her mind told her was right. Tonight she justified it by telling herself that she needed to know the latest about the homicide at Soldier Field; the sex was secondary.

Harry's phone rang. Coming from the bathroom, he answered it. "Yeah . . . uh huh . . . good. I'll be there in fifteen minutes. Wait around the corner for me. We'll go in together." He set the phone down on the nightstand and began to dress.

"That was Bobby. He's at the home of the witness I discovered at the museum. I'm going over there now. Bobby and me will find out if there was any eyeball on this one. There was no evidence at the scene, just like the first shooting, but I dug around a little and came up with the only lead without any help from your super hero team."

The lieutenant sat up in bed. "Good work. Listen, Harry, it's critical that we get something out of this interview. When I brief the chief today, he's going to want answers and to see some progress. The press is going to be all over this story until we grab the guy."

Strapping his holster to his belt, he cinched it up and put his jacket on. "Hey, Princess, I'm doing the best I can. This guy hasn't left a whole lot for us to work with, and the two prima donnas you gave me to work with are a pain in the ass."

"Harry, I already told you that was not my call."

"Yeah, yeah. I gotta get goin'. I'll see you in the office sometime this morning. Hopefully I'll get some kind of lead from whoever this witness turns out to be."

"Okay, Harry. Good luck."

"Yeah. Anyway, it was good, as always. I gotta go."

She followed him to the door and bolted it after him. *This is so wrong.* She got back in bed and willed herself to tune out her conscience quickly. Grabbing an oversized pillow, she hugged it to her body, allowing the afterglow of her time with him to relax her. In no time she drifted off to sleep. For now, Harry was not a problem. In fact, he was just what she needed.

"Who is it?" Rubbing his eyes, the man pulled the curtains aside to look out on his front porch.

"Police, open the door. I need to talk with you," said Harry, holding open his ID for the man to see.

Opening the door wide, the man stepped aside, allowing the detectives to enter. "What's this all about? It's two o'clock in the morning?"

"Yeah, we know. There was a shooting today at the Bears' game; a cop was killed. Your license plate came up as being in the area where we think the shot came from."

"What?" The man stammered, "I mean, I know about the shooting; I saw the report on the news before I went to bed. I wasn't there, but my son and his girlfriend were at the game, but they parked in the stadium parking lot in my usual spot. I have season tickets and a parking pass. Is that where the shooting took place?"

"No," said Harry. "Listen, something's not right here . . . Mr. Hermanowitz, is it?"

"Yes."

"What's you boy's name?"

"Ray."

"Is he here?"

"Yes, but he's sleeping."

"Wake him up," Harry ordered. "I need to talk with him."

The man looked at Harry as if to challenge him, but quickly thought better of the idea. A few minutes later, the teenager came down the stairs. Seeing Harry caused him instantly to shake off his grogginess. He sensed the tall cop wasn't in any mood to fool around.

"Ray, my name is Detective McKinnon; this is my partner, Detective Russo. Were you at the Bears game today?"

"Yes, Sir."

"There was a shooting—a cop was killed. Your dad tells me that you were parked in the stadium lot. Is that the truth?"

The boy pondered the question for a moment and deduced from Harry's icy stare that he already knew the right answer.

"Well, I was parked there for most of the game, but towards the end I left and parked over at the museum."

His father cocked his head. "Son, why would you leave the game and go to the museum?"

Realizing that it was no longer a good idea to keep his actions a secret, he confessed. "Dad, the Bears were winning so me and Barb decided to leave before the crowd did. We went over and parked in the lot at the museum so we could talk. We didn't do anything wrong."

Harry quickly realized this kid had no direct involvement in the shooting and was trying to save himself from telling his father that he was screwing his girlfriend in the family van. "Okay, Ray, nobody said you did anything wrong. I'm interested in what you saw or heard while you were parked there. We think whoever killed the cop was also in that lot, possibly parked right next to your van."

Recognizing that he needed to be forthright with his answers, he told Harry about hearing the shot and lying low until the van next to theirs had departed.

"So, other than noticing that it was red, you didn't get the plate or take a look at who was driving?"

"No, Sir; sorry."

"All right, kid. I may need to come back later if I have any more questions. Thanks for your help."

The detectives headed toward the front door to leave. Harry turned to the boy's father. "Sorry to bother you in the middle of the night, Mr. Hermanowitz, but courtesy goes out the window when a cop is murdered."

"I understand. Glad we were able to help out. Good night."

The man locked the door and turned to his son. "Ray, we need to talk."

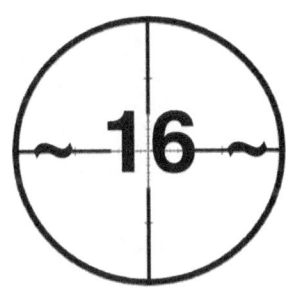

"Damnit, Darcy, I don't care. I want answers, and I need something solid I can give to the papers. When I go to the Superintendent with the crap you've given me, he's going to think I'm totally inept."

The chief of detectives was furious. Lt. Darcy had been ordered to meet with him as soon as she arrived at headquarters. She related the news that Harry had given her during their early morning tryst, but it wasn't enough to assuage the chief's anger.

"Chief, this guy hasn't made any mistakes; he hasn't left us anything to work with."

"Spare me your problems, Lieutenant. You said you have your best team on it, and I've given you two bright, energetic detectives to assist them. Two cops are dead! If we don't get this guy soon, we may have a third. Christ, my job is in jeopardy here! The Mayor will can my ass faster than a drunk reaching for his first drink in the morning. I guarantee you that if you don't grab this nutcase soon, you'll find yourself in charge of the freakin' motor pool."

"Chief, I . . ."

"Get out."

Walking from his office into the reception area, Darcy felt the rush of blood, fueled by humiliation, painting her face in a cherry red mask. *Is it hot in here?* Two other commanders were seated in chairs along the wall, awaiting their turn with the chief. Lord only knows what their encounters would be like. He was not in a very good mood this morning, to say the least, but she had little sympathy for them. She needed to figure out a way to get her team working harmoniously.   If she failed, she could find herself counting cars and ordering oil changes.

As they walked up the front steps of the bungalow, their nostrils flared as they breathed in the aroma of home cooking.

"Mmm, smells like bacon frying," said Marilyn, as her salivary glands ignited.

"Yeah," said, Pete, ringing the bell to the Hermanowitz residence. "Looks like someone's still home."

Seconds later, a man opened the door. Pete flashed his ID. "Mr. Hermanowitz?"

"Yes?"

"I'm Detective Shannon, and this is Detective Benson. May we ask you a few questions?"

"Is this about the officer who was shot?"

Marilyn shot a quick glance at Pete. "Uh . . . yes, did you see it happen?"

The man held the door open and gestured for them both to come inside. "No, I told the detectives last night that I wasn't there. My boy and his girlfriend were at the game in my van, but they only heard the shot."

"What detectives?" Marilyn frowned.

"Um, two guys, one tall who did all the talking. The other one was short. They were here very early this morning, woke us all up. They asked my son, Ray, some questions and then left. I was kind of upset at first; I mean who comes in the middle of the night? But after they told me what happened, I can see why they did it. I guess they'd been working non-stop trying to catch the guy."

"Well, sir, I guess we've all been so busy on this case that we haven't had time to update each other. Sorry to bother you, again.

Before we go, is there anything you may be able to add, anything your son may have forgotten to tell Detective McKinnon while he was here?"

"No, Ma'am. Ray told them he heard a shot and that he and Barb may have been parked right next to the van it came from, but that's all he could offer."

Marilyn closed her notebook and handed him her business card. "Thank you. If your son remembers anything else would you please call us?"

"I sure will."

Getting back in their car, Pete shouted and banged his fist on the dashboard. "Damn!"

"Easy, Pete, settle down."

"What is with McKinnon?" Pete said, throwing his hands up. "Why won't he work with us?"

"I don't know. But he must have gone to the museum right after I left and got the guard to give him the tag information. He probably figured out that I had already been there as soon as he spoke with security. In fact, he probably knew that we would wait till morning to do the interview. That's why he didn't hesitate to go and talk to the witness."

"Yeah," said Pete. "Shame on us for being considerate and waiting till morning to do the interview; Harry played us for chumps."

Marilyn headed the car toward the office. "We need to sit down with Darcy. This situation is not going to get any better, nor will it help us catch the creep whose killing cops."

As she finished her sentence, her cell phone rang. "It's Darcy."

The man walked into the diner and took a seat at the counter right where it takes a sharp turn toward the kitchen. Two other customers had already claimed their seats on the vintage stools which rotated fully around, allowing even the portliest of patrons easy access to the Formica countertop.

"Hey there, Hardcore, what's up?" One of the men seated at the counter waved to him. The old-timer was a regular at the greasy spoon restaurant, having been a customer for over twenty years. He knew most of the people who came in to eat and drink coffee in the morning. He set his newspaper down.

"Ain't nothin' to it, just need to get some coffee in my system to help wake up." Hardcore was the nickname given to him by members of his platoon while he was serving in the Army in the Middle East. The men had taken note of how he relished difficult situations and assignments, thriving during hard times when others complained and failed.

"Guess you haven't found a job yet; you're still walkin' around in that cammo field jacket. Hard to get the Army out of your blood, eh?"

The waitress set a cup of coffee in front of the younger man. "Anything to eat for you, sweetie?"

"Naw, just the coffee." He took a sip and looked over toward the man reading the paper. "Mind if I read some of your paper?"

"No, here, take the first section, I'm done with it," the younger man said. "The front page is filled with that shooting at the Bears game yesterday. Some folks are just plain crazy. Why would anyone want to kill a cop directing traffic? It makes no sense."

Hardcore put his cup down and reached over for the paper. He sat silently for several minutes while he read the story. *Yeah, that was a great shot. One shot one kill.* He remembered that mantra from his military sniper training. His instructors had drilled that notion into him and his fellow trainees. No warm-up, no practice, one shot is all a sniper gets to take out the enemy. He'd learned his lessons well, placing first in his class.

His tour in the Middle East found him to be one of the most accurate snipers in his division. During the battle of Baghdad, and then later as they swept through adjacent villages, he was personally responsible for at least thirty kills, most from a distance of two hundred yards or more. His comrades were in awe of his marksmanship; he was their first choice whenever a sniper was needed to take out a fortified position.

Things had been looking up for him. War was an environment in which he found he could excel. That is until he got drunk one night and saw that woman walking alone on the road. She spoke good English and seemed to like him, but when he walked her home and tried to kiss her as he said good-night, she became angry. He followed her into her home and was immediately confronted by her father and brother. They were no match for him. When he was finished with them, he refocused his attention on the woman. Two days later the MPs came to his unit, put him in cuffs, and threw him into the brig.

He swore she had consented, that she wanted to be with him. He tried explaining to the two goons that he had done nothing wrong, but they wouldn't listen. Instead, they roughed him up, belittled him by calling him nasty names, and refused to let him have a cigarette. "Hell, we're at war with these people. Why are you locking me up? Don't you know who I am?" Apparently they didn't. Hardcore was just another drunk G.I. as far as they were concerned.

The woman never testified at his court martial; nevertheless, he was found guilty of assaulting the father and brother. He served six months in the brig and was dishonorably discharged. All that time spent in the military . . . gone, wasted, no skills, other than killing people. He'd been home almost a year before he found a job as a painter's helper, but that didn't last long before he was let go. He was bitter. It seemed the whole world was working against him, and he was tired of it. He was ready to fight back. What better way to get even than to use their own training against them? He'd show them. Besides, it was something to do. It gave him a purpose. He was tired of filling out job applications and talking with people who lied through their teeth, telling him, "We'll be in touch."

Wrong. I'll be the one in touch.

Walking into St. Mary's for the ten-thirty Mass, Ed dipped his fingers into the basin of holy water and made the sign of the cross. He hesitated in the doorway, scanning the pews for Lisa. *I hope she's here.* Then he spotted her seated on the right side of the church, toward the front, near the statue of the Blessed Virgin. He made his way toward her, stopping to genuflect at the end of her pew before sitting next to her.

"Ed, you made it," she whispered. "I was hoping I'd see you here today."

"Hi, Lisa. Thanks for inviting me." Ed knelt and said a quick prayer before sitting.

"I think you'll enjoy this Mass. Our pastor, Father Mooney, always celebrates the ten-thirty and gives a great homily. Our choir sings the most beautiful songs."

"I'm sure you're right. In the short time I've been in Fredericksburg, this parish has been one of the highlights. The people are friendly, and from what I've read in the bulletin, involved in many worthwhile causes."

"You should talk with him about getting involved in one of them yourself. You'd be great." She picked up a hymnal and found the page for the day's ceremony just as the lector greeted the congregation. "We'll talk after Mass."

Ed watched intently as the ceremony unfolded, celebrating it vicariously, through Father Mooney. Being able to say Mass was the priesthood's greatest reward. He had enjoyed the blessing, the privilege. Indeed, he looked forward to each day's ritual. Now, his joy had turned to sorrow. He no longer was an active priest and no longer able to consecrate the bread and wine. *Father God, is this to be my lot in life?*

An hour later, the Mass ended with the final blessing, and the worshipers made their exit toward the pastor who was standing out front greeting the congregants. Lisa and Ed walked side by side as they approached the priest.

"Father, I'd like you to meet my friend, Ed. He recently moved here from Chicago."

Shaking Ed's hand, the priest remarked, "Chicago, eh? I bet you miss the pizza and hot dogs already."

Ed laughed. "You're right, Father. I guess you must have sampled them yourself."

"It's the first thing I do whenever I pay a visit to an old friend of mine who's assigned to a parish on the north side of Chicago. As soon as I get off the plane, I find the closest hot dog stand and get one with everything."

Warning bells went off inside Ed's head. *He knows a priest in Chicago. Will he know about me?*

"It's a pleasure to meet you, Ed. Lisa, good to see you again." The priest turned his attention to the other parishioners departing the church.

"Where are you parked, Ed?"

"Actually, since it's such a beautiful morning, I walked."

"I'm over there by the rectory. Say, if you don't have any plans, would you care to join me for brunch? There's a great place I like to visit a couple times a week called University Café. It's just down William Street, toward the river."

"That's a great idea."

A few minutes later they were seated in the café and ordering their food. Looking around the room, Ed liked what he saw. The restaurant had a wide assortment of tables, easy chairs, sofas, coffee tables, and a counter where folks could sit and watch their order being prepared. There was even a coffee bar and several flat screen TVs positioned on the walls around the spacious interior. Some patrons were lounging, engrossed in their laptops and enjoying the free Wi-Fi. Toward the front, a local author was signing his latest novel. "Thanks for inviting me, Lisa. This is quite an eclectic place, very comfortable."

"You're welcome. Now you see why I like this cafe so much." Their coffees arrived and Lisa continued. "So, tell me about yourself. Why did you leave Chicago?"

Uh-oh. He had dreaded this moment when people might ask about his past, but unless he intended to be a hermit the rest of his life, he had to tell them something. "Well, I was working for a small, non-profit, community group. We helped immigrants and homeless folks, connecting them with agencies that could address their needs."

"That sounds like rewarding work. Why did you leave?" Lisa's cell phone rang. "Excuse me, Ed. Hello."

He watched as she spoke on the phone, sensing the conversation was becoming unpleasant for her.

"James, please, I've asked you before not to call me again. No, I'm busy at the moment . . . good-bye." She frowned, turned off her phone, and placed it in her purse. "I'm sorry about that, Ed."

"That's okay. Are you all right?"

She sipped her coffee. "That was someone I used to date. I've asked him not to call me, but he just won't listen. Sometimes I feel like he's stalking me."

"That's serious. Have you thought about contacting the police?" Looking into her eyes Ed thought she looked frightened even discussing the man.

"I've considered it. The problem is that *he is* the police. He's a deputy with the Fredericksburg Sheriff's Department. I met him last year at the state fair. We dated for several months, and I thought that we had made a connection, but later, when I innocently brought up the subject of marriage and children, he was adamant about not wanting any kids. That was a deal breaker for me. I want a family. So, I tried to cool things down and end the relationship, but he refused to cooperate. He began treating me rudely, even pressuring me to have sex with him. He has become very controlling."

"He sounds dangerous, Lisa."

"I know, but I'm afraid to go to his supervisors. I don't know what he might do to me if I go to his job."

Ed pondered what she said for a moment. Were he still a priest and she was one of his flock, he would counsel her to go to the authorities. His experience told him that this type of individual, one who refuses to take no for an answer, would only become emboldened left unchecked. However, she was not his parishioner; she was a friend, so he decided to be a good listener.

"So, what do you expect to do about this situation? If you won't go to the police, can you at least threaten him with that?"

She stared down into her coffee cup. "I don't know what to do, Ed. He scares me so much that I've even gotten rid of my home phone, and there are days when I don't even turn my cell phone on. It seems whenever he calls, the rest of my day is ruined."

Ed felt sympathy toward her plight and instinctively reached across the table to grasp her hand. As soon as he did, she turned her hand to meet his and held him. Touching her was like a jolt of electricity jump-starting his emotions. His heart raced. He began to pull his hand back slightly, but she held on, firmly. For a moment, he was speechless, confused. "Lisa, I'm sorry to hear that. I'll pray that he leaves you alone."

Letting him go, Lisa said, "I'm sorry to involve you in my troubles. I meant for us to have a nice brunch so we could get to know each other. I'd really like to have a friend like you in my life. I can't explain it, but from the moment I met you, I felt like you were someone special, that you had kindness and compassion in your soul."

Their meals arrived, causing the moment to pass. "Well, then, let's do just that. Let's get to know each other," Ed offered.

"Yes, let's."

They talked for two hours, Lisa doing most of it, telling him about her childhood and family. She was an only child. Her father died shortly after she graduated from high school, but as a federal employee, he had ensured there would be money for his daughter's education. Not wanting to leave her mother alone, she attended the University of Mary Washington in town. After she graduated, she continued to live with her mother for several years until she had saved enough money to buy a modest home herself. She had dated several men in the past and was even engaged to one of them, but as the relationship progressed and the couple got closer to the wedding date, he told her that he didn't want to go through with it. He didn't think he could make a lifetime commitment.

"That happens a lot," Ed added. "It's not only men who fear commitment. Women also are guilty of calling it off at the last minute as well."

"I guess I never realized that," she remarked thoughtfully and then continued talking about herself. "After that I didn't date for two years, and then I met James. He was in uniform, working security at the fair. I asked him to help me because I had locked my keys in my car. He had the door unlocked in no time at all and then asked me if he could take me to dinner."

Ed put his fork down. "I guess he made a good first impression."

"Yeah, he did," she said, refilling her cup. "I really thought he was the one, but after a few months I saw a dark side emerge. At first, I thought maybe he had a bad day at work or something. Then I saw that he wanted to control me. In fact, our last couple of dates were horrible. He wanted to, as he called it, progress to the next stage—he wanted to sleep with me."

Listening intently, Ed could see how painful telling her story was for Lisa.

"Then, one night, after I had fixed dinner for him at my house, he refused to leave. He demanded to spend the night. I repeatedly told him no, that I had no intention of allowing him to stay. An argument ensued, and I picked up the phone and begin to dial 9-1-1. He roughly snatched it from my hand and threw it against the wall where it shattered. I was terrified and began to cry until he eventually left. I haven't seen him since, but he calls constantly."

"Lisa, he's trouble. I don't know if he's ever going to leave you alone. I really think that you need to get the authorities involved."

Lisa covered her mouth momentarily before saying, "I know you're right, Ed, I'm just scared to do anything. I can handle the calls; I just turn my phone off for awhile. But I don't know what I'll do if I actually see him. Anyway, you've been an angel for listening so patiently to me. I guess we should go, I've had all the coffee I can handle for one day."

Ed paid the bill, and they walked outside to Lisa's car. "I'm only a couple of blocks from my apartment, no need to drive me."

"Okay. Thank you for a wonderful time, Ed. I'm sorry to have burdened you with my problems, but you're so easy to talk to. Will I see you again at the library?"

"Yes."

"Good." She stepped in close and hugged him. "Thanks again. Have a great day."

"You're welcome. I enjoyed our time together. God bless you, Lisa. See you soon."

Ed watched as she pulled away and then turned to walk home, He didn't notice the sheriff's car parked discreetly around the corner.

"Margaret, have you heard anything from Father Ed?"

"No, Father, and I'm worried. You said he was only going to be gone for a few days, visiting a friend. It's been several weeks."

"I know. I was hoping maybe he'd call and speak with you while I was out. I'm worried too. Maybe something has happened to him."

The housekeeper was in the midst of preparing lunch for the pastor. Perhaps now was a good time for her to tell him what she knew about Magdalena, the woman who had accused Father Ed of molesting her son, Rodrigo. She set his lunch down on the table.

"Father, can I ask you a question?"

"Yes, of course."

"I've been thinking about the mess that Father Ed's involved in. I know him; I know that he's not the kind of person who would harm a child. The people here at St. Nicks love him, and I don't think anyone believes he hurt that boy."

Picking up his knife and fork, the pastor answered her. "I know, Margaret, but the police said the boy's mother informed them that Rodrigo told her Father Ed was inappropriate with him."

"Do you believe that?"

The pastor looked down and shook his head. "I'm not sure. Like you, I think I know Father Matthews. I can't imagine him doing anything improper to anyone, much less a child. But the police arrested him. Would they do that if they didn't have sufficient cause to do so?"

"No, but maybe they don't have all the facts."

Putting his fork down, the priest asked, "What do you mean?"

She sat down across from the priest. "A friend of mine, Bozena, is the housekeeper at St. Francis, you know, down on Roosevelt Road. She told me about Magdalena. She said Magdalena used to be the parish housekeeper at St. Francis, but had been fired."

The priest leaned forward. "Why?"

"Well, Bozena said that Magdalena was caught stealing money from the rectory. After the Sunday masses, the collection was brought into the pastor's office. They think she was skimming money from every bag before it could be brought to the bank for deposit on Monday mornings."

"Was she arrested?"

"No, I guess they couldn't get her to admit to it, but she agreed to quit if the pastor dropped the matter."

"That's too bad," he replied. "But what does that have to do with Father Ed?"

"A lot. A couple of years before that all happened, a priest in the parish was accused of molesting one of the school children. The mother got a huge cash settlement from the Archdiocese in exchange for her silence. She agreed not to go to the papers and put the Church in a bad light. It was later determined she lied about the incident, and she was arrested."

"So what?" The priest asked, resuming his meal.

"Father, that woman was Magdalena's sister."

The priest jumped to his feet as he was struck by the epiphany. "Margaret, you have to tell this to the police! Magdalena could be making this story up so she can sue the Church."

"I know; I've been thinking the same thing. And now that we haven't heard from Father Ed, I'm afraid we may never see him again."

He walked into the next room.

"What are you doing, Father?"

"I'm calling the detective who gave me her card. She said if I had any more information about the case I should give her a call. I'm certain she'll want to know about this."

"Pete, you look exhausted, another bad day?" Beth asked, as she and the baby greeted him.

"Yeah, we went to interview the owner of the van that was spotted in the museum parking lot at the time of the shooting. Turns out McKinnon had already been there."

"But I thought Marilyn had developed that lead."

"She did, but Harry must have deduced the same thing about the trajectory of the shot coming from the museum. He went in there and had the guard give him the same info he gave Marilyn, but he didn't wait to act on it like we did. He and Russo went to interview the owner in the middle of the night. I felt like a fool after the guy told me he'd already talked with the police."

She put the baby in the playpen and hugged Pete. "I'm sorry, honey. Did the man see anything that might help?"

"Actually it was his son and the boy's girlfriend who were in the van. They borrowed it to go the game. Apparently they left early and parked in the museum lot to make out. The kids heard the shot, but couldn't provide anything more than that."

"You should sit down and discuss this with Lt. Darcy, Babe. It seems like this partnership is impeding progress, rather than helping to solve the case."

Pete took his holster and cuffs off his belt and placed them on the shelf in the front closet. "I know; I need to do something before I lose my temper and confront Harry. I wanted to see Darcy this afternoon, but she told me she was unavailable, whatever that means. One of the guys told me she had a meeting with the chief of detectives this morning, and apparently it didn't go well."

Beth helped him off with his sports jacket and hung it in the closet. Then she wrapped her arms around him. "Honey, promise me you'll talk with her about this before it blows up into something bigger. You're letting it get to you. I've never seen you this upset about work. You love your job, but this past week you've been quiet. I think that even Pete, Jr. senses something's wrong."

Pete kissed his wife tenderly and went over and picked the baby up. "Is that right, little guy? Has daddy been ignoring you?" Kissing his son, Pete took Beth in his other arm and held them both. "I need to straighten this situation out. You both mean too much to me; I'm not going to allow McKinnon to disrupt my family life."

Hugging him, Beth said, "Good, we want the old daddy back, the one who laughs and smiles."

Pulling her car into the lot at the gym, Marilyn heard her phone ring. "Hello."

"Mar, how are you, Honey?"

"Joe, I thought you'd still be asleep." She grabbed her workout gear and locked her car.

"No, you know how it is the first few nights after you switch shifts from days to midnights. Your body can't tell if it's day or night. Anyway, I was wondering if you'd like to come over and have dinner with me. I've got some pork chops I can broil, and I'll bake a couple potatoes."

"That would be great. I just pulled into the gym. Let me get in a quick workout and I'll be there in about ninety minutes."

"Okay; call me when you're on the way."

She hurried inside and spotted Kim, her workout partner. "Gotta do a short one today. Got a dinner date with Joe."

"That's okay, I'm kind of fried anyway. We had two runs late last night. Seems like half the south side was on fire."

"I don't know how you do it, girlfriend, work twenty four hours at the firehouse and then go to the gym. I know the other firefighters can't be keeping pace with you."

The two friends chatted while they did their warm-up stretches. "Oh, there are a couple of guys who are as crazy as I am, but you're right. Most guys go right to their other jobs when they're off duty. They don't have any fitness regime. Then they come to me when they get hurt. They know I have a degree in kinesiology so they want me to rehab them."

"You know, you could be charging them hundreds of dollars."

"Yeah," she said, as the two loosened their shoulder muscles. "That will come someday down the road, but I've got too many years with the fire department to change careers just yet. I'm going to make sure I get that retirement first."

"Good girl."

"Say, how's Joe doing? Sounds like things are pretty much back to normal with you two."

"Yeah, he's healthy again. I'll tell you, Kim, that cancer battle just about destroyed him. But I really think his faith and all of the prayers from people who love him, got him through it. He's an amazing man. When I think that I almost lost him . . ."

Marilyn stopped her warm-up and covered her face with her hands. Then, looking through tear filled eyes, she said, "Kim, I don't know why, but whenever we begin to plan our wedding, something always seems to get in the way. First it was his cancer, now, it's this case. I almost feel a sense of urgency about it, like I need to marry him right away before something else happens."

Kim put her arm around her friend. "Don't worry, God put you two together for a reason. You draw strength from each other. The things you call obstacles are what He chooses to make you stronger. Have you stopped to think about how much more you love him since you've battled through adversity together?"

Wiping the tears from her eyes, Marilyn replied. "You're right; our love has never been any stronger than it is now. Helping Joe in his battle to beat cancer allowed us both to peer into each other's soul. Our love couldn't be any deeper, and our faith cemented our bond; I know we are blessed."

"Thatta girl. Now, enough with the negative feelings, let's hit some iron."

The two friends began their workout, but Marilyn just couldn't shake the sense that something else was going to thwart her plans to marry Joe.

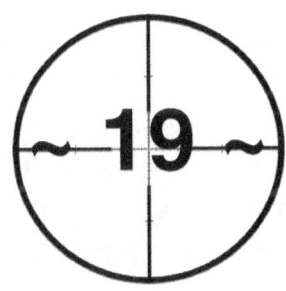

"Did you get any rest last night?"

"A little. I got in a quick workout with Kim and then went to Joe's house. He cooked dinner for us."

Pete was in the midst of checking his department emails before they had to see Lt. Darcy. "So, when are you two going to set a wedding date?"

"It's all set."

"What?" Pete spun around in his chair to face her.

"We did it last night, over dinner. It's going to be next year, November seventh."

"That's great, Marilyn. Congratulations to you both." He got up and gave his partner a hug. "You're finally going to be a married woman."

"Yeah, I can't believe it. I've been praying about it for so long, but the wait's been worth it. Joe is everything I've dreamed about in a man. You know, I wanted to set the date a little bit sooner, but he thought the year engagement would be more appropriate."

"Leave it to Joe," he said. "He's a perfectionist in everything he does."

"Yes, he is perfect, isn't he?" She laughed. "Anyway, there's just something about this case that unnerves me. I feel anxious about things, like wanting to get married right away and not wait."

"I know, Bens, it's making me crazy too. It seems like I lose my temper every day over something McKinnon does. I need to spend more time in prayer." Logging off his computer, he asked, "Okay, are you ready?"

"Yeah, let's go hear what she has to say."

They grabbed their coffees and walked over to Lt. Darcy's office. The door was open. "You wanted to see us, Lieutenant?"

Looking up from a report, she replied, "Yes, I did, come in."

They took the two seats directly in front of Darcy's desk.

"I had a meeting with the chief of detectives," she began. "He's not happy with the progress of our investigation into the murders of the two officers. I explained that the shooter is smart and that he's given us very little to go on. McKinnon and Russo came up with the only solid lead thus far. They found a couple who were parked next to our suspect's vehicle at the Soldier Field murder."

The two detectives looked at each other before Marilyn blurted out, "What?"

Darcy explained. "Harry spoke with a security guard at the Field Museum. He reviewed some surveillance footage with him and found a red van that just might belong to our shooter."

Leaning forward in his chair, Pete put his coffee cup on Darcy's desk. A crimson hue emerged upward from his collar stealing all traces of white as he spoke. "Lieutenant, that witness was discovered by Marilyn. She was the one who first thought the museum might hold some answers to the shooting, not McKinnon. He had to have gone there later, after she had already done the interview with the guard and got the license plate you're referring to, the same one Marilyn came up with."

"Pete's right, Lew. I got a CD from the guard with the footage from the camera. By then it was pretty late, so we decided to wait until morning to interview the potential witness. When we went to the address, we found that Harry had already been there."

Furrowing her brow, Darcy answered. "Harry never mentioned that to me. I understood he and Bobby had done their own legwork. In fact, that's why I wanted to speak with you both this morning. I was upset that you haven't been doing your share of the work."

Pete jumped to his feet. "Dammit, Lieutenant! McKinnon hasn't cooperated with us since day one. He's refused to work with us or share any information. Now, he takes credit for leads that we've developed? This can't go on."

"Sit down, Detective. I won't have you raising your voice at me."

"Sorry, I got a little carried away," Pete said, sitting back down. "It's just that when Marilyn and I found out we were assigned to work this case, we were excited to be able to help catch a cop killer. But since we started working with McKinnon and Russo, it's almost been like one team working against the other. We give and they take."

"He's right," Marilyn added. "We've gone out of our way to work with them, yet they ignore us. Most times they won't even speak to us."

"Lew, I hate to be a whiner. I'd much rather handle things myself, but catching the shooter is what's important here." Pete folded his hands and tried to regain his composure.

"I didn't realize the team had problems. As I told you before," said Darcy, looking at Marilyn, "Harry is a tough guy to work with. He's unconventional in many ways, but he has a successful track record. He's probably solved more homicide cases than anyone in the unit. Let me have a talk with him. In the meantime, continue to work with them on the case as best you can. And listen, I don't want the chief to get wind of this. He's already in a foul mood. Hearing about personnel problems will only set him off."

They nodded.

"By the way, Lt. King wants you to give him a call, something about a priest."

Ed hardly remembered going back to his apartment on Caroline Street after saying goodbye to Lisa. It was a beautiful fall afternoon in Fredericksburg; the sun warmed him as he walked, and for the first time he began to notice the many unique shops the town had to offer. The nice weather produced a wave of shoppers and tourists. The restaurants and cafes were doing a brisk business.

He thought about his morning with her. *What a sweet person.* He played back in his mind the moment he held her hand while she explained her problems with her ex-boyfriend. Not having much experience with relationships in the past, he wondered if his friendship with her might develop into something deeper.

Unlocking the door to his apartment, he opened it and walked up the stairs to the second floor. He spotted his cell phone lying on the table by the window. He walked over, picked it up, and turned it on. While he stood there and waited for the phone to boot up, he glanced out the window and saw a sheriff's patrol car driving past. *Hmm . . .* Checking the missed calls, he saw that both his parents had called, again, as well as his friend, Dan.

Ed hated not being able to call his folks, he wanted to speak with them, at least to ease their fears that maybe something had happened to him. Still he worried that the police might be able to track him if he contacted them. Dan was his best friend, and now, also his lawyer. He owed him a call, but . . . Then it occurred to him: *if I call Dan and have him tell my parents that I'm okay, Dan could claim attorney-client privilege.*

Just to make sure he covered all the bases, he decided to buy a phone card, rather than use his cell phone. He retrieved his car keys and walked back downstairs and around the corner to George Street, where he had parked his car. Down the block, just off Princess Anne Street, a sheriff's car sat idling by the curb.

I've got you on my radar screen now, Romeo.

"Hey, you two, how goes the homicide case?"

Pete and Marilyn walked into Lt. King's office in the Violent Crimes Unit. "Could be better," replied Pete. "Lt. Darcy said you wanted to see us?"

"Yeah, all I needed was a phone call, but this is even better. I have some new information on the case involving Father Matthews."

"Really?" Marilyn moved closer.

"I was going to have another team do the interview, but I thought that for the sake of continuity, and, if you had time to go to St. Nick's yourselves, maybe you'd like to hear what the housekeeper has to say."

"What's up, boss? Is there a witness?"

"I'm not sure. The pastor called looking for you, Marilyn. He said that he thinks Father Ed is being set up. Can you two go see him and the housekeeper, her name is . . . " he looked down at the phone message, "Margaret."

"Definitely, Sir. "We'll contact him immediately and see what's going on."

"Good, and Pete, just because you're detailed to homicide doesn't mean you're no longer part of my team. I still want you to work on your caseload if time permits, but if you guys are swamped with the murders, I'll give this lead to someone else."

Shaking her head, Marilyn said, "No, Lieutenant, we can handle this. In fact, we'd prefer to since we think the priest is innocent. Hopefully, this new information may confirm our suspicions."

"Okay, let me know what happens." King shook both their hands. "It's great to see you both. I kind of miss having you around."

Clasping both his hands around King's hand and shaking it, Pete replied. "You don't know how good that makes me feel,

Lieutenant. The sooner we get back here to Violent Crimes, the better off we'll both be."

"Ditto. Keep your heads down while you're tracking that killer. I want you both back in one piece."

"Roger that, sir."

Pete and Marilyn walked out of the office over to their old cubicle. Pete sighed, feeling the tension drain from his neck and shoulders. "Man, I feel rejuvenated. Just talking with King put me in a better state of mind. I didn't realize how much I enjoy working for him."

"I know what you mean," Marilyn smiled. "I don't mind telling you that I've been worried about you. Your fits of anger are so out of character. If I didn't know better, I'd think Satan is making inroads into your soul."

"No way, unless Lucifer is disguised as McKinnon."

"That may not be as farfetched as it sounds."

"Enough about McKinnon. Let's get a phone call into St. Nick's and find out when we can do an interview with Father DeSalvo and Margaret. After the past several weeks around homicide, this feels like coming back home. Thank you, Lord."

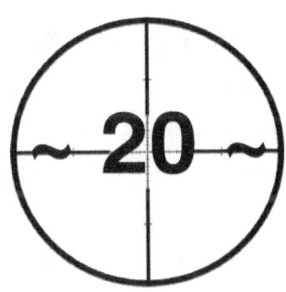

"Are you awake, Mar?"

"Yes, Joe, it's six o'clock. I've already had my first cup of coffee, and I'm about to go out for a run before I head off to work. How's your shift going? Were the natives restless last night?"

"Actually, it's been fairly quiet. A couple of auto thefts, one burglar alarm at the Pizza Hut on 63rd Street, and one drunk driver. Just enough to keep me awake."

"Midnights are tough, baby. I don't know how I survived them."

"I know. I'll be glad when this month's over. But that's not what I'm calling about. I thought you might want to hear some good news to start your day."

"Great, I could use some," she said, nursing the last of her coffee. "McKinnon and this homicide case are still causing us a lot of problems. We had a meeting with Darcy. We caught Harry in a lie. She claims she's going to talk with him about it, but there's something about that relationship that just doesn't seem right. I get the sense that Harry controls her, rather than the other way around."

"You could be right. When I was in the detective division, I knew Harry and Bobby. Harry was a player, got into a lot of jams, but he was street smart. He was able to wiggle out of them, and the bosses loved him because he produced the numbers they needed to make themselves look good. Bobby was never a problem, except to the extent that he did whatever Harry told him to, which sometimes got him in trouble."

"I know," Marilyn replied. "That's what Darcy keeps bringing up. Harry's clearance rate, it's the best in the unit. So, what's your news, honey?" She put her cup in the sink and began to lace up her running shoes.

"Well, last night after roll call, the watch commander called me into his office. He told me that beginning next month I'll be working on the Tac Team."

"Joe, that's fantastic! Congratulations!"

"Thanks, sweetheart. It will be good to get out of uniform and not be handcuffed by answering radio assignments. And I'll be able to work on the big cases in the district."

She finished tying her shoes and retrieved her knit cap and mittens from the closet. "It couldn't come at a better time. I've been worried about you since this creep with the sniper rifle started killing cops. It seems he's out looking for uniforms. Next month can't get here soon enough as far as I'm concerned. If anything happened to you, Joe . . ."

"Don't worry, Mar, I'll be okay. In a couple of weeks I'll be working plain clothes and riding around in an unmarked car. Besides, I've got to make sure nothing happens. I've got a big wedding to look forward to next year."

"That's right, my love. You're going to be my husband, finally. But, Joe, I'm still so anxious about the killer targeting uniforms. Are you sure we can't push the date up a little earlier?"

"C'mon, honey, we've talked about this. We have to have at least a year-long engagement; it's the proper thing to do. Besides, there's so much we need to get done, so many plans to make—find a reception site, invitations, and as we agreed, I've got to pick out a honeymoon location."

"Ooh, a honeymoon. I haven't given that much thought, Joe. Now my head will be swimming all day with ideas about where we'll go and what we'll do."

Laughing, Joe replied. "I think I already know what we'll do, Mar. I just have to figure out where we'll go to do it."

"Ah, you got me on that one. You're the best, honey. Will I see you tonight?"

"Let me call you after I get some sleep. Maybe we can go out for a late dinner."

"That'll be fine. I can meet Kim for a workout at the gym."

"Good, gotta go. I was just about to get another cup of coffee to help me make it through this last hour of work. I'll talk with you later. I love you."

"I love you too, Joe. I can't wait to be your wife. Bye."

"And I can't wait until I'm your husband. Goodbye, Sweetheart."

Marilyn hung up the phone, grabbed her house key, and went out the front door. Feeling energized from her conversation with Joe, she decided to add an extra mile to her run this morning. It would give her more time to think about the man she loved and less time thinking about catching the man she loathed.

Driving south on Kedzie, he caught the red light at 71st Street. Waiting for it to change, he looked over in the direction of the convenience store and spotted a squad car parked in the lot. As the light turned green, he saw the cop get out and head into the store. *Hey, why not?* He sped up through the intersection, cracked a quick u-bender, and headed back north toward Marquette Park. With over three hundred acres and a beautiful golf course and a meandering lagoon, it was one of the jewels of the Park District. He made the right turn into the urban oasis and parked his vehicle adjacent to the water. Jumping into the rear of his van, he checked his field of fire. *Damn, this won't give me a clear shot.*

His parking spot would not allow him to shoot through the back window like he'd done with the first two cops. He couldn't position the van the way he needed to without making himself obvious. He'd either have to pass this one up or take the shot from somewhere outside his sniper hide. He got out of the vehicle and looked around. Off to his left was a lagoon with a nice sloped bank. It would give him both cover and a stable shooting platform. Coming out of the van was risky, but that was how he rolled. He lived on the edge; he'd proven his mettle in combat. This kill would be a cake walk.

The cold, fall Chicago weather worked to his advantage. It allowed him to hide his rifle under his jacket, and the early morning darkness covered his movement. *Hell, these are perfect conditions.* He made his way over to the water's edge and found a spot next to an evergreen tree that would serve as concealment. Seconds later he had his rifle out and was adjusting the power and focus on his scope, waiting for the unsuspecting cop to exit the store.

"Good morning, Officer. How are you today?"

Putting a lid on his coffee cup, Joe replied. "I'm great, my friend. How are you?"

"Pretty good, sir, now that business has picked up with school back in session. Lots of the high school kids come in before the bus picks them up at the corner."

"I'm glad to hear that. Just start your shift?"

"Yes, Sir. My brother works the midnight shift; I relieve him at six, and my wife takes my place at three."

"You've got the whole family involved. Good for you."

"Yes, we're blessed to have a business that can support all of us. The bad part is I don't get to see very much of my wife. Because of our shifts, it seems like we're always apart."

Joe handed two dollars to the man to pay for his coffee. "Yeah, I guess everything has its downside, but the good news is that you and your wife are working toward one goal."

"Yes, Officer. We've been able to send our kids to college and live comfortably because of this store. Now I'm looking forward to the day when we can just relax and spend time together."

"I think we all share that dream, me included."

"Are you married?" asked the man, handing Joe his change.

Joe paused for a moment, remembering his deceased wife. "I was, but my wife passed away. Now I'm engaged to a woman who is the most beautiful person you'd ever want to meet." Putting his change into his pocket, Joe headed toward the door.

"I hope your marriage is a long and loving one, Officer."

"Thanks."

He walked out the door and stopped to take a sip from his steaming cup.

Power's right . . . focus . . . there . . . close enough to read the name tag—Officer Murphy. Good morning, Murphy, nice to meet you, but it's time to say good-bye. Hardcore took his three deep cleansing breaths and on the fourth, began his trigger squeeze. The shot broke. Adjusting from the recoil, he regained his position on the stock of the rifle. The officer was no longer in his scope. He dialed down the power to increase his field of view and saw his victim lying on the ground. Yes . . . His record was still intact—three shots, three kills.

Feeling exhilarated, Marilyn ran through Mt. Greenwood Park. Pete was right, this truly was the best time to run. There was just a hint of frost on the tips of the grass, and the multi-colored leaves on the ground made for a beautiful, tapestry-like carpet on which to run. Picking up the pace, she could see her breath, while thoughts of her and Joe as man and wife danced in her head. The honeymoon he mentioned just before they'd hung up had her excited. How great will it be for the two of them to get away from it all? She'd decided to let him plan that part of the wedding; he said he wanted to surprise her. *Can I wait an entire year for our plans to come to fruition?* It seemed like an eternity, and this homicide case had her worried. At least Joe would be in plain clothes and out of harm's way on the Tac Team.

Exiting the park at 111th Street near Central Park, she decided to head north toward 95th Street. Still thinking about her life as Mrs. Joe Murphy, she stepped off the curb.

Ted Sharp had been partying all night. After shutting down the bars on 111th Street, he and two friends spent the next few hours drinking wine and smoking marijuana. Unemployed for the last six months, he didn't have a job to worry about, so most days he did whatever he wanted. Lately, many of his days and nights had run together. So much so, that he rarely knew what day of the week it was.

Right now he was tired. He pointed his beat up 1990, red Toyota toward home. His buzz was beginning to wear off, so as he drove he rummaged through the glove box looking for one more joint he was sure he had stashed there. As he approached the intersection of 111th and Central Park, he kept his head stayed below the dash, focusing on his search for weed. He never saw the runner stepping off the curb. Suddenly, he heard a thump. Looking up, his windshield had morphed into a grotesque kaleidoscope of distorted frames, which momentarily held what appeared to be the image of a woman.

The young man slammed on the brakes, put the car in park, and sat transfixed, trying to comprehend what had just happened. Stepping out of his car, allowing the cold, crisp air to wash over him, the sound and cracked windshield all began to fall into place.

Twenty feet ahead of his car was the body of a woman, lying motionless, alongside the curb. *Holy shit . . .*

He quickly hopped back into his vehicle. Heart racing and having difficulty catching his breath, he stepped on the gas so hard he thought his foot would go through the floorboard. Despite the chill, sweat poured from his forehead. He couldn't take the blame for the accident. He was out of a job and out of money. His license was suspended. *Sorry, lady, hope you pull through.*

Officer Joe Murphy's body hit the ground at almost the same time Marilyn's did. As he lay dead outside the convenience store, and his wife-to-be lay injured in the gutter on 111th Street, neither one was aware of the tragedy that had befallen them both. A resident, who had been looking out the window for her child's school bus, saw what happened to Marilyn and dialed 9-1-1, before rushing outside to shield Marilyn from further harm.

Meanwhile, at the scene of the shooting, the store owner, thinking that perhaps Joe was sick and had collapsed, rushed out to render assistance to the officer. Once there, however, he was jolted by what he saw. The officer would not need his assistance; he was beyond help. Shaking, the clerk grabbed the officer's radio microphone. "Policeman shot . . . come quickly . . . a police officer is dying . . . help me . . . please."

At that very moment, St. Michael the Archangel, patron saint of all police officers, stood over Joe's earthly remains. Bending down, God's Principal Warrior gently lifted this valiant soul and began the final journey to eternal life. *Well done, good and faithful servant! You have been faithful with a few things . . . Come and share your master's happiness!*

~ 21 ~

As Pete turned onto 103rd Street from Kedzie Avenue, he had a strange feeling . . . a sense of urgency. He couldn't explain it, but this last mile home had to be run as quickly as he could. It was still dark, and his thoughts swirled around the upcoming day's activities. He was planning on visiting St. Nick's today. He and Marilyn needed to interview Margaret, Father DeSalvo's housekeeper, about the recent revelation concerning the allegation against Father Matthews, but that task shouldn't cause him to feel like something ominous was in the offing.

Pumping his arms, he headed home as fast as he could, almost as if the devil himself was chasing him. He passed by Queen of Martyrs Church and Saint Xavier University, finally slowing as he reached the mouth of his subdivision. He felt good physically; he was in great shape. He knew the importance of being fit—it had already saved his life once, but mentally, something was amiss. *Is it because of the disconnect between McKinnon and me?* He couldn't quite figure out this feeling of impending calamity.

He went into his house through the back door. Beth and the baby were still in bed, so he headed straight to the shower, remembering to bring his phone with him. Ten minutes later he was finished and went into the spare bedroom to get dressed for work. Beep. Looking at his cell he saw that he had a text message waiting from Lt. Darcy. He brought it up:

> another cop killed
> call me ASAP

Uncertain about whether his partner had received the same message, he dialed Marilyn's phone. It immediately went to voice mail. *She must not have turned it on yet.* He hung up without leaving a message and dialed Lt. Darcy's number.

"Shannon?"

"Yes, what's up, Lieutenant? Your message said there's been another shooting."

"There has, Pete. It's Officer Joe Murphy. He was killed as he stepped out of a store on 71st and Kedzie. I've got Harry and Bobby on the way to the scene. I didn't get an answer when I called Benson's number. Can you head over to her place? I don't want her anywhere near the scene of the shooting. I know those two were engaged; I can't have her see her fiancé lying on the ground."

Suddenly feeling light-headed, he sat down on the bed. This can't be happening . . . please, Lord, let it be a dream . . . make me wake up.

"Pete, are you there?"

"Uh, yeah, Lew, I'm here. I'm just trying to wrap my head around what you just told me. Was it a robbery or something?"

"No, Pete. It's probably the sniper."

"I can't believe it. Poor Marilyn. I'll head over to her apartment and break the news."

"Pete, I'd send the chaplain with you, but he's on his way to Murphy's mother's house to make the death notification."

"I understand."

"Listen, Pete, I'm sorry. I know he was a friend of yours. If you don't want to work this one I'll understand."

He thought for a moment. "No chance, I need to work it. In fact, I've got all the reason in the world to find out who this demon is—I owe it to Joe."

"Good, I'm glad to hear that. But for now, I want you to hang with Benson and keep her away from the crime scene. I don't know how she's going to react to the news, and I certainly don't want her hearing it on the radio or TV. Get over there, now."

"I'm on the way." Hanging up, he quickly began to dress, thankful he had a mission to perform to keep his mind off Joe's murder. A minute later, Beth walked into the room, rubbing the sleep from her eyes. "Honey, I heard you on the phone. Is anything wrong?"

With tears welling in his eyes, he went to her. "It's Joe Murphy; he's been murdered."

"No . . ."

"Darcy called to tell me. She couldn't get hold of Marilyn and neither can I, so I've got to get over to her place. I don't want her hearing the news on the radio or TV, and I certainly don't want her showing up at the scene while Joe's body is still there."

Sobbing, Beth held her husband tightly, wishing she could say something to make him stay. Things were getting worse, rather than better. This case was having an impact on their marriage, turning Pete into a different man than the one she knew, but more than that, she feared for his safety.

"Pete . . . I'm scared. Whoever is doing this is a maniac. None of you are safe. Now, Joe's been killed. I can't handle much more of this, I just can't handle it."

She sank to the floor, falling on her knees, covering her face with her hands as she wept. He knelt down and held her, feeling her body quiver as she sobbed.

"Listen to me, Honey. I know this is a shock. I don't know what's going to happen when I break the news to Marilyn. She's endured so much pain already. Just remember, this is our job, we're cops. This kind of thing happens. Satan doesn't play favorites; he's after every one of us. As upsetting as Joe's death is, I take consolation in knowing that he was ready to be with the Lord. He lived his life according to the Word. If anyone was ready for the Father to call him home, it was Joe."

She lifted her face to him. "Pete, this changes everything. I was feeling so good about us. Little Pete is happy and healthy, and our newest miracle is doing fine," she said, as she moved her hands to her protruding abdomen, caressing it lovingly. "Now I don't know what to think. It's hard to be happy knowing that any moment your husband might be taken from you."

"Beth, please, settle down. Nothing's going to happen to me."

"How can you say that, Pete?" she asked, as she looked at him with tears running down her face. "You've been shot once already. Who's to say that it won't happen again? I don't want to be a widow with two small children like Susan O'Hara."

Pete didn't have a comeback for that. His first partner, Joe O'Hara, had been killed by a thug they'd engaged in a gun battle, and Pete himself had been shot in the line of duty by a rogue cop. He knew she was right. How could he guarantee that it wouldn't happen again?

Hearing his parents in the next room, Pete, Jr. began to cry, sensing the conflict. While he held his wife and wanted to stay and allay her fears, he knew how urgent it was for him to notify Marilyn. Police families try to steel themselves to the horrors of the job. They somehow get through crisis after crisis, but some are more difficult than others, and neither Pete nor Beth knew if Joe's death would be the only one they would have to endure.

Hearing the loud noise nearly caused the young woman to stumble as she ran. *Was that a backfire from a truck?* She stopped momentarily, then continued her run across Kedzie Avenue, into the eastern half of Marquette Park. Although she loved the fall weather, she hated the early morning darkness that it brought. Her morning exercise routine was ingrained; some of her friends even told her she was addicted to it. No matter, it was what made her happy.

Summertime was when she enjoyed exercising the most. Running through the park at six in the morning, with the sun already shining brightly and the birds welcoming her with their melodious voices was the fix that allowed her to endure the worst of conditions. She'd made many new friends who were also runners. It wasn't unusual for her to be running with three or four others in at this time of day, but once the cold, dark weather moved in, she found that she was mostly on her own. She hated it, thinking the darkness hid unseen dangers, especially for a lone female.

Continuing along the path, she thought she spotted movement out of the corner of her eye, off to the left. Her body went on full alert. A figure by the water's edge . . . by the trees . . .yes, a man, getting to his feet. She slowed to take a better look. *A homeless person?* The stranger froze and looked in her direction. Her heart raced as panic seized her. She began to run as fast as she could, crossing the grassy area out onto the busy street. Her instincts told her to get to a well-lit, populated area.

Once on 71st Street, she turned and headed toward home. As she ran, she heard a trumpeting of police sirens in the distance, announcing the approach of men in blue. The shrill wail of the sirens caused the hair on the back of her neck to stand on end. Sirens were a harbinger of suffering and sinister acts. Minutes later she was inside her home. She said a prayer of thanks that she was safe. *What just happened? Who was that guy?* She couldn't shake the feeling that she had seen someone evil.

He put his weapon on safe and saw a runner coming his way. *Damn . . . where the hell did she come from?* Interrupting his concentration threw off his routine. He stood quickly, wanting to clear the area before the mob of blue and whites showed up. She looked directly at him and then took off running once again. *Yeah,*

you better run, sweetheart, you don't want none of this. Collapsing the stock of the weapon, he put it underneath his jacket and made a beeline for his van. Opening the door, he heard the approach of law enforcement. The van's engine fired, and he drove off in the opposite direction, his heart beating rapidly from the adrenaline rush. Taking the shot from outside his vehicle was a risk that reminded him of his sniper activity in Iraq. It psyched him.

Being able to safely clear the area after the kill was as critical as the shot itself. He'd had several close calls in his military career, almost getting caught a couple of times before he was able to extract himself from his hide. Fleeing the scene today brought back those memories and made him feel like he was back in the moment. This was his calling, his specialty. He should still be in combat; he was born to be a sniper. *Damn MPs.*

As satisfaction replaced excitement, he drove toward the coffee shop to have breakfast. He deserved a reward for a job well done. Much later, he would realize he had broken one of the cardinal rules for snipers.

Standing over the body, Bobby said, "Oh man, Harry, it's Murphy!"

"Yeah, too bad. He was a pretty good cop. Used to be a dick a couple years back, worked in area two."

"I know. He quit when his old lady got killed by a drunk driver. He came back on the job 'bout a year ago. I hear he was engaged to Benson."

"Wonder Woman?" McKinnon asked.

"Yeah, I overheard her and Shannon talking about a wedding."

Harry pulled the crime scene tape and a blanket out of the trunk. "Well, I guess Benson's gonna be a little upset when she sees what went down this morning. Maybe this'll get her off our ass. I'm tired of that bitch gettin' in my way."

"That's cold, Harry. I mean, she is a fellow cop."

"Yeah, whatever. Cover the body and then use the tape to cordon off this whole lot. The friggin' news people will be here any minute; I don't want them screwin' up the scene. Don't let anyone leave the store until we get their names and statements. Have a couple uniforms help you. Oh, and get a couple of coffees for us from the owner. It's the least he can do for us. The lab guys just pulled in. I'm gonna talk with them."

"Okay, Harry."

Man, Darcy's gonna be pissed.

The morning weather was uncharacteristically cold for Fredericksburg, but it was certainly nothing like Midwest winters he was used to. Ed wished he'd packed some warmer clothes before leaving Chicago. Now he'd have to buy a hat and gloves. Pulling out of the parking lot at St. Mary's church after the six o'clock mass, he was still thinking about the service. *I miss being a priest.* The ordeal of having been arrested for a crime he didn't commit and then being told he couldn't minister to his parishioners was becoming a heavy burden that consumed his every thought.

His new life, although physically comfortable, was unsettling in other ways, not the least of which was being unable to serve in a spiritual capacity. The Mass had always been the highlight of his day, when he took on the role of Christ's priest. Whether it was a high Mass at Christmas, attended by hundreds of parishioners, or simply one of the scores of daily Masses he'd said, where only a handful of the faithful were present, his spirit always soared. At that sacred moment, the Consecration of the bread and wine into the body and blood of Christ, Ed felt His presence. That reenactment of the Last Supper infused his soul with a deep, gratifying love for the Savior.

Now all that was gone; he longed for a solution. *Father, help me find my way.* He knew once ordained, a man was a priest for life, but what kind of priest could he possibly be if he wound up in jail? Thoughts of his overnight incarceration bubbled to the surface, the dreadful memory of confinement causing him to sweat despite the cold weather. As he drove down William Street he was suddenly blinded by a light reflecting off his rearview mirror.

A bright beam from what appeared to be a spotlight captured his vehicle, like an alien space ship. The light enveloped him and filled the inside of his car like an intruder, turning the gray morning as bright as noon. Slowing his vehicle, Ed pulled to the curb as blue lights from behind cast eerie shadows that danced on his dash board like phantoms from a science fiction movie. His pulse racing and heart beating piston-like, he knew . . . *a police car*. He waited for the officer to approach. *Is this it, have they found me?* He sat helplessly in the car, unsure if these would be his final minutes of freedom.

"License and registration."

Ed looked up at the officer through the rolled down window. The police car's spotlight was still directed at his car in such a manner that the reflection in the rear view and side mirrors did not allow him a clear vision of the police officer. "Is something wrong, Officer?"

"I said, license and registration . . . now!"

Ed fumbled with his wallet for the documents while looking at the cop with his peripheral vision. In the harsh glare of the police light the officer's breath was visible in the chilly morning air. He found the papers and handed them to the officer. "Here you are, sir. May I ask . . . ?"

Snatching the identification from Ed's hand, the officer began. "I stopped you because you were going thirty-three miles per hour in a thirty mile per hour zone. Stay in your vehicle; I'll be right back."

Blinded by the light, Ed couldn't see what the officer was doing. Time stood still while he waited, alone and afraid. His fate, indeed his very future was in the hands of this stranger who in one instant could very well turn his world upside down. *Three miles over the limit? Who gets stopped for that?* If this were Chicago, it might mean the cop was looking for some money. Ed wondered if his phony identification would stand up to whatever scrutiny the officer was giving it. If it didn't, would he find himself back in jail? A short while later, the officer returned.

Handing Ed back his papers, the cop said, "Here you go. I gave you a break on the speeding—I gave you a warning citation. When the posted speed limit is thirty, it doesn't mean thirty three. Understand?"

"Yes sir, thank you. It won't happen again."

"Where are you headed?"

"Home."

"Do you work?"

"Yes, sir."

"Where?"

"I work at the Visitors Center downtown."

"Okay. Remember, watch your speed."

The cop walked back to his vehicle while Ed sat in his car and put his documents and ticket in his wallet. Shutting off his spotlight and emergency lights, the cop pulled out and drove off.

Ed noticed that it was a Fredericksburg Sheriff's vehicle. Slowly regaining his composure, he had a thought: *I wonder . . .* He pulled out the ticket; it contained the officer's signature on the bottom: Deputy James Rogers. *Lisa's ex-boyfriend, James?*

Still shaking from the experience, Ed put his car in gear and continued his drive home. The realization of the tentativeness of his existence unnerved him. His daily life would never be free from these types of intrusions, any of which could send him back to jail. He found a parking spot close to his building, locked his car, and walked toward the door leading up to his apartment. Instead of going inside, he walked past the building. He needed to think, to analyze his situation. Was his plan really the best thing for him, or should he have stayed in Chicago and allowed his arrest and trial to run its course?

The problem was jail. Ed couldn't fathom spending anymore time in a cell. Although he did make bond and his stay was brief, what if after his trial, he was found guilty of the charges? Would they imprison him? And where? He'd heard horror stories about the state penitentiary, particularly the attacks on those convicted of child molestation. He didn't think he was strong enough—mentally or physically—to survive that environment. But how long could he endure this counterfeit life he was living? Being on the run would never allow for a moment of relaxation. The anxiety of knowing that the authorities were always searching for him would be like a Gordian knot he could never untie.

And now there was Lisa. She was presenting him with an entirely new dilemma. He was getting close to her, perhaps too close. He found himself thinking about her during idle moments, remembering things about her such as her smile and the touch of her hand. He felt, no, he knew, that this relationship was becoming more than just a friendship. What problems would it pose for him? Should he divulge his past to her?

Before he realized it, he had been walking for thirty minutes. He found himself in front of the Hyperion Espresso coffee shop. Feeling chilled, he walked in and was immediately assaulted by the bold aroma of ground coffee beans. Breathing in the delicious scent, he proceeded to the counter and ordered a large cup. He took his brew to one of the many mismatched tables, deciding on one by the window which offered a view of the busy intersection and the market square across the street.

As he sipped the strong blend, he watched as strangers walked the streets that George Washington once called home. Ed wondered if this city would be a permanent stop for him, or would it become just another place from where he would be forced to flee. Being stopped by the police had scared him and brought him back down to earth. He had been so confident before. Now he was worried he would be discovered. Moreover, was this officer who stopped him, the same one who used to be Lisa's boyfriend? He thought it was, but he had to ask her and confirm it. If the cop was stalking her, he was probably next on the cop's list.

Ed took another drink and let thoughts of Lisa comfort him. She was the only good thing that had happened to him since his arrest. He stared out the window, not seeing anything in particular, letting his mind play vignettes of time spent with her and producing previews of what might occur in the future. A family . . . children? No, he was a priest. Confusion reigned, so he turned his thoughts to his parents. He'd tried to keep those thoughts out of his head, but the reality they must be worried and anxious about him continued to plague him. *I should call.*

Finishing his coffee, he checked the time and decided he should go home and get ready for work. He was thankful for his job, not only for the income, but because it kept his mind occupied. The busier he kept, the less time he had to think about his situation. He didn't know how long he would live in Fredericksburg, but while he did, he wanted his stay to be as pleasant as possible. He walked out the door and headed toward his apartment. One thing he did know—he needed to ask Lisa her ex-boyfriend's name. He had an ominous feeling it just might be *James Rogers*.

Pete pulled into the parking lot at Marilyn's apartment complex and immediately spotted her car. He found a space close by and parked and then ran up the stairs to her apartment. Knocking on the door and ringing the bell, he waited impatiently for her to answer—nothing. He repeated the sequence, this time knocking more forcefully—still no response. Reaching into his pocket for his cell phone, he was about to dial her number when the phone rang. The caller ID flashed: Lt. Darcy. *Now what does she want?*

"Shannon?"

"Yes, I'm at Benson's apartment but I can't get her to respond. Her car is here so she must be home. I was just about to try her cell again."

"Don't bother."

"What?"

"Pete, there's been an accident. She's at Christ Hospital."

"What are you talking about? Her car is still parked here at the apartment. How could she be involved in an accident?"

"Listen to me, Pete. She was apparently out for a run this morning. Someone hit her as she tried to cross 111th Street. I was just notified by the on-duty ER nurse who recognized her from past visits."

"Is she okay . . . I mean . . . she's not hurt badly, is she?"

"I can't say, Pete. All the nurse would tell me is that she's unconscious. Get over there and let me know what's going on. McKinnon and Russo will handle the crime scene at the shooting, and there's already a unit from Major Traffic on scene at the site of the hit and run."

"Okay . . . okay. I'm on the way."

"Pete, are you going to be all right? Can you handle all that's being thrown your way this morning?"

Leaning against the wall, he slid down until he was seated on the ground. He closed his eyes as he felt a tremendous weight suffocating him, pressing him into the concrete.

"Are you there, Pete? Pete?"

"Yes, Lieutenant, I'm here. I'm just trying to digest everything that's happened. It's too much; nothing makes any sense."

"I know. I can't figure it out either, but we have to stay strong if we're going to be of any help. Get over to the ER. I'll be there after I check on the murder scene."

"Okay, Lew. Bye."

He somehow made his way down the stairs, back to his vehicle. Dawn was about to break, and as he looked east as the sun's corona began to color the ashen sky, he thought about how he might break the news to Beth. When he left, she was still upset about Joe's murder. Now, another friend lay in the hospital emergency room. Could she handle another tragedy? He wasn't sure. *Can I?* He wondered.

Getting into his car, he shut the door and turned to the only One he knew would have the answers. He shut his eyes and prayed. *Father, I know you have a plan for your children, that your plans are meant to help us. Please let Marilyn be okay. Right now, I need your divine intercession. I need your blessing and grace to help me understand what's happening. Strengthen me . . . give me the words I need to comfort my wife and the wisdom to find the killer responsible for Joe's death. Help me, Father . . . please help me.*

As he drove to the hospital, his resolve became inexplicably resolute. He didn't realize it yet, but God is closest to those with broken hearts.

"It's gotta be the same, guy." Harry's toothpick danced between his lips as he gave Lt. Darcy an update on the shooting. "The crime lab guys went over every inch of this lot, but came up empty on physical evidence. No bullet fragments or shell casings. They took a look at how Murphy's body was positioned and determined that the shooter was probably across the street, somewhere in the park."

Darcy looked over in that direction and saw the Mobile Crime Scene Unit and two techs searching the area. "What about witnesses?"

"Zip. I talked with the store owner. He didn't hear the shot, but he saw Murphy collapse and thought maybe he was sick. He went outside to see if he could help. That's when he discovered Murphy had been shot."

"Any other customers inside the store when it happened?"

"Yeah, two kids. They came outside when the owner went to see if he could help. Bobby interviewed them. One of the kids might help us ID a vehicle. She said she was looking around trying to spot her friend's car that was expected to come by and pick her up. I've gotta get permission from her parents to let the shrink hypnotize her to see if she saw anything that might help us."

"Good, Harry, stay on that and get it done quickly. The chief is going to be all over me now that a third cop's been killed and all by the same guy." She looked around the front of the store. "Any surveillance cameras out here?"

"Yeah, there's one right above the door, but it covers only the front."

"Grab the footage. Maybe our guy was here before, or maybe even after he killed Murphy. You know how macabre some of these people are; they like to admire their work. Get all the tags and run them."

"Yeah, okay." Harry looked over Darcy's shoulder. "Crap, the chief just pulled up across the street. Let's see if his fat ass can come up with anything. He couldn't catch a cold in a room full of snot-nosed kids. I wouldn't worry too much about him if I were you. Besides, you're a skirt, sweetheart . . . you're bulletproof. He can't boot your ass out without upsettin' all the PC types out there."

"Knock it off, Harry. This isn't the place for that kind of talk. Incidentally, you and Russo may have to work this on by yourselves."

"What happened, Batman and Wonder Woman get cold feet?"

"No, Benson's been in an accident, a hit and run. She's over at Christ Hospital, unconscious. I'm on my way there now to see how serious she's been hurt. I sent Shannon there ahead of me. Did you know that she and Murphy were engaged?"

"Yeah, Bobby told me this morning. Tough break, but at least those two won't be gettin' in my way for awhile. I didn't see them helping us catch the shooter anyway."

"Don't be too quick to criticize. I heard about the lead you stole from the guard at the museum."

"What?"

"We'll discuss it later. Right now keep working on this; it's your number one priority. I'm reassigning your other cases. I want you on this 24-7."

Lt. Darcy turned around and walked over to meet the chief of detectives as he made his way inside the cordoned area.

"Morning, Sir."

"Cut the bullshit, Darcy. Is it the same guy?"

"Yes, sir, it appears to be the same M.O."

"Damn, the boss is gonna be livid. Tell me you've got some leads and that we're close to identifying this guy."

"I wish I could, but . . ."

Eyes widening, the chief's unibrow went from a straight line to a curved one. He stuffed his hands deep into his overcoat. "Lady, you've got forty-eight hours to give me something solid on the shooter . . . a vehicle, a name, ballistics on the rounds being used . . . something . . . anything."

"Chief, you don't understand."

"No, you don't understand. I put you in charge of the Homicide Unit, and I can just as easily remove you." He looked around the scene. "Where're Shannon and Benson? Why don't you have the whole team out here?"

"Well, that's another thing, Chief. I just learned that Benson's in the ER at Christ Hospital. She was run over by a hit and run driver this morning. I've got Shannon there with her now."

Taking his hands from his overcoat pockets, the chief ran them through his grey hair. "Holy shit, what else can go wrong?"

Nervously licking her lips, Darcy took a deep breath and said, "Chief, Murphy and Benson were engaged to be married."

He threw his hands up in the air. "You gotta be kiddin' me." He turned and walked toward a gaggle of reporters who were standing outside the police tape. Stopping momentarily, he turned back to Darcy and said, "Forty-eight hours, Lieutenant."

As the night time stars went off duty, the brilliant sun relieved them. At the same time, Darcy's once bright rising star seemed to stop its ascent. She had two days before it would lose its place in the galaxy completely.

"Coffee?"

"Yeah, and give me a couple scrambled with bacon. I'm feelin' kinda hungry this mornin'."

Hardcore took his usual spot at the counter at his favorite breakfast spot. The regulars were already in their normal seats.

"Hey, young man. How you doin' today?" The paper reader asked him as he looked up from his morning newspaper.

"Hungry . . . been busy."

"Find a job?"

"Nah, nothin' yet."

"Well, keep lookin', somethin's bound to pop up."

"Yeah, right."

As the two bantered back and forth, the television in the corner was tuned to the morning news show.

. . . And on the city's southwest side, another police officer has been gunned down by what looks to be a sniper. Details remain sketchy at the moment, but what we've learned thus far is that the officer was murdered by what appears to be the same unknown gunman who shot and killed two other cops in earlier incidents. Police have yet to ID the wanted shooter, but the Chief of Detectives is said to be on the scene. We'll have details as they emerge.

"What the hell? This is getting out of control," the waitress said, as she set Hardcore's breakfast in front of him. "They need to catch this animal and get him off the street."

Hardcore picked up his silverware and began to butter his toast. "Animal? You're awful judgmental, Lynn. Maybe this guy's got a reason for what he's doin'."

"Sweetheart, ain't nobody got any kind of good reason to murder cops."

"I don't know. Seems to me some folks need killin,' maybe even some cops."

"Whatever," said the woman, as she walked away toward the kitchen.

The customer seated at the counter to Hardcore's right continued to read his newspaper, but he overheard the exchange between the two. He glanced sideways at the man in the cammo jacket. *Something's not right with this one.*

~ **24** ~

Beth finished feeding Pete, Jr., and set him down in the playpen next to the kitchen table. Putting on a pot of coffee, she stood at the window, peering out and seeing nothing except despair and uncertainty in her future. Their dear friend, Joe Murphy, a good man who had endured so much adversity and was about to begin a new life with a woman who loved him, was gone. Gone. Why? How to explain the unexplainable? And Marilyn—lying in the hospital—unconscious? What is happening? Nothing seemed to make any sense. Was her husband safe, or was he the next target of this Satanesque murderer?

Going to the kitchen counter with a cup of freshly brewed coffee, she reached to the shelf for a bagel but stopped before grabbing one. The pain of the unknown, the fear of not being in control of her life began to gnaw at her. The same gut feeling she had when she was battling the demons within after she had cheated on Pete. The agony she had stuffed far away in her mind was now as fresh as it was back then.

The only way she knew to ameliorate the hurt and regain some control had been to deny herself the simplest of things—food. Knowing of no other way to fight back, she quickly decided she needed that power again. She couldn't control her husband's life, couldn't protect him, but she could manage one thing in her life— what she ate. She had used this technique successfully in the past. Denying herself food and controlling the numbers on the scale, was a coping mechanism that had worked for her. With danger and death becoming commonplace in her life, she needed to do something. Being in control of her body would have to suffice until she found something else to take its place.

She took her coffee to the table and switched on the television. As the news program reported the tragic events of the early morning, Beth said a silent prayer that Pete would be safe. She didn't want to think of her life without him; she needed him. Looking down at the playpen, she saw that the baby had fallen asleep, and as she took another sip of coffee she felt movement in her womb. *We need him; we can't lose him.*

She loved Pete dearly. He was her life; her lover, friend. and confidant, the father of their children. *What would she do if . . . ?* She didn't want to think any more about losing Pete. Picking up her coffee, she went to the bedroom and turned on the shower. *Stay busy; don't dwell on it. He'll be fine, won't he?* She dropped her robe to the floor and stepped inside the stall underneath a torrent of soothing hot water that masked the tears that fell from her eyes. *He'll be okay.*

Pete rushed into the ER looking for any familiar face. Seated along the wall was Sgt. McNamara, the midnight desk sergeant at the 8th District. "Mac, what happened, how is she?"

Standing up to greet his friend, Mac took Pete's extended hand and then pulled him close in a warm embrace. The two cops had built a bond over the past few years, one that resembled a father-son relationship. "Not much word, I'm afraid. The docs have x-rayed her. She has a broken collarbone, a couple of fractured ribs, and some cuts and abrasions. The Major Traffic Accident Unit is still on the scene reconstructing, but for now all we have to work with is that small red car hit Marilyn and then took off. I'll check with them later to see if there are any more leads."

"Whew, that's not too bad. She should heal quickly," Pete sighed, as he sat down.

"You're right, except she's been unconscious since she arrived, and they don't know why. They're getting ready to take her up for an MRI to see if there's any damage they couldn't find with the x-ray."

"Oh, no." Leaning back in the chair, Pete closed his eyes momentarily. "Mac, this is horrible. You heard about Joe?"

"Yeah, I can't believe it. He was a good man, a great cop. I heard the call come over the radio as I was about to go off duty."

A fire department paramedic team burst through the ER doors with a patient on a gurney, causing Pete to sit upright. "Mac, what the heck's going on? It's almost like we're under attack, like it's open season on us."

"I know. I can't figure it out, and Joe's murder brings it much too close to home for me. Did you know he was just assigned to our district Tac Team?"

"Yes, I did. I only wish it had happened sooner. Being out of uniform may have saved his life."

"Maybe, maybe not. This guy is going after cops in uniform, but it's not difficult to spot one of us, even in plain clothes, if you know what you're looking for."

Pete rubbed his eyes. "You know what's frustrating? I'm assigned to find the guy doing the shooting, and I'm no closer to finding him now than I was on the first day."

"Aren't you working with McKinnon on this one?"

"Don't get me started on him."

"What? He's got a great reputation, Pete. He's supposed to be one of the best homicide investigators on the job."

"If another person reminds me about his reputation, I think I may vomit."

Mac sat down next to his friend and put his arm around his shoulders. "What is it, son, what's wrong? This isn't like you."

"I'm frustrated, Mac. McKinnon has thwarted our efforts to work with him and Russo. It seems we're working against each other. Marilyn and I rarely see him, and when we do, he gives us the cold shoulder. There's no sharing of information, and Darcy seems to turn a blind eye to it."

"I don't know your lieutenant that well, but her reputation . . ."

"Stop, Mac, I don't want to hear it. I'm sick of what's happening, tired of being powerless and not being able to track this cretin down and put the cuffs on him. And now my partner, my friend, lies unconscious after some creep runs her down in the street and doesn't have compassion enough to stop and help her."

Pete's raised voice was drawing stares from several people gathered in the waiting area of the ER and even caused a couple of uniformed officers who were there on other matters to pay him attention as well.

"Pete, settle down. You're hurt, I know, but you've got to pull yourself together. There's nothing you can do here; Marilyn's in good hands. They'll find out what's wrong with her. In the meantime, you need to get out to the crime scene and get back to finding the guy responsible for all this carnage."

Taking a deep breath, Pete stood. "You're right, I need to be working, focusing on catching the shooter. That way I won't have time to think about Joe and Marilyn."

Mac stood and took Pete's hand. "I'll be here for awhile. I'll give you a call if the doctors have any news about her condition. Listen, you're a good cop, Pete. Use your skills and keep your eyes and ears open. Remember, everyone leaves a clue or some evidence of who they are and where they've been. Don't give up; don't get discouraged."

The two friends shook hands. "Thanks, Mac, you've always been there for me."

"Hey, how's Beth doing? Do you need me to stop by your place on my way home?"

Pete hadn't thought about her since he'd left. She was probably hurting as much as he was. "Yes, please do. She's scared, and I probably haven't done much to comfort her. Joe was her friend, too."

"Okay, Pete. I'll make it a point to stop by."

Turning to leave, Pete said, "Mac, I'm grateful you're in my life."

"I feel the same way about you and Marilyn. I'll talk to you later. Good luck."

"C'mon, Angel." The woman called out to the dog that had apparently found something interesting at the water's edge and refused to come when called. Out for the animal's early morning walk with her two children in tow, she didn't have time to dawdle. "Colin , Courtney, run over and get her to come along, I have to get to work."

The two kids hurried over by the water to retrieve their pet. As they herded her toward their mother, the boy spotted something shiny on the ground. He bent over and picked it up, studied it for a moment, and then stuffed it in the pocket of his jeans. "C'mon, girl, let's go." They chased the dog up the embankment and then headed back toward their house with their mother.

The little girl pointed toward the corner store and asked, "Mommy, why are all those police cars there?"

Grasping her children's hands as they crossed the street, she replied. "I don't know, Courtney, maybe some bad guys did something wrong." She didn't want to hazard a guess. It wasn't unusual to see a squad car in the lot, since many cops liked to stop there for coffee. But she knew this wasn't a coffee stop. Too many cars and too much yellow tape, something evil has happened.

Later, on the drive to school the woman flipped on the radio in time to hear the news.

. . . And police are searching for whoever is responsible for the murder this morning of another one of their own. An officer was gunned down as he left a convenience store on the city's southwest side. Details are sketchy, but police say it's probably the same individual who shot and killed Officers Eduardo Gonzalez and William Wright. An anonymous source tells eyewitness news that the superintendent of police is unhappy with how the investigation is progressing. Look for changes to be made . . . soon. Today's weather . . .

She switched off the radio as she arrived at Tarkington Elementary and gathered her backpack stuffed with materials she needed for the day. Walking into her classroom, she set her things on the desk and prepared for another day of teaching her first grade class of special needs students. Her job required she be totally focused, yet she couldn't shake the feeling that this morning's cop killing would somehow play a role in her life in the days ahead.

~25~

She watched while brilliant, white light, unlike anything she'd ever seen, danced before her. It radiated out from the center and morphed into shapes for which she had no words . . . degrees of bright she couldn't fathom. The sound . . . comforting, soothing, emanating from somewhere . . . nowhere. Suspended as if floating, no pressure exerted anywhere on her body, she was neither standing nor lying, neither walking nor being carried, yet moving nonetheless. A sense of peace, contentment, wonder. Something was happening, something over which she had no control, nor did she want to control it. Anticipation. Something was about to occur—something. Voices. Unrecognizable, talking to her, or maybe about her? Wanting to answer, to say something, yet not caring if she did or not. Marilyn waited.

"We've got all we need, Pete, you can take him now." The mobile crime lab was wrapping up their investigation at the scene of the shooting. Measurements had been taken, photos, and a ground search for evidence. The three team members had given the store and surrounding parking lot a thorough going over. McKinnon and Russo had interviewed the store owner and several kids who had been in the area at the time of the shooting. The partners were now doing a house to house canvass of the surrounding area, looking for any potential witnesses.

"Thanks, guys," Pete said to the burly lab tech who had a camera strapped around his neck. "Any physical evidence left behind?"

Lighting a cigar, the tech replied. "Naw, it's just like the other two murders. Whoever did it took the shot from some distance. He never really physically enters the crime scene, so other than the bullet itself, we've got nuthin'."

"Damn."

"I made a copy of the surveillance camera footage," the man said, blowing cigar smoke while he handed the CD to Pete. "I didn't review it, but I captured fifteen minutes before and after Murphy was shot."

"Good. I'll sign the chain of evidence log before I leave. Thanks again for all your hard work."

"No need for thanks, Pete. It's what we do. Besides, Murphy was a helluva cop. It's a shame what happened."

"Yeah, I lost a good friend today."

A few minutes later, a wagon backed close to the spot where Joe's remains lay in a body bag. Pete helped the two officers assigned to the wagon put him on a stretcher and gently place him in the back, while a parish priest, Father Mike, recited prayers.

Lt. Darcy watched the solemn ritual take place. Spotting her standing nearby, Pete went to her. "Lew, I'm going to ride in the back with Joe. Can you have someone drive my car to the morgue?"

"Sure, Pete. Listen, I want you to know that I'm sorry for what happened to Joe. He didn't deserve to go like this, none of us do. The best way we can honor his memory is to find whoever did this and hopefully prevent it from occurring again."

"I intend to do just that, with or without McKinnon's help."

"Pete . . ."

Climbing into the back of the wagon, he shut the door quickly. He had no desire to listen to what she had to say. He was focusing on one thing—catching Joe's killer.

It was late afternoon by the time Pete made it back to headquarters. The trip to the morgue only served to put him in more of a somber mood. His thoughts turned dark, focusing on the monster that had killed his friend. He pictured himself with his weapon drawn, looking through the sights, aiming right at the killer's head, and then slowly squeezing the trigger, again and again. He'd never had these kinds of thoughts before, never dreamed about killing someone. Now that he had, the thought of killing another human being didn't bother him. *What's happening to me?*

The phone rang in his cubicle, snapping him back in. "Homicide, Detective Shannon."

"You're workin' with McKinnon, right?"

"Who is this?"

"Never mind, you don't need to know, but I'll bet he's probably drivin' you nuts."

"Listen, I . . ."

"Shut up for a minute, kid. Take the cotton outta your ears and put it in your mouth. McKinnon's playing you like a freakin' fiddle. He's a scumbag who don't care about nobody but himself. Only thing he's got goin' is he's street smart, got lots a snitches who tell him who to look for. How do you think he makes so many pinches? His partner, Russo . . . he's weak, man . . . just grabs McKinnon's coat tails and hangs on. He's useless as a snooze button on a smoke alarm. He should be back in uniform writin' parking tickets on cars double parked in front of gin mills."

Pete listened, then interrupted. "What's all this got to do with me?"

"Man, you ain't the brightest bulb, are ya? You're bein' played the fool. McKinnon's bangin' the boss. That's why she don't lay down the law with him, cuz she's too busy laying down with him. Don't you get it? He can't do no wrong long as she's doin' him, but if the old man finds out, she's through. The boss can't be screwin' the troops anymore; them days are long gone. So while McKinnon's sharin' the love, she ain't the only one getting' the shaft, if ya know what I mean."

Looking around nervously, Pete asked, "How do you know this?"

Laughing, the man replied. "You sure you're a detective? Can't you figure out what's goin' on? Did McKinnon welcome you as a partner, share any leads with ya? No . . . right?"

"Why are you telling me this?"

"Cuz Murphy was a good cop. He pulled my fat outta the fire one night on 63rd Street. I got in a jam off-duty; he handled the case. Probably saved my life and my job. I wanna see whoever killed em gets caught. McKinnon aint' gonna catch this guy, he's too smart, don't leave no clues. My advice to you, Shannon, is forget you're even on the same team as McKinnon and hunt this guy down yourself."

"Hey, can you . . ."

Click. The caller hung up. Pete put the receiver down and sat back in his chair. McKinnon and Darcy. That explained a lot of things, especially why McKinnon seemed to walk around with impunity. Standing up inside his cubicle, Pete peered over the top and looked around, wondering if someone on the squad had made the call. Not that it mattered. The information could never be documented, or even verified, at least not by him. Now he felt a sense of relief in knowing why there was a lack of cooperation among the four detectives assigned to the biggest case in the Homicide Unit, and it was up to him to make good use of this new information and focus on catching a ruthless killer.

An image slowly appearing before her, materializing out of nowhere, though nowhere was exactly where she was. She was somewhere she had never been before, someplace that existed in another world—not hers. She waited, devoid of physical sensation except for light and sound. Inexplicable, yet comforting, relaxing, inviting. Then the image became clear . . . Joe. He smiled, "I love you, Mar." As slowly as he appeared, he began to fade away. She wanted to reach out, to call to him, but she was unable to. Still floating . . . somewhere, nowhere. "I love you too, Joe."

Walking through the ER doors, the doctor went over to Sgt. McNamara. Mac had been joined by Marilyn's good friend and workout partner, Kim. The sergeant stood as the doctor approached. "What's the word, Doc? How's she doing?"

"Not much change, Sarge." The doctor looked at Kim. "Are you family?"

"Not by blood, but we're like sisters. We've known each other for years. She doesn't really have much family. Marilyn's mom is deceased, and her dad hasn't spoken to her since he and Marilyn's mother divorced."

"Oh, I see. That's too bad. Well, she's still unconscious, but the MRI revealed brain edema."

"What's that, Doc?" Mac asked.

"It occurs most often as a result of injury, in this case being hit by the car. It's brain swelling—it's serious—it can cause death because the skull doesn't provide much room for that to take place."

Kim's eyes began to well with tears. "Can you help her? Can you stop the swelling?"

"We're going to try. You see, if allowed to continue, the pressure inside her skull will increase. We call that intracranial pressure, or ICP. It can prevent blood flowing to the brain and deprive it of the oxygen it needs to function. ICP may also block other fluids from leaving, making the swelling even worse. I've called in one of our neurosurgeons. Your friend needs immediate surgery."

Mac thought about Pete, and about how he might take this latest batch of bad news. "What are her chances, Doc? Will it affect her brain function?"

"We won't know for sure until we get in there and see firsthand what's happened, but she's healthy and strong. Her chances for survival are very good."

"But what about being normal?" Kim asked. "Will she be the same old Marilyn?"

"We won't know that until she regains consciousness, but right now we need to focus on stopping the swelling. Once we do that, her chances for a normal life are excellent."

"Thanks, Doc." Mac shook his hand, and then turned to hug Kim. "I guess our next move is to pray."

Tears flowing down her face, Kim replied. "I've already been there and done that."

"Well, don't stop now."

"I won't."

"Good. I'll be right back. I need to make a couple phone calls."

~26~

Logging off his computer, Pete reached down and locked his desk. He swung around in his chair preparing to leave when his eyes locked on several photos Marilyn had hanging above her desk in their shared cubicle. One showed her and Joe together at Pete's house at a backyard barbeque where they had first met. Another photo showed them both with Pete and Beth at a church picnic. He sat and stared at the images, his mind bringing the memories clearly in focus. *The perfect couple . . . why, Lord? Why?*

"Got a minute, Pete?" Lt. King stood just outside his cubicle.

"Lew, what are you doing here?"

"I called you on the air but got no answer; tried your cell, same thing."

Blushing, Pete said, "Sorry, I guess I just shut everything out. It's been a horrible day."

Walking into the cubicle, King went to Marilyn's desk. "Mind if I sit and talk with you for a moment?"

"No, have a seat."

"I heard what happened to Murphy. I'm sorry, Pete. I know you two were good friends. If there's anything I can do . . ."

"Thanks, I appreciate your concern. I don't think his death has really hit me yet. That's why I'm trying to keep busy. I'm afraid if I dwell on it, I'll just fall apart."

King leaned forward. "I heard about the horrible accident with Marilyn."

Pete's eyes widened. "What have you heard? Is there any change?"

"I was on the phone with Darcy while she was at the hospital looking in on her. She told me Marilyn had undergone emergency surgery to alleviate some swelling of her brain."

"What?" Pete said, gripping the arm rests on his chair. "Brain surgery? What happened? I thought all she had was a couple of broken bones."

"Easy, Pete. The doctors were worried she was still unconscious so they did an MRI and discovered the swelling. They had to operate. She would have been in danger if they did nothing. Anyway, they went in and took care of the problem but she's still unconscious. From what Darcy says, the doctors are convinced she has a better chance of full recovery if they keep her that way."

Pete stood up and walked out of the cubicle. "I've got to get over there."

"Whoa, hold on, Pete."

"What?"

Walking over to where Pete stood, King gently grabbed him by the shoulders. "Relax for a moment. Get control of yourself. I know you've gone through a lot today, my friend, but take my advice—don't let your emotions control you. You're a cop; think logically. Don't stress out." King paused for a moment. "Besides, I have one more piece of news to tell you."

Pete walked back to his cubicle to get his coat. Putting it on, he asked, "What news?"

"I took a call from Dan Walsh."

Furrowing his brow, Pete asked, "Who's Dan Walsh?"

"He's Father Ed Matthews' lawyer. Seems he was at the rectory talking with the pastor and housekeeper. He turned up some interesting information."

Pete had entirely forgotten about calling the priest and running down the lead King had provided to him and Marilyn. "Lew, I'm sorry, we never got a chance to follow up on the information you gave us."

"That's okay, but listen, it turns out the mother of the kid who was allegedly abused by the priest has been involved in scams before where she tried to use the church as her private bank account. She was accused in the past of stealing some church funds and trying to frame a priest so she could sue the church for a big payday. I guess it didn't work out."

Pete put his coat on. "Finally, some good news. That's what we thought may have happened. The priest never exhibited any signs of guilt. Marilyn and I never made him for the crime."

"Well, he'll probably have the charges dismissed if he ever shows up."

"What do you mean?"

"He's on the lam, hasn't been seen for weeks. Now he's got problems. If he's left the state he's violated the terms of his bond."

"Thanks for the information, Lew. Sorry about not following up."

"I understand, Pete. You've got bigger fish to fry."

Pete started making his way to the exit. "I've got to get to the hospital. My partner needs me."

On the way down the stairs, he thought about stopping home first to see Beth, but decided Marilyn needed him more right now. Little did he realize that he could do more for his grieving wife than he could for his comatose partner. While he stayed away all day, and now what would be a big chunk of the night, Beth sat by the front window, nursing a cup of coffee, while her stomach growled from not having eaten all day. She desperately needed her husband to comfort and reassure her that everything would be alright; however, she was quickly sensing she would not get what she needed anytime soon.

Walking into the ER, Pete went to the nurses' station to inquire about Marilyn. An attractive woman was on the phone. Pete waited, impatiently, while she continued her conversation. After thirty seconds or so, he decided to interrupt. Looking at her name tag, he said, "Maria, I need some information, please."

The nurse stared at him for an instant, like a mother showing her displeasure with a petulant child, then finished her conversation, and put the phone down. "Sir, I can help you now. I'm sorry I had to provide information to one of our doctors who is caring for a patient and needed to verify a blood type, but I'm sure your request is much more important than his."

"I, uh . . . I'm sorry," Pete replied, his shoulders sagging. "It's been a long day. My good friend was murdered, my partner was run over by a hit and run driver, and my wife is afraid that something will happen to me. I'm afraid I haven't been thinking clearly today. I didn't mean to be rude."

"Okay, now you're making *me f*eel bad. I'm sorry for your loss. I take it you're a police officer?"

"Yes."

"I have a dear friend whose brother is also a cop; I know the worries families endure regarding their safety." She put aside a stack of reports. "What can I help you with?"

Leaning his forearms on the counter, Pete explained. "Detective Marilyn Benson was admitted this morning. I just learned she had brain surgery, and I'm wondering where she's at, if I can see her."

The nurse punched in a few keystrokes and then read from her computer. "Your partner's in ICU. Do you know how to get there?"

"Unfortunately, I'm all too familiar with where it is." He looked down by her computer where a photo sat of a little girl with long brown hair and gorgeous blue eyes. "She's beautiful.

Your daughter?"

"Yes," the nurse said, smiling. "Her name is Grace, she's nine."

He thought about his own little boy, Pete, Jr. "I have a . . . we have a little boy, Pete's his name. My wife is pregnant with what we hope will be a baby girl."

"Well, Officer . . ."

"Shannon, Pete Shannon."

"Officer Shannon, I'm truly sorry about your friend's death, and I hope your partner recovers quickly. I wish you and your wife the best with the new baby."

He thought for a moment about what she had just said. "Thank you, Maria, for reminding me what's important in life." He turned and headed toward ICU, thinking about his family. Arriving a few minutes later, he heard his name being called.

"Pete."

"Reverend Dean, I'm surprised to see you here."

"Why? Marilyn's a cop, she's hurt and in need of prayer. I am the police chaplain, aren't I?"

Shaking his head, Pete sat down next to his friend. "You're right, what was I thinking? Hey, I heard you were with Joe's mom earlier today. How did that go?"

"It's never good anytime you have to tell someone their loved one is gone. Only time will tell what kind of toll it will take on her. She's elderly, but still very sharp; I simply told her the truth. If you can find it in your heart, Pete, she'll need prayers to get through the ordeal of burying her son."

Pete flashed back momentarily to when he learned of both his parents' death in a plane crash years ago. "For sure, Dean, starting tonight. Now, tell me about Marilyn."

"Not much to tell. She had surgery this afternoon. The doc said it went well, but they have to keep her comatose to ensure she recovers. I was allowed in for a few minutes to pray. It's such a tragedy, her and Joe about to be married."

A man and a woman, both sobbing, holding each other, followed a nurse out of the ICU.

"I hate this place," Pete said, standing. "Nothing good ever happens here."

Getting to his feet, the priest stood next to Pete. "You've got a lot on your plate. Your emotions, understandably, are getting the best of you. A lot has happened today, much of it bad, but there's some good here as well."

"Tell me what could possibly be good? Joe's dead; Marilyn's in a coma, where's the good?"

Dean grabbed him by an elbow and led him to a chair. Sitting down, he explained. "To begin with, Joe is with the Father—he's home—he's happy and content. Yes, it's sad he was murdered, but Joe walked with Christ each day and now they're together. As for Marilyn, she's getting the best treatment possible. The doctors probably saved her life with that operation, so don't tell me nothing good happens here."

Leaning over in his chair, his elbows on his knees, Pete ran his fingers through his hair. "You're right, Dean, I'm sorry. This case . . . the murders . . . Marilyn . . . Beth . . ."

"What's wrong with Beth?"

"Nothing physically. She's just terrified that I might be the next cop murdered. It doesn't help that it's my case and that Joe was our friend. She's convinced herself that I'm in danger too."

Dean looked directly at him. "Pete, think about it for a moment. She's right, you are in danger. You're a high profile cop, working the biggest case of your career right now. You don't think she should be worried?"

Pete stared at the chaplain for a moment before answering. "Yeah, I guess you're right. I've just been blowing her off, not really taking her concern very seriously."

"Pete, you need to comfort her. You need to be honest with her. In *Proverbs* 24, the Bible tells us that 'An honest answer is like a kiss on the lips.' Be honest with her. Don't lie and have her believe you're not in any danger. She's your partner in life. Don't you expect honesty from her?"

"Yes, I do. I guess I've been a horrible husband the past few weeks; this case has been sucking the life out of me. I sometimes don't even recognize myself; I've said things I normally would never say, to her and to others."

"Snap yourself back in, son. Get your priorities straight. Remember what's important in life, and most of all, don't let yourself drift away from the Lord. Ask Him to keep you on the path and not allow you to get sidetracked."

Staring at the floor before he answered, Pete turned and said, "You're right, Reverend. I've got some amends to make . . . at home and with the Lord."

"Start right now by going home and reassuring Beth that you love her and understand her fears. There's nothing either of us can do here anyway, Marilyn's going to be in a coma until the doctors decide to bring her out of it. When that time comes, we're going to have to put our heads together and decide how we break the news to her about Joe."

Sighing, Pete stood to leave. "Thanks, Dean. As usual you're the voice of reason."

"I'll walk out with you," he said, putting his arm around Pete's shoulder. "I'll be praying that you'll find the clues you need to catch the shooter. I don't want to have to bury another police officer." They walked through the double doors into the hallway, wrapping up what had been a long, sad day for both of them.

~ 27 ~

It was late when Pete pulled his truck into the garage. He'd mulled over the events of the day on the ride home, particularly, the trip to the morgue with Joe's body. Despite having seen his corpse, Pete still couldn't grasp the fact that Joe was gone. The tragedy of his death, magnified by Joe's upcoming wedding to Marilyn and her accident this morning, rocked his soul. For a while, the calming words of Reverend Dean gave him respite from his sorrow, but now a flood of guilt began to wash over him. If he had done a better job of investigating the first couple of killings, Joe might still be alive. If he hadn't let McKinnon get to him, to distract him from his usual style—methodical, focused, and logical—maybe Joe would still be here. If, if . . . if.

Walking to the garage door, he opened it and stepped into the kitchen. All the lights were off. *They're sleeping.* He removed his shoes and tiptoed down the hall to his son's bedroom. Quietly, he moved to the side of the crib. Pete, Jr., lay on his back, one hand grasping the edge of his favorite blanket, the other hand up by his face, a tiny thumb in his mouth. The juxtaposition of having seen Joe lying on the ground and the sight of his son asleep in the crib caused his eyes to well with tears. An enormous feeling of love and gratitude infused his being. The innocence of his little boy, a soul entrusted to him and Beth, the enormity of the love he had for his family, struck him like a wrecking ball smashing against the side of a building. This was his life; this was his family. He had made a vow to Beth and to God, to love, cherish, and protect them.

Lately, he had been remiss in that promise. He was putting other things first, not paying attention to his family. Worse, he was allowing his thoughts to turn dark, wanting to take his own revenge on whomever the monster was that was murdering his brother officers.

Bending over the railing of little Pete's crib, he kissed his son lightly on the cheek, while inhaling the sweet smell of his baby's breath—the breath of life—life that he and Beth had created. He went into the spare bedroom, got undressed, and brushed his teeth. Before turning off the bathroom light, he took a long look in the mirror at the image staring back at him. *You've got to focus . . . get back to the things that made you a good detective in the first place. Shut out distractions; catch the killer . . . for Joe, and for Marilyn.*

He shut off the bathroom light and made his way into their bedroom. She was asleep. Slipping quietly beneath the blanket, he did his best not to disturb his wife. He knew she was struggling with anxiety, knew she was worn out. Concerned about him, pregnant with their second child, distraught over Joe's death and Marilyn's accident, she was neck deep in a churning sea of worry. Rather than grab her hand and pull her out, he had made that body of water even more difficult for her to stay afloat in. *I need to reassure her.*

Pete's last thoughts before succumbing to exhaustion were of Marilyn. How would it be to work without her? For that matter, would he ever again work with her? How long would she be in a coma, and what would she be like when she awakened? It was too much to think about, too painful, too unfair. He didn't want to blame God, but he found himself doing so anyway. *Father, I know you have plans for me, but how can what happened today possibly be in Your plans? Help me, help me to understand.*

"Pete . . . Pete, wake up, it seven o'clock. Are you off today?"

"What, off?" he said, quickly bolting upright. "No, I don't have a day off—it's seven?—I've got to get going; I'm late. Why didn't you wake me?"

"You were dead to the world, babe. You never heard Pete, Jr.cry; we've been up for an hour, eating and playing in the kitchen. Besides, I thought you needed the extra rest. I hardly see you anymore. You leave early and come home late and don't spend any time with us."

Throwing his legs over the side of the bed and rubbing his eyes, he looked at his wife. He wanted to scold her for allowing him to sleep, but he knew she did it because he did need rest. He was burned out, becoming the kind of cop he'd always complained to others about—jaded, negative, tired. Somehow he had to stop this downward spiral before it ruined him and his relationship with his family.

Shoulders slumping, she turned to walk away and said, "I'm sorry, honey, forgive me. I just want my Pete back, the man who used to love me above all else. The man who was my protector, and could make me believe that everything would be all right, even if it wasn't."

Pete stood up and took her in his arms. "Beth, wait. I want that man back as much as you do. I don't like what's happening to me. Things are so fouled up, I don't know what to expect anymore. This homicide case has drained me, making me question myself and my abilities. I used to have Marilyn to turn to for help, now she's gone."

As the couple stood clinging to each other, Pete felt his wife's body tremble slightly. She pulled back from him, and as a tear slid down her flawless, alabaster cheek, she said, "Pete, promise me you won't take any chances. Tell me you'll be careful. Convince me, please. I'm scared . . . so scared. I feel alone, trapped. I sit watching out the window, waiting, wondering if you're coming home, or if a department vehicle will pull in the drive with the chaplain, coming to tell me you're gone. Can't you understand what this is doing to me . . . to us?"

She fell back into him, and he held her tightly. "Listen to me, Beth, I thought about this last night. I'm off track; I'm not doing the things that got me and Marilyn where we are now. I'm going to refocus, re-engage, and try to eliminate all the distractions in my life. My primary job each day will be to come home safely to you and our baby. I'm going to ask St. Michael to help me, to lead me to Joe's killer. I can't promise you our life will be normal the next few weeks or months, but I will promise that I'll come home to you. There is no other one in my life who means more to me than you, honey. I love you so much."

Wiping her tears away, she looked into his eyes. "Pete, I want to believe you, but ever since you've been working in homicide you haven't been the same. You're cold; you're distant. You come home to eat and sleep. We don't spend time together as a family."

"What? Sure we do, I . . ."

"We do? When's the last time you made love to me, the last time we fell asleep in each other's arms?" She pulled away. "I feel like nothing more than a nanny who cares for your child and cooks your meals." She turned to walk out of the room but stopped short of the doorway. "And when was the last time we went to Mass as a family? Have you ignored Christ like you've ignored us?"

He stood silent, barely able to fathom her words. Sitting back down on the bed, he cradled his face in his hands, feeling as alone as Beth had just described how she felt. What had once been his safe haven, a warm loving family, was now becoming a place barely resembling what he once knew. It was all because of him—the faceless stranger—who reveled in murdering cops, and who now was killing Pete without ever having even fired a shot in his direction.

"Kim."

"Hi, Pete."

"How is she, have you been able to look in on her?"

Marilyn's workout partner stood and gave Pete a hug. "Nah, the nurse said I'm not family so I couldn't go in, but she told me there's been no change. Marilyn's still in a coma. Are you on your way to work?"

"Yeah, but I thought I'd stop in and see how she's doing. This will be the first time in a couple of years that I won't be working with her."

Kim took him by the arm and led him to a row of chairs along the wall. "Sit down, Pete. You look tired. Have you been getting enough sleep?"

"Hardly," he said, leaning back in the chair. "Who can rest with all that's going on?"

"I know what you mean. Usually after my twenty four hour shift at the firehouse, I'm all fired up to meet Marilyn at the gym for a workout. This morning when my shift ended, I felt drained. I thought about her all night, wondering if she's going to recover."

"Yeah, that's what's bothering me too. Will she be *our Marilyn* when she wakes up."

Shaking her head, Kim hesitated before responding. "I pray that she will be; that she'll be the old friend I know and love. You know, Pete, I think I've taken her friendship for granted, just been too comfortable with her warm, easy-going ways. She always goes out of her way for the people she loves, always put them first. She was like that with Joe. I used to have to listen to her talk about him during our workouts. To tell you the truth, it got kind of boring, listening to her always talking about him. When I'd tell her to knock it off, she start in about you—how you guys were working on a case, or an arrest you made. She never sang her own praises. I guess that's what drew me to her. She's a tough gal, but humble. She was always there for her friends, and in the last year, something else changed about her."

Pete leaned forward in his chair. "What, how did she change?"

"Maybe it was her engagement to Joe, or working with you, but I could tell she had a much closer relationship with God. She never used to mention her faith much before, but this past year she wasn't hesitant to discuss it at all. Heck, when we'd go out for a sandwich she'd bless the meal before we ate. I actually began to like it, and I started to get closer to God just by being around her."

Sighing, Pete hung his head. "Kim, I can't imagine working without her. Heck, I can't even imagine not having her in my life. She's been more than a partner; she's been a good friend. Actually she's like a member of my family. She has to pull through."

Kim rubbed Pete's shoulders as he leaned forward in his chair and rested his elbows on his knees. "I know, I know. I feel the same way, and just between you and me, I don't think God is done working through her just yet. I think He has plans for her."

Pete stood. "I hope you're right, Kim. Thank you for being here." He turned and walked toward the exit, wishing his faith were as strong as his partner's, but he felt the tug from the dark side pulling at him, causing him to picture himself standing over the body of the killer who was lying dead on the ground.

"That's him; that's my old boyfriend. His name is James Rogers." Lisa held the traffic ticket in her hands as Ed listened. "That's his writing," she said, her eyes getting bigger as she stared at the piece of paper. Ed sensed a hint of fear in her voice. "What happened? What did you do?"

"Nothing really, I had just pulled out of the parking lot at St. Mary's yesterday morning after Mass. I'd driven only a couple of blocks when he pulled me over."

"Why?"

Shaking his head, Ed replied. "I don't know. I didn't think I had done anything wrong, but when he stopped me he said I had been speeding." He took the ticket from her, folded it in half, and placed it back inside his wallet.

"Miss . . . "A homeless man, one of the regulars at the library, was standing behind Ed as he discussed the incident with Lisa. "Can I get a computer, please?"

"Certainly, sir," she replied, while she recorded his terminal number on her log and handed him a card. "Use number four, over on the right."

"Thanks."

Lisa stood up behind her desk in the computer lab. Wringing her hands, she looked directly at Ed. "I don't like this. I think he's trying to scare you, Ed. He must think you're my new boyfriend."

Pausing to think, Ed considered her last statement. *Boyfriend . . . me? I can't be her boyfriend; I'm a priest.* "Lisa, I . . ."

Collapsing into her chair, she looked up at Ed. "When will I ever be free of this man? I wish I had never met him."

The library security officer walked up to the desk. "Is there a problem here?"

Surprised, Ed turned and replied, "No, um, officer. She's upset about something."

The security officer looked directly at Lisa. "Is this man bothering you?"

A tear glistened on her cheek. "No, he's not a problem. I'm fine, Robert. Sorry to bother you. He's just trying to console me. Thank you for checking."

"Okay. I'll be over by the circulation desk if you need me." He turned toward Ed and gave him a stern look before walking away.

"Oh, great," Ed moaned. Now I've got James *and* this guy thinking I'm trouble."

"I'm sorry to get you involved in my problems, Ed. Can I make it up to you? What if I cook a nice dinner for you tonight? Can you come by around six-thirty?"

"Sure, a home cooked meal sounds great." Truth be told, he did miss home cooked meals, particularly the ones Margaret, the housekeeper at St. Nick's, used to cook.

Lisa grabbed a piece of paper. "Here's my address, I'm only about five minutes from here. I'll see you tonight." Handing him the paper, she said, "Ed, I'm sorry."

"Forget about it; I'll be fine." He turned and made his way out of the main doors and headed toward the Visitors Center. Just down the street a car sat parked at the curb, idling, waiting.

"Mom, someone's at the door. Should I open it?"

"Who is it, son?" Tina had instructed her children never to open the door for anyone they didn't recognize. Her son, Colin, remembered the lesson and refused to allow the stranger entrance to their home. "I don't know, Mom."

The woman went to the door and looking through the peephole saw a man standing with police identification open for her to see. "Who is it?" She called out through the closed door.

"Police . . . Detective Shannon. I spoke with you on the phone."

"Just a moment." Tina quickly unlocked the deadbolt and took off the door safety. Still holding open his police identification, Pete waited for an invitation to enter. "Sorry, Detective, I've taught my children never to open the door for anyone they don't know. C'mon in," she said, motioning for Pete to follow her as she walked into the kitchen area. "We just finished eating dinner. I have some coffee made. Would you care for a cup?"

"Yes, black, please." Pete took a seat at the kitchen table. "You said you had some information about the officer who was shot the other day?"

Placing a cup of coffee in front of him, she moved back to the counter to pour herself a cup. She stood by the counter, her two children by her side. "I'm not sure if this has a connection or not, but the day the officer was killed we were walking our dog, Angel, in the park. I was running late for work and the dog was doing what dogs do best—sniffing around. She wasn't interested in coming when I called to her, so I told the kids to get her away from the water's edge. They went to her and got her moving again, and as we made our way home we saw all the police cars at the store on the corner. I knew something bad must have happened, but it wasn't until I heard the report of the murder on the news that I realized we must have just missed being there when it happened."

"Did you or the children see anything?"

"Not exactly."

Pete put his cup down. "What does that mean?"

"Well, Colin," she put her arm around her son's shoulders, "picked something up that perhaps might have come from whoever shot at the policeman. Go ahead, Son, give it to the detective."

The boy reached into his jeans and pulled out a bullet casing and handed it over to Pete, who took a quick glance at it and immediately recognized it as a rifle round normally used by the military and police. "Where did you find this, Colin?"

"Right by a big evergreen tree, next to the water."

The mother quickly added, "We were in a hurry to get home at the time, and I didn't realize he'd picked anything up. The next day I was doing laundry and found that in the pocket of his pants. I asked him where it came from. That's when he told me he picked up at the park, and I made the connection. Do you think it may be related to the officer's death?"

Realizing that this may be the first solid piece of tangible evidence in the case, Pete placed the casing in one of the plastic evidence envelopes he kept in his pocket for such occasions. "I'm not sure, ma'am, but there's a good chance that it may. I'll take this to our crime lab. They can do an analysis on any markings made on it from the rifle, and when we come up with the murder weapon we can do a comparison. Colin, that's a great bit of police work. Thank you for your help."

The boy was shy and turned to his mother to hug her. She smiled and said, "I hope it helps catch the person responsible. I just can't believe anyone would have a reason to go around shooting at our police officers. We're praying for all of you, Detective."

Standing to leave, Pete picked up his empty cup and took it over to the sink. He went to the boy, grabbed his hand, and shook it. "Thanks again, Colin. You've given me a big clue in a puzzle that so far has been difficult to solve." Pete made his way to the door. "It will take a while to find out just how this piece of evidence fits in, but I'll let you know what happens."

"Thank you, Detective. Good luck and God bless you."

Walking back to his car, Pete realized that an eleven year old boy had just found a bigger piece of evidence than the best detectives on the Chicago Police Department had come up with thus far.

Getting into his car, Pete drove toward the park and arrived there in a couple of minutes. It was dark, the same conditions that early morning when Joe was killed. Pete grabbed his flashlight and made his way toward the water. The streetlights in the park made it unnecessary for him to turn on his light. As he approached the edge of the lagoon he saw the evergreen tree the boy had described—it was large and full—perfect concealment for someone with evil intentions to use as cover. Slipping into a tactical mindset, he lay down beside the tree where the embankment sloped gently down toward the water. He propped himself up on his elbows, assuming a shooting position, while looking toward the convenience store. *With a scoped rifle, this is an ideal firing position. Joe never had a chance.*

He sat up and turned toward the water, staring. *Joe . . . Marilyn . . . both struck down . . . the same day, the same hour, why?* The enormity of the dual tragedy bore down on him and pressed the air from his lungs. He pulled his knees to his chest and rocked back and forth, like he was in a trace, in the fashion of so many veterans returning from battle who'd seen things no one should have to see. He was alone, looking at a murky, inky, strip of water that took on the dimensions of a blank palette where he superimposed images of better times—Joe and Marilyn, happily sharing a meal at a restaurant; his wife Beth, holding their son; his first partner, Joe O'Hara and his wife Susan at the parish picnic— pleasant memories scarred by tragedy.

As those thoughts fueled his emotions, like logs piled on top of an already raging fire, he wept. The stress and recent tragedies were all becoming too much, and there was no end in sight. He sat and rocked, and cried, and thought, and suddenly he felt a hand on his shoulder. "Friend, are you okay?"

Startled, Pete looked up to see an older man looking down at him. "I said, are you okay? Can I help you in some way?"

"Uh, no . . . I mean, yes, I'm fine, I was just thinking."

The man sat down beside him. "Sometimes that can be trouble. We let our mind go off in directions we can't control, taking us down paths we really shouldn't travel."

Inexplicably, Pete felt comforted simply by this stranger's presence. Although his police experience told him to always be wary of strangers, in his grief he ignored this basic instinct.

"I've done it myself, Son, sat right here and stared at the water looking for answers."

"Did you ever find them?"

"Not the answers I was looking for, but I discovered how important it was to take time to reflect and figure out where I'm going and why."

Pete thought about that for a moment. "Yeah, I guess that's what I need, to find out where I'm going. I need to find a direction; I've been off course lately."

The man put his hands on his knees and stared ahead. "You're right. Sometimes we lose sight of what matters most, simple things like a kind word to a stranger or a quick 'I love you' to a spouse. Things that by themselves seem inconsequential, but over time mean a whole lot, particularly if you haven't said them." The man stroked his beard. "Human beings are funny, they run on emotions, like love and affection. A lot of times they forget that these intangibles, these feelings and emotions, mean more much than material things. They get thrown off course, thinking stuff they accumulate means more than the people who love them. They believe what they've acquired defines who they are."

Pete listened and looked straight ahead.

"Think about it. When you're feeling down, do you seek comfort from a new car or an expensive suit? Probably not. You seek out those you love for comfort. Worldly things will never ease your pain; love and friendship hold the keys to the quality of your life. Faith and works are what heal a soul that's been hurt; they're what keeps us on the right path."

"You're right. I've allowed myself to be led down the wrong road. I've been selfish and self-absorbed; I need to get back on track."

"You will; I know it. You've got a lot on your plate right now, and there's more to come. But I have faith in you, Pete, and a plan. Go home to your family. Beth needs you."

The man stood and walked behind him before Pete fully understood what he had just heard. He jumped up and quickly turned around. "What? Hey, how do you know my name?" But there was no one there; Pete was alone again.

The next forty-eight hours were a blur for Pete. He left early each day and came home late. As a result he saw very little of Beth and little Pete. He was there to sleep and shower, nothing else. So focused was he on his task, that he eschewed his usual morning run in favor of rest. His life was becoming one-dimensional as his obsession with the killer intensified. Other than a quick stop at the hospital on his way to and from work each day to check on Marilyn, he had no other diversion to distract him.

This morning, after another day of few words with her husband, Beth resigned herself to the fact that her marriage was in trouble. Were it not for having to care for their little boy, Beth had a notion she would likely be sharing her troubles with another old friend, alcohol. It had been an escape for her before when she had problems in her life, but she couldn't turn to it at this point. For now, she'd have to channel her frustration into mastering the numbers on the scale and her daily calorie count. Yesterday had been a good day—only about 500 consumed. Each day became a little easier. The hunger felt good. It took her mind off Pete's gradual abandonment. She knew the baby inside needed nourishment, but she rationalized her behavior by eating "good" calories in fruits and vegetables. Besides, she felt she had sufficient stores of fat for the baby to draw from.

Pete had good reason to leave early each day. He'd decided to see who used the park in the early morning hours. He sat in his car near the big evergreen tree with the motor turned off, watching and listening, to get an idea of what it may have been like on the morning Joe had been murdered. The first day, all he saw were the same people who had found the spent bullet casing: the mother and her children, walking their dog, just as they had done on that morning. He waited fifteen minutes past the time when Joe had been shot and then headed to work.

The following day he parked in the same spot and experience the same results until just as he was about to start his car to leave, he glanced in the rear view mirror and spotted a young woman jogging in his direction on the park sidewalk. When the woman was about ten feet away he got out of his vehicle. "Miss, may I . . . ?"

Startled, the woman veered off the path, shouting, "No. No. Get away!" She ran onto the grassy area that separated the park's sidewalk from the busy nearby thoroughfare.

Stunned, Pete stood motionless for a moment, then ran after her. "Police . . . stop!" Grabbing his ID from his jacket pocket, he held it out in front of him while he ran. "Stop, I'm a police officer; I just need to speak with you."

Undeterred, the woman continued her sprint toward the street, which streamed with motorists intent on getting to work on time. As she reached the curb, a city bus passed in front of her, causing her to stop abruptly. Turning to look for her pursuer, she found he had caught up to her. Pete grabbed her, yanking her away from traffic. The woman resisted—kicking and trying to punch him. Pete had no choice but to wrap her tightly in a bear hug. Holding her firmly, he felt her heart beating like that of a frightened animal.

"Stop, listen to me, I'm a cop; I just need to talk with you." He waited a few seconds, before explaining. "Please, calm down. I'm holding my police ID in my right hand. Look down. Do you see it?"

Breathing heavily, the woman, nevertheless, did as requested. "Yes, I see it, now let me go."

"Okay, but promise you won't run. Look, we're standing out in plain view, people all over the place. No one's going to hurt you. I'm a detective; I just want to ask you about the cop who was murdered several days ago."

His words seemed to register with the woman, and when Pete released her she took several steps back, but she didn't run. "Let me see that ID again." She took it from him and compared the photo on his identification while looking at him. "I guess you are who you say you are," she said handing it back to him. "You scared the life out of me when you jumped out of your car."

"I'm sorry," he said, putting his credentials away. "I've been sitting here the past couple of mornings, trying to see if I could find anyone who might give me an idea of who killed the police officer that day."

Her heartbeat slowly returning to normal, the woman nodded. "In a way I guess I'm glad you caught me. I *was* out for a run that morning."

Pete's eyes widened. "Did you see anything unusual or maybe hear a shot?"

"Maybe. I thought it was a backfire from a truck or something. Traffic's heavy that time of the morning, you know, rush hour and busses. But I also saw something, or should I say *someone*. I've been meaning to call, but to tell you the truth, I was scared. This is the first morning I've run since that day."

Pete fidgeted and put his hands on his hips. "Tell me, please, what did you see?"

"Well, I was running down the same path as today. As I got to the spot where you car is parked," she said, pointing to Pete's car, "I saw something out of the corner of my eye—some movement. I turned to look, and that's when I saw a man. He was crouching right by that big evergreen tree by the water." She paused and indicated the big evergreen tree. "At first I thought it was probably some homeless guy. There are a few of them who live in the park, and when I took a few more seconds to get a better look, I saw he was getting to his feet."

"What did he look like?"

She shook her head. "I'm not really sure. He was white, and he had on . . . like some kind of Army jacket, you know, the camouflage type."

Pete had his notepad out. "What about his age or hair or anything else you might remember about him?"

Looking down at the ground, the woman thought for a moment. "I honestly can't think of anything else. It all happened so quickly." She looked up. "Wait, there was one other thing. He put something inside his jacket and then zipped it closed."

Pete leaned closer. "What did he put in his jacket?"

She looked directly at him. "I'm not sure, but it looked like it could have been a rifle."

An hour later, Pete was pulling into the parking lot at police headquarters. Before realizing what he was doing, he caught himself looking around for Marilyn's car, something he'd done routinely each day he arrived. His temporary high from the jogger's new information about Joe's killer, spiraled downward, like a fighter jet struck by enemy fire. *Marilyn, get well, I need you.* He made his way up the steps, purposely avoiding the elevators. Since he hadn't run the past couple of days, he knew he should do something physical. Entering the homicide unit, he made his way toward Lt. Darcy's office. He wanted to tell her about the latest information he'd acquired.

Nearing her door, he saw a tower of boxes stacked outside. He stuck his head inside the office and found a painter repairing the nail holes in an empty wall. "Hey, what's going on? Where's Lt. Darcy?"

The corpulent city worker stopped scraping and turned to face him. "Don't know no Darcy. All's I was told was to take down all the pictures, patch up the holes, and put on a fresh coat o' paint. They don't tell me why, they just tell me when."

Glancing at the door, Pete saw the lieutenant's name tag missing. "Did you take her name off the door?"

"Yep, the boss told me to pack it all up cuz someone new's gonna be movin' in this afternoon. Now if you don't mind, bud, I gotta finish up."

Puzzled, Pete turned and walked to the cubicle he shared with Marilyn. He sat down at his desk and saw the message light flashing on his phone. Dialing the code, he found he had two messages waiting.

Message One:

"Pete, it's Bill Sherlot from the lab. Hey, good news. That bullet casing you submitted from the park yielded good results. We weren't able to get any prints from it. Looks like it was cleaned up pretty good—not even any gunpowder residue—but I was able to get an excellent firing pin impression, and the rim had some fairly decent marks made by the extractor. The other thing is, one of the bullet fragments recovered from Joe's body was big enough for me to be able to catalog the rifling from it. I entered all of it in IBIS. All I'll need now is for you to give me the murder weapon to make a match. Stay with it; this guy's bound to screw up."

Message Two:

"This is Captain Prince Samuels. Effective immediately, I am your new commanding officer. Unless you have an arrest or a scheduled court appearance, I expect to see each of you in the unit squad area at 1500 hours. We'll discuss the new direction of our unit."

Hanging up the phone, Pete gathered his thoughts. Sherlot's information about the casing and bullet fragment was a giant step in the right direction. Being able to enter the bullet into the Integrated Ballistics Identification System would increase the chance of identifying the weapon, and therefore, the shooter.

The second message worried him though, and he wondered what this new development might mean for him. Captain Samuels was not someone he knew, and with Pete being assigned temporarily to homicide, it meant a new CO could get rid of him with the stroke of a pen. *That might not be so bad.* He quickly reconsidered. He didn't want to leave; he wanted to finish the case and either catch or stop, the killer who had wreaked so much havoc in the lives of so many people, especially his own.

What if the new CO is a buddy of McKinnon? Pete went over to the file and grabbed the folders associated with the murders. The new information he'd discovered had to be included in the file, but he also wanted to review everything about the case while he waited for three o'clock to arrive. He logged onto his terminal and began typing his report. *No sense worrying about it now.*

"Ed, welcome. Please, come in." Lisa answered the door, dressed in a navy blue skirt and sleeveless red blouse with a décolletage that made him uncomfortable. "Dinner is just about ready; I hope you're hungry."

"Yes, and I'm looking forward to a home cooked meal. " Ed glanced around. The building was an older, colonial-style house, built in the early nineteenth century. "Lisa, this place is amazing. I love the way you've maintained the flavor with the antique furnishings."

"Thanks, Ed. It's an ongoing project, and it's even on the Historic Register. Maintaining the integrity of the structure is difficult, but it's something I enjoy doing. Here, let me take your jacket."

She hung his coat in a closet off the dining room and invited him into the kitchen. "I hope you like pork. I've prepared a roast, with potatoes, carrots, and onions. I rarely get the opportunity to cook like this. Eating alone means mostly microwave meals."

"I know." He breathed in the aroma of the meat and vegetables sizzling in the roasting pan. "It smells delicious. "

She pointed to a bottle on the counter. "Will you open the wine? You do like wine, I hope."

Thinking back on the daily celebration of Mass, the miracle of turning wine into the blood of Christ, he answered. "I love wine." He opened the bottle,   poured a small amount in each glass, and then offered one to Lisa.

Turning from the oven, she took the glass from him and said, "To us." Then she gave him a quick kiss on the cheek.

Ed wasn't expecting a gesture like that and was momentarily flustered by it. He didn't comment, just took a sip from his glass without responding.

Removing the roasting pan from the oven, Lisa carved several slices of meat then put the vegetables into bowls, which she handed to Ed, asking him to take them into the dining room. In a few minutes they were seated at the table, prepared to eat.

"Shall we bless the meal?" Ed asked.

"Yes." Lisa reached over and took his hand.

Again, Ed hadn't anticipated she would do that, but he began the prayer. "Father, we ask you bless this meal prepared by your servant, Lisa. May this food strengthen us, making us better able to spread the word of the Gospel. In Jesus' name we pray, amen."

"Amen," Lisa replied, squeezing his hand before releasing it.

Ed brought his fork to his mouth and tasted the roast. "Lisa, this is delicious. It reminds me of my mother's cooking."

"Thanks, that's quite a compliment." She smiled. "So, tell me, Ed, what was your childhood like. Are your parents still alive? We've talked about my past, now tell me about yours."

Suddenly losing his appetite, Ed sipped the wine while trying to decide how to answer. "Uh, yes, my folks are still alive and live in Chicago."

"Any brothers or sisters?"

"No, I'm an only child." He finished his wine and set the empty glass in front of him.

"Where are my manners?" Lisa got up and retrieved the wine bottle from the kitchen counter. She filled his glass and then poured some more for herself. "Continue, Ed, I'm eager to hear more about your life in Chicago."

His heart beating faster; beads of sweat popped out on his forehead. He used his napkin to wipe away his anxiety. He was still uncomfortable lying about his past, for he wasn't good at deception. He brought his glass to his lips and took another drink. "Actually, the job I had with a non-profit organization didn't look very promising. I didn't see much of a future with the company, and the economy being what it is, there aren't a lot of jobs available like that in Chicago so I decided to look elsewhere."

"Well, you came to the right part of the country. The D.C. area is loaded with jobs—particularly government ones. Not too many people out of work here."

Silence.

"What about girlfriends? Do you have one back home?"

"Uh, no, no girlfriends."

"Are you telling me the truth?"

He picked up his glass. "What?"

"You're lying, aren't you?"

Taking a long drink, Ed finished his wine. "What do you mean?"

"A good-looking guy like you doesn't have a woman waiting for him? C'mon, Ed, you won't hurt my feelings if you tell me you've got a girlfriend."

"No, Lisa, honestly, no girlfriend. I, uh, I guess I was too involved with my work to have time for that." He pushed his plate forward, suddenly losing his appetite.

She grabbed the wine bottle and quickly filled his glass again.

"If you're finished eating, let's talk in the living room, where we'll be more comfortable." This is going to be trouble.

She took him by the hand and led him into the living room where she sat on the couch. Patting the seat next to her, she said, "Ed, please, sit down."

He reluctantly did as she requested, sitting near, but not right next to her. But as soon as he was settled, she moved closer to him so that their bodies touched. "So tell me, have you decided on whether Fredericksburg will be your new home?"

"I'm not really sure, Lisa. For now, I'm enjoying living here, well, except for Officer Rogers."

"Oh, yes, James. I'm sorry about him pulling you over. I'm sure he thinks you're my boyfriend—he's the jealous type." She reached to the coffee table and picked up her wine glass. "Ed, what do you think about that?"

"About what?"

"About . . . us. I know it's rather forward of me, but I really enjoy your company and I'd like to see a lot more of you in the future," she said, as she let her hand rest on his leg.

The talk and closeness was beginning to become much more than he'd bargained for. He stood quickly and stepped to the middle of the room. "Lisa, I've been lying to you."

Nodding her head, she said, "I knew it. I knew you had a girlfriend, or is it a wife? You're married, aren't you?"

"No, there is no woman in my life."

"You're gay?"

"No, it has nothing to do with any of that." He sat down in a chair across from her, nervously folding his hands in front of him. "Lisa, I think you're a wonderful person, someone I consider a friend, but it can't be anything more than friendship between us."

Leaning forward, she asked, "Why?"

He knew he was putting himself at risk by exposing his past, but his conscience told him it was the right thing to do. "I'm not who you think I am. I didn't lie to you when I said I was from Chicago, that much is true. But my name isn't Edward Michaels; my name is Edward Matthews . . . I'm a Catholic priest."

She leaned back against the couch, her mouth agape, allowing time for what he had just told her to sink in. "You're a . . . a priest? Why would you lie about something like that?"

"Lisa, believe me when I tell you I never wanted to lead you on, but I was afraid to tell you the truth. I didn't know if I could trust you to keep my secret."

"What secret, that you're a priest? That's hardly anything you wouldn't want anyone to know. Being a priest is an honorable calling."

"There's more to it than that. Lisa, listen to me. I need to know I can trust you, that if I tell you why I'm here, you won't share the information with anyone. Can you promise me everything I say to you will be held in strict confidence?"

"Yes, of course Ed, but what's going on?"

He stood and paced back and forth in the room, the same way he had paced in his cell. "I've been on the run from the authorities in Chicago. I was falsely accused of a crime and arrested. I spent a night in jail. I made bond the next day, but that brief experience behind bars convinced me that I would never survive if I was convicted. I decided to just leave everything behind, particularly after the Archbishop forbade me from serving my parishioners. I didn't tell anyone about my plans or where I was going, not even my lawyer. You're the first person I've told. Lisa, please be the decent person I know you are and not share this information with anyone."

Finishing her wine, Lisa put a hand over her mouth. A few seconds later, she spoke. "This is all so unbelievable, I never dreamed that you . . .   Ed, I apologize for my inappropriate behavior," she said as she adjusted her neckline upward. "If I had known you were a priest . . ."

"No apology needed. I led you on. It's me who needs to apologize. Can you forgive me?"

"Yes, of course, but how did all of this happen? Why were you arrested?"

He knew he couldn't avoid telling her the whole story. He sat down in the chair and related the events of the past to her, finishing with, "I hope you believe me when I say that I've never harmed anyone."

"How terrible. Your life is all but ruined, but are you sure that running from the problem is the right thing to do?"

"That's a good question, one I struggle with each day. When your old boyfriend stopped me, I thought for sure it was all coming to a head, that my brief stint of freedom was about to end. I don't know that I can continue to live this kind of life, one where I have to lie every day."

"What about the priesthood? If you're cleared of the charges, can you go back to being a priest?"

"If I can beat the charges—yes. That's the battle I'm waging within myself. The priesthood is my life, and it seems the further I run from Chicago, the more difficult it will be for me to clear my name and return to the service of our Lord."

They sat quietly, staring at each other, neither one wanting to say the wrong thing. Finally, she broke the stalemate. "As shocking as your revelation is, I've seen the type of man you are. I believe you when you say you're innocent."

Ed breathed a sigh of relief. "Thank you."

"You have my word that I won't share anything we've said here tonight, but if you want my opinion, I think you're going down the wrong road. I think the best thing you can do is to return to Chicago and fight for your life. Fight for the truth."

"But what if I lose?"

Leaning forward, she looked into his eyes and said, "What if you win?"

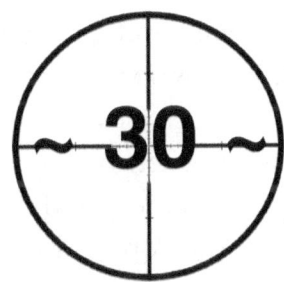

The temperature dipped below the freezing mark overnight, balmy weather for November. A dusting of snow caused the Chicago streets to become as slippery as an ice cube on a summer day. Hardcore was restless; he had yet to find a steady job. He was living hand-to-mouth, doing odd jobs just to pay the rent and buy food. Even gas for his van was becoming difficult to afford.

Shivering from the cold, one hand on the wheel, the other between his legs to keep it warm, he drove toward his favorite diner for breakfast. *Damn Ford products . . . heater ain't worth a crap.* His attitude reflected his circumstances. Coming to a stop sign, he misjudged his ability to brake and slid through the intersection. Before he knew it, blue lights strobed in his side view mirrors.

Pulling over to the curb, he immediately thought about the rifle in the back of his vehicle. *If the cop finds, it I'm toast.* The officer appeared at his driver's side window, Hardcore rolled it down.

"Mornin' sir. You went through the sign back there without stopping. I need to see your license and registration."

"Yeah, Officer . Hey, it's slippery out here . . . the snow, ya know?"

"Right, but I still need to see your license, registration, and proof of insurance."

Hardcore could ill afford to get a ticket and tried to placate the cop with a tale of woe. "Hey, man, I been outta work for a while; I'm barely making it. Is there any way you can give me a break on this?"

The cop drew a deep breath and gave Hardcore a stern look. "I don't know anything till I see who you are. Now, for the last time, license, registration, and insurance card."

Reaching into his back pocket for his wallet, Hardcore pulled the documents out and handed them to the officer.

"Stay in your vehicle," the cop said abruptly and returned to his patrol car.

Just my luck, gettin' pulled over by a cop with an attitude.

Ten minutes later the officer walked back to the van. "Today's your lucky day. I gave you a break on the stop sign violation, knowing you're out of work and all, but I had to write you a citation. Your insurance certificate's expired. Here's your court date," he said, pointing to a box on the ticket. "Just bring proof of current insurance with you to show the judge, and the ticket will be dismissed."

"Man, I told you I'm outta work."

"You and hundreds of others pal, but it doesn't mean you can drive around here without proper insurance. What if you woulda hit somebody when you blew the stop sign?"

Snatching the ticket from the cop's hand, Hardcore quickly folded it and put it in his wallet, along with his other identification. "Thanks for nuthin," he said as he rolled his window up. "I put my ass on the line for you, humpin' through the dessert, and this is how you repay me?" He watched the officer go back to his car. Hardcore stayed put while the cop pulled out around him, making sure he gave him a hard look as one final gesture of defiance. *You dumb shit. You coulda solved a big murder case if you knew how to do your job. Cuz o' you, some cop's goin' down.*

Closing the cover of the case file, Pete got up from his chair in his cubicle at homicide. He stood and surveyed the squad area. It was almost three; time to meet the new boss. Several new faces were scattered among the rest of the unit members. He didn't recognize them as anyone he knew on the job. He took a minute to study them. Definitely cops—they had that look—but why hadn't he at least seen them in the course of his career?

Pete drifted over to the open area just outside the CO's office where Lt. Darcy used to conduct the squad meetings. McKinnon and Russo were there, standing off to one side. Pete felt he should probably stand with them, after all, they were a team. *I wish Marilyn was here.* Bobby Russo greeted him as he neared. "Hey, Shannon, guess we're about to find out if any head's are gonna roll."

Puzzled, Pete responded. "You really think he wants to get rid of anyone?"

Russo shrugged. "Maybe. I know when they made him CO at the Gang Crimes Unit, he transferred four guys the first week and brought in replacements from his old unit. He's not afraid to shake things up, 'specially if he thinks you're not doin' the job."

Pete looked sideways at Russo. *Speaking of not doing the job.* "So, other than that, what do you know about him?"

"Harry worked with him years ago, when they were both in uniform assigned to Area Two Special Operations," said Russo, tilting his head toward McKinnon who was standing next to him, trademark toothpick in his mouth. "He said Samuels was a pretty aggressive street cop, never backed down from a fight. I guess he used to be an Army Ranger. Likes to keep in shape and go to the range a lot—people at the Academy say he's a regular there—does a lot of combat shooting."

Pete nodded. "Sounds like my kind of cop."

"Yeah, he doesn't play around. He got in a shootout with a couple of bank robbers—killed 'em both."

"Man, I like this guy without even having met him." Pete smiled. "He's a major league change compared to Darcy."

McKinnon's toothpick began to dance in his mouth at the mention of Darcy's name.   He pulled the smooth sliver from between his lips and pointed it at Pete. "You might be wishing she was back here once 'The Prince' starts leanin' on your ass to catch our shooter."

Before Pete could respond, a tall, well-built man, dressed in a tailored, dark blue suit, strode confidently into the sea of detectives and made his way to the podium. Standing as straight as a steel rod, he turned to face the anxious gumshoes.

"Good afternoon, ladies and gentlemen. My name is Captain Prince Samuels. I recognize a few of your faces, others I've not seen before, but rest assured in a very short while we will know each other quite well. I'm not one to equivocate, so let me get straight to the point. The chief is concerned about the murders of our fellow officers. The fact that the creature responsible is still at-large is not only disturbing, but it also means we can probably expect he will strike again."

Samuels paused and removed a folded sheet of paper from his inside jacket pocket. "I'm well aware this unit is staffed with diligent, professional investigators. Your homicide clear up rate is exceptional. There's absolutely no question about your ability to catch murderers. Nevertheless, we are faced with an extraordinary situation that has thus far stymied us and taxed our manpower, thereby impeding the progress in our other cases."

Samuels unfolded the paper and laid it on the podium. "To alleviate the burden on this unit, I've been given approval to form a joint-agency task force and to initiate what will hereafter be referred to by the code name: SNIPEOUT. I've recruited three highly-experienced investigators to team with our own personnel. I'd like to introduce them to you.   First, Detective Timothy Beckham, from the Illinois State Police. Next is Detective Stan Larsen, Cook County Sheriff's Department, and finally, Special Agent Tameka White from the FBI."

As each person was introduced, each one nodded and looked around at their new squad members.

"Bringing these additional bodies on board will allow us to utilize the resources of the county, state, and federal governments. It is by no means a reflection of the work done thus far by the team assigned to the case. On the contrary, it will allow us to devote more time and follow more leads to ensure we prevent another murder from occurring. Let's not kid ourselves; we're dealing with a serial killer. We need to stop whoever is committing these murders before we have another one on our hands.

"I'll be meeting with each of you in the coming days to get a sense of your strengths and to ensure you are aware of what I expect in terms of behavior and performance. Right now, I'd like to meet with the members of SNIPEOUT in my office. The rest of you may resume your normal activities."

The detectives fanned out from the meeting, gathering in cliques to assess the new CO and additional personnel. Together with Pete, McKinnon, and Russo, the three newest members of the unit filed into Samuel's office. Pete looked around at the room's new décor: several photos of the captain posing with Army brass; others of him at various pivotal moments in his career—promotions and awards ceremonies. The Army Ranger logo hung next to the FBI National Academy Associates logo, indicative of his attendance at the Bureau's leadership school. The one photo behind the captain's desk, displayed prominently on the credenza was a picture of a woman in a CPD uniform. *His wife?*

"Have a seat, everyone." The office renovation did not include a sofa, as was the case during Darcy's tenure, but there were three chairs directly in front of the desk and six others along the wall. A police radio tuned to the investigative channels droned low in the background, while a plasma TV screen, displayed an all-news station, sans sound, causing the newscasters to appear like children mouthing words to their playmates.

Prince Samuels unbuttoned his suit jacket and sat behind his desk. "First, some administrative thoughts. This is not a routine homicide investigation, like most others where the shooter and victim know each other. We don't really have any clear idea of who it is we're looking for. That said, we need to utilize outside help in developing some leads. Thus far, there's been no word on the street, nothing from informants," he said, glancing toward McKinnon. "We need someone to drop a dime on this guy, so I'm offering a reward of ten thousand dollars for information leading to the arrest and conviction of the sniper."

Looking around at each other, the detectives in the room nodded in agreement.

"The money should be enough to loosen some tongues out there. I'll be holding a press conference tomorrow morning; I want Shannon and White to be there with me. I need to put a face on this investigation, and you two are it."

McKinnon smirked. *So what's new?*

"I'll be putting out a hotline tip number for the public to call with any information that might help us track this guy down."

"Who's manning that, Captain?" Russo asked.

"It won't be any of you. I've set up a rotating schedule for the rest of the squad. I want investigators taking the calls, not someone unfamiliar with homicide investigations, which brings me to the subject of partners. Everyone in this room is a good investigator; otherwise, you wouldn't be here. Sometime we get too comfortable in our routine and become a bit sloppy or apathetic and miss some things we wouldn't normally miss. So I'm going to experiment and break you up into new teams: McKinnon, you and Beckham will work together. Russo, you'll be teamed with Larsen, and Shannon and White will work together."

The new partners looked at each other. Some were excited; McKinnon stared at the wall.

Samuels picked up three folders from his desk. "I've had a

searchable database created for this case. Every bit of information we've acquired to date has been or is in the process of, being uploaded. It will allow you to do a quick search of a name, vehicle, location, and any number of other items. From now on, in addition to filing your reports in the case file, you will also give the information to the squad secretary who will load it into the searchable database."

Looking at the ceiling, McKinnon sighed heavily, indicating his displeasure. It was noted by Samuels.

"These new teams and procedures are meant to cut quickly through the minutiae and cumbersome machinery we normally face when conducting complex investigations. Get used to it; it's not going away," he said, looking directly at McKinnon. "We can fine tune the process as needed, but right now this is the road we're all going to go down."

Captain Samuels looked at Pete. "Shannon, you and White will be flying to the FBI Academy in Quantico, Virginia, immediately following tomorrow's press conference. While I attended a National Academy session there several years ago, I formed a relationship with Steve Land, the Unit Chief of the Behavioral Science Unit. I've asked him to try and develop a profile of our shooter, but I want you there to speak with the agents compiling that picture. You've had enough exposure to what we've gleaned thus far. Agent White will facilitate the visit, since she's familiar with FBI protocol on accessing the site and the institution itself."

Pete shifted uncomfortably in his seat. *I won't be able to see Marilyn.* "Captain, I wonder if you might be able to send someone else on the trip."

"No, Shannon, I want you to go. See me afterward if you have a problem."

"Yes, sir."

Samuels handed the folders to the teams. "Larsen and Russo, I want you to get busy ID'ing the vehicle. We have several witnesses who've mentioned a van, and there are a couple of surveillance tapes that need reviewing. Get them down to Tech and have them enhanced. McKinnon, Beckham, get into the database and pull up everyone we've interviewed thus far. I want them re-interviewed. What happened with the youngster from the convenience store, the one who was to have been interviewed under hypnosis?"

McKinnon clenched his teeth so hard his toothpick broke in half. "Cap'n, we haven't been able to follow through on that yet."

Staring at McKinnon, Samuels isolated him from the others and said with a voice as cold as ice, said, "Schedule it today."

McKinnon nodded and stared back, the tension between the two flashing like sparks from a downed electrical wire.

"Okay, that should do it for now. Get busy on your assignments. Tomorrow's press conference should begin to generate some leads once the hotline number is made public. Hopefully, we'll be swamped with new leads."

The investigators got up and began to file out; Pete stayed behind. "I'll wait out here for you, Shannon," said Agent White.

"I'll just be a minute," Pete replied, as he closed the door. Turning to face Samuels, he began. "Sir, I don't mean to get off on the wrong foot, but my partner, Marilyn Benson, is in the hospital."

"I'm aware of that, Shannon; I had a briefing from Darcy before I took the unit over."

Pete moved over to one of the chairs in front of Samuel's desk and sat down. "Sir, the doctors have been keeping her in a coma, and I'm not sure when they're going to bring her out of it, but I really need to be here when they do."

Folding his hands on the desk and leaning forward, Samuels replied. "Look, Shannon, I admire your loyalty and concern for your partner. I'm aware of Benson's history. You've both done some really fine police work, and I'm proud to have you onboard.

But this case takes precedence; we need to stop this lunatic before another one of us is murdered."

"You're right, sir. It's just that she's like family. In fact, she has no one else, no brothers or sisters, her mother's deceased, and we have no idea where her father is. I just don't want her coming to and being all alone."

Samuels stared at his hands in front of him, which had now taken on the form of a steeple, while he considered a suitable answer. "Okay, find out if the doctors intend to bring her out of the coma in the next few days; you'll only be gone two. If they tell you they're going to wake her, I'll send McKinnon."

Pete sighed. "Thank you, sir, I owe you one." He got up and went to the door.

"I'll see you and White at the conference in the morning—0900."

"Yes, sir."

The next morning Pete woke early and went for a run. The previous day's light snowfall had disappeared from the paved surfaces, but a light dusting still rested on the lawns, like powdered sugar on top of a cake. As he ran, he thought about the recent turn of events, particularly, his new partner, FBI Special Agent Tameka White. *An FBI agent.* He'd always been in awe of the Bureau, particularly, its ability to investigate big cases which sometimes took years to solve. *Maybe she can give our case some direction.*

Turning the corner onto 103rd Street, Pete ran past Queen of Martyrs Church, making the sign of the Cross as he went by. He immediately thought about his encounter with the stranger at the park. *Could it have been . . .? Was it real, or did I imagine it?* Last Sunday he worked all day and had missed Mass. In fact, he hadn't even realized it was Sunday until later. His routine was in a shambles, his otherwise orderly life resembling so many jigsaw puzzle pieces strewn about randomly on a table.

Before leaving the house, he had all but finished packing his overnight bag for the trip to the FBI Academy. He left it open on the bed so he could put his toiletries inside after his shower. He'd come home late last night, and Beth was already in bed so he hadn't told her about his upcoming trip and press conference. He'd have to make sure she knew about it before he left. Things were not good between them. He hoped he could somehow make them better, but with as much time away from her as this case demanded, the prospect dimmed with the passing of each day.

Beth awoke slowly to the soft sound of cooing coming from her son's room down the hall. The sound rescued her from her fitful sleep. Another sound, the grumbling from her stomach demanding to be filled caught her attention as well, but that wouldn't be happening anytime soon. She was still in control and would supply only the bare minimum—she would not be broken. Pete had worked late again last night. There had been no phone call, no communication between them. They lived alone . . . together.

Getting up she grabbed her robe and started toward her baby's room. As she passed by the spare bedroom, she was startled by something she saw. An open suitcase lay on the bed. Still groggy from sleep, she ambled over to take a better look. Pete's clothes were packed inside. *He's leaving. He's given up on us.* In an instant her resolve disappeared, like a handkerchief in a magician's hand. She stumbled back to bed, threw the covers over her head, and felt a gut-wrenching sorrow seize her frail body.

Her tears were brief. She'd exhausted most of the supply over the past few days; the reservoir was near depleted. Her stomach convulsed in waves of anxiety, and then the new life in her womb, sensing her distress, began to move. She was caught in a conundrum: continue to deny herself nourishment for the sake of her mental well-being, or eat normally to ensure the baby's health. She was alone; she needed someone to help her, to shore her up before she collapsed like an aged wall in the face of a gale force wind. *Mom.*

She got up quickly, packed a bag for herself and her child, and pulled on a jogging suit. She went into Pete, Jr.'s room and prepared him for the short ride to Grandma's house. Within minutes she was in her car, backing out of the garage, en route to a place she knew would give her what she needed most—love. As she drove down the block, she glanced in her rearview mirror at a house that was once the cradle of her being, a place where no problem was too big to overcome. Now, that once safe haven, that place of comfort and warmth, represented failure and sadness. She turned the corner, the image and the hope it represented fading with each block.

"Good morning, ladies and gentlemen. My name is Captain Samuels. This morning I'd like to brief you on the latest developments in the homicide investigation involving three of our officers." The new CO of the Homicide Unit stood behind a podium, flanked by the U.S. and Chicago Police Department flags. "The Superintendent has initiated a multi-agency taskforce that includes the county, state, and federal governments. If you check your briefing sheet, you will find a toll-free tip-line number that will be activated at noon today. We expect that given the additional resources available so we can bring this case to a speedy resolution.

"Standing behind me are FBI Special Agent Tameka White and Detective Peter Shannon of the Chicago Police Department." Samuels turned and gave an identifying glance toward the two investigators. "They will be leaving to consult with profilers at the FBI Academy in Quantico, Virginia, at the conclusion of this press conference."

Samuels gave a few facts concerning the case and held a Q & A session for several minutes. Cameras flashed from the gallery of print, radio, and television media. The captain was an impressive figure, and as much as the reporters tried to provoke him, he refused to be cowed.

Several minutes later, the captain closed his folder. "That will conclude our meeting this morning. Thank you for your attention." Samuels turned and walked off stage to the anteroom; White and Shannon were close behind. He held the door open until the investigators were inside and then closed it.

Reaching into the manila folder, Samuels removed an envelope and handed it to Pete. "Here are your tickets; the flight leaves at one. My friend, Steve Land, from the Behavioral Sciences Unit, will be expecting to meet with both of you at four. At that time, he'll introduce you to his two profilers. I've already sent him information from the case database, but it's important for the profilers to speak with an investigator who's working the case. You'll be staying onsite overnight. The next morning I've arranged for a profiler from the Baltimore PD to brief you on a similar case that occurred several years ago in his jurisdiction. We may have a copycat here."

The captain closed the folder and looked at Pete. "Shannon, did you get the information you needed at the hospital?"

"Yes, sir—status quo for the time being."

"Good, I want you totally focused on this investigation. You may wonder why I picked you for this trip. It's because you bring a fresh perspective. Traditional methods haven't been working thus far. You're new, not mired in routine, which is exactly what this case needs. Between your perspective, and Agent White's investigative experience and resources, I expect we'll make great strides."

Pete turned to his new partner with a nod. "I hope to learn a great deal from her, Sir. Thanks for the opportunity."

Samuels turned to leave. "You'll return home late tomorrow night. Just let me know if you need anything. I've included my cell phone number in the envelope. Good luck."

"Hey, Lynn, can I get a refill here?" The paper reader was in his usual spot at the diner counter, devouring both his breakfast and the newspaper.

Walking over with the coffee, the waitress poured him a fresh cup and then paused as the TV played the news conference being held at Chicago Police headquarters. They both watched as Captain Samuels explained the latest direction of the case. Hardcore was also watching from his spot at the end of the counter.

"Hey, Ron, looks like we've got some major league help working on the murders now," the waitress offered.

The paper reader took a sip of the freshly poured brew. "Yeah, bringing in the FBI is a smart move."

Hardcore seethed, still resentful about being stopped by the cop and given a ticket. "That don't mean shit, it's all political. I mean, look at what ya got—a black guy takes over the case and first thing he does is bring in the feds. It's all a big show, man. Hey, the FBI girl's black too. The mayor probably told him to smooth things over, make everything look good, ya know, all that PC crap. The publicity was gettin' too hot."

The waitress simply shook her head and retrieved a customer's order from the kitchen.

The paper reader spun on his stool to face his fellow diner. "Man, you are a bitter son of a gun. I don't know what happened with you in the Army, but whatever it was, you need to let it go."

"Yeah, whatever."

"You find a job yet?"

"Nah, there ain't nuthin out there. Nobody's hirin.'"

Ron turned back to the counter, grabbed his coffee, and then spun back around. "Listen, I can give you some work if you're willing to bust your butt. I run a painting service, corporate work, painting office complexes. I'll team you up with a guy who's been with me for a long time, and he'll show you the ropes. It's hard work and long hours, but it pays well."

Hardcore thought about the offer. He hadn't worked in months and could use a job, but this sounded like it was too much of a commitment, too many hours. Besides, he didn't really want to have to *work* for the money, especially if it meant working hard. "Let me think about it."

Frustrated that his goodwill gesture had been rebuffed, the man turned back to concentrate on his paper. *This guy is a loser. He'll either wind up in jail or the cemetery.*

An hour later, Hardcore was underneath the El tracks. Sparks rained down from the elevated structure like overturned bottle rockets, as the wheels contacted the electrified third rail. Most people avoided this area; the steel behemoth was a magnet for thugs. That's why Hardcore was here. He had developed a liking for marijuana while he was away. When he came home, he found this seldom-travelled area was one of the spots where he could score his drugs, mostly Amp. Although he smoked daily, he liked to treat himself every so often to a couple joints laced with PCP. He drove to his usual spot and saw his connection. Getting out of his van, Hardcore walked over and got inside the dealer's car.

"Hey, Holmes, whadup? Ya' got anything for me?"

The wiry Hispanic youth, his head constantly bobbing from either drugs, music, or both, looked out through the windshield. "Yeah, man, I got yer two, but ya gotta help me with somethin'."

"Whadya talkin' about?"

"I gotta chance to score some heavy weed, man, but I need the bens."

Hardcore laughed. "I hope you ain't lookin' to me for any dough, I aint' got jack."

"Man, I know that. I need ya to help me do somethin'."

Squirming in his seat, Hardcore said, "Hey, dog, let me get my two and get outta here."

His head still bobbing, the dealer adjusted his hat atop his greasy hair and looked at Hardcore. "You're not listenin', man, I need you, and your ride, to get some things, then ya can get your weed."

"What the hell's goin' on, man? I'll pay you for my two."

The dealer reached under his seat and retrieved a joint. Putting it in his mouth, he lit it, took a long drag, and held it. He released the noxious smoke toward the windshield where it spread like ivy on a brick wall. Then he handed the stick to Hardcore.

"Here's the deal, man. My boy works for a dude's got a store with 'lectronic stuff—computers and what not. He closes the place on Thursdays; the owner got some kinda meetin' he goes to. So my boy's gonna make sure the back door don't get locked and the alarm don't get set." The dealer turned up the music as another train screeched overhead.

Hardcore took his toke and handed the "J" back. "So what?"

Taking another hit, the dealer began to answer while holding the gasses in his expanded lungs. "You and me . . . gonna grab much as we can . . . throw it in your van." He exhaled a cloud of smoke, adding to the already hazy interior. "I got some dude gonna buy whatever we get outta there. Once I get it to him, I can get my stuff. Then you can chill with some premium weed or whatever else ya wanna fly wit."

Hardcore took another drag. *Sounds a lot easier than paintin' every day.* "Awright. I'm in."

The dealer's head bobbed again. "I knew you was a smart dude. Be here tomorrow 'round ten."

"What about my stuff, man?"

Smiling, the dealer handed the joint to Hardcore. "Here ya go, my man. This'll hold ya till tomorrow—no charge."

"Where to, folks?" The taxi driver at Washington Reagan National Airport in D.C. loaded their bags in the trunk and then hopped behind the wheel.

"Quantico," said Tameka, getting into the back seat.

The man flipped up the flag and directed the cab through a maze of cars and busses with the deftness of a surgeon dissecting a path through layers of tissue. Minutes later they were on I-95, heading south to Quantico, although moving didn't seem quite the appropriate description for what they were doing.

Pete looked around at the traffic which was barely moving. "Wow, and we're in the express lanes, Tameka?"

She laughed. "Yep, this is what they call the HOV lanes, high occupancy vehicles only. Get used to this kind of gridlock whenever you travel out East. And by the way, Pete, you may as well call me by my nickname, Meka. Everyone else does."

"Meka? Sounds good. Hey, sorry about sleeping on the plane. I've been exhausted the past couple of days. Lots going on and all at one time."

Gesturing with her hand, she replied. "Don't worry about it, I only wish I was able to do the same. I've never been able to fall asleep on planes; I guess I just don't feel safe enough to close my eyes."

"Not safe enough? How can you not feel safe when you're flying armed?"

"Oh, that. Wearing our weapon isn't a choice when we fly—

we have to wear it.   The FBI has primary jurisdiction aboard aircraft, which means we're responsible to take action onboard if something should occur."

"Like the air marshals?"

"Kind of like that.   Believe it or not, there aren't a lot of marshals on flights.   On any given day, there are probably more FBI agents flying somewhere than marshals. Anyway, I don't feel comfortable closing my eyes, especially after 9/11."

The taxi hit a patch of open road and sped ahead, while traffic in the local lanes moved as if driving through a tar pit. Pete turned to his new partner. "So, Meka, tell me, how long have you been an agent, and what led you to the FBI?"

"Well, ten years ago I was teaching in the public school system in Little Rock. One of my students was having difficulty so I had her mother come in to discuss her child's problems. As we were talking, I discovered that she was an FBI agent. We became friends, and she encouraged me to submit an application. I wasn't sure about changing careers. Teaching was a job that paid fairly well and had a good future, but something was missing in my life."

Pete interrupted. "What did your family think of you changing careers? "

Biting her lower lip, she paused, pondering Pete's question. "My husband was opposed to the idea. He had a good job; he worked for the local power company as an attorney. He knew that if I got the job, we would be transferred somewhere other than Little Rock. He didn't want to leave the place he had lived all of his life, and he didn't want to leave his friends."

Traffic slowed once again as the vehicle passed over the Occoquan River and moored boats danced solo, while tethered to their wallflower slips.

"I guess he got over it."

She shook her head. "No. A year later I was accepted and

reported for sixteen weeks of new agent training at the academy. After eight weeks, he came out to visit for a weekend. I could tell the relationship was strained. We both knew that when I got my assignment our marriage would face a critical test. Two weeks before graduation I received orders for Houston. That was the beginning of the end.

"I had thirty days to report to my new office, which included finding a place to live. To his credit, my husband was honest and said he was not moving to Houston. He gave me an ultimatum: quit my job or we were through. I didn't quit."

Her story caused Pete to think about the state of his own relationship with his wife. Things had gone from bad to worse. This morning when he had returned from his run, he found the house empty. Beth had taken the baby and gone somewhere, probably to her mother's house. He wondered why she hadn't left a note or waited to tell him her plans? He called her cell phone but got no answer. He called her again before he left for D.C., but again he still wasn't able to connect with her.

The taxi passed beneath a sign extending over the Interstate:

Exit 148 Quantico Marine Corps Base

Slowing to exit on the ramp, the driver asked Tameka, "Right or left?"

"Make a right turn at the bottom of the ramp. The FBI Academy is about eight miles down the road. You can't miss it." She turned to Pete and continued her story about her marriage and her job with the Bureau. "I regret that we divorced, I thought we were so in love that we could overcome anything, but I don't regret taking the job. It's the best thing that's ever happened to me."

Ten minutes later, the cab pulled to a stop in front of the Jefferson Building, the main entrance to the academy. After gathering their bags, Pete and Meka walked through the front doors to the reception desk. Pete looked around. "Wow, what a place. It's massive."

She was busy checking them in, getting visitors' badges for both of them, and dialing Steve's extension. "I know, it's huge, and all of the buildings are connected by covered walkways. Most people who leave here refer to it as the gerbil cage." She spoke into the phone. "Steve, it's Meka. We just arrived."

Pete watched as a formation of trainees ran down the street outside the building, each one lean and fit-looking, their instructor reminding him of his drill instructor in the Army.

"Okay, we'll see you in ten minutes." Tameka hung up the phone and picked up her overnight bag. "Partner, let's head over to BSU."

Pete picked up his bag. "I don't mean to be rude, but BSU?"

"I know; I thought the same thing when I first heard that acronym. Sounds like it stands for bullshit unit, but it actually means the Behavioral Sciences Unit, although a lot of folks in the Bureau insist that BSU actually represents what you were thinking, and that it's a rather appropriate moniker."

Pete laughed as he followed her through the glass security doors, which were activated by their badges. As they ventured deeper into the sacrosanct edifice of law and order, his thoughts drifted back to when Meka referred to him as partner. *Marilyn, I hope you're okay.*

The halls were relatively empty as they passed through one of the connecting tubes leading to the building that held the profiling offices. "In another hour, this place will be teeming with bodies," she said as they walked toward the door to a stairwell that would take them to the sub-basement. "It will be dinner time. This building also houses the dining hall, and everyone eats here, staff included. I think you'll enjoy the atmosphere. It's extremely collegial, and the food's not bad either."

"I'm looking forward to it. I haven't eaten since breakfast."

They walked down four flights of stairs and then through a door that opened to an expansive reception area. Tameka checked in with the unit secretary while Pete looked around the room. On one wall was a gallery of photos of the unit members. A unit logo sat prominently below the visual roster. On an adjoining wall was a display case containing mementoes from famous FBI cases, as well as a huge FBI insignia. Pete was studying the artifacts when a door to his left swung open and a tall, thin man walked through it and spotted Tameka.

"Meka, good to see you!" He walked over and hugged her.

"Steve, hi,. You know I try to get back here for a visit whenever I can."

Backing away from her, the man extended his hand to Pete. "Hi, I'm Steve Land, and you must be Detective Shannon, I'm pleased you could come and meet with us."

Pete shook the unit chief's hand. "Thank you. I've only been on site for about twenty minutes and already my head is swimming. What a facility."

"We're proud of it, and we have high expectations for the people we train, like Meka," he said, nodding in her direction. "She's another one of our success stories."

"So I'm learning," Pete said.

Land began to walk down a narrow hallway lined with plaques on either side. "Please, follow me to the conference room, I have two colleagues waiting to speak with you about the murders."

The trio walked to the end of the hall which then took a turn to the right and ended at a double door. Land flashed his badge at a reader on the wall and both doors opened simultaneously, almost like a scene from a Hollywood movie. Pete expected to see a translucent cloud with soft light and heavenly music playing when the doors began to move slowly inward; instead, he saw two men in suits seated at the end of a massive oak table.

Land guided the two visitors in their direction. "Gentlemen, I'd like you to meet Chicago Police Detective Peter Shannon."

The two agents stood and shook Pete's hand.

"Detective, meet Ron Fresno and Charles Sandow. They've been analyzing the data your captain sent, but they'd like to speak with you before they come up with a preliminary profile of who you might consider a suspect. Gentlemen, you already know Meka."

Everyone found a chair and sat on either side of the long, thick table. Land took a position at the head. "Detective . . ."

Pete quickly interrupted. "Please, just call me Pete."

Land began again. "Okay. I'm not sure how familiar you are with what we do here at the Unit, how we develop a profile, so let me give you a quick overview. We first try to accumulate as much evidence as we can about the crime, which includes the act itself, the scene, the victim, type of weapon, if any, and any interaction between the victim and offender before, during, and after the crime. If there are any witnesses, we examine their statements. Then we study any crime scene photos, autopsy reports, and all other reports submitted by the requesting agency.

"After we've examined all that, we try to initially classify the subject into one of two categories: organized or disorganized. The murderer in Chicago has now committed three similar acts, and he appears to fall under the organized classification."

Ron Fresno nodded in agreement with what Land had just said. "Steve's right. Whoever you're looking for is definitely not impulsive either in terms of planning or in the commission of the act."

Opening his folder, the other profiler spoke. "This last murder, the one at the convenience store, seems to verify that since the possible offender was seen in the open. The previous murders appear to have been committed from inside a vehicle. It would be helpful to determine why he changed his routine for that particular victim."

"Good point, Charlie." Land continued, "The mark of an organized murderer is one who takes care in planning and carrying out the crime. For instance, they ensure that little evidence and few clues remain after they've killed their victim. They probably have advanced social skills that allow them to hide in plain sight without drawing attention to themselves."

"That makes sense," Pete offered. "Our guy hasn't really given us much to work with—no eyewitnesses while he's committing the act and hardly any physical evidence left anywhere."

Ron stood and slid a folder across the table toward Pete and Meka. "Here's a chart of the murders which lists the evidence for each crime."

Pete and Meka looked at the chart while the agent spoke.

"As you can see, there's definitely a pattern established. And what's particularly significant is that there's no contact with the victim before the murder. So while it appears he chooses his victims randomly, he is targeting a certain type of victim: the police."

Land removed his phone from his belt, read a message on it, and then returned it to its carrier. "I have another meeting to attend. Ron and Charlie will continue the discussion, but what I wanted to add is this: it appears that whoever the murderer is, he does not want to be caught. Many times criminals will send a message to the media, or even to the police department, to taunt them or give them clues. It's generally a sign that they are hoping the police will arrest them. This killer hasn't done that. He does not want this reign of terror to end, he's probably enjoying his success, and therein lies the problem—he's likely to kill again."

Pete breathed out a sigh and shook his head. "We can't let that happen."

Getting up from the table, Land made his way toward the door to leave. "I agree. Ron and Charlie will spend some time with you to see if you may have some clue that hasn't been recorded in all of the reports or perhaps some theories you may have. Don't hold back, Pete. Every inkling you may have about the killer is important. Even if it sounds ridiculous, we want to hear it."

Opening a side door, Land hesitated before walking through it. "I'll see you both tomorrow before you leave for Chicago. Meka, great seeing you again."

"Thanks, Steve."

Charlie took out a pad of paper and looked at Pete. "Let me ask a question. Why do you think this shooter has been so difficult to catch? Or, perhaps, just as important, what has hindered you in your investigation?"

One word: McKinnon. Pete shifted in his seat. "To begin with, my sense is that we're dealing with a guy, and I use that term in a generic sense, for all I know it could very well be a woman, but whoever is committing the murders is some kind of professional— a cop, or maybe military. The tactics are such that he picks his spots, ensuring his environment disguises the sound of the shot and his location."

Charlie looked up from writing. "That's good, Pete, and it would account for the lack of evidence at the first two homicide scenes."

"Yeah, that's why I think our guy is operating out of a van of some kind. His weapon remains hidden, the brass is ejected inside after the shot, and the report is muffled because the shot is taken in an enclosed area."

"Good theory," added Fresno. "No eyeballs or evidence of the shooter at either of the first two murders."

Leaning forward, Pete placed his elbows on the table and rested his chin on his hands. "The third shooting was a departure from the pattern. For some reason, he decided to take the shot from outside his vehicle, as evidenced by the casing found by the little boy at the park. I can't figure out why he would do that when his first two shootings went so well for him."

"That's a good point," said Charlie as he stood and walked to the whiteboard in front of the room. He took a black marker, hastily sketched a diagram, and then turned back toward the table. "We wondered about that also, so we went to Google maps and brought up a satellite view of the area." He pointed to his sketch. "If you look at the way the street is configured and its position relative to the store where the officer was shot, two things come to mind: his vehicle is out in the open, there are no trees or shrubbery in this area, and, depending on his vehicle—we're assuming it's a van—the way he would have had to park may not have afforded him a good shot."

Pete's mind formed a mental picture of the scene as the agent continued.

"Google Earth, once you enlarge the area by the water, shows brush and several trees which would camouflage his shooting position, particularly if he was prone."

"This area," said Ron as he pointed with his pen at the board, "is probably the reason he deviated from his normal routine. His impulse was to get a better shooting position, which also plays to your theory, Pete, that this guy probably has a law enforcement or military background."

"Exactly." Charlie drew a line from the water's edge to the van. "From the lagoon to the van is probably fifty yards. Early morning winter darkness might conceal his movement, so his impulse to improve his position was a result of one of two things: either he didn't perceive it to be a risk, or, and this is another characteristic of this type of offender, or it was a risk. He may be one of those people who are risk takers, someone who gets his kicks doing dangerous things. It's a challenge; it's a high."

Meka looked up from the chart in front of her. "Charlie, it says here that the woman runner saw a guy in a camouflage jacket. I think Pete's onto something here. Maybe we should be concentrating on former military types."

"That's certainly an area we were going to suggest."

Pete stood and ran his fingers through his hair. "But why, what's his motive?"

"If we knew that, Pete, it would make things much simpler." Charlie returned to his place at the table. "Something may have happened in this guy's past . . . a run in with an officer, an arrest, even something as simple as a traffic ticket. When a person is mentally unstable, the slightest inconvenience or a wrong word can set him off and cause him to do all kinds of irrational things. This guy may think he's getting even by killing cops."

"We just don't know," said Ron. "It could be something at his job, or if he is military, something that happened to him there, and now he's taking out his revenge against very visible authority figures like cops."

Meka turned to Pete and asked, "Anything else we haven't covered?"

Pete sat. "No, I think we've established that our guy is definitely organized and probably professional. He knows how to kill."

The others rose from their seats and they all headed toward the double doors. "We'll work on this and send it out to you as quickly as possible. I understand you have a meeting in the morning with Nelson Croke."

Meka waved her badge past the reader by the doors. "Yes, he's driving down from Baltimore in the morning. Captain Samuels arranged for us to meet with him before our flight leaves for Chicago."

"Ah yes, Nelson," said Charlie. "He was an intern here for two years while he worked on his doctorate. He's a good man; tell him we said hello."

As Pete and Meka began their trek up the stairs, she turned to him and said, "You know, there's an elevator we can use if you'd like."

"No thanks, I prefer the stairs."

"My kind of man. May I make an offer?"

Pete gave her a sideways glance as they passed the first landing. "Depends."

"Would you care to join me for a run before dinner?"

"How far?"

"Three miles or so, out to Lake Lunga."

"Sure, I got one in this morning, but I'm always up for another workout. Besides, I'd love to see some of the campus up close."

"Great, but it will be rather dark. We'll be in the woods and it's late fall. Bring a flashlight if you want to see anything. Five-thirty in front of the Jefferson?"

"You're on."

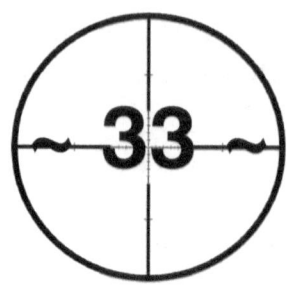

~33~

"Your phone's ringing again."

"I know, Mom. It's Pete. I can tell by the ringtone," said Beth, as she sat in the family room of her parents' home.

"Why don't you just answer it, for goodness sake? How long are you going to drag out this drama?"

"I'm not sure, I'm mad at him for ignoring us." She shifted the baby in her arms.

Beth's mother put down the magazine she had been reading. "He's ignoring you? What did you do this morning? Weren't you the one who left the house without telling him where you were going?"

"Yes, but I was frustrated. I've hardly seen him the past few weeks. I guess I wanted to give him a dose of his own medicine."

Her mother inched forward in her chair. "Beth, this is not the time for adolescent behavior. Think about what Pete's going through. Marilyn is lying in the hospital, his friend has been murdered, and from what you've told me he's working long hours, and things at work aren't going very well. Put yourself in his shoes. He's trying hard to stop a deranged killer, and his only refuge, his home, is hardly the welcoming place it needs to be. How would you handle the same situation?"

She laid the baby on the rug and picked up her coffee cup, giving some thought to what her mother had just said.

"One other thing, honey."

"What, Mom?"

"You've been here all day, yet I haven't seen you eat anything. Please, tell me you're not slipping back into your old ways. It was bad enough when you had the bout with anorexia a while back, but you're pregnant now. You're not only putting your own health at risk, but the baby's as well."

Sipping her coffee, Beth felt her eyes well with tears. She nodded slightly. "Mom . . ."

Her mother got up from her chair and sat next to her daughter on the couch. Wrapping her arms around her daughter, she said. "It will be okay, dear. I'm here for you; that will never change. We'll get through this rough patch—together. But you have to promise me that you'll take care of yourself and the baby."

"I want to Mom, believe me I do. It's just that when things aren't' going well for me, I need a place to hide, somewhere I can be comforted. Denying myself food has worked for me."

"Has it? Has not eating solved any problems for you? Has it ever made anything better or made problems disappear?"

"No, but . . ."

"What happened the last time you had problems and turned to the disorder?"

"I know, Mom, nothing got better, but it allowed me to set the problem aside for a while."

"That was then. It was bad enough you damaged your own health. What about the baby growing inside of you? Are willing to risk hurting the baby's chances of developing?"

Her mother reached down and picked up Pete, Jr. who had crawled over to them as if to comfort his mother. "We all need you; your husband needs you. Pete has never abandoned you and I know he never will. You and the baby mean more to him than anything else in this world. Don't put yourself and the baby at risk and don't ignore him at a time when he needs you most."

Beth's tears flowed freely as she leaned into her mother and child. "You're right, Mom. I guess I've been selfish lately, not realizing what he's going through. Pete's been trying to tell me how he feels, but I've shut him down. What's wrong with me, why am I have been so inconsiderate?" Beth took the baby from her mother's arms.

"Listen, it's not too late to fix things," she said, as she wiped the tears from her daughter's cheeks. "Call him. Let him know you're here and that everything is fine. And tell him you're sorry."

"I will," she said, smiling. "Lord knows He's forgiven me and my problems before."

"Good. Now, Honey, one more thing."

"What?"

Her mother got up and walked toward the kitchen. "Let's fix you something to eat."

"Mom."

"What?"

"Thanks."

Clouds covered most of the sky, but a slight opening, radiant with a golden hue, foretold of a pleasant day for his flight home. As he ran across the baseball fields behind the physical training building at the FBI Academy, Pete saw groups of new agents working out: timing each other on laps around the track, running sprints, doing pushups and pull-ups. He realized these were focused men and women ensuring they would master every component of their new agent training, including fitness. They were future warriors.

He crossed a paved road and jogged down a gently sloping dirt path, the one Meka had shown him last night on their run before dinner. It had been dusk when they began, and by the time they finished, it was dark. He had been barely able to see the road. This morning, with dawn about to explode and rain light on the woods around him, could enjoy the beauty of the area.

The undulating path was soothing, taking his mind off the turmoil that had engulfed him the past weeks. Yesterday, he hadn't been able to call Beth on his cell phone; Meka explained about the shield that intercepted and blocked radio frequencies in the area. But just before he was about to go to bed, his room phone rang. The front desk had a call transferred to him. It was Beth, calling on a land line. She had called his unit and discovered he was at the academy. He replayed their conversation in his mind while he ran.

"Pete?"

"Beth, honey, are you okay?"

"Yes, I'm fine . . . now. I'm at my mom's house with the baby. Pete, I'm sorry about leaving without telling you. It was stupid of me to act that way, but I've been concerned lately about where we're headed. We're drifting apart at a time when we should be closer than ever."

"It's my fault. I've been ignoring you and little Pete; I'm spending too much time on the case, trying to stop whoever is behind these killings."

"I don't blame you, so much has happened—Joe and Marilyn—I can't believe how things have gone so wrong."

He sat on the bed in his dorm room. "Beth, let's not try to place blame. Let's just try to move on and make things better. There is no other person in my life who means more to me than you; I can't imagine life without you. I love you so much; I promise to do a better job of being there for you."

She stifled a sob as she listened to the words she so desperately needed to hear. "Babe, I love you too. I've missed *us*, the couple whose lives were so tightly woven together. Let's not make this mistake again. We need to always talk things out, not just when there's a problem, but each day, letting the other one know what's going on in our lives."

"You're right. I've forgotten my priorities, but it won't happen again."

They talked for an hour, each of them coming to tears several times. She explained how she had felt ignored and alone, like he was no longer there for her. He apologized. He told her he was wrong for allowing work to consume him. And as their lines of communication opened, the wall that had formed between them slowly began to crumble. By the time he hung up he felt the best he'd felt in a long while. He slept soundly, even dreaming about the early years of his marriage when it seemed they didn't have a care in the world. He woke refreshed and without a single thought about the murders he was investigating in Chicago.

Pete turned down a winding path that led to the foot of a recreation area where a large portion of Lake Lunga was visible. The vista was spectacular, the surface quiescent with just a hint of steam rising from the water. Like a huge mirror, it reflected the sky above. He paused to take in the splendor of God's creation, and at that moment the eastern sky bathed him in a heavenly light. *I'm sorry for ignoring you, Lord. Guide me, walk with me, never stop calling my name.* Pete felt His presence and got down on his knees and recited the Lord's Prayer. When he finished, he thought about the many blessings in his life—family and friends, his health, his job. He had been given much, but he had given back little.

He turned and ran back the way he had come. Today he would make a new beginning. After his meeting, he and Meka would fly back to Chicago. His first stop would be home, and after he made amends to Beth, he'd go to the hospital to check on Marilyn.

"That's it, man, it's the one with the steel door and bars." Hardcore drove slowly down the alley that was littered with garbage and broken glass. The lights from his van reflected in the eyes of hungry rats, giving them an eerie appearance as they scurried from their buffet of trash, angered by the intrusion into their nocturnal domain. With no one to upset their daily foraging, the creatures grew disturbingly large. Hardcore killed the van's lights and rolled to a stop beside the door.

"Lemme check it." The dealer got out and pulled the burglar bars aside and tried the doorknob. He twisted it, opened the door a crack, and then returned to the van. "Just like my boy said. It's all good; let's go."

Hardcore got out and looked around. Half of the buildings on the block were either abandoned or in a state of disrepair. Discarded mattresses, old tires, and other eclectic debris piles dotted the alley, like some kind of bizarre urban obstacle course. He followed the dealer through the back door where they stood in partial darkness; the interior lit only by a neon sign glowing in the front window.

"Dog, you bring a flashlight?" the dealer asked.

"Yeah. Let's grab some stuff and get outta here. Man, I got bad vibes about this place."

"It's cool, my man. Nobody gonna bother us," said the dealer, as he aimed his light at a wall of shelves. "Bam—there's the mother lode—sweet. Grab some boxes, Homey. Yeah, it's Christmas in the ghetto, Bro."

Picking a couple of packages off the shelf, Hardcore nervously looked around the interior. "You sure there ain't no cameras gonna see us?"

"Man, I told ya, my boy took care o' everything."

The thieves made several trips to the van with armloads of merchandise. On one of the trips, Hardcore spotted movement a couple of buildings away. He grabbed the dealer. "Shhh , someone's over there," he said, pointing toward a dumpster. He crept slowly, crouching as he went and using his military training to minimize any sound. Reaching the corner of the dumpster, he pulled his knife from the pocket of his jacket and deftly extended the blade with one hand. He readied his flashlight and then quickly stepped around the side.

"Hey, man, whatcha doin?" said a bum who sat on the ground against the side of the dumpster, wine bottle in one hand, the other hand trying to block the blinding light directed at his face. "Uh, sorry, Officer, I ain't done nothin' wrong."

"Shut up, fool." Hardcore turned his light off. "Stay put and nurse that bottle; you don't want none o' me."

"Yes sir. I ain't hurtin' nobody."

CRASH. Hardcore heard a loud noise and hurried back to the van where he saw a broken TV set lying on the ground.

"What the . . . ?"

The dealer cocked his hat and looked down at the damaged set. "It slipped."

"You stupid . . . someone's gonna hear us." Hardcore looked around and then stepped out toward the middle of the alley, looking both ways for any sign of the police. "Let's go man; I'm leavin' before 5-0 gets here."

"Hey, I gotta few more things to get."

"I'm gone, man. You stay if you want, but I'm outta here." Hardcore shut the side door of the van and then went around to the driver's door. Getting in, he looked up and saw a video camera installed just under the eaves, by the gutter. "Damn!"

The dealer shut his door, and as Hardcore backed out, he looked over at his passenger. "You see that camera?"

"It's cool, man. My boy say he turned everything off. Anyway, we put dat bogus plate on yo ride. What you worried about?"

"Yeah, what am I worried about?" Hardcore turned out of the alley. *This was a mistake; this pothead's gonna get us both locked up.* He was already thinking about how to ditch the van.

"I'd be afraid of gaining weight if I ate here every day." Pete peeled a banana as he and his new partner, Tameka, ate breakfast in the dining hall at the FBI Academy. "There's so much to eat, but I see that the majority of it seems to be nutritious."

Setting down her glass of orange juice, she answered. "That's certainly a possibility. In fact, we do have some trainees who leave here weighing several pounds more than when they reported. Hopefully, most of that is muscle. But if you want to eat healthy, the choices here will allow you to do so. Usually there are three entrees available, and of course, the salad and fruit bar is always open."

Trainees scurried about the dining hall, some wearing their range clothing and protective vests, others in business attire. The morning meal was not a time for socialization; the students' priority was to fuel up for the busy morning of training.

"Everyone looks so focused."

Tameka pointed to a table in the far corner. "Take a look over there, Pete. See that group with the backpacks and books?"

Pete turned to look at a table where several students appeared to be quizzing each other. "Yeah, looks like they're kind of stressed."

She smiled. "They are. I can tell by the book they're using. They're taking the law exam this morning. It's one of the more difficult tests they'll take. There are two three-hour tests. Fail both and you're out."

CRASH! Pete snapped his head around, startled by the sound of a tray dropped by someone at the breakfast bar.

"Happens a lot. "Meka smiled. "Students get stressed, and many of them don't get enough sleep, but the whole training cycle gives us a clear picture of how the trainee will adapt to the job. There will be plenty of stress from complex investigations, long hours, road trips, and deadly confrontations. If they have a problem here, there's a good chance they won't be able to handle problems in the field."

Pete shook his head. "Wow, it's certainly high-energy around here. I have a new-found respect for FBI agents. I never imagined the training was so rigorous."

"Thanks, Pete." She put her plate and glass on her tray. "Finished?"

"Yep."

"Okay. Let's head over to the library for our meeting with Nelson."

"Nelson?"

"Nelson Croke, don't you remember? Captain Samuels told us he's the profiler with the Baltimore PD. Steve set up the meeting so he could brief us about a case he worked several years ago that has similarities to ours."

"Oh yeah. Sorry, I forgot. I've got a million things running through my head."

They picked up their trays, set them on a cart near the kitchen, and then headed down the steps. Walking out the door on the first floor, they encountered a long line of trainees wearing ballistic vests and baseball hats. "What's all this?" Pete asked.

"They're lined up to check out their weapons for firearms training. The gun vault is around that corner," she said, pointing off to their right. "Everyone's firearm is checked in and out of the vault. They're not allowed to keep them in their rooms or carry them into the complex. It's a safety issue."

"Good idea," Pete said, "especially if they fail the law exam."

"Pete!"

"Sorry, poor attempt at humor. Let's get to the meeting."

After a five minute walk through another gerbil tube, the pair arrived at the FBI Library. "Beautiful," Pete remarked, looking three-stories upward toward the skylight that diffused direct sunlight into soft incandescence. "What beautiful architecture."

"It's quite the place. Three floors of books, surrounded by chairs, couches, and desks, all well-suited for everything from casual reading to intense research. I spent many a late hour here when I went through new agent training. It's open all day, every day."

They walked up to the main desk where a woman was logging in returned books. "Can I help you?"

"Hi, I'm Tameka White. I have a scheduled meeting with Detective Croke, from Baltimore."

The woman smiled and pointed behind Meka and Pete. "He's already here. He's waiting in the Hoover Room."

"Thanks."

They walked through the door and saw a middle-aged man hunched over a stack of journals. Hearing the pair enter, he stood. "Hi. Just going over some criminal justice abstracts while I waited. I enjoy coming back to the academy. I get to see old friends and peruse the library's collection of law enforcement subscriptions."

Tameka extended her hand toward the man. "I'm Tameka White; this is Pete Shannon. Steve Land told us you might be able to shed some light on a case we're working in Chicago."

"Nice to meet you both. Yes, Steve forwarded the information to me about your case. He thought there were some similarities between your case and one I worked some time ago."

"And what do you think, are there?" Meka asked, as she and Pete had a seat at the table.

"Yes. The biggest similarity in both cases is that the shooters used a vehicle to take the shot from. In my case, there were two subjects involved, although I didn't know it at the time. One masterminded the operation, while the other subject, seemingly, was there only as a driver and errand runner."

"What kind of vehicle did your subjects use?" Pete asked.

"Our guys were in a beat-up old sedan, a very inauspicious looking one. What's interesting is that because it was an older model, it had a huge trunk. These guys took their shooting position from inside of it, and had the barrel of the rifle protruding from one of the taillight assemblies. They fashioned a spring hinge that allowed them to open and close the shooting portal at their convenience."

Tameka leaned forward toward Pete. "I remember some things about that case. When they spotted a victim, they'd get their car into position, and the shooter got into the trunk through the back seat. He'd take the shot from inside, which meant the noise was muffled and the spent cartridge was contained within the trunk, leaving no physical evidence and no eye witnesses."

"Ingenious."

Nelson got up from his seat and walked near the window. Resting on a credenza, he continued. "They killed three people before I was brought into the case, and I pored over the incident reports, trying to give the investigators an idea of who to look for. I have to admit, at first I was way off in my conclusion. I thought the subject was probably black. And, based on the police reports, I felt the shots probably came from a van, since at two of the crime scenes, witnesses reported seeing a white van."

"What happened? Why were you wrong?" Pete frowned.

"Their next victim was a black man, an early morning newspaper delivery guy. That's when I had to reassess what I had previously concluded. I practice what's called 'offender profiling.' It's different from psychological profiling. I'm looking solely at the behavioral evidence and drawing conclusions from it. And when there's a scarcity of it, as in our case, we grab on to the most logical correlations. Sometimes we get it wrong."

Pushing back from the table, Tameka stood and walked over to a floor-to-ceiling window that looked out into a beautifully landscaped courtyard. "The good news is that you eventually got it right, and the two shooters were arrested and convicted. But are we looking at the same thing?"

Nelson spread his arms. "Let me cut to the chase. The Baltimore case involved a guy who was full of hate and thought society had dealt him a losing hand. He was more concerned with picking the venue than with the victim. He randomly picked people to kill. He just happened to see more white people than blacks wherever he set up. And he enlisted the help of an accomplice who was easily duped into believing whatever he told him. Although they came up with a great idea regarding shooting out of the trunk, their actions afterward were amateurish. At the scene of the fourth shooting, a woman watched from her front window as the shooter crawled out of the trunk and into the backseat. He then got out of the car and opened the door to get into the passenger seat in front where the driver was waiting to drive them away from the scene The woman ID'd both guys—they were white. Your guy, on the other hand, is a pro, and I say your 'guy' because I'm convinced we're dealing with a single subject."

"Explain," said Pete.

Nelson started to walk around the room, like an attorney giving final arguments to a jury at trial. "First, no witnesses. He's careful about where he sets up. Second, his skill. Each victim has been taken out by a kill shot. Snipers train to take what's referred to as a cold-bore shot. They aim for a one-inch band, basically, an imaginary strip that covers both eyes. The bullet penetrates the skull and severs the cervical spine, causing instant incapacitation and death. Your guy has made three identical shots—he knows what he's doing. My guess is he's probably ex-military or maybe even police. My shooter just tried to hit his target center mass."

Pete reached over to the center of the table and poured himself a glass of water from a pitcher that had been put there for the meeting.   "What else? Any more differences or similarities between your case and ours?"

"Yes, just like in my case, your guy will continue to kill until he's caught, particularly, because he has probably made a living doing it and enjoys it. He thinks it's his job or calling.   However, here is a major difference: your guy is targeting a specific victim — cops.   My two guys picked out whoever was convenient.   The excitement, the thrill of killing is magnified for your shooter because he's killing warriors—cops—and the likelihood that he might get caught makes it even more of a rush for him."

"Just uniformed cops?"

"No, Tameka, any cop he spots.   If you're looking for us, we're not difficult to ID. We all but wear a sign that screams COP. Bad guys, in particular, can smell us a mile away.   Face it, now that you're part of the case, you're at risk. Now it's personal, isn't it?" Nelson looked at his watch.   "That's about all I've got, Steve has all the germane investigative case serials from our arrest if you need to refer to them.   I've got to head back to Baltimore. You know how D.C. traffic is."

Pete laughed. "I found out yesterday."

The profiler moved toward the door.   "One more thing. There was an agent who worked on the case after we formed a task force consisting of multiple jurisdictions. His name was Jim Toppe. He was assigned to the Washington FBI Field Office at the time but was later transferred to Chicago. You might know him, Tameka."

"Toppe?"   She answered, raising her eyebrows.   "I do know him. He's on the Financial Crimes Squad; he's also on SWAT."

Nelson opened the door and paused before leaving.   "You might want to talk with him. He knew a lot about the case and was on the arrest team when they took both guys down."

"Thanks, Nelson. Have a safe trip back."

"I will. Call me if you have any more questions," he said and walked out.

Pete and Tameka looked at each other. "Well, what do you think, Pete? Are all of your questions answered?"

Pete cupped his chin. "All I know for sure is that our guy is probably a trained sniper and that we're all in danger. I hope Steve can shed a little more light on a possible suspect."

"Me too. I guess we'll find out when they finish their assessment, but my guess is that we're not going to catch this guy unless he gets sloppy, or somebody drops a dime on him."

"I agree. Hey, I'd like to talk with Agent Toppe. Do you think you can arrange that?"

The duo headed for the door. Tameka had a big grin on her face. "I know of one surefire way to talk with him."

"What's that?"

"Jim's a runner. I'll set up a workout when we get back. Be ready for a long run, he's a marathoner."

"Great, thanks."

They headed back to their rooms to pack for the trip home. Although Pete enjoyed his visit at the Academy, he was eager to get back to Chicago. He had a long to-do-list to get started on.

~ 35 ~

Father Ed didn't know what to think after leaving Lisa's house. He felt relieved that he no longer had to lie to her about who he was, yet he'd broken his own promise to himself not to tell anyone the truth about his identity. Circling the block looking for a parking spot, he pondered his next move. What if Lisa was right about going back to Chicago to clear his name? After all, he had a great attorney and his past was impeccable.

He found a parking spot just down the block and pulled to the curb. He got out, locked his car door and began walking down the street toward his apartment. It was getting close to Thanksgiving, and the town of Fredericksburg had just hung Christmas decorations along William Street. Bright banners hung on old lampposts, and thousands of miniature lights adorned the trees, creating a glorious, living oil painting. A gust of wind blew open his jacket, chilling him. He thought he might walk to the end of the block and get a coffee to go.

Walking past his apartment, he noticed a flier of some sort hanging on his door. He grabbed it, stuffed it into his jacket pocket, and continued his trek toward the cafe. Several doors down he saw a vehicle parked at the curb with its lights off and engine running, the cloud of exhaust evidence of the cold night. Coming along side it, he glanced at the driver—a cop—James Rogers!

Ed jammed both hands into his pockets and quickened his pace. A couple of minutes later, he opened the front door to the coffee shop and stepped inside. His first inclination was to lean on the door and not allow anyone inside. He felt his heart racing and a bead of sweat trickled down his chest. *What does he want with me now?* Taking a deep breath, he walked up to the counter and ordered a large coffee. A minute later, he was seated at one of the tables in the corner and away from the windows. He had thought to enjoy his drink at home, but he changed his mind after seeing the cop. He removed the lid from his cup, his hand shaking while he did so. Steam rose from the hot liquid, and Ed stared into the vapor like a psychic reading a crystal ball.

A few moments later, his spell was broken by a group of teens entering the store. His shoulders relaxed, and he leaned back against the booth. He took a sip of coffee and analyzed his situation. His life was controlled by everyone but himself. As long as he had to hide his true identity, moments like the one he'd just experienced would be the norm rather than the exception. He watched the young people seated around a table, enjoying a beverage and each other's company. More than anything else, he noticed their apathy about everything outside their little world. They were young, probably high schoolers or college freshmen.

The priest took another sip and reached into his pocket absentmindedly. He felt the piece of paper he had found on his door. Taking it out, he unfolded it. It was the front page of a recent edition of the local paper. The headline read: Man's Body Discovered in Quarry. Written across the photo, which showed police removing a body from the water, were the words

you could be next

Ed quickly read the accompanying story which explained that fishermen had discovered a body in the Fredericksburg quarry adjacent to the Rappahannock River. The body had apparently been in the water for a long time and was unidentifiable. A forensic examination was pending.

He folded the paper and put it back in his pocket. The cop.

Panicked, he closed his eyes and prayed. *Father, what am I to do?* The coffee shop door opened once again, jarring him from his prayer, but it was not what he imagined: James Rogers barging in gun drawn, ready to take him down to the river and kill him. An elderly couple walked up to the counter and ordered. He picked up his coffee and while he drank, he saw the same car drive slowly by the coffee shop.

For the next twenty minutes, he debated with himself about what to do. Finally, he made a decision. He finished his coffee and walked out the door toward his apartment. He looked around but didn't see the car. Arriving at his building, he unlocked the downstairs door and hurried up the stairs, two-at-a-time. Once inside, he knew what he must do. He grabbed his belongings, threw them in his suitcases, and carried them to his car. He closed the trunk and drove toward Route 3. Approaching the I-95 overpass, he had a decision to make, continue west, out of town to who knows where or get on the Interstate. A bright green and white sign appeared:

I-95 South Richmond

Ed eased his car onto the ramp and headed south. He'd never been to Richmond before, but it was a big city, easier to get lost in and remain anonymous. Fredericksburg had not been such a wise choice, but he had learned a valuable lesson: don't get close to anyone.

"Marilyn . . . Marilyn, can you hear me? Time to wake up." The doctor massaged Marilyn's hand as he spoke to her. He turned to the others in the room. "This may take a while. She's been unconscious for a week so all of her reactions have slowed considerably."

"Marilyn, it's Kim. Can you wake up now?" Marilyn's best friend and work out partner was at her bedside, along with

Chaplain Dean, Detective Sanela Latarski, and Beth. When Pete got word the doctors were going to bring Marilyn out of her induced-coma, he wanted plenty of support to be there for her.

"C'mon, partner, time to get out of bed. We've got work to do."

Marilyn stirred. "Pete, Pete?" What's happening? Am I dreaming? So hard to open my eyes . . . tired . . .

Kim bent over the bed and brushed the hair aside as she rubbed Marilyn's forehead. She whispered in her ear, "C'mon, Bens. Open your eyes, we need you awake."

Marilyn's eyelids opened slowly, as is they were weighted. The light was harsh; she had been one with the darkness for so long. Through blurred vision, she saw several figures standing around her bed. Closing her eyes again, she hoped that once she opened them she would find herself at home, in her bedroom. Through slits, the bright light once again stabbed at her vision, but she struggled to keep her eyes open and focus.

"Hey, partner, it's about time you woke up."

"Pete?"

"Marilyn, welcome back." She looked to the side of the bed to see Beth and Kim. Turning her head, she saw Reverend Dean, Sanela, and what looked to be a doctor. She opened and closed her eyes several times and then stared at the ceiling for a moment. "Where am I?"

Pete moved close to her bed and took her hand. "You're in the hospital; you were involved in an accident."

"An accident? I don't remember that."

Pete looked toward the doctor. "Doc . . ."

"It's not unusual for the patient to be unable to recall a traumatic event," he explained. "The mind has a way of blocking certain memories. It aids in allowing the patient to minimize discomfort and speed up the healing process. As she recovers, you can fill in the blanks for her."

Marilyn moved as if to sit up. "Ow . . . I'm sore all over." She looked at the IV line running into her arm. "What's this?"

"Nourishment, we didn't want you to waste away," said the doctor. "The soreness is primarily from a couple of cracked ribs. It will fade away, along with the bruising. And we had to shave a little patch of hair from the back of your head, but you won't even notice it."

She reached back and felt her head. "Why?"

"You had a pretty substantial trauma to your head as a result of striking the windshield of the car. You had some bleeding within your skull, and we had to relieve the resultant swelling."

Marilyn rubbed her hand over her stomach, feeling its concave surface. "I feel like I've been on a crash diet."

The doctor was at the end of the bed, making notations in Marilyn's chart. "Not eating solid food for a week will do that."

Marilyn's eyes widened. "A week? I've been here a week?"

Her doctor walked around to the side of the bed and took her vitals. "Everything appears to be as it should be. I'll be back in an hour to look in on you. Try to drink some water; I've ordered a light meal for you. In the meantime, enjoy your company, but don't try to get out of bed just yet until the nurses are with you."

As the doctor walked out into the hallway, Pete caught up with him. "Hey, Doc, got a minute?"

"Sure."

"The chaplain and I have been trying to decide how to break the news to her about her fiancé's death. Should we wait for a better time to tell her?"

"You mean the officer who was shot last week?"

Pete nodded. "Yes, but she knows nothing about it. The hit and run happened at almost the same time as the shooting. When she asks where Joe is, do we tell her the truth or should we wait?"

Shaking his head, the doctor answered. "I'm not a psychologist, but based on what I've seen happen in cases like this, I'd be inclined to tell her the truth as soon as she inquires about

Joe. To withhold such a tragedy from her will only exacerbate the problem. She needs to deal with her emotions. Besides, is there ever a good time to break such news?"

Beth walked from the room and stood beside Pete. "Thanks, Doc."

"You're welcome. I'll be back shortly."

"Pete?" Beth took his hand. "Bad news?"

"I don't know. I wanted his opinion about how to break the news to Marilyn about Joe's death. He thinks we should tell her the truth."

Beth squeezed his hand. "I think he's right. When you were shot, the first thing they told me was that you were in a scuffle. When they drove me to the hospital to see you, it was swarming with cops and reporters. I knew right away they had lied to me."

Pete looked down into his wife's eyes, the memory of that night flashing in his mind. "I'm sorry you had to go through that, Babe."

"It's okay, it wasn't your fault. The point is, the truth is always better than a lie. Marilyn needs to know about Joe, and there's no easy way to tell her."

Pete put his arms around his wife and kissed her lightly. "You're right. Let's go back inside."

As they re-entered the room, Kim was kidding around with Marilyn about how she might smuggle a hot dog with everything into the hospital for Marilyn. "And I'll bring plenty of greasy fries."

Marilyn smiled. "I don't think I'm quite ready for that, Kim. Maybe in a day or two. Right now food doesn't sound very appealing."

Pete thought about how good it was to see Marilyn awake and engaged in conversation. He had been worried that she may have suffered some impairment from the accident.

Marilyn looked over to where Pete and Beth were standing just inside the door. "Pete, it's been a week, any new developments in the case?"

Pete welcomed the question; it meant that he didn't have to deal with telling her about Joe. For the next ten minutes, he explained to her about the change of supervisors and teams, and his recent trip to the FBI Academy.

"Wait a minute, you're working with a new partner? What about me, am I still on the squad?"

"Captain Samuels hasn't said anything to the contrary, but right now; you just need to get back on your feet again."

Marilyn paused to think about what Pete had just told her. "Just give me a few days. Hey, speaking of partners, where's my Joe? Why isn't he here?"

The mood in the room suddenly turned somber. "Pete? Where is he?" Marilyn asked, her voice cracking and her eyes fixated on Pete.

Pete and Beth approached her bedside; Beth took her hand as Pete broke the news to her. "Marilyn, Pete's gone—he was killed by the sniper." Pete's hand went to his mouth, as if trying to retrieve the words that he knew would devastate Marilyn. His eyes filled with tears.

"What? What are you saying . . . how could you . . . please . . . no, Pete, no . . . please, not Joe!"

Beth grasped Marilyn's hand between hers. "Honey, listen, I hate to have to tell you this, but Joe was killed the same morning you were involved in the accident."

Marilyn pulled her hand from Beth's and covered her face as the tears streamed through her fingers. She made no attempt to hide her agony, her body racked with physical pain and from a new, penetrating wound that invaded her soul.

Pete leaned into her. "Marilyn, there was no good way to tell you. I'm sorry."

Marilyn pushed him away, her once pale complexion now red,

her sight blurred through a veil of tears. "Please, everyone, go . . . just leave."

Pete hesitated. "Marilyn, please . . ."

"Go! Leave me alone!"

Reverend Dean began to shepherd the group from the room. "C'mon, Pete, she needs to be alone. She needs to grieve."

They assembled just outside the door, where Marilyn's sobs could still be heard. "Dean, I feel so helpless," Pete said, his own eyes moist with tears. "I mean, she's right there, so close and in so much pain."

"I know, but right now she's dealing with it the only way she can. Frankly, had she not reacted the way she did I would have been worried. But I know that the Father will get her through this. Her faith is strong, and it will save her. For the moment, the best thing we can do is to give her a little space and, of course, our prayers."

Sanela took the chaplain's hand. "Reverend, can we pray?"

"Yes, of course." The small group joined hands, and Dean prayed. "Father, you are a loving God and a compassionate parent. We ask that you comfort and heal your child, Marilyn, from both the physical pain from her injuries and the emotional trauma inflicted by the loss of her loved one. Help her to accept your plan and recognize that Joe is with you in your Kingdom. Dear Father God, strengthen us and help us to get our dear friend on the road to recovery. In Jesus' name we pray, amen."

Marilyn stared at the ceiling and felt more alone than she had ever felt before. Her thoughts drifted back to when she and Joe had first met at the barbeque at Pete and Beth's home. And the first date at the coffee shop, where they talked about their faith and she realized this man would be more than just a friend. She reached over for a tissue to dry her eyes and then recalled the difficult battle with cancer that Joe had fought and won. His illness had been a difficult time for them, but it had convinced her that this was the man she wanted to spend her life with.

The news about Joe's death was the worst thing she could imagine. Their marriage plans and their future, now nothing but a memory. As tears rolled off her cheeks on to the pillow she closed her eyes and looked into the darkness. *Why, God, why? Is this your plan for me, that I should be alone?* And then she remembered . . . the dream. She had seen Joe, somewhere, heard him, "I love you, Marilyn, goodbye." *Was that supposed to comfort me, Lord? Was this the bone you threw me? I thought you were a loving God, a Shepherd who took care of his flock. You stole from me; you took the best thing that ever happened to me. Why? What good was faith . . . why pray to a God who doesn't listen? Why even try . . .*

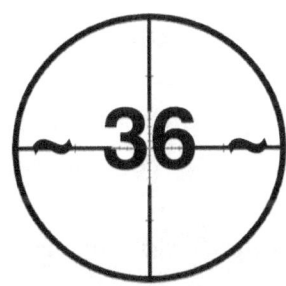

Hardcore spotted the dealer's car parked in its normal spot beneath the EL tracks. Although all the windows were up, he could hear the loud music coming from it. He was anxious to get the money and dope promised him after the break-in. When he got them, he was finished with this fool. Approaching the passenger side door he tried the handle—locked. Banging on the window, he looked at the dealer who appeared to be nodding off. *Man, he's baked.*

He walked around to the driver's side, took out his knife, and banged on the glass with its handle. Stirring, the dealer turned to look toward the noise and stared directly at Hardcore. He rolled down the window, "Dude, whaddup?"

"Open the door, man."

"Sure."

Hardcore went over to the passenger side and got in. He reached over and turned down the music. The car reeked of dope; Hardcore saw a crack pipe lying between the seats. "I'm here for my money, dude, and my two."

"Hey, man, chill. I got your stash, it's right under your seat."

Hardcore reached underneath and found a long crumpled foil package. He opened it and saw two joints that had been soaked in PCP. He re-wrapped the package and put it in his pocket. "Cool. Now, just give me my cut.—I got shit to do that don't involve you."

The dealer sat a little straighter. "What's your hurry, Dog? Let's get high."

"I ain't got time for that right now I just want my money."

The dealer reached into his coat pocket and removed a small plastic bag. He tried to open it and take out the rock that was inside, but he was too stoned and fumbled the effort. "Hey, man, help me out here . . . let's fire one up."

Hardcore was getting impatient. "I told ya, dude, just give me my money so I can get goin'."

"You ain't got time for yer homie?"

Hardcore banged his fist on the dash. "Cut the crap! Where's my dough?"

"Easy, Dog. No need for violence. I had a little prob gettin' rid o' some of the stuff. Things is hot now . . . my boy got talked to by 5-0, but don't worry, he ain't gonna dime nobody out—he's solid."

I knew I shouldn't of trusted this mope.

"So when am I gonna get the money?"

The dealer's head was bobbing again. "Soon, Bro, soon."

Hardcore was not in the mood for games and couldn't be sure if either this crackhead or his friend at the store might finger him. He knew what he had to do. He reached over and took the packet with the crack from the dealer's hand. "All right, let's get high." He took the rock out and handed it to the man and then retrieved the crack pipe.

While the dealer was engaged in lighting the pipe, Hardcore surreptitiously reached into his jacket and slowly withdrew his knife. Unfolding the six-inch serrated blade with one hand, something he'd practiced hundreds of times, he got a firm grasp on it. With his other hand, he reached forward, and turning up the music, he looked at the dealer. "You ready, dude?"

"I'm trippin', homie." Holding the pipe in his mouth, he held the lighter beneath the bowl, moving it slowly back and forth while inhaling. He never saw the knife, which entered his throat just below his Adam's apple, penetrating the full length of the blade. Hardcore was a good student; the military had taught him well about the fine art of killing. He twisted the blade several times, and in seconds, the dealer's head flopped forward like a ragdoll.

Quickly looking around to see if anyone was nearby, Hardcore withdrew the blade, wiped the blood on the dealer's coat, and then went through the man's pockets. A few hundred dollars and several more rocks were all he found. He looked in the glove box and under the seats and came up with a dime bag of weed. Not enough to justify killing the man, but what he just did was all about getting rid of a threat, not about killing for money and drugs. He never should have hooked up with this loser in the first place. Now he wouldn't have to worry about him talkin' to the cops.

Hardcore shoved the quite dead body up against the door, grabbed the dealer's hat, and placed it over his face so that it appeared he was taking a nap. He switched off the radio and quickly glanced around before stepping out of the car. Walking casually back to his own vehicle, he got back in and started the engine. Hopefully, his boy at the store did just as he promised — turned off the cameras. If not, Hardcore was prepared to get rid of him as well. *Nobody better mess with me.* But he couldn't be sure, so he had to get rid of the van. He still had a score to settle with the cops, but first it was time to enjoy the fruits of his labor.

"Let's get you untethered," said the doctor as he began to remove the lines and monitors that crisscrossed Marilyn's body. "Then I want you to sit up and eat that snack," he said pointing to the tray the nurse had placed on her table. "The quicker we get you back on solid food, the sooner you can leave." He finished taking all of the lines out, save one. "We'll leave this one so we can monitor your heart and blood pressure, but you can remove it yourself when you get up, which I want you to do often. You need to be on your feet, moving around." The doctor took the bed control and raised the back to an upright position.

"Whoa, I'm feeling a little lightheaded," she said, as she sat up for the first time in a week.

"That's normal. You've been lying down for so long." The nurse brought the bed table over with a serving of Jello, crackers, and water. "I want you to eat this and drink the entire glass of water so we can get your digestive system working normally again. After you've finished, the nurse will take you for a short walk down the hall. Don't be surprised if you feel lightheaded once again, and your legs will probably feel weak. The muscles have begun to atrophy slightly because of inactivity."

"All that work in the gym, down the drain," Marilyn said, as she pulled the covers aside and looked at her legs.

"Don't worry. Once you're up and about, the muscle tone will quickly return."

"I hope so."

The doctor made a notation on her chart. "The nurse will be back to take you for your walk. In the meantime, I'd like you to try and finish your snack."

"Fine."

The nurse and doctor left the room. Marilyn took the first bite of Jell-O, swirled it around in her mouth, and was surprised at how satisfying the taste and texture was. She took a drink of water, put the glass down, then picked it up, and finished the rest. It felt good to be in control of her body again. After taking several more spoonfuls of the Jell-O, she thought about her situation. Why had this tragedy happened, and how? Her plans were finally about to come to fruition, and then in an instant, they had been destroyed. Joe, the man she loved and wanted to spend her life with gone.

Closing her eyes, she thought about their life together, the wonderful times. Even when they battled his cancer, they did it together. How close they had become when they were unsure about how much time they might have if the battle was lost. She recalled their joy when Joe's doctor pronounced him cancer free. They had finally set the wedding date and had begun to make plans in earnest for their big day. She recalled her anticipation of their life together as husband and wife, finally being with him completely. *Why, Lord, why? I never got to say good-bye.*

Marilyn took the remote in her hand and lowered the hospital bed. Pulling the sheet over her head, she turned on her side, away from the door, wanting to shut out the world around her. She felt alone; she felt abandoned. A solitary tear splashed on her pillow like a wave crashing on the shore of a remote beach. *How could you, Father, how could you?* Hearing the annoying sound of the television, she pulled the sheet off her head, reached for the remote, and switched off the power to the intruder in her space. As she was about to pull the cover over herself again, she spotted the Bible on the bedside table. She took a deep breath and then swept the book on to the floor. *Lies . . . all lies.*

Father Ed had been driving south on I-95 a little more than an hour when he entered the Richmond, Virginia area. It was the middle of the night, and he was drowsy. Glancing at the gas gauge, he saw the needle creeping toward empty. He had passed a sign indicating a gas station at the next exit, so he eased on to the ramp and spotted the beckoning sign down the block. He pulled next to the pump, filled the tank, and then went to the store to pay. It was late; the door to the station was locked but bore a sign with an arrow pointing to a small sliding window off to the side. Ed walked up to the window and saw a man slumped on the counter. He tried opening the slider, but it was also locked. Taking his keys from his pocket, he tapped on the glass. After several attempts to arouse the attendant, the man raised his head and looked in Ed's direction. He slowly stood and walked over.

"Yeah . . ."

"I got gas."

Wiping his eyes, the man looked at his electronic register. "Twenty bucks."

Ed took a bill from his pocket and passed it through the window. "Thanks. Hey, can you recommend a cheap hotel around here?"

The man took Ed's money and placed it in the register. "You tryin' to be funny? Do I look like some kinda dumb redneck?"

"What?"

"Look behind you, Slick. There's a friggin' hotel right there."

Turning around Ed saw a sign: Richmond Arms Hotel. It was a one-story drive-in, L-shaped, with what looked to be about a dozen rooms. "Is it safe?"

The attendant sneered. "You got your gas, now get outta my face." He slammed the window shut and went back to the counter, spread his arms out in front of himself, and resumed his prior position. *Welcome to Richmond.*

Tired, and once again finding himself in a place he knew nothing about, Ed got back in his car and drove across the street to the hotel. Pulling up to the office, he saw a sign flashing: No Vacancy, yet he saw only two other cars parked in the lot. As long as he was here, he decided to try his luck and see if there was a room available. He pulled open the screen door and tried the door knob—locked. Peering inside he saw a counter that ran the length of the office, but no one was visible so he pounded on the door. A moment later an elderly woman's face popped up like a jack-in-the-box, just above the chest-high counter. She took Ed's inventory and then pressed a button. When he heard the lock buzz, he pushed the door inward. Stepping inside, he said, "Hi. I saw the

No Vacancy sign but thought I'd ask anyway. Do you have any rooms available?"

"Oh, that," said the woman as she pulled out a file box from a cubby hole behind the counter, "it don't work. You stayin' for more than a hour?"   Her best days were obviously behind her, much like the hotel in which she worked. Her thinning, gray hair, short and worn in the fashion of a man's, matched her dull and lifeless eyes. They had obviously seen too much of life's underbelly and had taken on the color of the attitude of the person looking through them. As she bent over to sort through the index cards, her oversize, shapeless house dress gaped open, presenting Ed with a view of her saggy breasts, which hung like two giant squash. Ed turned away and looked around the office.

The décor was stark. Ed saw easy chairs, one which had its cushion missing and each appearing to have been re-upholstered one too many times, and a coffee table with a chrome ashtray that was bent and dented and containing the burnt remains of countless numbers of cigarettes. Off to one side stood a vending machine with coffee and hot chocolate as the only two selections, both of which were negated by the handwritten piece of paper taped to the front: Out Of Order. A large sun-bleached photo of the Virginia State Capitol building hung on the wall between two windows, both decorated in early American burglar bars. A door leading behind the counter also bore a sign: No public toilet—use your own. In the far corner, sleeping on the missing chair cushion was an aged beagle, whose breath Ed could smell from across the room.

"Ahh, here ya go. I got a end unit for ya, mister; it's non-smoking. Had to look through the availables cuz some o' the plumbing don't work good in the rooms. This one's pretty nice; got a big double bed, a clock radio, and a brand new lock on the door. Damn vagrants like to force 'em open when it gets real cold." She handed him an old ledger, the outside edges yellowed with age, but it seemed more appropriate for financial records than registering guests. "Just fill in your name and address under the last one," she said.

Ed turned the old hardcover book around and read the name of the last guest: John Smith. As he wrote in his information, he glanced further up the page to discover there appeared to be a huge Smith family presence in the Richmond area. He counted the Smith name on eight separate dates. He finished writing and then turned the ledger back toward the woman who gazed at the entry.

"Ed Michaels, huh? Sounds like that might be your real name. Don't get much o' that around here. You stayin' one night or what?"

"Let's make it for one night. How much do I owe you?"

The woman smiled, revealing a crooked set of teeth, some of which were missing. The remaining ones matched the aging pages in the register. "Well, the rate is nineteen ninety-nine a day, but if you want to stay a week I'll jist charge a flat hunnerd dollars."

Although Ed had yet to see the room, he knew one night here would be enough of a challenge for him. No sense enduring more than that. "One night will be fine." He handed the woman a twenty dollar bill.

"Need a receipt?"

"Uh, no, but thanks."

"Okay." She pulled out the drawer beneath the cubby hole and grabbed a key. "Here ya go. Suite number six, all the way at the end."

Ed took the key from her.

"Ya got much luggage?"

"Why?"

"Well, ya know, yer all the way at the end; better bring it in yer room so nobody steals it from yer car."

Ed shook his head. "So you're telling me it's not safe around here?"

"Not sayin' that, but ya know it's nighttime an' all. Tell ya what, leave yer car parked here by the office, and I'll watch it fer ya."

"Okay," he said turning to walk out of the office.

"Five bucks."

"What?"

"Five bucks. I'll watch yer car all night fer five bucks."

Surprised, Ed answered. "You're going to charge me five dollars just to look out the window at my car?"

"Hey, I'm doin' ya a favor. Ya want yer car safe er not? Scuse me . . ." The woman leaned over to the side and spit into the waste basket. "Stopped smokin' a couple years back but still gotta have that neckatine. " She refocused on the business at hand. "C'mon, what's five bucks to a guy like you? Ya know, I gotta eat too. This ain't no Holiday Inn."

Shoulders sagging, Ed reached into his pocket and found a five dollar bill. "Right. Here you go, thanks." Ed waited at the door for the buzzer, then walked to his car, and removed one piece of luggage. He carried it to the last unit of the L, which was situated in the darkest corner of the property. The overhead light had only the filament and screw base visible; light was not an option in the parking lot of the Richmond Arms Hotel.

He inserted the key and opened the door. A strong stale smoke smell assaulted him as soon as he entered the room. Although it was late November, a thin sunflower design bedspread covered the bed. It did little to disguise the fact that the old mattress was as lumpy as a bowl of mashed potatoes. He dropped his suitcase on top of it and surveyed the rest of the room. A rickety night stand held an old wooden lamp in the shape of a Civil War musket. *Must be a tribute to the former Confederate Capitol.* The highly vaunted clock radio was a blue light special with numbers so dim they could have been interpreted to read any time one wished it to be. Ed walked into the bathroom. At first glance he thought the top of the vanity was some type of contemporary art design, until he switched on the forty-watt bulb. A platoon of cockroaches sprinted back to their encampments, leaving what Ed realized was simply hundreds of scars left from cigarettes mindlessly left to burn themselves out in this non-smoking room. He glanced at the shower; the tile around the tub had not been cleaned or grouted since Grant took Richmond.

Sighing, Ed decided not to unpack or even clean up. Instead he simply moved his suitcase and collapsed, fully clothed, on top of the bed. In an instant he was asleep. Sleep was the only thing that had yet to betray him; the only thing he looked forward to each day.

"Is that it?"

"Yeah," said McKinnon. "It's the one with the big front porch and the white rocker."

Beckham eased the unmarked state police vehicle to the curb of the heavily treed avenue lined with sixty-year-old brick bungalows. "I'm gonna call it in before we get out." He picked up the mike from the dash and keyed it. "Squad, 6203 out at 5623 S. Mozart, in the city."

"10-4, 6203. Got you 10-7 on the southwest side."

Harry glared at his new partner and then inserted a fresh toothpick.

"What?" The detective asked Harry, noticing his stare.

"I don't use the radio unless I need help; I don't like anybody to know my business."

"What if you get in a jam and no one knows where you are?" Beckham asked, replacing the mike and shutting off the car.

Harry's toothpick began to move up and down. "I make sure that doesn't happen."

Beckham rolled his eyes. "Whatever." This new partnership was not what he'd envisioned. Since teaming up with McKinnon on the task force, Beckham had to pry every bit of information from him. Today they were following up on a lead provided by the tip hot line, and Beckham had no idea of how to interact with his partner. "Harry, how do you want to work this?"

Harry opened the car door. "I'll do all the talkin'. When we get inside, you take a quick look around, see if this guy's got any guns lying around or if there's anyone else in the house. I'll take care of makin' sure he's not gonna hurt us."

The team walked up the front steps. Harry pulled open the flimsy storm door and pounded on the heavy wooden door.

"Might be at work," Beckham offered.

"Or still in the sack," Harry said, as he pounded on the door again. The caller said this guy's a heavy drinker. Those types don't get up early to go to work." Harry banged more heavily this time.

Hands appeared through the slats of the blinds at a window next to the door, pulling them apart and exposing a man's face. Beckham flashed his police credentials up against the window pane. "Police. We need to speak with you."

The hands disappeared, and the blinds returning to their closed position. A few seconds later the door opened and a short, stocky man dressed in boxer shorts and a tank top stood before them, rubbing his eyes. His black hair was coarse and unruly, and thick tufts of body hair stuck out on his arms and chest, much like a cave man. "What's up?"

Beckham once again displayed his credentials to the man. "Are you Billy Logan?"

"Yeah . . . why?"

Harry pushed the front door open the rest of the way and then shoved the man in the chest, forcing him through the short front hallway and into the living room. "You alone?"

"Hey, what's all this about?" The man was no longer groggy and began to protest. Although a head shorter than McKinnon, the man was powerfully built and now stood his ground. "What the hell do you want?"

"Shut up! Beckham, take a look around." Harry stared down at the man. "I asked if you're alone?"

"Yeah . . . why?"

A minute later Beckham walked back into the living room. "It's clear."

"Someone gave us information you've been runnin' your mouth about what a good shot you are, said you been braggin' about bein' able to take out a cop from two hundred yards."

"Do you have any rifles in the house?" Beckham asked.

Harry quickly glared at his partner and then re-focused on the man in front of him. Pulling the toothpick from his mouth, he pointed it at the man's face. "What do you know about the three cops who've been murdered?"

His eyes opening wide as silver dollars, the man quickly replied. "What? I don't know anything about no cops bein' murdered. You gotta be kiddin.' I work every day, man, down at the mills at Cal Steel. I work nights, been there fifteen years."

"We got information you think you're some kinda hot-shit sniper, that you've been talkin' trash about how the cops that were killed was an easy shot, that you coulda taken them out from twice as far."

The man thought for a moment. "Oh, hell, man, that's just booze talk. I stop most nights after work for a few cold ones with the boys. We get to talkin' and pretty soon we start braggin' about shit that don't even make sense."

"I don't believe you," said Harry, as he pushed the man down on the couch. "You got a rifle in here?"

The man bounced up from the couch. "Hey!"

Harry shoved him back down. "Stay put, asshole."

As Harry towered over him, the man looked up and decided the couch was safer than standing. "You got this whole thing blown outta proportion. Yeah, I was runnin' my mouth about the cop killings, said I coulda taken those shots from farther away. I used to be a sniper in the Corps years ago, was pretty good too, but I ain't had a rifle in my hands since I got out. I'm tellin' ya, it's all me just bullshittin' with the guys from work."

"Why would someone want to accuse you?" Beckham asked.

Harry's head whipped around instantly as Beckham posed the question. "Damnit, shut up!" He glared back down at the man on the couch. "You care if we look around, see if you have any guns in here?"

"Yeah, I care. You got no warrant to even be in here talkin' to me. I ain't got nuthin to hide, but, hell, you can't come bargin' in here."

Harry grabbed his toothpick and snapped it in half, throwing the pieces at the man. "Let me explain something to you, Shithead. I'm lookin' for a killer, and right now somebody dropped a dime on your ass. I gotta make sure you're not the one I'm lookin' for. Now, we can either do this my way or yours, but either way we're gonna do it. My partner here will babysit you while I look around. If I don't find anything, we'll leave, and you'll never hear from us again. If you want to continue giving me a bunch of crap, I'll make your life so miserable you'll wish you'd never met me. I'll have a squad car on your tail, and I'll catch you dirty somehow, some way. Now, it's your call. Do I have a look around or not?"

The man considered the question for a moment. "Go ahead, but you won't find nuthin."

"Where're your car keys?"

"For what?"

"I need to check your car too."

"Damn." The man was about to get up, but Harry was quick to respond.

"Stay put; just tell me where they are."

"On the kitchen table," the man said with a sigh. "Car's in the garage, the door's unlocked."

Without a word, Harry began to look through each room in the house and eventually went out to the garage to search it and the car. While he was busy doing that, the man regained some of his composure and asked Beckham, "What's with that guy? Is he always like that?"

I'm wondering the same thing. "He's wound a little tight. Try to understand, his friend was one of the officers who was murdered. He's not usually like this." *I hope . . .*

"I guess I can kinda understand that, but man, he's way over the top."

"If you're being honest with us we'll be out of your hair and not bother you again."

A while later, Harry walked back into the living room. "Okay, I didn't find anything. For your sake, I hope you're not bulljivin' us. You don't want to see me mad." Harry moved toward the door to leave.

Beckham shook the man's hand as he remained seated on the couch. "Sorry to bother you, sir. If you do hear anything about the murders, don't hesitate to call me." He handed the man his business card and followed Harry out the door. Getting into the car, Beckham slammed his door shut. "What the hell was that all about?"

"Let me tell you something," said Harry, as he retrieved a fresh toothpick from his jacket pocket. "When I tell you I'll do the talking,' I mean it. Don't interrupt me. I scare the shit outta people; that's how I get them to cooperate and tell me things they wouldn't normally tell other cops. You wanna baby people, get a job at a daycare."

Beckham rubbed his hand over his mouth and was about to say something, but then thought better. He put the key in the ignition, started the car, and grabbed the mike. "Squad, 6203 is 10-8."

"Roger, 6203."

Beckham pulled away from the curb and began the drive back to police headquarters. *If I work much longer with this guy, I'll either be fired, indicted, or both.*

"That was a great breakfast, Babe." Pete finished his scrambled eggs, picked his plate up, and walked it over to the sink.

Beth smiled as she looked up from her own breakfast which she had yet to start on. She shifted Pete, Jr. around to begin to burp him after his bottle. "I'm glad to you enjoyed it. Pete . . .?"

He stopped at the counter and looked at her. "What?"

"It's good to have *us* back again."

Walking over to where she sat with the baby, Pete knelt on one knee. "I know. How did we let ourselves fall into that trap, honey? How is it that we let pride get in the way of our relationship?"

Patting her son's back, she replied. "I think we got too comfortable and let things distract us from what's really important."

Pete leaned in and kissed them both. "You're right, as always. You two, I mean, you three," he said, as he rubbed her belly, "are what mean the most to me. I can't let the job interfere with my duties here at home. I promise you I'll do my best not to ignore you; I love you."

"I know you do, it's what keeps me going." She stood with the baby and walked over to the playpen where she laid him down. "Are you going to stop by the hospital to visit Marilyn before you go into the office?"

"Yeah, she needs all the support we can give her until she gets back on her feet. Last time we left her, she was really depressed. I don't know how long it will take her to recover from Joe's death, but she's going to need help and plenty of support."

Beth walked over to the counter and poured herself a cup of coffee and then went back to the table to start on her breakfast. "I suspect it will be a long time. Her physical health will heal before her mental health. I can't imagine what she's going through right now."

Picking up his gear bag, Pete walked over to his wife and bent down to kiss her goodbye. "She's a strong woman. She wouldn't have accomplished all that she has if she wasn't a fighter. But you're right, this challenge is like nothing she's ever had to face. I'm afraid for her." He headed toward the garage door. "I'll call you later."

"Thanks, Honey. Be careful."

Opening the door, he looked over his shoulder. "I love you, Beth."

"I love you more, Sweetheart."

The night had been mostly sleepless for Marilyn. Images of Joe and what could have been flashed in and out of her mind all night. She switched on the TV with the bed remote and watched as the news readers recited a litany of crimes that had occurred overnight. ". . . and on the South Side, a man was murdered as he sat in his car under the L tracks. Police suspect robbery may have been the motive." *More like a drug deal*, thought Marilyn. *Nothing good ever happens under the tracks.* The weather segment was about to begin when the doctor walked into her room.

"Good morning, how are you feeling today?"

She pressed the button on her remote to raise the bed higher. "I can't sleep in this place; I want to go home."

Removing the bandages on her head, the doctor checked the incision. "Is that some kind of not so subtle signal you're trying to send me?"

"We call that a clue in my business, Doc. Seriously, I need to get out of here."

He studied her wound for a moment and then checked her chart for vitals and blood results. "I think that might be possible, Detective. How would you like it if I scheduled you for discharge this afternoon?"

"Doc, I would absolutely love it."

"I guess you do," he replied. "That's the first smile I've seen on your face since you got here."

He made a notation in her file, then closed it, and set it on the end of the bed. "Just so you know, Detective, it doesn't mean you can automatically go back on full duty. You still need to mend another three to four weeks before I can fully release you to resume your normal routine. And I'll want you to come in for a final examination before I sign off on full duty. Remember, you were hit by a car. That's pretty serious stuff."

"I know, Doc. I lost that battle, but I can heal much quicker at home than I can here."

"And so you shall. I've notated in your chart that you are to be discharged after three this afternoon, so start making some calls to have someone pick you up."

"Thanks, Doc."

Moving toward the door, he had to sidestep as Pete entered the room. "Now that was quick. I didn't even see you pick up the phone," the doctor joked.

"Did I miss something?" Pete asked, a quizzical look on his face.

"She'll explain," said the doctor as he walked out.

Moving to her bed, Pete bent over and took her hand. "How are you, Partner?"

"Good enough to get out of here, according to the doctor."

"You're kidding."

"Pete, can you come by this afternoon and take me home?"

"Of course, we were just . . ."

She stared at him, expressionless. "Just you, not your partner."

"Sure, Bens, I'd love to take you home." He paused. "Listen, I know you've been through a lot lately. Everyone's surprised at how well you're holding up."

Glaring at him, she blurted, "Are they surprised? You and

everyone else, you think I'm some kind of super woman that this will just eventually pass and not have a lasting effect on me? Don't you realize what I've lost, that my life is over?"

Sitting down on the side of the bed, Pete tried to reason with her. "Bens, wait . . ."

She snatched her hand from his. "Wait for what? We're not even partners anymore, you've moved on."

"No, you're wrong; it's just temporary until you're well enough to come back. I'm not looking for a new partner; I've already got the best one I could ever hope for."

"Whatever. It didn't take you very long to team up with someone new."

Pete chewed on the inside of his cheek for a moment before responding. "Listen, Bens, your first job is to get well. When you're released for full duty, it will be you and me again, just like before. I'm praying for you, we're all praying for you."

She pulled the covers up to her chin. "I don't need your prayers or anyone else's. They're just words, they don't mean anything."

Pete's eyes grew wide, surprised at what he was hearing. "Bens, please, you don't mean that."

"Don't tell me what I mean, Pete. What good have all of my prayers been? Did they save Joe?"

Running his hand through his hair, he said, "Sometimes bad things happen . . ."

She cut him off. "Spare me. Will you come by at three to take me home or not?"

"Uh. . . yeah, sure."

"Good. I'll see you then. Now, I need a nap, I'll see you later. Thanks." She turned so her back was to him."

He stood. "Okay, see you this afternoon." He turned, walked out, and made his way down the hall to the bank of elevators. Pressing the down button, he leaned against the wall trying to analyze what had just happened. Joe was gone, and he hardly recognized Marilyn.

Walking into Homicide, Pete spotted Meka in their assigned cubicle. She saw him at the same time and waved. Pete made his way over and set his coffee on the desk. "Morning, Meka."

"Good morning, Pete. How are you today?"

"I'm still trying to decide."

"Did you stop by the hospital to see Marilyn?"

He rubbed his chin, "Yes. In fact, she's being discharged today."

"Fantastic! She is one tough lady."   Meka looked at him. "What's wrong, you don't look very pleased about it?"

"I'm not . . . I mean, I am, but it's her attitude that has me worried."

"What do you mean?"

He sat down in his desk chair, collapsing in the seat as if he would welcome having the chair swallow him up. "She's down in the dumps; there's no spark in her. She's always been so bubbly, so energetic."

"Pete, she just lost the man she was engaged to, and on top of that, she was the victim of a hit and run. What do you expect?"

He sipped his coffee. "I know . . . I know. But, it's more than that. She's always been so grounded in faith. Heck, we used to pray together in the car. This morning, when I mentioned that lots of people were praying for her, she didn't even want to hear it, said it was all just words, that prayer didn't work. Meka, I've never heard her talk like that."

She shook her head. "She's in a bad way, all right. Sounds like she thinks God has given up on her. That's not going to help her get well, nor do much for her self-esteem and confidence."

Leaning back in his chair, Pete stared up at the ceiling. "I'm scared for her—no parents or a sibling to comfort her. She's alone in that apartment."

Meka stared. "Pete, you don't think she'd . . . um . . . try to harm herself?"

He frowned. "You mean suicide?"

"Well, yes."

"I can't imagine she'd ever contemplate that. I mean, we're Catholics."

She smiled. "Pete, religion is a vehicle by which we worship. It helps people to be a part of a group that praises and honors God. But when times are bad, when one's faith is tested, the laws and customs of any religion are the least of the person's concerns. Going to church doesn't make one spiritual; it's one's own personal relationship with God that matters most. When you have the feeling that the relationship is no longer there, it's easy for dark thoughts to blot out your reasoning."

"That's just it; I really thought she was close with Him. Both she and Joe were strong in their faith."

Meka stood up to leave. "I hope you're right because this is truly a test for her. It's easy to believe when times are good; the real challenge is to believe in the Lord when your world is upside down." She continued to walk out. "Hey, I have to get a file. We've got some leads from the tip line to run down today."

"Okay. By the way, Marilyn asked me to take her home from the hospital. I have to be there at three. Can you handle it alone this afternoon?"

"Sure. There's a couple things we need to look at together this morning, and I also have a call in to Agent Toppe to set up a meet. Are you still up for a run?"

He nodded. "Definitely, anything to take my mind off Marilyn."

"Okay, be back in a few."

He watched her disappear down the hall and then leaned back

in his chair again, his hands clasped behind his head. Lost in thought, he lurched forward when his desk phone rang. "Detective Shannon."

"Pete, Sgt. Castro. How are you?"

"Hey, Sarge. We're up to our neck in alligators here, but it's good to hear your voice."

"Likewise. I know you and Benson are assigned to the sniper case. How is Marilyn doing?"

"Actually, she's going home today."

"Great. We were afraid she was so banged up she'd be laid up for a long time."

"She's doing pretty well, physically, but mentally, she's got a long way to go." Pete said. "She's heartbroken about Joe's murder. Sarge, I've never seen her so low. I'm worried."

"Can't say I wouldn't feel the same if I was in her shoes. I know you both are strong believers, but given all that's happened to her, you might consider putting in a call to the chaplain."

Pete switched the phone to his other ear. "That's a good idea, I'll do that."

"Yeah, Reverend Dean has seen it all. If anyone can get her through this, it's Dean."

"I hope you're right, Sarge."

"Pete, the reason I called is I got a call from a friend of mine. He's a businessman, operates a service that cleans office buildings. Anyway, he's a regular each morning at a diner on the south side—likes to eat breakfast there and read the paper. Apparently there's some guy who comes in for coffee every once in a while, who according to my friend, is kind of shady."

"In what way, Sarge?"

"I guess he's made some strange remarks about cops getting killed, stuff like that. It could be just this guy blowin' smoke, but I thought I'd let you know."

"Thanks."

"I'll send you all the info in an email."

Pete made a mental note to be sure and look for the missive. "I'll put that on our list of things to do today. Our tip line has generated a ton of leads."

"Good," said Castro. "Best of luck. Tell Benson I said hi."

"I will."

Pete was about to hang up when he heard Castro say, "Oh, Pete, I forgot to tell you — this guy's supposedly an out of work vet, used to be in the Army."

There was silence on the other end of the line. "Pete . . . did you hear me?"

"Uh . . . yeah, Sarge. We'll get on it."

Hanging up the phone, he stared ahead at the cubicle wall. The *Army keeps popping up in this puzzle.*

~38~

"Damn." Hardcore looked at the sleeve of his jacket as he took it off. The dealer's blood had stained it, making it obvious to him or anyone else that it was exactly what it appeared to be. *Gettin' too cold to wear it now anyway.* He tossed it in the corner of his room. Reaching in his pocket, he pulled out a wad of cash he had taken during the robbery. Today he'd have to pay Mrs. Schiller the monthly rent. Thanks to his late dealer, that wouldn't be a problem. He'd be set for a while, at least until he found a job or, better yet, another loser like the dealer.

Stoners were an easy mark since most times they hardly knew where they were, much less what was happening around them. And to his surprise, killing the dealer came easy and provided a quick solution to possible problems in the future. Now he didn't have to worry about gettin' ratted out to the cops. He dwelled on his bloody handiwork for a moment, pondering the impact it might have. Other than the possibility of being caught, killing people seemed to have no downside. The process was challenging and gave him a sense of purpose.

Walking down the stairs to the first floor of the two-flat, he looked out the front door. "Crap," he muttered. "More snow." He banged hard on the solid cherry wood door to Mrs. Schiller's apartment. When he first moved in, it seemed it took forever, waiting for her to answer her door after he rang the bell. He found out later that she was hard of hearing, particularly, the door bell. And since her husband died several years ago, she was reluctant to

answer her front door at all. Hardcore had arranged for a signal
between them, two knocks, pause, then three more. It worked.

Mrs. Schiller opened the door slowly at first, just a crack, to
ensure it was her boarder, then fully to allow him to enter. "Good
morning, Steven. Please come in."

Hardcore walked past her into the living room. Shutting the
door, the woman shuffled silently over to her chair while leaning
on her cane. After years of use, her favorite chair bore the imprint
of her tired bottom, thereby allowing a custom fit. On the table
next to her were her daily accouterments: the Bible, several bottles
of pills, an AM radio, a water glass, and a framed picture of her
and her husband, Frank, taken on their wedding day over fifty
years ago. She set her cane aside and looked at Hardcore.

"I came to pay you the rent for November." Pulling the cash
from his pocket, he counted the amount out loud and handed it to
her. She took it and set it on the table.

"Thank you, Son."

"Okay." He looked around the room which always appeared
to be frozen in time. It seemed nothing had changed in the year he
had lived here. Each time he visited her, everything was exactly in
the same place as before. Although there was an old console TV
along one wall, he had never seen it turned on. Instead, the radio
always played, the volume set just high enough to drown out the
deafening silence.

"Well, I guess I'll be going, unless you need me for anything."
He turned to leave.

"Steven . . ."

"Yeah."

"I'm thinking I'd like to get rid of our car. I haven't driven it in
over a year. I used to go out to the garage every so often to start it,
but now even that has become too much for me. Do you know
anyone who would like to buy it?"

He thought for a moment. He'd seen the car in the garage one day when he'd carried some storage boxes out there for her. It was a black Cadillac Coupe Deville, in mint condition. *This might be the answer to my problem.*

"What year is that car?"

She answered quickly. "Mr. Schiller and I bought it brand new in 2006—paid cash for it. Frank always wanted to own a Cadillac, a black one, said it made us look important. The only time we used it was to go to a restaurant or to church. The sad thing is he died a year later so we barely got to enjoy it. I never drove it while he was alive; he always said a husband was supposed to chauffer his wife around. A few weeks after he passed, I tried to pull it out of the garage to go to the store, but I just can't turn my head around that well to see behind me. For a while I had a neighbor who used to take it shopping for me. I'd give her a long list of things to get. That way I didn't have to do any shopping myself."

Hardcore rocked back and forth on his feet as he listened to the woman explain about the car. "What happened; why'd she stop?"

"She died."

"Oh."

"So if you could ask around for me, see if anyone might be interested. I'd be grateful." She continued. "It would be to your advantage too. You could pull your van in the garage and keep it out of the weather."

Keep it outta the weather, hell. I can hide it from the cops. "Ya know, Mrs. Schiller, my van is pretty much shot. I been lookin' for another car. What are ya askin'?"

Taking a sip from the glass of water on the table next to her, she thought about it. "Well, I don't really know much about prices of cars. I don't even know what my Frank paid for it when we bought it. But since it's for you, why don't you tell me what a fair price would be? I know you're out of work and don't have a lot of money. I'd be willing to work something out so you could pay me a little every month."

This is too easy. Hardcore crinkled up his nose and pursed his lips, trying to appear as victim-like as possible. "You're right. I can't seem to land a job, but I definitely need a car, even if it is kinda old. I mean, it's been sittin' there for so long . . . might even be somethin' wrong with the engine."

The old woman raised one hand toward him. "Oh, I don't want you to buy someone else's troubles. You're right; maybe it has been sitting too long." She paused. "Tell you what, why don't you take it to a mechanic and have it checked out? Make sure everything's working properly, and I'll pay for the checkup."

Smiling, he answered. "Good idea. Gimme the keys, and I'll take it to one right now. If he tells me it's in good condition, I'd like to buy it."

Mrs. Schiller's face beamed as she grabbed her cane and got up from her chair. She walked to the kitchen and came back several minutes later with a set of keys and some cash. "Here you go, and the garage door key is on the same key ring as well. Mr. Schiller had a remote door opener installed. We were both too weak to open it ourselves. Just push the button on the ceiling of the car, and the door opens automatically."

Hardcore took the keys. "Thanks. I'll be back later." He moved to leave as she sat back down in her chair. As he closed the door after himself, she said, "Good luck, Steven." The old woman imagined he was the son she and her husband never had, but all Hardcore could think about was the money that had instantly appeared.

The wind at the Adler Planetarium stung exposed skin like a whip. It came from seemingly all directions as it punished the tiny peninsula of land that jutted out into Lake Michigan. What little snow there was had been blown off into the icy water, leaving only frozen tundra covered with dormant brown-colored grass. Pete and Meka sat warm and toasty in the front seat of their Bureau car, waiting for FBI Special Agent Jim Toppe to arrive.

"You sure he'll want to run in this cold?"

"Oh, yeah. Toppe doesn't let a little thing like cold weather stop him from getting his run in." Meka adjusted the laces on her running shoes. "Did you take Benson home from the hospital this afternoon?"

"Yeah," replied Pete, his shoulders sagging at the mention of her name. "I tried to get her to open up, but other than hello and goodbye she had nothing else to say."

"She's in a bad way. What did you expect?"

"I understand that, Meka, but it's just so unlike her."

"Give it some time, Pete. If she's the woman you say she is she'll come around."

Tap, tap, tap. Startled, Pete simultaneously reached under his seat for his pistol while looking through the window. A lone, skinny figure stood just to the rear of his door, jogging in place.

"That's Toppe," said Meka.

"Man, he scared the life out of me."

Meka opened her car door and got out. "Hi, ready for a run?"

"Yeah. Let's get going, the longer we stand around, the colder we'll get."

Pete opened his door and got out, extending his hand to the runner. "Pete Shannon; nice to meet you." The two shook gloved hands. "Where are we headed?"

"Good to meet you, too," Toppe answered, while continuing his perpetual motion. "I have a lot of respect for Chicago cops. You guys are on the front lines 24/7." Toppe pulled his hat down over his ears, protecting them from the icy wind blowing in from the lake. "Let's head up toward North Avenue, okay?"

"Sure. Ready, Meka?"

She pulled on her mittens. "Yep, let's go."

Pete locked the car with his remote and the trio set out along the jogging path that parallels the water. Chicago's magnificent lakefront was a legacy to the original Mayor Daley. The entire stretch of shoreline within the city limits was zoned for parks and recreation only; no industry was permitted to build there, lest it foul the water or view of the lake. The joggers ran by the Aquarium and then eased down the path that carried them alongside Burnham Harbor, which was normally filled with sailboats and powerboats, but now it was empty, the boats' occupants hibernating elsewhere in warm shelters.

"Meka tells me you were involved in a similar case to ours, one involving a sniper," Pete shouted above the wind and traffic noise.

The anorexic-looking agent kept his gaze forward as they ran. "Uh huh . . . case in Baltimore. You probably know the one, it was in all the papers. Anyway, I helped investigate the shooting while I was assigned to our Washington Field Office. Heads up!" He quickly pointed out a patch of black ice to his fellow runners. "Gotta watch out. You hit that stuff, and you'll wind up on your butt."

"Toppe's also a profiler," said Meka. "Quantico has a complement of them scattered in our 56 field offices around the country."

"Yeah," added Toppe. "I prefer to work in the field, rather than the FBI Academy. I still enjoy working cases and putting the cuffs on people who've broken the law. I specialize in white collar crime. Besides, I couldn't be on SWAT if I went to Quantico."

"Sounds . . . like . . . the best of both worlds," said Pete, who had to force his speech because of the effects of Toppe's quickened pace.

"Yeah, I'm fortunate. Anyway, I've been following the exploits of your guy here in Chicago. He's a bad one—no conscience, the type who gets enjoyment from killing people. Once he starts, he's unable to stop. Killing and getting away with it emboldens him and gives him a rush so that he begins to almost crave it. I wouldn't be surprised if once you grab the guy, you find out he's responsible for other murders besides cops."

Meka found herself beginning to struggle with the pace. "Hey, Top, ease up a little. We're not in a race here."

"Oh; sorry,"Toppe apologized.

Thanks, Meka. "Do you have a theory about why he targets cops?" Pete huffed.

"That's a tough one. It could be something as simple as the guy has a problem with authority figures. Cops in uniform are a vivid representation of authority. Then again, maybe this guy had a run-in with a particular cop, and it left a bad taste in his mouth so he wants to get even with all cops. There's really not enough info yet to be able to pinpoint a single reason."

The runners passed Buckingham Fountain on their left. The huge summer attraction was now turned off, all bundled up for the harsh Chicago winter. A little farther along they passed by the baseball fields at Grant Park. Traffic on Lake Shore Drive moved beside them, a sea of red brake lights in brilliant contrast to the deep dark waters of the winter lake on their right.

"Meka tells me you don't have a lot of physical evidence at this point."

"I gave him a synopsis of what we have," shouted Meka, who was beginning to drop slightly off the pace.

"Yeah, it's pretty sparse—a red van, a casing from what looks like a .223 round, and a bullet fragment."

Toppe looked over at his two companions. "Watch yourself ahead. Before we get to Navy Pier, we have to cross over the bridge. It gets icy in some spots." He slowed the pace so they could catch up and also shorten their stride. "I do have one theory."

"What's that?" Pete looked down at the bridge grating while he spoke.

"I think your guy is a military veteran."

"Why do you say that?"

"The shots, they're all good, solid sniper-type shots. Precision. He knows what he's doing; he's disciplined, knows how to get in, take the shot, and then get out, undetected. That's the mark of a sniper. If I were you, I'd be all over the database of military types living in the area, particularly recently discharged vets. I'd focus first on guys with dishonorable and general discharges. They're the ones with problems that might give you some insight as to why he's committing the murders. I know what you're going to say: too much data. You're right, but get somebody with a background in accounting, somebody who doesn't have a problem pouring over records. I'm a bean counter myself. We love finding things no one else can."

Pete made a mental note to do just that.

"One other thing," added Toppe. "I wouldn't hold any more press conferences. He may interpret them as a personal challenge. It could cause him to go out and add another notch to his gun. Play everything close to the vest and don't cause him to deviate from his pattern; otherwise, you'll be back to square one. Let him keep doing what he's doing. After a while, this type of killer develops a sense of confidence that causes him to become sloppy and leave more clues behind."

Passing Lake Pointe Towers, the commuters on their left began to gain speed as traffic thinned and they left downtown Chicago behind. The wind had picked up considerably, swirling around the runners, sometimes in their face, other times blowing them off their stride, for it now battered them from the lakeside.

"Pete . . ."

"Yeah?" he said, turning to Meka.

"My hands are numb. Whaddya say we head back?"

Toppe looked at his companions. "'The Hawk' is definitely out today. Tell you what, let's turn around at Oak Street Beach. It's just ahead."

Pete nodded. "Fine with me. Meka?"

"Okay," she shouted, as the wind continued unabated.

"I think that tip line was a great idea," Toppe said. "Money talks. This guy has probably made some enemies along the way, or just acted strangely enough around others to leave an impression. Somebody's bound to drop a dime on him."

"I hope you're right. I appreciate you giving us your input on this, although I wish it was spring rather than winter. Thanks."

The group came abreast of the Oak Street Beach sign and turned around to retrace their steps to the Planetarium. "My pleasure. Unfortunately, I'm afraid someone else will have to die before we get a handle on this guy's identity."

"That's what scares me," said Pete to no one in particular.

Hardcore guided the big black Cadillac down 69th Street. The old woman had been right. The car had hardly been driven in the year her husband owned it—twelve hundred miles and change. *It's a freakin' new car.* As he put the vehicle through its paces, speeding up, braking, backing, he couldn't find anything wrong with it. Not that he thought he would; he'd only concocted that story so the old lady would feel sorry for him. No, this car didn't need a damn thing . . . didn't need to be checked out, but he would tell her that he had done just that, so he could justify keeping her money. Now he could rest easy. He'd put the van in the garage and keep it there, out of sight.

Needing to kill some time, Hardcore drove toward the diner. Might as well spend some of the woman's cash on a nice, big breakfast. *Maybe even show off my new ride to that tight-ass waitress and the other misfits.* Minutes later he arrived, and after finding a parking spot down the block he walked toward the eatery. As he approached, he noticed a car parked close by the diner that he immediately recognized as an unmarked police car. Cop cars were easy to spot; Hardcore prided himself on his ability to do so. Walking across the front of the restaurant, he looked inside and saw two strangers in suits, a man and a woman, standing by the counter talking with Ron, the newspaper reader. Cops!

He continued past the door, not wanting to arouse any suspicion. He certainly couldn't risk going inside. *So the cat and*

mouse game has begun, has it?   How the hell did they track me?
Walking past several store fronts, he crossed the street and
doubled back to his car. He got in and slouched down low in the
seat, waiting for the pair to exit the diner. Several minutes later,
the duo stepped through the door. *It's him, the guy from the press
conference. Yeah, Mr. Detective and his arm piece, the FBI agent.*

Hardcore watched as they got in the car he had spotted earlier
and pulled away. *Scratch that joint off the list.* He'd have to find a
new place to eat, this one was too hot. He headed south, thinking
that it was time to put the cops to the test. *Time to find another
target.*

Pete and Meka walked out the door of the diner. "What do
you think, Partner?"

Meka folded her small notebook and put it in her jacket pocket.
"I think there may be something to it. The guy . . ."

"Ron."

"Yeah, Ron, he said the guy with the attitude is a veteran,
former Army, refers to himself as, Hardcore. That would square
with what we've heard from several people so far, that we should
be looking at returning vets. He also said this Hardcore guy
maybe had some problem in the military, like he's holding a
grudge or something."

Pete unlocked the doors, and they both got in the car. "Right,
but what really got my attention was the red van, the same color
van spotted at a couple of the crime scenes."

"Yeah, and according to the waitress, Lynn, the guy wears a
cammo jacket. I think we need to put a unit on this place in the
mornings so when this guy shows up again we can get a tag off the
vehicle."

Pete pulled away from the curb. "I don't know, I'm just
wondering about the info."

"Why, Pete? It makes sense, I mean both the waitress and the customer say this guy has a chip on his shoulder about something, and he's pulled a tour in the Middle East."

"That's what I mean—it's too easy—maybe even too good to be true. I don't think this case can be solved this simply."

Meka pulled out her notes again. "Stranger things have happened. Anyway, I'll let Captain Samuels know what we have. He'll have to authorize surveillance units to stake out the diner."

"Okay. What else is on our plate today?"

Looking at her notes, she replied. "I took a few addresses from the tip line. We can check them out and talk with the callers. Then I have a couple locations the analysts ran through DMV where a search revealed red vans. We've got a busy day ahead of us."

"Good. I need to keep my mind occupied; otherwise, I'll be thinking about Marilyn all day."

"I know," she replied. "That girl's probably feeling like she's been kicked to the curb."

Pete turned their car to head south on California Avenue toward their first address, which was located in the Chicago Lawn area.

"What about tomorrow, Pete?"

Confused, he looked at Tameka. "What about it?"

"It's Thanksgiving. Are you going to include Marilyn in your plans?"

"Oh, man, I completely forgot it was tomorrow. I'll stop by and invite her to eat dinner with us. I can't leave her all by herself on a holiday."

She nodded. "Just be ready in case she declines your invitation. She may not be in the holiday spirit after all she's been through."

"You may be right, but I still have to give it a shot."

"Ah . . ." After some effort, Marilyn sat up in bed with her legs hanging over the side. Normally, the first thing she did each morning was go out for a run. That wouldn't happen for a while. Her ribs still ached and she felt weak. After Pete drove her home from the hospital yesterday, she made her way to her bedroom and lay down. She thought she would only take a nap, but before she knew it, it was morning. The ride home and the walk up the one flight of stairs to her apartment had worn her out. *Man, I'm really out of shape.* Pete had wanted to stay and talk, but she had been in no mood for it. She was still angry about everything—Joe's death, her accident, his new partner. Everything in her life was coming apart.

She walked slowly into the bathroom and turned on the shower. *Maybe this will get me going.* Filling a glass with water, she used it to gulp down two pain killers. She looked out the window and saw the grass covered with a pristine layer of fresh snow, just enough to change the color from a lifeless brown to a brilliant white. As the water became hotter, steam filled the bathroom. She dropped her robe and stepped inside, letting the soothing water massage her aching body. She soaped up and rinsed, but the water felt too good to get out just yet, so she stayed underneath the torrent, the water cascading over her like waves, helping wash away her physical pain. She finally stepped out and dried herself, but despite having showered, it didn't help cleanse her emotionally. Nothing could erase those scars.

Sitting on the edge of the tub to steady herself as she toweled dry, she buried her face in it and wondered what her future held. Her marriage was to have been the beginning of a new life for her. Finally, a family of her own. No more envying others' lives and marriages. She and Joe had even discussed having a child, not right away, but they both agreed that children would be a part of their life together.

Now she was alone . . . again. She had come so close to having what she'd always wanted, so close to her dream becoming a reality, that she felt as if she'd fallen into a deep dark hole that she'd never be able to climb out of. She'd been there before, but she'd had always fought and clawed her way out. She used to take solace in the fact that she was strong; she could handle any adversity that came her way. She no longer felt that way. Everything had failed her, even God, the one thing that had been a constant in her life.

She walked back into the bedroom and slipped into a baggy sweat suit. Returning to the bathroom to comb out her hair, she looked into the mirror and then dropped the brush in the sink. *What's the use?* She flipped off the light and made her way to the kitchen. Opening the pantry door, she found a can of coffee and brought it over to the kitchen counter. She pulled open a cabinet door to get a coffee filter, but she just stared at the open cabinet, forgetting why she had even opened it in the first place. She turned and walked away, back to the bedroom where she fell face down on the bed, feeling as small and insignificant as a blade of grass on a hillside pasture.

Father Ed awoke, somewhat chilled from having slept on top of the bed spread rather than underneath it. His clothes were bunched and wrinkled, and his feet were numb from having slept with his shoes on. He limped to the bathroom, pins and needles seeming to prick his feet. He switched on the light, much to the dismay of the other occupants of the room. The bugs scurried en masse behind the counter top. Looking in the mirror, he was startled by his appearance. *I'm beginning to look like my dad.* With a few days growth of beard, uncombed hair, and a few new worry lines etched on to his forehead, he seemed to have aged ten years.

He was certain of at least one thing—he needed coffee. Putting his jacket on, he departed the room and headed toward the motel office. It was cold; he could see his breath. His car, covered with frost, was still parked in front of the office. *That's a good sign. Funny what five dollars can do.* He knocked on the door expecting to see the old woman, but instead he saw a man appear from a hallway near the desk. Ed knocked on the door and was rewarded with the sound of the electronic release which allowed him to enter.

"Morning."

"You must be the guest," said the man. "You checkin' out?"

He looked at the man who sported a white stubbled beard and a Confederate flag baseball hat. A burning cigarette dangled from his mouth, the ashes dropping on the desk while he spoke.

"Not sure yet. Would you have any coffee available?"

"Not here, machine's busted," he answered, pointing to the vending machine with the note on it that Ed had seen last night. "Used to have a pot we kept goin' all the time, but we don't get many guests anymore." The cigarette burned dangerously close to the man's lips as he spoke. Ed stared for a moment, wondering if the man would remove it or not.

"Okay; is there a restaurant nearby?"

Pausing to remove the cigarette with his nicotine-stained fingertips, the man set it on an already full ashtray in front of him. "Yeah, one down the street, but it ain't gonna be open today, Thanksgivin' an' all."

Thanksgiving? "Oh, uh, yeah, I forgot it was a holiday."

"'Bout the only thing's gonna be open today might be the Mackdonalds. Most places is closed. You on your way to visit somebody?"

"Uh, yeah, going to visit with family."

The man grabbed another cigarette, lit it, took a long drag, and slowly let it out before placing it back in his mouth where the other one had been. Ed wouldn't be surprised if the man's driver's license photo showed a cigarette in it as well.

"Well, checkout's at noon."

Feeling depressed about not only the hotel, but now the holiday, Ed made a quick decision. "I guess I'll check out now."

"Okay." The man looked at the ledger and made a notation. "Oh, you was in one of our best rooms. Everything meet with your satisfaction?"

Letting out a quick laugh, Ed replied, "It was a little chilly, but otherwise very comfortable."

Smiling, the man pulled the ledger off the counter. "Good, the owner don't give that room out to everyone checkin' in here, lessen they look okay. You got lucky. Need a receipt?"

"No, I don't think I'll need one. I'll just get my things and put them in my car."

"Make sure you drop off the key 'fore you go."

Ed turned to leave. "Sure." The man buzzed the door, and Ed walked back to his room. He grabbed his suitcase, put it in the trunk, and then dropped off the room key. *Guess I'll have to find some fast food joint for breakfast. Thanksgiving.* He drove south on Route 1, the only car on the road.

Time had eluded him; he felt he had been running away forever. He longed for the structure of his former life: the Church, his students, and most of all, his family. Thanksgiving was a huge event at the Matthews' home. His mom would begin early in the morning, baking and cooking. She and dad would take time out to attend whichever Mass Ed would be celebrating that morning, and then they'd head back home where Dad would drink coffee and read the paper, while Mom continued to prepare the Thanksgiving feast. After Mass, Ed would visit with sick parishioners and others who were homebound, some of whom would ask him to stay and share their holiday meal. Ed always declined their invitations, opting instead for his mother's special creation. Today would be a sad day, not one for which he could give thanks.

And what of his parents? How must they feel about their son

not being with them on this day, or for that matter, not even knowing his whereabouts?" *Should I call?* He banged his fist on the dashboard. "Damn! Father, take this burden from me!" He shouted at the top of his voice, his words echoing around him, bouncing off the closed windows, and coming back to him—mocking him. Pulling over to the curb, he felt the tears stream down his face while he gripped the wheel, holding it as if he were holding on to the last bit of a life he once knew. He rested his forehead on the wheel and closed his eyes. *Father, if you love me, help me . . . please . . . help me.*

Bang, bang, bang. The noise startled her and she immediately rolled over and reached to her waist for her gun, but felt nothing but the band of her sweat suit. Staring at the ceiling in her bedroom, she tried to gather her senses. Bang, bang. "Marilyn . . . Marilyn, it's me, Pete. Open the door."

Gingerly getting up from the bed, she moved toward the front door of her apartment, measuring her steps as she went. Looking through the peep hole, she verified that Pete was there, unlocked the door, and opened it.

"You are home," he said, with a sigh. "I've been calling you all morning. Why haven't you answered?"

Opening the door wide for him to enter, she replied. "Sorry, my phone's turned off. I didn't want to be bothered."

He came in and sat down on the sofa. "I understand, you're probably tired, but today is Thanksgiving. Beth and I would like to invite you for dinner, and little Pete would love to see you."

She shut the door and sat down on a chair across from him. "Thanks, but I'm kind of worn out. I'd better stay home. Besides, I'm not your partner anymore so we don't have much in common."

Pete frowned. "Wait a minute, that's not true. We may not be partners right now, but it's only because you're on sick leave. I don't know what you're thinking, but as soon as you're cleared to return to full duty, we're back together."

"Really? So if I go in tomorrow, your new partner goes back to the FBI and I take over like nothing ever happened?" she replied sarcastically, staring at him.

"C'mon, Bens, we both know that's not going to happen. You need some recovery time; you need to get strong again. That's why I'd like you to come to dinner and have something substantial, something healthy to eat today. Did you think Samuels would have me working alone? Heck, he brought in a bunch of guys from other agencies on this task force. Everyone has a new partner."

"Oh?"

"Yeah, he split up McKinnon and Russo, too. McKinnon is fuming."

Marilyn leaned back in the chair, tucking her legs underneath her. "I imagine he must be driving his new partner insane," she said, with a smile.

Pete looked at her as she did. *Thank you, Lord. I never thought I'd see that smile again.* "You can bet on that. But the guy is from the state police, he's sharp and I'm sure he won't take very much of McKinnon's BS before he brings it to the boss." He paused and collected his thoughts, trying to say anything that would get her engaged in her job and distract her from Joe's death. "You know, Samuels has created this new database that contains every piece of evidence and written report ever generated in the case. I think you could come back on limited duty, dive into that information, and find some leads that others wouldn't even think were valuable."

She remained quiet, tossing the idea around in her head, and then replied, "Maybe."

"Yeah, just let me know when you feel up to it. I'll run it by the Captain. Now, how about dinner? I can come by and pick you up.

What do you say?"

"I don't think so; I'm not strong enough yet. And besides, I'm not in the mood to celebrate or be thankful for anything."

"Aw, Bens, I really wish you'd reconsider, I mean, no one should be alone on Thanksgiving."

Marilyn knew he was right, but his answer inflamed her and ignited a passionate chord within her. Leaning forward, she planted her feet firmly on the floor, as if she were preparing to attack an enemy. "No one should be alone? You don't think anyone should be alone? Look at me, Pete. Do I look like someone who is ready to be thankful . . . someone who should be rejoicing about anything? I am alone, dammit! I have nobody. Nobody! No parents. No brothers or sisters. No husband. I'm alone!"

Pete stood and moved toward her. "Marilyn, please, I'm sorry. I didn't mean to upset you. Please, take it easy."

Angry, she moved forward to within a few inches of his face. "Take it easy? I should take it easy, like I have no right to be . . . upset, as you call it? Well, I am upset; I'm angry; I'm pissed off, Pete. My life is screwed up beyond belief. Did you forget that Joe is dead? That maybe I might be a little mad that some bastard took the best thing that ever happened to me? And you want me to settle down?"

Pete backed up as she continued her tirade, her face turning red, the veins in her neck straining in bold relief beneath her skin. "I'm sorry, Bens. I'd better leave."

Her vision clouded by tears of rage and self-pity, her soul bleeding from a wound of enormous proportion, Marilyn watched as Pete went to the door.

"I'll pray for you, Bens. I don't know what else to do or say. Just know that I care about you and that you're on my mind."

Still in a rage, she spit back. "Don't bother; I don't need your prayers. Prayers are for people who believe."

Shaking, he opened the door and left. As he walked down the apartment stairs, he suddenly felt disoriented, having witnessed a total transformation of someone he thought he knew. *Call Reverend Dean.*

Marilyn sat back down in her chair. Facing the wall, she stared at it, the kind of stare worn by those who have cheated death but wish they hadn't.

~40~

Time to get back to work. Hardcore had slept most of the day after feasting on Mrs. Schiller's Thanksgiving meal the day before. It had been a long time since he'd enjoyed such a treat. In fact, the last time he had turkey with all the trimmings was while he was still in the Army. His landlord, however, had insisted he join her, even sent him to the store in his new Cadillac for the ingredients. Allowing him in her apartment had given him the chance to explore it. Talking with her and pretending to really care about her life caused her to reveal some interesting facts that would work to his advantage in the future. *Old people are naive fools.*

Even though it was a used car, the Cadillac looked and felt brand new. It was comfortable and cozy; he set the temperature on a toasty seventy-five degrees. No more icy windows on the inside, causing him to have to scrape them while driving. This car had all the conveniences. Cruising around the south side, he got stares from people who normally wouldn't give him a second look. He'd transferred his rifle from the van into the trunk of the car after he parked the van in the woman's garage. Losing the advantage of being able to shoot from inside a vehicle would be tough, but his training was good, and it would just mean he'd have to hide himself using available cover wherever he decided to take his next shot. Hell, he'd done that over in the sandbox every day.

Driving south in rush hour traffic on Kedzie Avenue, he approached the always congested intersection where 79th Street, Southwest Highway, and Kedzie all merge together. It was one of the busiest areas in the city, a confusing, frustrating jumble of streets difficult to navigate, particularly during rush hour. To help alleviate the bottle necks, the traffic division placed a couple of cops there on week days to direct traffic and expedite the flow. As he crossed Southwest Highway, Hardcore suddenly saw an officer with his hand up, frantically blowing his whistle. Hardcore slammed on the brakes and slid partially into the intersection.

The red-faced police officer hurried over to Hardcore's window and signaled for him to put the window down. "Hey, pay attention, Dummy! Didn't you see me signaling for traffic to stop?"

"Uh, sorry, man."

"I oughta write you a friggin' ticket. Next time keep your damn eyes open!" The cop walked back and resumed his duties in the middle of the street.

Dummy, huh. I'm a dummy? We'll see who's the dummy.

A minute later, the cop signaled in his direction and blew his whistle for southbound traffic to resume. As Hardcore drove past the cop, he gave Hardcore a stern look. Hardcore gave it right back to him. *You just messed with the wrong dude.* He drove several blocks ahead and then turned east into a neighborhood he knew would have an access road to an overpass containing the myriad railroad tracks that ran above the giant intersection. It was dusk; his car blended in well with the surroundings. Black dirt roads, stacks of railroad ties, and a collection of parked rail cars provided plenty of cover for what he had in mind.

Getting out of his car, he did a quick visual of the area. He saw three sets of rails; the one closest to his intended target had a partial line of cars parked on it. The middle set was clear, and the rail line furthest from him had a long, slow freight train heading his way. *Perfect.* Hardcore walked back to his car and waited until the lumbering train reached his location. Once the engine passed, he quickly went to work. He got out, looked around, and then took the rifle from the trunk. He found a position behind a three-tiered stack of fresh ties. Darkness was chasing any remaining light, and as he readied himself he breathed in a mixture of diesel from the passing engine and creosote from the railroad ties. He was just to the left of the steel overpass, well-hidden from any passing motorists or pedestrians.

Reaching forward, he removed the rubber cap from the eyepiece and married his eye to the scope. Using the variable power adjustment, he first found his target—the arrogant cop. Once he had the object in his scope, he dialed in a higher power to make his precision shot. The cop was animated, signaling with his arms, bending this way and that, and occasionally turning completely around. This shot would be Hardcore's toughest one yet.

It reminded him of the time in the Middle East when his platoon had been pinned down by enemy sniper fire. He had been assigned to take the guy out and had devised an ingenious plan in which a fellow sniper took a shot from one position, thereby drawing the enemy sniper's fire to his colleague's position. When the unsuspecting enemy sniper prepared to fire at what he thought to be his only adversary, Hardcore blew his head off.

This one would be challenging, but not quite as dramatic as that shot. With the traffic noise and constant drone of the passing train, it's heavy wheels yawing against unyielding iron and screeching loud enough to scare flocks of pigeons away, his shot would be sufficiently muffled. As Nature was about to drop the curtain on the sun's remaining light, Hardcore trained his rifle on the cop's head. It was doubtful he would be able to take a frontal shot, but it didn't matter. Bullet placement was what was important.

With everything lined up, Hardcore began his three cleansing breaths and took up the slack on the trigger. On the last breath, he held it for a moment and then slowly let it out while squeezing the trigger at the same time. The round exploded from the muzzle, the spent casing ejecting from the chamber and onto the ground behind him. The projectile ripped into the back of the officer's skull, fragmenting itself and the bone as it travelled through vulnerable tissue that only a moment ago defined a dedicated cop and loving husband and father. Officer Tommy Blackburn collapsed on the ground in a lifeless heap.

Hardcore nonchalantly retrieved the spent casing, folded the stock of his weapon, and walked back to his car. Placing the rifle back in the trunk, he got behind the wheel and drove the two-track down the embankment that had allowed access to the railroad property. As he was about to turn back on to the pavement, he spotted a boy walking his dog. Hardcore gave him a hard look, causing the boy to look away. He rolled down his window and yelled: "Go home, kid, before you get hurt." Driving down the residential street away from the area, he looked in his mirror and saw the boy making his own retreat. *Screw you, punk.* In moments Hardcore was safely out of the area.

He felt good, and hungry. Stopping for a hot dog a few miles away, he took his time eating, all the while feeling a sense of contentment. His marksmanship skills were better than ever, enabling him to take a shot from wherever he chose to. Doing what he did best made him feel useful; that he had a purpose in life. Sure, he'd rather be utilizing his skills in the Army, but its leaders had turned their back on him. *Their loss.* He knew one thing—he had an answer for anybody who tried to mess with him. The cops picked the wrong guy to harass; Hardcore was nobody's fool, and they were paying the price. With all of their detectives and FBI agents, they had no clue who he was or how to catch him. *Sorry bastards.*

That cop at the diner asking questions with his FBI agent partner was beginning to get under Hardcore's skin. Because of him, he could no longer eat there. It wasn't the greatest chow in the world, but he had gotten used to stopping there and kind of relaxing and talking with a few of the regulars. Of course, they had probably dimed him out. *Screw them, too.* Hardcore thought for a moment about killing Ron, the newspaper reader, who thought he knew it all. *Gonna offer me a freakin' manual labor job? I don't think so.* Besides, he was pretty sure his landlady could be persuaded to cough up enough dough to keep him in drugs and whatever else he needed. No, there was no need to waste time on Ron, he was a nobody. Anyway, killing him wouldn't have the impact that killing the cop or his partner would have.

He finished his meal and got back in his car. Smiling as he found a rock station, he cranked up the volume. It was time to celebrate, just like he'd always done in the Army when he took somebody out, but he'd left his weed in the van. *I need a drink and some company.* He continued south to 111th Street to a bar, Erik The Red, which featured live bands. He'd been there before and recalled that it was loud and attracted plenty of frisky women. Still flush with cash from his unsuspecting landlord, he had money to party. *Hell, maybe gettin' kicked out of the Army wasn't so bad after all.*

Walking in the front door of the corner bar, the scent of beer, smoke, and over-active pheromones enveloped him. Still high from the murder, his senses were on fire. He elbowed his way through the crowd of people, all eager to fill their drinks and lower their inhibitions. Stepping up to the bar, it took several minutes to attract the attention of one of the two female bartenders. There was no way to have a conversation with either of them though, too many customers and too much noise; Instead, Hardcore let a twenty dollar bill speak for him. He ordered his drink and signaled for her to keep the change, thus ensuring himself quick service for his next one.

He took a drink from the long neck bottle and surveyed the bar. He saw more women than men—his odds were good tonight.

On the dance floor, several couples were gyrating to the music played by a band that seemed to be more into themselves than their audience. They were loud and wild and provided the perfect environment for people to become the same. To his left stood a cluster of women, one of whom caught his eye. She was blonde and green-eyed, wearing fire engine red lipstick and a tight blouse cut low enough in the front to reveal what could have passed for a deep valley separating two huge mountains.

Hardcore looked her in the eye, his usual tactic. Sipping her drink through a straw, the woman smiled back. *Yeah, I thought so.* Without hesitation he approached her.   The music was loud, giving him a reason to lean into her. In doing so he breathed in her intoxicating mixture of sweat and perfume. "Hi, can I buy you a drink?"

"In a while . . . I'll let you know," she said, as she lifted her glass to show him she still had some left. "What's your name?"

"Steve. What's yours?"

"Terri."

Hardcore took a drink of his beer. "Are you here with anyone?"

"Just some friends. We're celebrating."

"A birthday?"

"Naw, the weekend, man!" She laughed at her own words.

"Good enough reason. Mind if I celebrate with you?"

"Sure, that's why I'm here." She looked at his hair, which he chose to keep in a military-style cut. "You in the Army?" she asked, while she rubbed her hand over his head.

"Naw, been out for a while. Got tired of it—too many rules."

"Yeah, you look like a military guy, and you look like you're in good shape," she commented, as she looked him up and down.

Hardcore took another drink. *This is going right where I want it.* "Yeah, I like to keep myself fit." He stared at her body. "You look hot."

"Thanks." She smiled, looked down into her drink, and stirred it. Leaning into him, she asked, "Did you ever have to kill anybody?"

"Here or in the war?"

Laughing, she replied, "In the war, silly."

"Yeah, but I can't talk about it."

She sipped her drink again, finished it, and then said in his ear, "I'll take that drink now, vodka and cranberry juice."

Taking the glass from her, making sure he touched her hand as he did, Hardcore returned to the bar and signaled the same girl with a ten dollar bill. Within minutes he was back with the woman's drink. She leaned into him once again. "Thanks," she whispered and then kissed his cheek.

The band started a new set, and one of her girlfriends came over. "C'mon girl." Grabbing her by the hand, she had just enough time to give her drink to Hardcore before the woman dragged her out to the dance floor. Seconds later, she and the woman were on the edge of a crowded group of dancers. Hardcore took a good long look at her. She was lean and fit, her muscular legs shooting out from under a tight, clingy skirt that left little to the imagination. She performed rather than danced, her routine sexy and seemingly directed at him while she moved to the music, staring at him every few seconds.

Although Hardcore was standing still, he was working up a sweat. He watched and drank as the woman hypnotized him with her body. By the end of the song, he had finished his beer and was eager for another. Smiling, she returned to where he stood. Shaking her hair from her face, she gathered it behind her head trying to cool herself, the gesture causing her already prominent breasts appear even larger. "Looks like you need another one, Steve."

Not taking his eyes from her chest, he shot back. "Yeah, maybe I need more than a beer. Hey, do you smoke?"

"Yeah, you got some weed?"

"Not here, at my place."

Gulping her drink, she asked, "Where's that?"

"My apartment, about ten minutes away. Want to go for a ride?"

She eyeballed him, playing with him and dropping her eyes toward his waist. "You live by yourself?"

"Yeah."

"Okay, let me tell my friends I'm leaving." She went over to her group and explained to them that she would be leaving with Hardcore. A couple of the women looked in his direction and smiled knowingly. Two minutes later, she was back. "Okay, Army boy, let's go."

A short time later Hardcore and the woman were at his building. She accompanied him to the garage where he retrieved a dime bag of marijuana from the red van and then followed him up the back stairs to his apartment. He set the bag on his dresser in the bedroom and retrieved a pack of rolling papers from his nightstand. After carefully rolling the J, Hardcore lit it and passed it to the woman who didn't hesitate to accept it. Nodding her head while holding the smoke for as long as she could, she finally released it. Smiling broadly, she said, "Mmm, great stuff."

"Yeah, I got a good connection. Keeps me hooked up whenever I need it."

The couple talked and joked until the roach turned into a mere ember. "More?" Hardcore was ready to roll another reefer and stepped over to the dresser to grab a paper. The woman followed and stood behind him, wrapping her arms around his middle. As the couple watched each other in the dresser mirror, her hands found his belt and began to undo it.

Seconds later, driven by alcohol, drugs, and lust they were naked in his bed, selfishly going after what each of them had come here for. The more Hardcore took control and dominated her, the more she enjoyed it, until finally, they lay exhausted and bathed in sweat. A few minutes later, the woman got up. "I gotta pee." He watched her as she went into the bathroom and shut the door.

Sighing contentedly, Hardcore reviewed his day while the woman tended to herself. He'd killed a smartass cop who'd tried to give him shit, even took the shot without using the van. And he'd scored a hot chick with very little effort. *Life is good.*

A while later, the woman opened the door and came out, her breasts leading the way; Hardcore got up. "Gotta use it myself," he said and closed the door behind him. The woman looked around the room while she heard his stream find its mark in the toilet. Typical guy—clothes strewn all over the place. She could never live with someone with habits like his, but he was good in bed, at least for tonight. *Time to go.* She walked around collecting her clothes that had somehow landed at various spots around the room. Retrieving her blouse, she looked at a cammo jacket lying on the floor next to it. The sleeve had a dark stain. Blood? There was a big spot and then what looked like several other drops. All of it t must be blood. Working as a receptionist at a clinic the past two years made her familiar with what blood looked like wet or dry. She paused to think. *Well, he said he had been in the Army. Definitely time for me to go.*

Hardcore came out of the bathroom and found her stepping into her panties. "Ready to blaze up?" he asked

She continued to dress. "No, I don't think so—I gotta get going. Take me back to my car."

Puzzled, he asked. "You sure? I got plenty. What's yer hurry?"

"Thanks, but I'm done," she said, forcing her abundant bosom into what seemed to be an inadequate amount of material to restrain them. "If I don't go home soon, my husband will be pissed."

Husband? That answer was all Hardcore needed to hear to cause him to get dressed himself. "You didn't say you were married."

"You didn't ask."

A while later, he pulled his Caddy next to her small import. She got out, looked back at him, and said, "Thanks for the weed." She unlocked her car, started it up, and in seconds was a memory.

Driving home, Hardcore thought about Mrs. Schiller. She obviously had some money lying around her place since she quickly came up with a wad of cash for him to take the car to be checked out. There must be more hidden around her apartment. He'd have to pay her a visit and find out just how much his landlord was worth. *I might never have to work again.*

Finishing the last bite of his breakfast, Father Ed looked around at his fellow customers in the fast food restaurant. A homeless man sat huddled in a corner nursing a coffee that had long ago turned as cold as the weather, all of his worldly possessions bound together in a pack which he carried with him. The vagrant nervously looked around; waiting for what he knew would happen sooner or later—the manager would ask him to leave. He'd use the excuse that the man's odor was offensive to his customers and that loitering was illegal. Until then, he would play the role of a diner, enjoying his coffee.

In a table near the back, a couple of teenagers, neither dressed for the weather but rather for their own convenience and pleasure, furtively explored each other as best they could while seated in a public place. A family, happily kidding among themselves, probably travelers taking a break from a long drive, shared two tables close to Ed's. He was able to hear bits and pieces of their conversations as they enjoyed their breakfast and each other's company.

Watching the family interact, Ed felt both jealousy and loneliness. A scene that would have otherwise brought him joy now caused him pain. To see them content and happy while in the midst of the simple act of eating a meal together reminded him of his abundant despair. *How long can I survive like this?* He picked up his trash and deposited it in the bin and then went to the counter to get a refill of his coffee.

"Travelling today, huh?" the manager asked him, as he poured the coffee.

"Uh, yeah."

"Where ya headed?"

Ed hesitated. "I, uh, I'm going to visit a friend who I haven't seen in a while."

The manager finished pouring his drink. "Well, have a safe trip and enjoy your visit. I'm sure your friend will be happy to see you, especially on Thanksgiving."

"Thanks." Ed walked out to his car, thinking about the lie he had just told the man inside. *I have no place to go, no friends to visit. Lord, what am I to do?* He sat for a moment, weighing things in his mind. *I can't do this any longer.* A flood of emotion swept over him, compelling him to make a decision that would alter his future. Sobbing, he pulled out of the lot while reaching into his jacket. He pulled out the cell phone he had purchased in Fredericksburg. Pressing in the numbers he had dialed hundreds of times in the past, he waited for the connection to be completed. Ed heard the phone ring once . . . twice . . . and a third time. *Please, answer.* As he was about to press the button to end the call, he heard a voice on the other end. "Hello."

Pete walked in the back door and entered the kitchen where Beth and little Pete were engaged in a conversation consisting of unintelligible words and strange gestures, a code of sorts, developed between mothers and their children. He could smell a roast in the oven and saw that the table had already been set. A tray of fresh dough sat on the counter top, waiting to be baked into soft, warm dinner rolls. Beth sat on the floor against the cabinets, holding the baby up on his still unsteady legs. "Hi, Daddy!" She grabbed the boy's arm and helped him wave to Pete.

"Hello, Daddy's Boy; hi. Mommy." He went over to them and joined them on the floor. "How was your day, Sweetheart, did you get any rest?"

"A little. His nap time is my nap time. How about you? Is there anything new on the case?"

Pete loosened his tie and unbuttoned his collar. "Nothing big, but we've gone through a ton of leads, most of which have proven to have no connection to the murders. The problem is we can't ignore anything. No matter how insignificant it may appear, we have to run it down and eliminate it."

"So, I guess that tip line the captain started is both a blessing and a curse."

Pete leaned over and kissed his wife. "That's a good way of putting it." He stood up and bent over to pick the baby up. "Hey, little guy. C'mon with Daddy while he gets into some play clothes."

Beth watched as the two men in her life walked toward the bedroom. Pete set his son on the bed and watched him while taking off his jacket and removing his gun, spare magazines, and the handcuffs from his belt. "Daddy's gonna lock up all his work stuff and then we're going to play." Grabbing his pager, he felt it begin to vibrate. *Uh-oh.* He pressed the top button, activating the message screen which displayed an urgent message:

Officer down 79th kedzie task force respond ASAP.

"Beth!"

Marilyn sat at her kitchen table, nursing a cup of coffee and a piece of toast covered with peanut butter. She didn't really feel like eating, but she didn't like being weak either, so she forced herself to eat while thinking about the direction her future was headed. While she was fixing her coffee, she had robotically switched on the TV and half-heartedly listened while the newscasters reported the big event of the day: Black Friday. It was being reported that shoppers had inundated the local malls and department stores, taxing not only the store personnel, but the police as well—traffic was congested all over the city.

Taking another bite from her toast, a story snatched her attention, riveting her eyes to the screen as a breaking news story was announced.

"This just in: A police officer has been gunned down on the city's south side, at 79th and Kedzie. The officer's name is being withheld, pending notification of family members. Channel 7 news has learned that this murder bears the trademark of the sniper who has killed three other Chicago police officers in recent weeks. More on this breaking story as it develops."

Pete. She sat upright, instantly alert and trying to analyze what she'd just heard. Another officer murdered: her case, or at least it used to be. *Who was the officer? Please, don't let it be Pete.* She went to the bedroom, located her phone, and turned it on. She had to find out some information, but before she could dial, the message alert went off, indicating she had voice mail. She dialed the number and discovered her mail box was full, a result of not having had her phone on for days.

She hung up and made a decision to call Beth. She would know whether Pete was okay or not. Seconds later, she heard the woman's voice on the other end. "Pete?"

"No, Beth, it's me, Marilyn."

"Oh, I thought it might be Pete calling me with some information about the shooting."

"Yes." The tension relieved, Marilyn sat on the bed and fell backward. "Thank goodness; I just heard on the news that an officer was shot on the south side. Sorry to bother you, but I just had to make sure."

"Wait, Marilyn, don't go. Are you okay? Pete told me things aren't going so well."

"Yeah, that's a good way of putting it, I suppose." She placed her hand over eyes, thinking she didn't really want to have this conversation.

"Marilyn, there are no words I can possibly say to comfort you, but I want you to know that I am here for you, just as you were there for me when Pete was shot. You're family to us, just like Joe was. Please, don't ever forget that. When you hurt, we hurt. Please, let us in; let us help."

Marilyn didn't know what to say, so she said nothing. A part of her wanted the help, wanted to let someone in, but there was also the feeling that she deserved the pain and wanted to endure it for as long as she could.

"Marilyn?"

"I'm here, Beth, I'll call you later."

"Okay." Beth waited before hanging up at her end. A few seconds later she heard Marilyn again.

"Beth . . .?"

"Yes?"

"Thanks." Click. Marilyn let the phone slip out of her hand and continued to lie on the bed, staring at the ceiling. Her first instinct was to pray, but what good had that done her lately? It seemed God had closed His ears to her, turned His back, her prayers seemingly returned without being opened. So much was happening. She needed to get back in the fight. She wanted to be part of the investigation, even if it meant sitting behind a desk rather than out on the street searching for the creep who had ruined her life.

As she sat up, the doorbell rang. *Pete?* She hurried to the door and looked through the peep hole. No Pete, just two men in suits—cops. She opened the door, keeping the chain in place just in case. "Detective Benson?" asked one of the men, holding his ID for her to see.

"Yes."

"I'm Tom Lanigan, and this is Willie McGee. We're with the Major Traffic Accident Unit. Can we have a few minutes with you to talk about your accident?"

Marilyn had completely forgotten about that aspect of her injuries, the fact that there was an on-going investigation to determine who had struck her. Undoing the chain, she opened the door and beckoned them to come inside. "Let's go in the kitchen."

The two men found chairs while she turned off the TV. "Any news on the officer who was shot?"

"Detective Benson..." Lanigan began, but she cut him off.

"Please, call me Marilyn."

Lanigan continued. "Thanks. They haven't released a name yet, but from what I've heard, it's one of the two uniforms assigned to direct traffic at that intersection. We heard your task force members responding to the scene." The detective rubbed his forehead. "This has gotten totally out of control. Every cop in the city is frustrated that we haven't caught this guy yet."

"Agreed."

"Marilyn, we're here to take a statement from you regarding the morning you were struck. Obviously, we weren't able to do that while you were unconscious, but we do need it for our report. Do you feel up to it?"

"Sure. I know you need to complete your report," she replied, "although truthfully, I really don't recall very much of what happened."

"That's okay," McGee smiled, "because we've also come to tell you that we've made an arrest of the individual responsible, and that after confronting him with the evidence, particularly your DNA on his car, he confessed to hitting you and then leaving the scene."

Marilyn leaned forward on her elbows. "Wow, guys, that was quick. Nice work. Who was it?"

"Just another pothead, high on wine and weed, with no license, no insurance, and no job. I'm not saying we don't work like this on all our cases," Lanigan offered, "but seeing that it was one of our own that was the victim, we put in plenty of overtime."

She reached across the table and held both their hands. "Thank you both, I am very grateful."

"You're welcome," said McGee. "So, how are you feeling? Are you going back to work soon?"

"I'm still a little weak from lying around in the hospital, but I'm getting there. Believe me, I need to go back at work."

"Good. You know, a friend of mine works for the FBI. She's part of the task force working the sniper case. She said there's a ton of phone leads coming in that have to be sorted through. They need all the help they can get."

"So I've heard. I'm still not good enough to hit the street. I have to get released from the department med section first, but maybe I can go back on light duty."

"Well, God speed your recovery," said Lanigan. "You probably already know that a lot of us have been praying for you, knowing the ordeal you've been through." He lowered his voice. "Some of us knew Joe," he paused momentarily. "He was one of our best."

She didn't think the mere mention of Joe's name would spur her emotions, but her vision quickly blurred through tears. "Thank you. He would have appreciated you saying that."

The accident investigation detectives took a short statement from her, consisting mostly of what she had done preceding the event, and then had her sign it. "Thanks for your time," said Lanigan, as he closed his notebook and got up to leave. "There won't be any trial since he's already confessed, so we'll let you know the outcome of the hearing when the judge sentences him. In the meantime, get well and hurry back to work. We need you."

Marilyn shook hands with each of them and saw them out the door. Their visit had been like a water hose turned on the fire of self-pity and apathy that had been consuming her inside. She went in the bedroom and found her phone. *Time to answer these messages and climb out of the pity pond.*

"Edward, is that you, son?"

"Dad, it's so good to hear your voice."

"Where are you? Your mother and I have been worried. Are you okay?"

"I'm in Virginia." Clutching the phone, Ed tried to control his emotions. Finally, he felt what had been missing in his life while on the run—love. "Dad, I'm fine. Well, not really. . I mean, I've been running away from a problem that will never get any better if I don't face it. I thought about it and prayed about it too, I need to come home and resolve this situation one way or another. If the Lord decides I need to go to jail, then like St. Paul, I'll have to resign myself to His will."

Ed heard a voice in the background. "Is it him? Is he coming home?" He could hear his mother's strained voice. It brought him comfort and joy, things he had sorely missed. "Son, you need to call Dan Walsh. He has some good news. We've been hoping you'd call so we could tell you."

Sitting ramrod straight in anticipation, Ed asked, "What are you talking about?"

"Oh, uh, here, let me put your mother on the phone."

A moment later, he heard her sobbing. "Edward, we've been praying you were okay and that you would come home. Praise God."

Trying hard not to weep, Ed interrupted her. "Mom, please, what's Dad talking about? What did Dan tell you?"

"He said the charges against you were going to be dropped. The woman was lying about you so she could get money from the church."

Ed breathed a sigh filled with vindication and briefly enjoyed a moment he thought might never come. *The truth has set me free*. He could almost see his mother's smile through her voice and momentarily laid his head back on the seat while resting the phone by his side.

"Edward . . . Edward?"

"Yes, I'm here," he said, smiling, bringing the phone back up to his ear. "I'm here. Mom, I've missed you so much."

Seconds passed as neither of them were able to find their voices, the reality of the inevitable reunion momentarily controlling their ability to speak. "Edward, why haven't' you called? Didn't you think we would be upset not knowing where you were or if you were okay?"

"Mom, I'm sorry. I was afraid to contact anyone, lest the police use their technology to track me down."

"What are you doing in Virginia?"

Smiling, he said, "I don't know, Mom. I'm asking myself that same question. Now tell me, what is this about the woman? You say she confessed to the police that she lied about me and little Rodrigo?"

"I guess so, Son. A detective came by. It wasn't either of the two that I saw in court with you."

Confused, Ed asked his mother, "What happened to Detectives Shannon and Benson?"

"Well . . . uh . . . here, let me put your Father back on the phone."

Ed heard the rustling as the phone changed hands again, and his mother told his father to explain. "Ed?"

"Yeah, Dad."

" I don't know for sure what's going on with those two, but one night we saw on the news that the guy, I guess, Shannon's his name, he's now working with a girl from the FBI and they're working on the sniper case."

The sun was getting warmer, heating the inside of the car, causing Ed to turn down the heat while he sat along the curb. "Dad, what sniper? What are you talking about?"

"Oh, gosh, Son, I don't know. Some guy is shooting cops for no reason; killed four of 'em so far."

"Oh my gosh, that's terrible. Do you know if Detective Benson, the lady who was working with Shannon, if she's okay? Even though they arrested me, neither one of them thought I was guilty."

Ed could sense his Father was getting anxious about answering the questions Ed kept asking. He could picture his dad running his hand through his hair like he always did whenever he was frustrated. "You gotta call Dan. He's the lawyer, ask him. We don't know what's going on, but you need to come home."

Looking around at the strange city he found himself in, he replied. "You're right, Dad. I do need to come home."

Hardcore pounded on the old lady's door, using their arranged code. Mrs. Schiller opened it and greeted him. "Good morning, Steven."

"Hi . . . uh, I was wondering . . . I have a chance to buy some tools from a guy I know who went out of business. I was thinking, now that I have a good car and all, maybe I could start my own, like, handyman service."

Mrs. Schiller opened the door wide. "Come in and let's talk." She shuffled over to her chair, while Hardcore took a seat on the couch across from her. "So, you say you would like to start a business? I think that's a marvelous idea."

"Yeah, right. Ya know I've been outta work for a while and don't have a lot of money, so I was wonderin' if you might be able to help me out a little till I get back on my feet, ya know, to buy the tools an' all."

"I understand. How much money do you think you'll need?"

Sliding forward on the couch, he said, "'Bout a thousand dollars. This guy has some real good power tools, way too expensive for me to buy brand new, but he needs the money cuz he's behind paying his house note. It's a real steal."

The old woman sat frozen; Hardcore thought maybe she had fallen asleep with her eyes open, but the next moment she spoke. "I think that's a good idea, Steven. I can lend you the money, and when your business gets going you can repay me."

"Great." He smiled.

"Wait here a minute; I'll go get it." She got up from her chair, continuing to lean on one of the arms of the chair until she retrieved her cane to steady herself. Moving toward the rear of her apartment, she took advantage of every piece of furniture along the way to help steady herself and maintain her progress.

He waited, giving her a chance to locate the money, and then crept to the rear bedroom where he found her bent over a box in the closet. Sensing she was not alone, she looked toward the doorway to find him watching. She saw not Steven's face, but that of a demon sent from below.

"Steven!" In an instant she realized her mistake. The bills she held in her hand dropped to the floor as she slowly stood upright and clutched her cane. Feebly trying to raise it in a defensive manner, she felt it swept aside like a mere toothpick, as Hardcore sprang forward and struck her with a blow that shattered her face. She dropped instantly, as if that one punch had somehow disintegrated her entire skeletal structure.

He opened the sliding closet doors all the way and found the cardboard box that held the money. *Damn.* It contained thousands of dollars. *Payday!*

"Ugh . . ." Hearing the woman groan, he turned around to find her still eying him. "Thanks for the loan, Granny," he said, as he wrapped his powerful hands around the old woman's neck and squeezed until her body felt like a deflated balloon.

She chose not to struggle, knowing that she was about to be reunited with her departed husband. They had been apart too long. Ironically, the attack was the best thing to happen to her since Frank's death. Now there would be no more loneliness, she was finally going home.

42

"Are you finished with the body?" Captain Samuels was on the scene of the homicide, personally taking charge ensuring nothing slipped through the cracks.

"Yeah, Captain, I think we can let the coroner remove it."

"Good." Samuels had stood by the fallen officer's remains since arriving on the crime scene, guarding it against any harm or disrespect, like a parent shielding a child who's been hurt. "I want a uniform to accompany the body to the morgue to collect all of the officer's personal belongings."

The investigator from the crime lab didn't question the captain's orders. "Will do, Sir."

"Where are the rest of your people, and what are they doing?"

Not accustomed to anyone questioning what the crime scene team was doing, the lead investigator let Samuels' questions pass in deference to the captain's rank and uber sensitivity regarding the fallen officer. "Sir, they're finishing up with the measurements, and establishing a trajectory of the bullet. The immediate area here in the kill zone is finished. We didn't find any bullet frags on the street, either because they're all contained within the victim or because the passing traffic picked them up and carried them away from the scene."

"Okay, thanks. As soon as you're finished, let me know so we can get the fire department to hose down the street. I don't want the family driving by and seeing their loved one's blood out here."

Samuels walked toward his car and got inside so he could use his phone to contact the police superintendent with an update. Knowing how things worked in Chicago, the captain was certain that he could expect an ass-chewing from the boss, questioning him as to why the sniper has not been caught. The superintendent would then himself be taken to the woodshed by the mayor, not because another cop had been murdered, but because it made the mayor look bad.

"It's pretty steep. What do you think, want to try it?" Pete and Tameka were on the street, looking up toward the embankment that led to the railroad property. The crime scene tech told them the shot had most likely come from somewhere near the overpass.

"Let's do it, Partner," Tameka answered. It was cold and dark on the hillside and it took several minutes to negotiate the slippery slope leading to the rail yard. At the top, a distant flood light cast spooky shadows as it illuminated the tracks and hulking freight cars sitting in formation. The duo searched slowly and diligently around the area, their movements preceded by the beam of their flashlights, as they looked for anything of evidentiary value.

"Tameka."

"Yes?"

"Come here for a minute." Pete was at the steel bridge that formed the structure allowing the track beds to pass over the street.

"Yeah, Pete, what have you got?"

Pointing toward the intersection where the officer had been shot, Pete said, "This must be the vicinity where our guy took the shot. With a scoped rifle, this spot is ideal."

Tameka looked out to where the officer was being removed. "I agree. It's a commanding view of the convergence of streets and affords numerous cover opportunities."

"Yeah, and if there were any trains going by when he took the shot, the noise factor probably worked in his favor as well." Pete looked around the area behind them, shining his light at the ground. "If it's the same guy, he probably took his brass with him, but let's look anyway. Who knows, he may have got careless."

"Okay, we can do a cursory search right now," Tameka added, "but we need to get someone back out here at first light to do a more thorough job."

"Good idea," Pete concurred.

As the two sleuths shone their lights searching for any clue that might be connected to the killer, Pete bent down to investigate a shiny piece of metal. He leaned in close and directed his beam directly on top of it. "Tameka!"

She hurried over. "What is it," she asked, looking down at the ground.

"It's a logo . . . a car logo . . . a Cadillac." Pete said.

"Uh huh." Tameka looked closer. "It looks like it's one of those things you find on a key fob, you know, the kind the dealer gives you when you buy a new car."

Pete took a plastic bag from his pocket, and sticking his hand inside the bag, he used the bag to protect any fingerprint evidence as he retrieved the key fob. "Exactly, and it's clean, like someone recently dropped it."

"Our guy?"

"I don't know, Tameka, but somebody has been up here recently, and I don't think it's a coincidence."

"Let's hope it came from whoever did the shooting. We desperately need a break."

The pair continued their survey of the area. While one team from the task force was assigned to stop vehicles and ask if they'd seen anything, another began a neighborhood canvass in a several block radius emanating from the intersection.

An hour later, Pete's cell rang. He checked the caller ID. "Captain?"

"Where are you?"

"We're up on the overpass. We've come up with a couple of things which may be important."

"How do I get up there?"

Pete and Tameka had traversed the entire area, discovering the access road. "Come up from the south, there's a two-track leading to the top. We'll meet you there."

"Okay."

Several minutes later, Samuels' car captured Shannon and White in its headlights. He got out and approached them. "What did you find?"

Taking the bag from his coat pocket, Pete held it in front of him. "We found this on the ground near the spot where we think the shot may have been taken. It's clean, no marks or dust on it, like someone just dropped it."

"Good."

"Captain, we also found some fresh tire tracks. We've got crime scene tape protecting the area for now," Tameka said, as she pointed in the direction by the railroad ties. "We need to get the forensic guys out here in the morning to make a cast and do a better search than we can do in the dark. If you don't mind, I'd like to bring in the FBI's Evidence Response Team to take care of that."

Samuels nodded. "Yeah, I'll authorize that. Make the call now. In the meantime, I'll get some uniforms out here to protect the scene. Good work."

"Thanks." Pete replied.

"Listen, this murder changes everything. I spoke with the mayor on the phone; he wants a press conference in the morning. He insists we give the public everything we have, in terms of who the shooter might be. With the election coming soon, he doesn't want the sniper to damage his chances of being re-elected."

"Okay." Tameka answered.

"He wants you two to be there."

"Uh, Captain, do you think that's a good idea?" Pete asked.

"No, but his political mind tells him it is. He thinks the whole black and white thing, the male and female team, cops and feds working together is a way to assuage the anger the city is beginning to show about our inability to stop the sniper. It's his version of damage control. He's nothing if not tied to all things politically correct. The other thing is, in some of our, shall I say, less-desirable areas, the thugs are cheering for the sniper to step up the pace and kill more cops. We need to grab this guy before he turns into another urban legend."

"Yes, sir. See you in the morning," Pete said, nodding.

The black Cadillac cruised south on Pulaski past 79th Street. Hardcore was hungry and looking for a new restaurant to have breakfast. He wasn't about to go back to the diner, not after he saw the cops there. He was too smart for them. They didn't have a clue about who he was and would never find him, but he was angry that they had forced him to leave the diner. He kind of liked the people in there. The waitress wasn't bad lookin,' and Ron at least knew where he was coming from, although Hardcore didn't agree with him sometimes.

He spotted a restaurant on his left: Grecian Garden. *Kinda classy, but I got dough now. Why not?* Pulling into the lot, he parked his car near the front so he didn't have too far to walk. The winter was closing in fast, and December was just around the corner. Gray days and mounds of snow were the norm for Chicago, and Hardcore didn't look forward to enduring the unpleasantness winter created.

Entering the eatery, he surveyed the place: nice, filled with comfortable tables and booths, mirrors and pictures on the walls. The hostess had watched him park and opened the door for him as he approached.

"Nice car. Table for one, sir?"

"Yeah."

"Follow me, please."

Gladly.

She led him to a booth by the far wall. "Is this suitable? It gives you a good view of the TV?"

Hardcore looked over where the plasma screen was mounted on the wall. "Yeah, thanks. This is good."

"Coffee?"

"Uh-huh."

The waitress walked away and he followed her with his eyes. *Not too shabby, tight waist and a nice rack. This place might work out.* He looked at the menu and decided on his breakfast just as his waitress returned with a cup and a carafe of coffee.

"Here you go, some nice hot coffee to warm you up on a chilly day. Now, what can I get for you." She took his order and went to the register to punch it in. Looking around the restaurant, Hardcore saw a mix of people, some older retired-looking types, as well as a smattering of young people, probably from the nearby junior college. A table behind him held a group of several people who were discussing the news stories they had just read in the paper.

"It says the cops all but know who the killer is," said one.

"Then why haven't they caught him?" asked another.

Just then, one of them said, "Shhh, there's the press conference."

Hardcore looked up at the screen and saw the two detectives he had seen questioning Lynn and Ron at the diner, the same two he had seen when the news was on one day as he ate at the diner. They stood behind a uniformed cop with two bars on his shoulders. *A captain, huh?* He listened intently, for the man seemed to be looking directly at him while he spoke.

"Tragically, we had another officer killed in the line of duty last night. Officer Tommy Blackburn was gunned down as he was performing his duties at the intersection of 79th and Kedzie, on the south side. We believe the person responsible for this officer's murder is the same individual who committed the murders of three other police officers. At this time, we have assembled a profile of who we think our suspect may be, based upon behavioral analyses, recovered evidence, and tips from our hot line.

"We believe our suspect is most likely a white male in his 20's, probably a military veteran, who may have been recently deployed in one of our overseas military theatres, possibly assigned as a sniper. Some of our eye witness accounts indicate this wanted individual may be driving a red van. Our hot line continues to function around the clock, and we encourage anyone who may have information about the identity of this individual to contact us immediately. Through the generosity of our local business community, the reward for information leading to the arrest and conviction of the individual responsible for these murders now stands at fifty thousand dollars.

"Detective Pete Shannon and FBI Special Agent Tameka White, standing behind me, are part of the multi-jurisdictional task force that has been working diligently to apprehend the subject. They assure me his arrest is imminent. We will not rest until we bring this killer to justice."

Behind him, Hardcore could hear the conversation that ensued, each one concurring that the situation was out of control and that the cops had better catch the killer soon. He began to feel anxious; he hadn't realized the cops had compiled as much information he'd just heard. Shannon and White, you're going to arrest me? We'll see about that. He knew then what he had to do.

~ **43** ~

"Ed, where the heck are you?"

"That's a fine way to start. No hello, or how have you been? C'mon, Dan, I thought we were friends."

Taking his father's advice, Father Ed had dialed Dan's number as soon as he hung up with him. He was trying to be coy, still somewhat giddy about the news that the woman had recanted her testimony which had accused him of molesting her son.

"Geez, Ed, I've been worried sick about you. No calls or emails, I must have sent you a hundred of them."

"I know. I'm sorry, Dan, but I was afraid to get in touch with anybody for fear the police would track me down. I wound up on the east coast in Virginia."

"Why there?"

"It's a long story. Anyway, it's good to hear your voice. Now please, my dad said the woman who accused me told the cops she lied. Is it true?"

"Yes, it is, but that doesn't mean you're out of the woods yet. There's a little matter of you violating the terms of your bond."

Ed scratched the back of his head. "Yeah. To be honest with you Dan, after that one night in jail, I didn't want to take the chance that I might be found guilty and spend more time locked up."

"Why didn't you tell me that before you just up and left?"

Shaking his head, Ed replied. "I should have, Dan. I'm sorry. Being arrested shook me to my core—I even questioned my faith."

"I won't lie, Ed. I'm disappointed you left and never contacted me, but we may still be able to salvage this thing. When can you make it back to Chicago?"

Ed took a minute to think. "I'm a long way from there, but I can be home sometime tomorrow."

"Okay. Let me contact Detective Shannon and set a time to meet with him the day after tomorrow. We'll arrange for you to surrender on the bail charge. You'll probably have to be booked again, and I'm going to have to convince the judge you're no longer a flight risk. It shouldn't be too difficult since the felony charge will no longer be pending."

The mere thought of being back behind bars, even briefly, caused Ed to break out in a sweat. "Dan, I don't mind telling you, I'm terrified of going back and being taken into custody again, but I'm at the end of my rope. I can't run anymore."

Dan's soothing professional manner comforted him. "Listen, the case was one-sided from its inception. Even the detectives advised the judge they had questions concerning the testimony of the complainant. Based on what I've dealt with in the past, I'm fairly confident we can convince the judge to be lenient."

"Lenient?"

"Yes. I think he may impose a fine or probation, maybe some community service, but once you satisfy the requirements, you'll be fine. We can probably even have your record expunged."

"Whatever that means. Hey, Dan, what happened to Detective Benson? My parents said she was hurt?"

"Oh, that. What a tragedy, Ed. Apparently the guy she was engaged to, another cop, was killed by a sniper. And at almost the same instant that he was shot, she was out for a jog and was struck by a hit-and-run driver.

Opening the window to get some more fresh air inside his vehicle, Ed recalled how well the cops had treated him. "Is she okay?"

"I hear she's out of the hospital, but I don't know how she's doing. Listen, call me when you get close to the city tomorrow. By the way, what number are you calling from?"

Smiling, Ed told him. "It's a Walmart phone. When the minutes expire, you just throw it away."

Laughing, Dan replied. "You need to come home; you're turning into a professional criminal, using all the tricks most thugs use to avoid getting caught."

"Nah, I don't think so. I'm too scared to become a crook. I just want to get home and be a priest again. I've missed serving my parishioners."

"Oh, thanks for reminding me about that. I'll call Father DeSalvo and let him know you're coming back. He has an apology ready for you, Ed, a well deserved one, I might add."

Ed rolled up his window and checked for traffic before pulling out. "I'm on my way, Dan. I feel like a kid who just woke up on Christmas morning."

"Good. I can't wait to see you, my friend. Drive carefully."

"Bye."

Ed turned left at the next intersection to go around the block and head toward the Interstate. Navigating the next corner, he saw a Catholic church, St. Jude the Apostle, patron saint of the impossible and of lost causes. The parking lot wasn't quite full, but obviously Thanksgiving Day Mass was in progress. Ed pulled his car in the lot and got out. *This is not a coincidence, finding St. Jude's.* He walked in through the heavy oak doors and made his way to an empty pew in the middle of the church. Kneeling down, he watched the priest as he consecrated the bread and wine into the body and blood of our Lord, Jesus Christ. *Thank you, Lord, for not giving up on me. I'm home once again, on Thanksgiving Day.*

Marilyn opened the door, "Hi, Reverend."

"Hi, Marilyn, thanks for inviting me. I hope you don't mind, but after we spoke on the phone, I called Kim and asked her to accompany me."

Reverend Dean and Kim walked in, and Marilyn shut the door. Kim hugged her friend and said, "I've been calling you for days, but you wouldn't answer. Thankfully, Dean called and said he was on his way to see you. He asked if I would come along. Don't be mad. I've been worried."

"I'm not mad, Kim, I just haven't had the desire to talk with anybody," she said, as they all found seats in the living room."

Smiling at her best friend and workout partner, her voice soft and a bit unsteady, Kim said, "Bens, I just wanted you to know how sorry I am about your loss. You haven't let anyone comfort you, and those of us who love you are hurting too. We need to share your pain, to help you get through this horrible event and recover from it. You're an important part of my life, girlfriend. Please, don't shut me out."

Kim wept softly; Reverend Dean handed her his handkerchief to dry her tears. "Marilyn, I realize this is a turbulent time right now, particularly regarding your faith. Whenever tragedy occurs in our lives, the first thing we try to do is assign blame. Often times the only one we can find to blame is God, so we raise the questions: if He is such a loving God, how could he allow this to happen? Why didn't He save my loved one? Why does He allow innocent people to be killed? They're all good questions, and I guess if I had the answers, I'd be divine as well. The truth is I don't have the answers. I can only speculate as to His reason for doing anything.

"Joe's death was indeed a tragedy. It came at a time in both your lives when your future together was about to blossom. And knowing both of you, seeing how your relationship grew into a loving, supportive partnership, Joe's murder becomes even more tragic."

Sitting across from him, Marilyn quickly sprang from her chair. "Dean, no disrespect, but I don't need you to tell me Joe's death was a tragedy. Nor do I need to hear about whom to blame. Yes, God didn't pull the trigger, but He didn't prevent it from being pulled either. Now, you tell me you don't know why He does things? Well, I think I do—I think He couldn't care less about me. I think after all of the prayers, the pain, and hard work that Joe and I put in to see him through his struggle with cancer, God turned His back on us. What kind of parent turns away from their child like that?" She was pacing, pointing at Dean, as if he were the Lord, and she was accusing him directly.

"Marilyn, you know that's not true. Your faith . . ."

She stopped him. "My faith? What faith would that be, Reverend? Would that be faith in a loving God who I believed would always be with me, who would shelter and protect me, who would reward me for being a good Christian? Is that the faith you're referring to?"

Standing, Dean interrupted. "Marilyn, listen for a moment."

Turning her back to him and continuing to pace the room, Marilyn continued. "Do you know how difficult it was, Dean? Do you have any clue about what Joe and I endured . . . his pain and suffering, his unselfish devotion to his faith? Even when he could barely get out of bed, he would limp to church, not wanting to miss Sunday Mass. Is that the kind of faith you're trying to explain, Reverend?" Her voice rising along with her blood pressure, Marilyn made her way back to the chair and fell back into it.

Dean stood his ground and looked at her. "Yes, what you described is exactly the type of faith I'm referring to. Joe was a perfect example. Why did the Lord call him home when He did? Because he knew that at that moment Joe was ready. Think about your relationship together. You came into Joe's life at a time when he was searching for something . . . anything that would relieve his pain. He had lost his wife, had given up his police career, and had fallen away from his faith. Then you two met at Pete and Beth's home during a barbeque. There was a physical attraction certainly, but the one thing that drew you both together was your faith."

Listening intently, Marilyn felt the tension slowly drain from her body. Still not willing to forgive, she nevertheless watched as Dean continued.

"The entire foundation of the life you were building together was grounded in faith: you were faithful to God and to each other. You, Marilyn, were instrumental in restoring spiritual life in Joe. You brought him back to the Lord. Your faith allowed God to work through you and save a soul. And when your work was finished and the Father was certain that, indeed, Joe was once again a child of His, He knew there was no better time to grant him eternal life."

Dean sat back down and leaned forward in his seat. "For all we know, Joe could have succumbed to the cancer, but perhaps our Lord knew that at that point he still needed more strengthening, needed more time here before he was truly ready. The Lord continued to work through you, knowing that your faith was strong. You served as his teacher, his role model as it were. You showed Joe the meaning of faith, never giving up, never showing weakness.

"Faith is something we can't see, Marilyn, yet we know it's there. Just like reason or intelligence, we know it exists, yet we can't see it. Faith in a God whom we can't see is similar. We believe even though we can't see Him, yet we know He's there because we see the result of His love every day. Think of Christ's disciples. Although they saw Him every day, some still had doubts. Yet we who have never seen Him believe and trust in Him."

Tears welled in Marilyn's eyes. She sat with her hands on her heart as if she could massage the pain from it. "If He is such a loving God, Reverend, how could He break my heart? How could He take my Joe at this time in my life?"

Like a father talking to his child, Dean explained. "When would you have wanted the Lord to call Joe home? Would there ever have been a time when you would say, 'Take him now,' and would you also want to know when that day would arrive? Marilyn, God loves you both so much that He ensured you would prepare Joe by rebuilding his faith and opening his eyes which had been cloaked in sadness. Joe died a happy man, in love with a woman who he was convinced had saved him from his darkest days. That is indeed faith, my child, and that is exactly how the Father works."

Marilyn was silent. She leaned forward to retrieve a tissue to dry the tears that came from deep inside. She knew Dean was right, but she didn't want to give in, didn't want to rid herself of the anger she felt. She knew she must; otherwise, she'd be right where Joe was when they met—bitter, angry, shutting out everything around her. She didn't want that kind of life anymore; she wanted only fond, loving memories of their love.

Feeling as if she had just fought a battle, she wanted to stand but felt too weak to do so. Sensing Marilyn's surrender, Kim went to her, falling into a mutual hug that brought a cascade of tears from them both.

"Marilyn, let me back in."

"I will, Kim, I will. I'm sorry I shut you out. I need your friendship now more than ever." After a few moments, she composed herself and Kim released her. Marilyn stood and went over to Reverend Dean who stood to meet her. Giving him a hug, she said, "Thank you Reverend. I needed to hear that. I think I'll be okay."

"Good, I'm glad. Healing will take a while, it doesn't happen overnight. Don't ever give up on yourself or the Father. Life is tough, especially if you're a cop. Know that He is always there and that you don't have to do anything alone."

"I will."

Dean made his way toward the door. "I've got some other business. I'll leave you two ladies to talk. Thanks for allowing me to come over, Marilyn."

"You're welcome, Dean."

The two friends instinctively made their way to the kitchen. "Coffee?"

"You bet."

~ 44 ~

It was Saturday; most people were relaxing at home, that is, unless you were a cop working on SNIPEOUT. Captain Samuels gathered the task force members in his office at homicide. He had received a board from the graphic arts people that depicted the cogent facts about the sniper, known only as FNU LNU.

Pete whispered to Meka, "Who or what is a FNU LNU?"

"That's an acronym we use in the FBI, it stands for fist name unknown; last name unknown. Once we determine the correct name of the subject we change it. We either use that or UNSUB when referring to a person for whom we have yet to identify."

"You feebs have an odd way of communicating."

Seeing that all of his people had gathered in the office, Samuels walked in. "Good morning. I'm not here to pat you on the back, at least not yet, but in the past couple of days we've made substantial progress. I just hope the press conference the mayor had us conduct doesn't spook our guy."

The captain picked up a folder and opened it. "Detective Beckham is presently in Judge Audrey Sheehan's chambers with a search warrant affidavit for a two-story apartment building located in the Marquette Park area. It's the building that our suspect took a girl to after meeting her in a local bar. We ran it through records; it comes back to an elderly couple, Frank and Florence Schiller. While we were at it, we ran them through the city clerk's office— the husband is deceased—so it's just Mrs. Schiller residing there. She apparently has a renter, but there are no records indicating who that might be. That's not unusual for that area, lots of retired folks rent to other seniors who may have lost their own homes.

"Russo and Larsen did a drive by to see if there might be a red van parked nearby, but failed to see one. That is until they crept around the garage and spotted one when they looked through a window. They weren't able to get a license number and didn't want to spend any more time there for fear of alerting our guy or the neighbors."

Meka spoke up. "Captain, any word on the evidence we found from the homicide at 79th Street?"

He opened the folder. "Damn good stuff. You and Shannon may have hit the mother lode there. We fanned out from the two-track you showed me. Just down the street, McKinnon and Beckham did a canvass and found a kid who spotted a black Cadillac driving down from the rail yard around the time the shooting took place. The kid said the driver rolled down his window and yelled at him. He described the man in the car as a white male in his twenties."

Pete and Meka looked at each other. "What about the tire impression, Sir?"

"It matches up with a tire GM installs on their Coupe de Ville models," he answered Pete. "That logo you found in the dirt came from a key fob the local dealership hands out to its new customers. The dealership ran a check on every black Caddy sold at their dealership in the last five years. One came back to Frank Schiller of Marquette Park. Your ERT guys from the Bureau worked round the clock on that tread impression, Meka. Thanks for the suggestion."

"Yes, Sir."

Pointing to the board on the wall, Samuels drew their attention to a forensic analysis from the ballistic section of the crime lab. "Bill Sherlot has positively ID'd the bullet fragments from the officer victims—they all came from the same rifle. And, with the extractor and ejector marks on the bullet casing found by the boy in the park, all we need now is the weapon to make a conclusive match."

"Captain?" Pete signaled.

"Yes?"

"What about the cammo jacket. We had our shooter in the park wearing one. The woman who was out jogging saw it, as well as the waitress and customer at the diner where he eats breakfast."

Samuels nodded. "Yes, and after that we didn't hear any more about that jacket. Detective Russo has been like a man possessed, going through the most promising leads from the tip line. On the day Officer Blackburn was gunned down, a call came in from a young woman later that night. She said she wanted to speak with a detective about something.

"Russo gave her a call. The woman told him she had met a guy in a bar that same night. She left with him in his car, a black Cadillac. They went to his apartment in Marquette Park. After their, shall we say, visit, she was getting dressed and looked around the room. She spotted an Army camouflage jacket that appeared to have blood on one of the sleeves."

"Bingo!" shouted McKinnon. "Let's move on this asshole, now. What are we waitin' for?"

"Not so fast. Nobody's gonna jump the gun on this until we have the paper on the building in our hands."

McKinnon took the toothpick from his mouth and broke it, but he thought better of throwing it at the Captain.

"In the meantime, I have a surveillance team watching the apartment. We believe our shooter is, for whatever reason, using the Cadillac that belongs to the Schillers. The Caddy is out of pocket right now, but they'll let me know once they spot it. After we get the search warrant signed, we'll hold off on serving it until we find out where our guy is at. Until that happens, I want each of you to be on call."

The group nodded.

"Okay, hopefully, this thug will soon be an inmate at the county jail, and we can let our guys and gals in blue relax. Dismissed."

As they began to file out of the office, Samuels pointed at Pete. "Shannon, stay behind for a minute."

The captain sat behind his desk and opened a notebook. "I got a call from your boss at Violent Crimes."

Uh-oh. "What's up, sir? Am I going back to my squad before we make the arrest on the sniper?"

Samuels smiled. "No, no, apparently you and Benson made an arrest on a case involving a priest, who later jumped bond."

"Yes, Father Ed Matthews."

"Well apparently he's seen the light, no pun intended. He's going to surrender here at VCU tomorrow morning. He'll be with his lawyer, uh . . . Dan Walsh," he finished saying, after looking at his notes.

Pete pouted. "Captain, what if we're in the middle of taking our subject down? I don't want to miss that."

"I know," the captain said, reassuring him. "If we get our guy returning to the apartment, I'm going to need everyone to help in the arrest and subsequent search of the building. Catching a cop killer takes precedence over a bail jumper."

"Thank you, Sir."

"That's all, Shannon. Stay available."

"Yes, Sir."

Pete made his way to his cubicle. Meka was nowhere in sight, but she had left a note for him; it was Saturday and she had some things she needed to do. He looked around the cubicle, his eyes resting on the photo of Marilyn and Joe. *I should call her to let her know Father Matthews will be turning himself in tomorrow; she could probably use some good news.*

"Damn!" Hardcore was about to turn the corner and head down the block leading to his apartment when he spotted a car parked near the corner with the motor running. The exhaust cloud drew his eye to the government-looking four door Crown Vic—cops! He drove past, not making the turn, but he was able to see a man behind the wheel, looking through binoculars in the direction of Hardcore's building.

He nervously gripped and re-gripped his hands around the steering wheel. *Damn, I'm toast!* Realizing that sooner or later he would be caught, he decided he wasn't going to roll over like he did when the Army arrested him and booted him out. He wasn't going to be treated by Chicago cops the same way he allowed the MPs to treat him. *Hell no.* This whole mess was personal now. In fact, if Detective Shannon was so confident about arresting him, then Shannon was going to be the first to pay the price.

Turning his car eastbound, he headed toward Chicago Police Headquarters. He'd be there whenever Shannon showed his face. After all, a rat always returns to the nest eventually, and when he did, Hardcore would be there to blow his head off. Besides, he had nowhere else to go and no place to hide. This new mission gave him a purpose; it reminded him of the long days and nights spent hiding in buildings and fields when he was a sniper in the military. Now he'd focus on Shannon and not worry about anything else. *Yeah, one thing at a time. Shannon, you're dead to me.*

"Marilyn?"

"Oh, hi, Pete."

"Is this a good time?" Pete asked, mindful of the treatment he'd received from her on his last visit.

"Sure," she replied and then paused momentarily. "Pete, I owe you a big apology for some things I said to you, as well as for the way I've been behaving."

Sitting in the chair in his cubicle, Pete leaned back and rolled it into the corner where he could shut out any ambient noise and focus on her conversation. "No, Bens, I understand."

"Please, let me finish. I haven't been myself lately. I've ignored and disdained help from people who love me, people who I've come to know as the only family I may ever have. I was so bitter about losing Joe that I even turned my back on God, blaming him for what happened. I couldn't see, or maybe I didn't want to see is a better way to put it, that rather than feel angry about Joe's death I should be thanking God for the time we had together."

Staring down at the desk, Pete listened intently.

"Reverend Dean and I talked."

Good old Dean. Pete continued listening.

Marilyn went on, "I never saw how the Lord was working through me, but Dean did. He explained the blessing that had been given to me, the gift of faith that I was able to share with Joe. Pete, I was able to play a role in Joe's spiritual salvation. Knowing that fact comforts me and brings with it hope for the future, something I badly needed."

"I, uh, I don't know what to say, except that I'm grateful to have the old Marilyn back."

"Thanks, Pete. By the way, let Beth know I didn't mean to be short with her the other day on the phone."

"I will, and believe me she understands what you've been through. Listen, the reason I'm calling is that I have some good news: Father Ed Matthews has surfaced."

"Holy cow! Where has he been all this time?"

"I don't know yet, but tomorrow he and his lawyer are meeting with me at headquarters so he can turn himself in on the bond violation. I was thinking that maybe you'd like to be there. I know you're still on medical leave, but if you're strong enough, I thought you'd want to hear his story first hand."

"Yes, I'd love that, anything to make me feel human again. Besides, I'm tired of lying around. Thanks, Partner."

As soon as she referred to him as her partner, there was silence on both ends of the phone. Marilyn was first to speak. "Pete, uh, I'm sorry. I didn't mean to imply anything."

She couldn't see his smile through the phone. "Sorry? You just made my day, Partner. We *are* a team, and as soon as you return to duty, we'll definitely be working together again."

"That's my hope," she sighed.

"Oh, one thing I didn't tell you. We're set up on a building in the Marquette Park area where we think our sniper lives. He's out of pocket right now, but if he comes back before Father Ed shows up, I have to respond with the task force."

"I understand. Pete, would you mind if I rode in with you tomorrow?"

"Heck no, I'll pick you up."

"Great."

"It's good to have you back, Bens."

45

De La Salle Institute was a Catholic high school on Chicago's south side. Its large campus occupied some of the most valuable real estate in the city. It was home to a beautiful collection of buildings, but that wasn't what drew Hardcore there. No, the high school complex sat directly across from Chicago Police Headquarters at 35th Street and Michigan Avenue. It was also a location that would be free of students on the weekend, particularly on a Saturday night.

Driving around the area, Hardcore did a site survey, something he always did before setting up to take a shot. His Army instructors had taught him the importance of not only knowing your target but also the area in which it will appear. They also drilled something else into him—get in quickly; get out quickly—and never leave any evidence that you've been there. That was the mark of a good sniper, one who dealt death from afar, the victim never realizing he was in any danger. He noticed the Michigan Avenue side of the police structure was probably one which the public utilized. The employees had their own entrance around back, where there was also a huge parking lot, and where the metro line ran, carrying passengers all the way downtown.

Saturday night. *Not many cars in the lot; cops have sweet jobs.* Hardcore checked out the rapid transit line that rested on a berm above the lot, but it lacked cover. He'd be spotted for sure. He turned out of the lot on to 35th, driving toward State Street, and spotted a coffee shop: the Blue Light Java. It was closed now but probably opened early each morning so the pigs from headquarters could feed from its trough. *Hundred bucks says Shannon stops here every day.* He pulled the Caddy to the curb and got out to look at the hours of operation. *Yeah, five to five, seven days a week. He'll be here.*

While he stood in front, Hardcore surveyed the area, looking to find a place that would afford him the best shot. Street level was taking too much of a chance, for it was the first area people scanned. Besides without the van, he'd have to take the shot from somewhere outside. He looked across the street at the high school. *Perfect.* Next to the school building was a detached three-story structure that functioned as the school's power plant. It had several air conditioning condensers sitting on top of its roof that would afford good cover. Even better than that was the foot-high wall that encompassed the entire roof. *This is going to be a breeze.*

Darkness was closing in. He needed to work on finding a place to hide while he still had some light remaining, and he had to get behind that building to check for access to the roof. Getting away quickly on this mission would be imperative. As soon as Shannon's body hit the ground, Hardcore needed to be up and out.

He made his way into the school property and found the alley way leading to the plant. Checking the doors on the building, he discovered that all of them were locked. He walked around to the west side of the structure and found a fire escape. *Damn!* It was just out of reach. Looking around, he spotted a dumpster, and after a couple minutes of exhausting effort, he moved the heavy steel container underneath the fire escape's pull-down ladder. Grabbing hold of it, he climbed to the first landing and then made his way up to the roof.

The sun's daytime heat had melted the trace of snow that had fallen yesterday. Unless it snowed tonight, footing would not be a problem. He crept toward the front edge of the roof, and when he was just a few feet from the edge, he got down on his hands and knees and crawled the rest of the way. Peeking over the lip of the wall that prevented anything from slipping off the edge, he spotted his target. Blue Light Java would be a fitting resting place for Detective Shannon. *Too much caffeine can be bad for your health.*

Doubling back to the fire escape, he navigated the stairs and finally the ladder and was quickly on the ground. He dug out his keys and unlocked the Caddy. As he was about to start the vehicle, he looked at them, noticing that the Cadillac emblem was missing. *What the . . .?* Panicked, he tried to imagine where he might have lost it. He switched on the car's interior lights and looked on the floor by the driver's side; he checked the seat cushion and then underneath—nothing. *The roof of the building?* No time now, he needed to get some chow and find a place to crash for the night. He had to be set up early in the morning before anybody bothered him or asked him what he was doing. Sunday morning was going to be a life-changing day, or should he say, life-ending.

"Edward?"

Father Ed closed the door of his parents' home and made his way to the kitchen where Peggy and Bill Matthews were having supper. "Hi, Mom; Hi, Dad. I'm home."

Ed's mother stood so quickly from her chair that it fell over backward while she went to greet her son. Hugging and kissing him, her joyful tears flowed freely while her husband wrapped his arms around them both.

"Praise God, you're safe. We have been just sick with worry," she told him. "We kept calling Dan to see if he had been in touch with you."

"Yeah," his father added. "I started to think that Dan was lying to us, that he knew where you were but wouldn't tell us."

Wiping his eyes, Father Ed looked at his parents, "He didn't know anything. I left in the middle of the night and never told anyone my plans."

"Come, sit down and have some spaghetti with us," his mother said, directing him to the chair he had occupied most of his life. While his mother prepared his plate, his father asked, "So, Edward, where have you been all this time?"

His mother set a dish in front of him and then sat down. While he ate, Ed filled his parents in on his flight from the law, pausing only to devour his mother's homemade cooking, something he'd missed and quite frequently fantasized about.

"More, Son?"

"No, Mom, I'm full. It's so good to taste your cooking again."

His father asked, "So what now, Son?

Ed put his elbows up on the table, folded his hands, and rested them under his chin. "In a couple of minutes I'm going to the rectory at St. Nick's and speak with Father DeSalvo. I need to resume my priestly duties, something I've sorely missed. Then, first thing in the morning I intend to celebrate Mass, and believe me, I can't wait."

"What about the police, Edward?" His mother frowned and began to rock slightly back and forth in her chair like she did whenever she was worried. "We don't know how this thing works . . . this trial stuff."

Ed reached over and took one of his mother's hands. "Try not to worry, Mother. Dan called me and said he made an appointment for us to meet with Detective Shannon at police headquarters around ten tomorrow morning. I may have to spend the day or maybe even stay overnight in jail."

"Oh, Edward . . ."

"I know, Mom, I dread even the thought of another second behind bars, but I have to face what I've done. I violated the terms of my bond. Hopefully, Dan can implore the judge to be lenient towards me."

"I don't think I can take anymore of this jail stuff," his mother lamented.

Nodding, while he played with a long strand of spaghetti on his plate, Ed said, "I know, and I'd rather you and Dad didn't go with me tomorrow. Either I will call you, if I can, or Dan will and let you know what's next."

Ed stood and took his dishes to the sink, something his parents had taught him to do since he was a little child. "Right now I'm going home to my room at the rectory and back to being a priest."

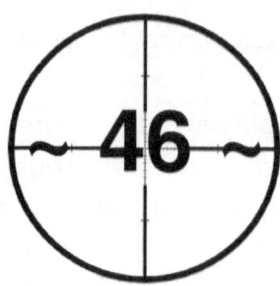

~ **46** ~

Driving east on 95th Street, Pete headed toward the Dan Ryan Expressway, which would take them quickly to police headquarters at 35th and Michigan. Sunday morning was the best time to drive around Chicago, for very few cars choked the streets. Most people were off from work; the others slept in. Dropping down onto the Interstate, he kept pace with a lone rapid transit train as it powered effortlessly down the tracks between the north and south bound lanes. Pete eased into the sparse traffic and soon slid ahead of the sleek silver silhouette.

"You're rather quiet this morning, Partner," Pete looked across at Marilyn who was busy looking out the window.

"Oh, sorry. I'm not ignoring you; it's just that after a week in the hospital I have a greater appreciation for things. I know it sounds corny, but all the times I've driven this expressway I've never actually taken the time to look around at the city."

Pete thought about that for a minute. "You're right. I guess I'm in that same boat. We take a lot for granted, but when you stop to really look at it, Chicago is a beautiful town."

"Yeah, it would be even better if we could get rid of all the thugs who threaten to turn it into a war zone."

"Now that's the old Marilyn I know," Pete said with a smile. "This morning while I was on the way to pick you up, I had a voicemail from Captain Samuels. He said Russo came up with the tag on the black Cadillac that's registered to the property owner of the apartment building. He put out a lookout message citywide.

Our guy is still out of pocket, and surveillance hasn't picked him up anywhere near his home."

"I know."

Glancing quickly at her, he said, "What? How?"

"I know all about it; I got the same voicemail. I guess maybe I still am a part of the team."

"C'mon, Bens. That's what I've been telling you all along."

U.S. Cellular Field, the home of the Chicago White Sox, began to loom large on their left. It was Pete's visual reminder to jump off the highway and on to the exit ramp that would take him east toward Michigan Avenue.

"I know you've told me, Pete. I was just being difficult, and, a probably a little jealous too. I'm torn between hoping we catch the sniper quickly, and not finding him until I'm back at work. I just want to somehow be a part of the end of the case."

"You are a part of it. You've worked the case from the beginning."

She smiled. "Thanks. Hey, can we stop at the Blue Light and get a coffee to go? I'm in the mood for a latte."

"A foo-foo drink? Sure thing."

"Dan, is this going to be like a trial? I mean, what's going to happen today?" Father Ed and his lawyer were in the Blue Light Café getting coffee to take to their meeting with Detective Shannon.

"No. This morning we're going to sit down with Shannon and tell him your story. Afterward, I'll contact the assistant state's attorney and ask if you can appear before the judge in the morning. Ed, I'm going out on a limb for you. I'm guaranteeing your appearance in the morning so that you won't have to spend the night in the lockup."

Breaking out in a broad smile, Ed replied. "Thanks. That's

more good news added to what I heard yesterday."

"What would that be?"

"Well, I spoke with Father DeSalvo. He told me the Archbishop is reviewing my status, and based on what happens with this bond thing, he's fairly certain that I can resume my normal duties very soon. Until then I'm still saying Mass, alone in the chapel, but still, that's a blessing.

"You know, this morning as I celebrated Mass, I made peace with the Lord. I realized I had been blaming Him for my problems, wondering if He was trying to tell me I should leave the priesthood. But once I began the ceremony, particularly when I recited the Act of Faith and then consecrated the bread and wine, I knew I was meant to be His priest, that He had been testing me, wondering if I really believed what He told us in John 3:16, that whoever believes in Me shall not perish, but have eternal life."

Dan nodded. "You always did know how to put things in perspective." The two friends continued to chat when a couple of customers walked in through the front door. "Ed, there's Detective Shannon now."

Closing the door behind him, Pete glanced around the interior, as he did each time he entered any room. Spotting Father Ed, he nudged Marilyn and said, "Hey, there's our guy now." The detectives walked over to the table where the two men were seated.

"Morning, Detectives," Dan said, as he rose to shake their hands. "I'm surprised to see you, Detective Benson. Last I heard you were just released from the hospital."

"Yeah, it's only been a couple of days. I haven't returned to duty yet, but to tell you the truth, I was interested in hearing Father Ed's story, his reason for jumping bond."

Looking sheepishly, Ed extended his hand to Marilyn. "I apologize for my conduct. I know I was wrong, but I want to make things right."

"Well, let's see if we can do our part and help get your life back on track," said Pete. "Let me get a couple coffees to go, and we'll head upstairs and talk about it."

Hardcore spent a long night sleeping in his car waiting for dawn to arrive. As the daylight washed the darkness clean, Hardcore parked the Caddy near the mouth of the alley that led to the power plant at De La Salle High School. He made his way up to the roof. No snow had fallen overnight, but the temperature had dropped below freezing, pasting a light coating of frost on the silver colored roof. He moved slowly to the front edge, setting out his rife and estimating the range of the shot he'd be taking. *Seventy yards, no problem.*

Even though it was a Sunday morning, he had expected his intended target to arrive around eight. When that time came and went, Hardcore grew restless. As nine o'clock passed, he became angry. By ten, he was about to leave when he saw Shannon walk in the front door of the coffee shop with a woman he couldn't quite place. He knew it wasn't the one he had seen at the two press conferences. This was a white woman; Shannon's partner was black. *Maybe she's a lawyer.*

No matter, Hardcore went on high alert. He improved his shooting position by propping himself up on his elbows, thereby taking the muzzle of his rife just over the parapet, but not extending beyond it. He dialed in more power, narrowing his field of vision within the scope so that he would have his bullet strike the victim at eye level. *C'mon on out, hero. I got somethin' for ya'.*

Bobby Russo was a changed man. After so many years of working with McKinnon, he had resigned himself to playing second fiddle to Harry. Indeed, many times he even acted as an errand boy for the taller and more dynamic of the two investigators. Now, he realized Harry had been holding him back, stealing all the glory himself without acknowledging Russo's legwork.

This morning, Bobby reported for work at seven, digging in where he had left off the night before, searching the database for anything that might ID the shooter. Away from McKinnon, Bobby embraced the diligent and methodical scouring of information. He knew the information was somewhere in the maze of disjointed information. He just needed to find it. This morning, with a clearer head and rested body energized from a double dose of Starbucks, he hit pay dirt. He dialed Captain Samuels' phone.

"Samuels."

"Captain . . . Russo here," he said, excitedly.

"What's up?"

"I have a positive ID on our guy; I have a name and an address that matches the apartment building."

"You sure?"

"Positive. I've been poring over the data base for two days. Last night I was in the middle of searching all the traffic citations issued the past six months, sorting them all kinds of ways, like time of day, area of the city . . . you name it, I did it. Anyway, I came up with a ticket written by a cop in the 8th District. He stopped a guy for going through a stop sign."

"Okaaay," said the Captain, impatiently.

"It was a red van, Sir. The cop listed it as a cargo van on the citation, the same kind of van that was spotted parked in the garage at the apartment building. The tag on it was registered to the building's address under the name of Steven Lattimore."

"Great work, Russo. Run that name and . . ."

Russo didn't let him finish. "Did that already, Sir. Lattimore is a vet, got out over a year ago, but the Army tossed him out. He was busted for rape while he was in the Middle East and did time in the brig."

"Russo, you just made my day. Listen, do an expedited records check through the FBI, tell them I authorized it. See what this guy's assignment was while he was on active duty."

"Done, Sir."

"What?"

"I already did it. I'm kinda used to usin' people's names to cut through red tape; hope you don't mind."

Samuels paused before answering, knowing he couldn't very well jump on Russo at such a watershed moment. "Okay, Detective, what did you find?"

"The final piece of the puzzle, Sir. Our guy was assigned as the platoon sniper."

Father Ed and Dan put travel lids on their coffees as Pete walked back to the table with his two cups. "Gentlemen, shall we head over to the office?"

"Yes, let's get this over with." Ed stood and followed Pete and Marilyn to the front door. His hands filled with coffee and car keys, Pete used his shoulder to open the door and then held it with his foot to allow Marilyn to exit. Once she did, he let it go. As it closed partially, Ed quickly pushed it back open and into Pete's arm, causing him to drop his keys.

Seeing what happened, Father Ed immediately stopped short and said, "Sorry." CRACK. As Pete bent over to retrieve the keys, a shot rang out, its ominous sound reverberating across the near empty street and echoing off the buildings.

"Pete!" Marilyn instinctively hit the ground, pulling Pete with her. While she did, she spotted movement on the roof of the building across the street. Her gut told her to get up and give chase, but she had to check on her partner first.

"Pete, are you okay?" She was afraid to look; afraid not to. She pushed him on to his side."

"Yeah, I'm good; the sniper!" Looking behind him, he saw the lawyer leaning over Father Ed, who, except for a bullet hole on the side of his head, had a peaceful look on his face, almost as if here were asleep.

Jumping to his feet, Pete barked out commands. "Marilyn, handle the scene here. Call it in on your cell. Let dispatch know I'm on foot across the street at the school, in plain clothes!"

"Will do. Pete, be careful."

He never heard her warning. By the time she had finished the sentence he was almost on the other side of the street.

"Shit!" He had Shannon right where he wanted him, had the reticle fixed on the bridge of his freakin' nose. No time to think about it now. Hardcore sprang to his feet and looked around for his spent casing. *Where the hell is it?* He scanned his three-sixty and found nothing. *Damn, must have ejected over the side of the roof.* He was losing precious time. He folded the stock and started to run across the rooftop toward the fire escape.

The early morning sun was just warm enough to begin thawing the thin layer of frost that had formed overnight. Taking his first step, the slippery surface caused him to fall flat on his back. WHACK. His head slammed against the roof. Groggy, Hardcore got to his feet, intent on making his escape. After several more steps, he slipped once again, this time on to one knee, cracking his kneecap, causing a sharp pain to jolt through his whole body. He decided to crawl on all fours the rest of the way, even though it would slow his progress.

Running around the corner of the building, Pete desperately searched for an access point for the roof from where the shot had come. The first two doors he tried were locked. Frantically shouldering and kicking at them, he found neither would budge. Making his way around the corner, he saw an alley and sprinted toward it.

Almost at the fire escape that would lead him to freedom, Hardcore fell once more as he stood to complete the final few yards. He lay dazed for a moment, looking at the sky, as stars danced before his eyes. He sat up quickly. Running his hand around to the back of his head he felt a warm, slick substance, and when he brought his hand forward he saw what it was blood. Struggling to get back to his feet, he finally stood and reached forward and grabbed the railing.

Pete turned the corner of the alley and stopped as if yanked back by a tether. Parked partially in an alcove near a loading dock was a black Cadillac. His pistol out, Pete approached slowly, leaning into the building while he did, as if trying to become a part of the brick and mortar. He did a quick visual on the car's interior before passing it by. Then he focused on the three-story building in front of him.

Dazed, Hardcore slowly started his descent. Holding his rifle with one hand while wavering from his injury, he misjudged the distance. He fell down several of the hard iron steps, his rifle clanging on the landing, while his face slammed against the unforgiving surface. "Ughh . . ."

Pete heard the noise and looked up. **"POLICE! STOP!"**

Transitioning to survival mode and hallucinating that he was back in combat in the Middle East, Hardcore took up a defensive fighting position. He rolled over and brought his weapon to his shoulder, firing a couple of rounds for cover in the process. Both bullets skidded harmlessly along the wall, ten feet above Pete's head. Hardcore tried to use his scope, but between his blurred vision and having knocked the instrument in his fall against the steel structure, neither could guarantee an accurate shot.

Pete took cover in a doorway. **"DROP THE WEAPON, DO IT NOW!"** He shouted at the prone figure pointing the rifle in his direction.

Hardcore squeezed off two more rounds, sending Pete deeper into the door way.

Can this be the sniper? None of his rounds have even come close. No time for speculation now. Pete returned fire and then advanced to a position just under the fire escape, next to the dumpster. From here he had a clear shot at the man, particularly since the steps and landings were grated, with large openings to allow for debris to fall through. He aimed his Glock .40 caliber at the man. **"LAST CHANCE; DROP THE GUN!"**

Shannon was directly below Hardcore, but to get a shot at him, Hardcore would have to lean over the side. Jockeying for position to enable his weapon to fire downward, his head and shoulders became a perfect aiming point for Pete.

Pete pressed the trigger three times when he saw the rifle pointing toward his position. In an instant, the rifle tumbled from the man's hands and landed on top of the dumpster. In case the rifle discharged as it struck the top of the dumpster, Pete ducked out of the line of fire. Then he looked up to see the gunman lying motionless, one arm dangling over the ledge of the landing as blood fell like raindrops through the still, crisp air.

"Pete!" Marilyn appeared at the rear of the Caddy, gun drawn. "Pete, are you okay?"

"Yeah. Did you call it in?" Pete asked, hearing sirens at the same time. Seconds later a phalanx of blue and whites appeared at the mouth of the alley, their occupants moving toward the building like a swarm of ants.

Pete and Marilyn hurriedly ID'd themselves by showing their police stars. "Police officers!" The point man checked Marilyn and moved tactically beyond her to Pete's position and performed the same task. "They're on the job!" he shouted to his other colleagues.

"I think he's dead," Pete said, pointing toward the downed subject, "but I'm not taking anything for granted."

"Agreed." The assisting units took up positions of cover, while an officer cautiously made his way up the fire escape. He checked the body and then shouted to the others: "Clear!"

Pete took a cleansing breath and let it out slowly. He began to shake; the realization of what he had just been through finally hitting home. Just as in most deadly force incidents, the adrenaline kicks in and propels the officer through the crisis. It's not until the incident is over that the gravity of the situation comes to the forefront and creates emotions that sometimes drive officers to seek help.

Marilyn approached him. "Father Ed?" Pete asked.

"Gone."

Looking down at the ground, Pete shook his head. "What a waste of a good man, a man of God."

Putting her arm around him, Marilyn nodded. "He didn't deserve it, that's for sure. If it's any consolation, his lawyer told me that Father Ed celebrated Mass this morning at St. Nick's and made peace with the Lord. I'm positive he's right where he needs to be."

His eyes glistening, Pete looked at her. "Yeah, Partner, both Father Ed *and* Joe have earned their eternal reward. God bless them."

The Aftermath

All the members of Operation SNIPEOUT returned to their previous assignments except for Detective McKinnon. After reviewing many of Harry's informant payments and having verified the detective's former relationship with Lt. Darcy, Captain Samuels held a closed door counseling session with Detective McKinnon and convinced him that it was in his best interest to retire.

Detective Bobby Russo was honored by the Chicago City Council for his diligence in discovering the identity of the sniper. He is now the senior detective on Captain Samuels' Homicide Squad.

The body of Mrs. Florence Schiller was discovered inside the red van parked in the garage at the apartment building. During the execution of the search warrant at the building, more than fifty thousand dollars in cash was recovered. Paint from the red van was matched to the parked vehicle that was struck at the scene of the first murder.

The bullet fragments recovered from the victims' skulls and shell casings found at Marquette Park, De La Salle High School, and inside the red van were all positively matched to the rifle used by Steven Lattimore, aka, Hardcore. Fingerprints from the bullet casings and the Cadillac logo found at the rail yard also matched his prints.

Hardcore's DNA was found on the cigarette butt found by Marilyn in the museum parking lot near Soldier Field where the second officer was murdered. The blood found on Hardcore's cammo jacket, was matched to that of the murdered drug dealer.

Magdalena Mendoza was arrested, charged, and convicted of filing a false police report and lying under oath while giving testimony for an arrest affidavit. She was taken into custody by federal agents and deported to Mexico with her son, Rodrigo.

Detectives Pete Shannon and Marilyn Benson returned as partners to the Violent Crimes Unit.

Pete's wife, Beth, gave birth to a baby girl. Marilyn, and Sgt. Mike Castro served as the child's godparents at the baptism.

Acknowledgements

As was the case with my first two books, my wife, Chris, has been one of my most valuable critics, pointing out flaws in my sometimes skewed sense of reality. She keeps me grounded and prevents me from jumping over the cliff when I get too near the edge.

A big thank-you goes to the wonderful members of the Monday evening critique group at Borders Books and the local chapter of the Virginia Writers Club. The Riverside Writers has provided me with insight and support, the value of which cannot be measured.

Retired FBI Special Agent Roy Hazelwood, a world-renowned profiler, generously agreed to review my work regarding behavioral profiling to ensure its accuracy. Roy has co-authored two books: _The Evil That Men Do_ and _Dark Dreams_, and is in demand all over the world to speak on the topic.

Thank you, Roy.

A gifted friend, Kate Lehman, was kind enough to read the manuscript and suggest several key changes. Thank you for your kindness and discerning eye.

Another debt of gratitude is owed to retired Chicago Police Officer, William Sherlock, an expert firearms and tool mark examiner. Bill honed his skills working for years in the Chicago Police Crime Lab. He later had a second career as a firearms examiner with the Illinois State Police Crime Lab. His knowledge about evidence and its collection can be found in a textbook he helped author: _Evidence Collection: Joseph J. Vince Jr., Joseph J. Vince, William E. Sherlock._

Thanks to my publisher, Bruce Moran, of TotalRecall Press, who continues to encourage and support me in my writing.

The Author

John spent thirty three years in law enforcement, working the streets in Patrol, Special Operations, posing as an undercover agent, and as a street survival instructor. He is the recipient of two of the highest awards given for valor by the Chicago Police Department, and has worked violent crime, organized crime, and drugs while an FBI Agent. He has published dozens of articles on training and police survival. This is his second novel in the Chicago Warrior thriller series.

John is retired from the Bureau. His last assignment was as an Instructor at the FBI Academy, in Quantico, VA. He lives with Christine his wife of thirty-nine years. They have been blessed with three fantastic children and four marvelous grandchildren.

Contact John via www.johnmwills.com

Be strong and courageous! Do not be afraid of them! The Lord your God will go ahead of you. He will neither fail you nor forsake you.

Deuteronomy

- Title: *Chicago Warriors*™
Midnight Battles in the windy city
- Author: John M. Wills
- Price: $27.95
- Publisher: TotalRecall Publications, Inc.
- Format: HARDCOVER, 6.14" x 9.21"
- Number of pages: 352
- 13-digit ISBN: 978-1-59095-843-8
- Publication: 2009

A Chicago Warriors™ Thriller

Chicago Police Officer Pete Shannon's life is about to take a dramatic turn. His wife has a dark secret that she's about to reveal to him; his partner's life is about to be in jeopardy, and worst of all one of his own colleagues will present him with one of the biggest challenges of his life. Pete's strength, both physical and spiritual, will be put to the test as he and his partner work the "graveyard shift" on the mean streets of the "Windy City."

Fellow officer Marilyn Benson doesn't realize it yet, but her life is about to change in ways that she could have never imagined. Forces of good and evil will do battle for her soul and her faith, both of which have lain dormant for many years. It's an issue that she can no longer ignore. St. Michael the Archangel, patron saint of police officers, is about to engage in his biggest clash since throwing Satan out of Heaven.

Praise
"I spent a lot of years with John Wills in the law enforcement trenches of Detroit, a place where Christian faith is rarely a survivor. Somehow John's flourished. In Chicago Warriors, he has created a unique narrative demonstrating how the worst of man can be defeated by the best in man. It is a parable of a morality that is vanishing from the American landscape."
--**Paul Lindsay,** author of The Fuhrer's Reserve, Traps, The Big Scam, Freedom to Kill, and Witness to the Truth.

Praise

"I spent a lot of years with John Wills in the law enforcement trenches of Detroit, a place where Christian faith is rarely a survivor. Somehow John's flourished. In Chicago Warriors , he has created a unique narrative demonstrating how the worst of man can be defeated by the best in man. It is a parable of a morality that is vanishing from the American landscape."

    -- **Paul Lindsay,** *author of The Fuhrer's Reserve and Traps: A Novel of the FBI*

"Wills covers issues that are timely today, including date rape, violence associated with prostitutes, steroid use among body builders, young criminals and police corruption....By today's standards it is also acceptable for readers of most any age. There is no problem with language, sexual content or violence."

    -- **Marilyn Olsen,** *President of Public Safety Writers Association*

"Chicago Warriors is the true voice of a battle tested street cop. A well written testimony of a Chicago Lawman. "A real cop's words, a real cop's experiences, John Wills knows how to tell a story!"

    -- **Randy Sutton,** *Author of "A COP'S LIFE", and "TRUE BLUE*

"Midnight Battles in the Windy City explores the dark underside of police work while illustrating the characters' moral values--all under the greater theme of good versus evil."

    -- **Andrea Nealon,** *Free Lance Star Reporter*

"What a great story! Chicago Warriors is a wonderful, inspirational read, and it was hard to keep a dry eye throughout. John Wills puts in words what every law enforcement officer knows in his heart...that forces of evil roam the earth and oftentimes ordinary men and women behind a badge have first contact. As a retired federal agent and author, like John, I have called upon Saint Michael to pull me through many perils like the characters in his book."

    -- **Mike Angley,** *Author of the Child Finder Series*

"The story carried me along. The characters are like so many I've met over the years. You know you're reading a good police novel when you go to work and find that: life imitates the art you're reading.

    -- **Dean C. Kavouras,** *Police Chaplain*

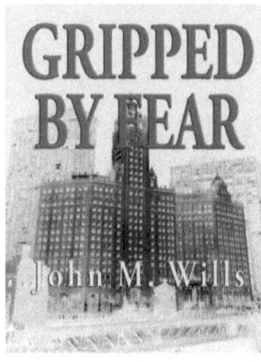

- Title: *Gripped By Fear*
- Author: John M. Wills
- Price: $27.95
- Publisher: TotalRecall Publications, Inc.
- Format: HARDCOVER, 6.14" x 9.21"
- Number of pages: 288
- 13-digit ISBN: 978-1-59095-772-1
- Publication: 2010

A Chicago Warriors™ Thriller

Pete Shannon and Marilyn Benson find themselves working their biggest case yet in their new role as Chicago Police Detectives. In this second book of the Chicago Warrior Thriller Series, a madman has inexplicably targeted women who labor as office cleaners in downtown Chicago, sexually assaulting them as they travel to and from their job.

As the number of victims begins to mount, the two investigators are pressured by their boss to solve this horrendous crime pattern. Local community organizations soon stage protest rallies at City Hall, convincing the media that the city has become "gripped by fear" as a result of the rapes. The Mayor demands quick action by the Police Superintendent to end this reign of terror. The heat is on, as summer in Chicago begins to sizzle, forcing the two detectives to put their lives on the line as they attempt to capture this demon of the darkness.

In the midst of it all, Marilyn learns some disturbing news that forces her to choose between her loyalty to Pete and the man she loves....and in the dramatic climax Marilyn's Christian faith plays a major role in saving her life.

Praise

Once again John Wills delivers a nitty-gritty true-to-life "you can taste the atmosphere" story about the life of police officers on the often violent streets of Chicago. Captured in the language and with a feel that only a cop from Chicago can deliver, Gripped By Fear, second of the Chicago Warrior Thrillers, reveals some of the heroism, fears, motivation and courage cops everywhere can relate to.

Frank Borelli,   *Editor in Chief of Officer.com*

"*Gripped by Fear* is as authentic as it gets. John Wills brings all of his law enforcement experience as well as his writing skills together to bring us a terrific read."

--Lt. Randy Sutton,   *Las Vegas Metro PD's "most highly decorated officer in department history";*
Author of True Blue and A Cops Life Law Enforcement Commentator, Fox News

"*Gripped by Fear* is Christian fiction's equivalent of Law and Order: gritty yet filled with hope in the ultimate triumph, delivering a thrilling read that Christian readers will appreciate."

--Alex Jurek,   *INDenverTimes.com*

"...*Gripped by Fear* is a not only a good mystery but also an exploration of the many challenges faced by today's law enforcement officers. It will be of special interest to readers who enjoy books with a strong Christian theme."
--Marilyn Olsen,   *President, Public Safety Writers Association*

"John Wills...takes you to the heart and soul of the Chicago undercover police force...taking note of every movement, every sound, things out of place—details only a veteran of law enforcement could provide. Woven through this police thriller is an inspirational message of faith. Gripped by Fear is a great read and a book you won't want to miss."
--Margaret Oleska,   *Richmond Book Examiner*